Pierced by Love's Lightning

Desire swelled within her. Vanessa moved her hands up and down his shoulders. Her mouth was open to him, her body rejoiced in the powerful weight of his. When he pulled away from her, she almost cried out with dismay.

But he was only stripping off his coat. She watched as he threw it to the floor, followed quickly by the rest of his clothes. He was so beautiful as he stood there, a powerful stallion.

When finally he came to her, Vanessa trembled. She clung to him, to the strength of him. And soon the night splintered into the shattering white light of pure sensation. . . .

Highland Sunset

Joan Wolf

AN ONYX BOOK

NEW AMERICAN LIBRARY

NAL BOOKS ARE AVAILABLE AT QUANTITY DISCOUNTS WHEN
USED TO PROMOTE PRODUCTS OR SERVICES. FOR INFORMATION
PLEASE WRITE TO PREMIUM MARKETING DIVISION, NEW AMERI-
CAN LIBRARY, 1633 BROADWAY, NEW YORK, NEW YORK 10019.

Onyx is a trademark of New American Library.

SIGNET, SIGNET CLASSIC, MENTOR, ONYX, PLUME, MERIDIAN
and NAL BOOKS are published by NAL PENGUIN INC.,
1633 Broadway, New York, New York 10019

First Printing, October, 1987

1 2 3 4 5 6 7 8 9

PRINTED IN THE UNITED STATES OF AMERICA

The rose of all the world is not for me.
I want for my part
Only the little white rose of Scotland
That smells sharp and sweet—and breaks the heart.

—HUGH MACDIARMID,
The Rose of All the World

I

Scotland and England, 1745

He either fear his Fate too much,
   Or his Deserts are small,
That puts it not unto the Touch,
   To win or lose it all.

—JAMES GRAHAM,
   Marquis of Montrose

1

The January day was cold and unusually windless. The brilliant blue Highland sky looked down on two figures riding sturdy hill ponies along the shores of Loch Morar. Suddenly a feminine voice called out, clear as a chime in the thin, cold air, "Can't catch me!" There came a whoop of joy from the other figure and the two ponies exploded into action.

Lady Vanessa MacIan laughed breathlessly as she led her brother on a chase along the hard white sand, across pools of ice that glinted between rocks, down to the very edge of the water where the small white-crested waves rolled up onto the frozen shore. Her long black hair streamed out from under her Highland bonnet, the only sign that the slender figure in tartan trews and enveloping plaid was not a boy.

Niall cornered her against some rocks, tagged her, and whirled away, with Van giving chase this time. The dogs who were with them barked and jumped and raced alongside, delighted by the game. The riders finally subsided, both bent over gasping for breath. The ponies' breath was steamy vapor in the cold air. The dogs, seeing the fun was over for the minute, went down to the water's edge to sniff around.

"We haven't played that game in years," Niall finally said.

"You haven't been home in years," Van retorted. "You were playing in Paris, not in Morar. And I'll wager you didn't play the same games in France, either, my dear brother."

Niall's face took on a look of exaggerated dignity. "I was in Paris for an education, not to play games, little sister."

Van's fine lips curled in a distinctly sardonic look. "You *were*," she agreed ironically.

Niall grinned. "I did attend some lectures, you know." The two ponies began to walk side by side along the sand. "Alan was more diligent than I," he added with seeming casualness. He looked at his sister out of the corner of his eye.

"That doesn't surprise me," Van returned serenely.

"Father said this morning that the MacDonalds are coming to Morar tomorrow." Niall gave his sister another look.

"All of them?"

"Well, Lochaber and Lady MacDonald . . . and Alan." The Chief of Lochaber was a friend of Lord Morar's, and Alan MacDonald, his eldest son, had been at the University of Paris with Niall for the last three years. Niall went on, "We've been home only six weeks, and I've seen as much of Alan as I did in Paris."

"He must miss you," Van said imperturbably.

"It's not Morar's *son* that Alan is interested in," Niall returned mischievously. "For some unfathomable reason, Van dear, Alan is interested in you."

"And whom are you interested in?" Van asked, neatly turning the tables. She did not wish to discuss Alan MacDonald. "Who is this mysterious French lady who keeps sending you letters? Mother is getting worried. Home six weeks and you've already had three letters from Paris—and all in the same feminine handwriting."

Niall looked uncomfortable. "Nobody Mother need concern herself with," he mumbled.

"Oh?" Van gave him a shrewd look. "You're not in trouble, Niall, are you? Or gotten some wretched girl in trouble?"

"No! No, it's nothing like that." His handsome face, reddened with cold, looked more uncomfortable still. "It's just a girl I lived with in Paris," he said in a burst of confidence. "Dash it all, Van, she was a girl off the streets! I took her in and she kept house for me and cooked and . . . and . . . well, you know When I left I gave her all the money I could spare. But she keeps writing how she loves me, and misses me . . ." His voice trailed off. "I wish she'd just leave me alone," he said after a minute.

Van felt a stab of pity for the poor little French girl. "Is she in want of anything?" she asked.

"No. I left her a decent sum of money." He seemed to come to himself. "I shouldn't have told you all this," he said guiltily.

"On the contrary," Van replied, "it's a good thing you did. I'll reassure Mother. And the letters will stop after a while if you don't answer them." She looked at him curiously. "Didn't you care for her at all?"

"Care for her?" He looked surprised. "Well, she was pretty. And nice. And . . . convenient."

"I see," Van replied dryly. Poor little girl, she thought again. Niall had graced her with his good looks and his careless charm and had hardly even noticed her at all.

"I really *shouldn't* have told you that," Niall said, turning to look at her. "It's not at all the sort of story one should share with one's younger sister. The thing is . . ."

"Yes?" She looked at him a little haughtily. Van had always felt Niall's equal in everything.

"The thing is . . . you're not just a younger sister. You're a friend." Van looked up quickly and he grinned at her. Then he glanced at the sky. "Come on," he said. "If we're late to tea, Father will be furious."

Frances MacIan, Countess of Morar, found her husband waiting for her when she came into the drawing room for tea. She paused for a moment on the threshold to watch him as, back to her, he rearranged a log on the fire. Even after twenty-four years, she thought, her heart still caught at the sight of him.

The earl was dressed for evening in his good scarlet tartan kilt and black velvet coat. His dark hair, more gray now than black, was tied neatly back in a queue with a black velvet ribbon. He sensed her presence in the doorway and his head turned.

She smiled and came into the room. "Hello, darling."

He smiled back, his face softening as it did only for her. He answered her and they took their seats, speaking in English, as usual. Frances, although she had learned to speak Gaelic quite well, was more comfortable in her native tongue.

The tea table was laid as customary at a little distance from the fire. One could not sit too close to the drawing-room fire, no matter how cold the day. The fireplace opening was so wide that half a dozen people could stand there easily and the fire that burned in it was blazingly fierce.

Alasdair looked around and frowned. "Where are the children?" he asked. At that moment Niall came around the embroidered screen Frances had placed at the drawing-room door to keep the fire from dragging a huge draft across the room.

"Good evening, Mother," he said. "Good evening, Father."

Frances looked with pride and love at the figure of her son crossing the room toward her. Built like his father, of medium height, slim and strong, he was also dressed in a scarlet kilt and velvet jacket. The hair neatly tied at the nape of his neck was ebony black. He bent to kiss his mother's cheek and she looked up into his dark, fine-boned face. He took his seat and Frances poured him a cup of tea. Alasdair frowned again. "Where is Van?" he demanded.

On cue from the doorway came Van's voice. "Right here, Father." Three dogs came in with her, two Highland deerhounds and a spaniel. The dogs advanced toward the fire with dignity and took up what were obviously their usual places. Van sat down, and the earl and Niall, who had risen at her entrance, resumed their own seats.

Van was dressed for the evening as well in a gold satin evening dress. Her black hair was braided into a crown on top of her head, leaving the lines of her jaw and throat and cheekbones clear and uncluttered.

She was so beautiful, Van, Frances thought as she gave her daughter her tea. So beautiful and so unaware of her beauty. Unlike her brother, who was all too conscious of the power of his careless smile.

They were so alike, her children. Both slim and dark, with the same fine bones, the same high-bridged straight nose and light eyes under coal-black brows and lashes. So alike and yet so different.

It was Van she worried for. Niall was comfortably placed in the male Highland society of his father. One day Niall would be chief, and he would be good at it. He had his father's example to follow. But Van . . . What was Van going to do with her life?

The huge fire crackled and a log fell. Alasdair said gravely, "I received a message today from Lochiel. Murray of Broughton is to be at Achnacarry on Friday."

Niall put his teacup down with a small click. His face was blazing. "Any news of the prince, Father?"

Alasdair's face did not mirror his son's excitement. "We will see on Friday," he replied. "I shall bring Lochaber as well, since he is to be here."

Van's great light eyes were fixed on her father. "Has Murray come from France, Father?"

"Aye," said Alasdair. "He has."

Frances suppressed a sigh. Ever since England had declared war on France over the Austrian succession, the Highland chiefs who were Jacobites had been hopeful of winning French aid to help restore the throne of Britain to the exiled Stuart king. Frances did not think anything would ever come of it, and she hated to see her husband wasting his hopes and his energies on such a futile cause, but she listened to him talk now and, prudently, said nothing.

She had known from the minute she met Alasdair MacIan, Earl of Morar, that he was a Jacobite. When the Stuart king, James II, had been dethroned in favor of James's daughter Mary and her husband, William of Orange, in 1688, the MacIan family, like most of the Highland clans, had declared for the Stuarts.

But England, it seemed, did not want the Catholic Stuarts. Rather than see the Stuarts return after Queen Anne's death, the English Parliament invited the German Elector of Hanover, a Protestant cousin of the Stuarts, to take the throne. The Highlands had risen in protest and, after an indecisive battle at Sheriffmuir, they had been put down ruthlessly by government troops. A number of peers had lost their heads.

Alasdair had fought at Sheriffmuir. Frances watched

her husband now as he talked to his children, his dark, arresting head rimmed by the light of the fire, and her heart contracted for him. He had been twenty years old when, after Sheriffmuir, he and his father, the third earl, had been forced to flee to France for safety. The earl had died in France. Two years after Sheriffmuir the government had granted pardon to all exiled rebels and Alasdair had returned to Scotland. He had lived quietly ever since, administering his vast property, dispensing justice and charity to all his clan, the very model of an enlightened Highland chief.

But in his veins throbbed the passionate, vengeful, long-memoried blood of the Celt. He had not forgotten. And he had passed his loyalties and his dedication on to his children. For as long as there were schemes and plans to restore the Stuarts to the throne of Britain, the MacIans would be in them.

Alasdair, Niall, and Van had switched to Gaelic, unconscious most probably that they had changed languages. It was at moments like these that Frances was most conscious of being a stranger. It was not that she could not understand what her husband and children were saying—she understood Gaelic perfectly—but she could not feel what they were feeling. She was English, and the gentler, more moderate blood of the south ran in her veins.

She looked from her husband's face to her daughter's. It was because she was English, Frances thought, and had known another sort of life besides the Highlands, that she wanted more for Van.

Alasdair himself was not untraveled or uneducated. He could speak Gaelic and English and French. He knew Greek and Latin. He, like Niall, had studied at the University of Paris. He drank French claret and wore French lace at his throat and could dance as well as any English courtier. But his life was his land and his clan, and he ruled over both with as much authority as did any king.

It was a life he loved, and Niall loved it as well. But it was a relentlessly masculine world and Frances could see no place in it for her daughter.

Yet how to approach Alasdair on this matter? How to suggest to him that life in the Highlands was inadequate for Van without also suggesting that it was inadequate for her as well?

For it was not. She missed many things, true, but she had always had him. A great love, the kind they had, made up for so much. If Van should find that kind of love, Frances would not be so concerned for her. But there was no one in their circle that Frances could see who was likely to awaken that kind of feeling in her daughter.

Alasdair said something and Niall laughed. Van's face was serious, intent on what her father was saying. They all three appeared perfectly oblivious of Frances.

The thought that Van should go on a visit to her cousin Katherine in England had come to Frances several months ago. She had pondered it silently for weeks and had finally written to Katherine. Katherine's answer had come that morning. Her cousin would be delighted to have Van come for a visit in the spring.

The problem now, Frances thought, as she sat at her tea table that cold January night, the problem now was to convince Alasdair that Van should go.

Frances was the first one to retire for the night. She left Alasdair and Niall playing a game of chess and Van reading a book by the drawing-room fire and, putting her lined velvet cloak over her shoulders, began the journey to her bedroom.

The name of the castle in which the MacIans lived was Creag an Fhithich, in English, Raven's Rock. It was very old and so full of turrets and lofty buildings, spires, and towers that it was more like a small city than a single building. The original keep had been built in 1220 by Alexander II to protect the coast against attacks by Norse and Danish raiders, and shortly thereafter it had passed into the hands of the MacIan family, where it had remained until the present day. Successive generations of MacIans had added a variety of wings to the central tower and they radiated outward like the arms of an octopus, all of different styles, all built on different levels.

Rooms led off other rooms, passages twisted, stairs spiraled dizzily. And all the passages and unused rooms were bitterly, frigidly cold, so that Frances' cloak was a necessity and not a decoration.

Her own room, when finally she reached it, was lit by a blazing fire and Frances was able to put aside her cloak and comfortably let her maid undress her and brush her yard-long brown hair. As yet she had found only a stray gray hair in the shining mass, an encouraging sign, she thought. Alasdair had been far more gray at forty-four. Now, at age fifty, he was as much gray as black. But gray hair didn't age a man the way it did a woman, Frances thought. No one in his right mind would ever think of Alasdair as old.

Frances got into the big bed, warmed for her by brass warming pans, and pulled the covers up to her chin. She stared absently at the fire as the maid put away her things. The girl did not put out water for, once the fire died down, the temperature in the room would freeze a jug of water solid by morning. Margaret would be back before Frances arose to relight the fire and to pour hot water into the washbasin.

"Good night, my lady," the girl murmured.

"Good night, Margaret," Frances replied kindly, and watched as the girl left the room. Once she was alone, however, Frances did not settle herself to sleep. She lay propped against her pillows, gazing into the fire and thinking.

An hour later she was still in the same position when there came a draft of cold air from the door and she turned to see her husband enter the room.

"Awake still, m'eudail?" he asked in surprise. "You went to bed an hour ago."

"I know. I've been dreaming a little, I think." She smiled at him and he came across the room to look down into her face.

"Were you now?" His voice was soft and the hand that reached out to touch the shining top of her hair was gentle. He was a hard man in many ways, authoritarian, inflexible, demanding; but with her he was always so gentle. He went over to the window and opened it. No matter how frigid the night, Alasdair always slept with an open window.

"Are you worrying yourself about that woman of Niall's in Paris?" he asked. He took off his coat and began to unbutton his shirt.

"No." She took a slow breath. "It's not Niall who worries me."

His hands stopped and he looked up. "Oh? Who is worrying you, then, mo cridhe?"

"Van."

"Van?" His black brows rose in surprise. "What has Van done?"

"It's not what she has done, Alasdair, it's what she hasn't done that worries me. Do you realize that apart from a few trips to Edinburgh over the years, she has never left the Highlands?"

He was frowning now. "Why should she leave the Highlands? She loves it here. You know that."

"Yes, I know that." She leaned a little toward him in her earnestness. "Van's heart is as strongly rooted here as your own. But that doesn't mean she shouldn't be exposed to other places, other cultural influences. She should see something of the world, darling, just for her own education. After all, we sent Niall to Paris for that reason."

"Niall is a boy. It's right that he know something of the world."

"Van should have her opportunity too," Frances insisted. "When I was a girl I was taken to concerts, the theater, the opera, and I led a very sheltered life. Van has had none of those experiences, and she would love them, Alasdair."

He had finished unbuttoning his shirt but he made no move to take it off. "Do you want to send her to Edinburgh?" he asked.

"No." She spoke with calm determination. "I want her to go on a visit to my cousin Katherine in England."

His face closed. "England," he said. "I do not want Van to go to England."

Well, she had known how it would be. Still, she must make him see this her way. "England is not the inferno, Alasdair," she said, "and my cousin is not the devil. *I* am English, if you remember. You didn't mind that when you married me."

"You are different," he replied simply. "And Van will marry Alan MacDonald."

Frances sat bolt upright in bed. "Oh? When was this arranged?"

"It has not been arranged," he replied patiently, "but surely it is obvious. Ever since he returned from Paris Alan has doted on Van."

"If Van wishes to marry Alan, fine," Frances returned, her voice sharp. "He is an extremely nice boy. But she must have her chance in England first."

Alasdair walked to the foot of the bed and stood staring at his wife out of suddenly hard gray eyes. "Are you thinking of marrying my daughter off to a Sassenach?" he asked.

And there it was, Scot against English, all the ancient hatred fierce and alive in his heart. Frances stared back, refusing to be intimidated. "No, I am not. I simply want her to have a chance to encounter wider cultural opportunities than she has here at home. Good God, Alasdair, she spends her days here galloping her horse along the beach and roaming through the mountains like some wild creature!"

"Make her help you around the castle," he said.

"Yes," she returned ironically. "It is so easy to get Van to do what she doesn't want to do."

There was a long pause. Then he leaned his hands against the footboard of the bed. "This is not the time to be sending Van out of the country, Frances." His voice was sober. "There is great talk of a French expedition."

"There is always talk of a French expedition, Alasdair. If we wait until there is no talk, Van will be as gray as you are."

Another long pause. "Is your cousin a Jacobite?"

"Her father was," Frances returned with perfect truth. She did not mention the fact that Katherine's husband, the Earl of Linton, had been a staunch supporter of the Hanoverian succession. After all, the earl was dead now. "I certainly do not wish Van to be presented at court," she assured him. "She will not have to curtsy to the elector or anything of that nature, Alasdair. I simply want her to meet a wider variety of people than she has had a chance to here at home, and I want her to have a chance to hear some music!"

"For how long would she stay?"

Her heart leapt in her breast. He was thinking of it! "Through the summer, I thought. She can leave for England in March, when the weather breaks a little."

He straightened up, stretching the muscles in his back. "This is important to you, isn't it?" he asked slowly.

"Yes, Alasdair," she replied. "Yes, it is."

He nodded and began to take off his shirt. "All right," he said, "she can go. But only until the end of the summer.'"

She smiled at him, a warmly beautiful smile. "Thank you, darling."

"And when she comes home," he continued imperturbably, "I expect that she will marry Alan MacDonald."

2

Van was up by six-thirty the following morning, her usual hour. In summer the sun was bright at six-thirty but in January she rose by the light of the stars. Winter or summer made no difference to Alasdair, however. Everyone in the castle, with the exception of his wife, rose very early.

After a breakfast of tea and bread and butter, Van went into the drawing room to the harpsichord. She lit a few candles, as it was still dark, and then sat down at the instrument.

It was one of the favorite moments of Van's day, the moment her fingers hovered over the keys, delaying for a moment to touch them, the way a lover might delay touching his mistress's skin, just to prolong his pleasurable anticipation. Van had been playing the harpsichord since she was four years old. She had never had any teacher other than her mother, but Frances was a very skilled musician.

It was because of Frances that the harpsichord stood here in the drawing room of Creag an Fhithich. Alasdair had brought it from Paris for his wife two years after they were married, when he had realized how much she missed her music. He had sold an Italian Renaissance painting in order to pay for it, and Frances, who knew how he hated to part with any part of his heritage, had been touched and grateful.

It stood now near one of the five large windows, as much a part of the drawing room as the glass-fronted cabinets, the Oriental rugs, and the Louis XIV chairs. Van took a deep, long breath, placed her hands on the keys, and began to play.

Two hours later, as she finished a piece by Bach on which she had been working for weeks, she became aware that her mother was in the room. Van swung around on her stool.

"When did you creep in, Mother? I didn't hear you."

"The house could burn down around you while you were playing, Van, and you wouldn't notice," Frances returned humorously. "That last piece is sounding very polished."

Van did not look satisfied. "It isn't quite right. Perhaps you could help me with it, Mother."

Frances smoothed the skirt of her blue morning gown. "You see, darling," she said gently, "you've gone beyond me. You are at the point where you need a professional teacher."

Van's light eyes, gray-green as Loch Morar in summer, widened. Imperceptibly her whole body tensed. "Would that be possible?" she asked. "Would Father get a teacher for me?"

"I'm sure your father would if he could, darling," Frances returned calmly. "But a musician of the excellence that you require is not going to come to Morar. Professionals of that caliber are only to be found in places like Paris, Rome, Naples, London."

"Oh," said Van quietly.

"Which is why," Frances continued briskly, "I have arranged for you to visit London for some months."

Van stared at her mother as if she had taken leave of her senses. "Visit London?" she echoed. "Whatever are you talking about, Mother?"

"I have arranged for you to visit my cousin Katherine, Lady Linton. You've heard me mention Katherine, Van." Van nodded numbly. "She is a widow with only one son and no daughters. She is delighted at the thought of having you. And she has promised to engage a music teacher."

A look came over Van's slender face that gave her an unmistakable resemblance to her father. Her back was ramrod straight. "I do not want to go among the Sassenach," she said.

"*I* am a Sassenach," Frances returned. Her voice was perfectly pleasant. "I do not think I am so very terrible."

Van stood up. "Of course you're not terrible, Mother." She herself sounded impatient. She began to pace the room.

Frances watched her in silence for a few moments. Then she said very seriously, "Listen to me, Van. There is more to the world than the glens and hills of Morar. There is another kind of life beyond the clan. In London you will mix with people of culture, people with a wide range of interests. There will be concerts and theater. There will be the opera. There is a whole world out there, my darling, of which you know nothing."

Van had stopped pacing and now she stared at her mother in astonishment. "Don't you *like* it here in Morar, Mother?"

"Of course I like it here. This is where your father is. But do I miss the company of intellectual people, people to whom books and ideas seriously matter? Yes, I do. Do I miss music? Yes, I do."

Van was looking appalled. "I had no idea you felt this way, Mother. Why haven't *you* ever gone on a visit to England, then?"

Frances looked amused. "Because, once I was in England, I would miss your father even more."

Van smiled uncertainly in response. Then, "But *I* am perfectly happy here," she said.

"'I know you are. And you have had the advantage of growing up in what is perhaps the most beautiful place in the world. But you are eighteen, Van, not a child any longer. We sent Niall to Paris so he could see something of the world. I would send you to France as well, but I have so few connections there now. It will be best if you go to England.'"

"England," Van said. She raised an eyebrow at her mother. "And Father agrees?"

"Your father agrees."

Van's rare smiled dawned. "That must have taken some doing."

Frances smiled back serenely. "Your father in his youth spent several years in Paris. It was in Paris that we met, as you know. He thinks you need a little polish as much as I do."

Van sat down on the harpsichord stool. "What if there is a French landing?"

"If there is a French landing, of course you will come home."

"Your cousin, Lady Linton, is a Jacobite?"

Frances scarcely hesitated. "She was brought up to be as good a Jacobite as I. Our fathers were brothers, you know, and both Papa and Uncle James were dedicated Tories." What Frances did not mention was that the family into which Katherine had married, the Romneys of Linton, were among the most prominent Whigs in England.

Van drew a deep, uneven breath. "I feel as if someone has just hit me over the head," she said frankly.

Frances looked at her daughter tenderly. "You will

enjoy yourself, Van. I would not send you were I not convinced of that."

Van frowned. "When am I to go?"

"In March. You will stay until September. That is the period of the London social season. Which reminds me,"—Frances looked purposeful—"you will need a whole new wardrobe."

"I have my gold satin dress," Van said.

"You have had it for two years at least," Frances agreed cordially. "We will have Marie make you one or two dresses, and I'll let Katherine supply the rest of your wardrobe in England."

Van's finely drawn black brows came together. "It sounds very expensive, Mother."

It would indeed be expensive, but Frances had some money of her own put by. Alasdair, she knew, was not likely to finance the sort of wardrobe she planned for Van. The MacIans were rich in land and Creag an Fhithich was filled with priceless things brought back from Europe by previous MacIan travelers, but cash was always short in Morar.

"Don't worry, darling," she said now to her daughter. "I have been saving your grandfather's money for you."

Van stared at her mother in amazement. Frances rose to her feet. "If the MacDonalds are coming, I had better go to the kitchen and order the food," she said.

Van stretched her shoulders. "Hmmm," she said. "Wait until Alan hears I'm going to England."

Frances looked sharply at her daughter's face but could find nothing in its expression beyond a faint amusement.

The MacDonalds arrived early in the afternoon and

were greeted warmly by all the MacIans, including Van. The sun set at three in the afternoon in the winter and company in the long Highland evenings was always welcome.

The following morning all the men except Alan went out hunting. The mountains of Morar were filled with stag, wolf, cat, and deer, and hunting was one of a chief's main pleasures. When Alan begged off, however, no one protested. And Niall looked smugly at Van.

After the men had departed, Frances and Lady Mac-Donald settled in front of the fire for a long gossip. Alan asked Van to go for a walk with him. They both wrapped themselves in plaids and took the path that led from the castle down to the loch. When they reached the shore, Van turned to look back at her home.

Creag an Fhithich had one of the most spectacular locations in all the Highlands. It jutted up from the rock that had given it its name, its turrets, spires, and towers standing out against the magnificent mountains that backed it. At its front stood Loch Morar, a salt-water inlet of the Sound of Arisaig. The loch was surrounded by mountains, which on clear days one could see mirrored, purple and blue, in its depths. The sands of Loch Morar were almost purely white. Van thought that her home was, beyond qualification, the most beautiful place in the world.

"I wonder if Murray will have news of the prince," Alan said beside her.

Van looked at him. Alan MacDonald was taller than Niall, but he had the same narrow-boned look of the Celt. His hair was brown with a distinct tinge of red in it and the eyes that were looking back at her were a clear hazel. Van smiled. "The prince, the prince," she said teasingly. "That is all you and Niall think about. Charles Edward certainly made an impression on you two."

"He must make an impression on everyone he meets," Alan said. His hazel eyes began to sparkle. "If only the French king would give him an army! Then we could chase the elector back to Hanover and set King James on his rightful throne. A Stuart king come into his own again."

Van smiled at Alan's ringing tone and ardent face. "That, of course, is what we all desire," she said. She frowned thoughtfully. "Do you think it will happen soon, Alan?" If it did, Van knew, her trip to England would be canceled. To her profound surprise, she felt a pang of disappointment at the thought.

"I don't know," Alan returned. "Niall and I met the prince in Paris last July. The French are so involved in this war with England that they have little extra manpower." Alan gave an impatient snort. "Or so they tell the prince." Alan's face set. "Niall and I told him to come anyway," he added defiantly. "We don't need the French. The clans alone can put King James back on his throne."

Van's long lashes lifted in surprise. "Are you serious, Alan? I know Father and Lochiel have said they will support the prince only if he comes with an army."

"So has my father," Alan said disgustedly. It was obvious what he thought of such caution.

Van changed the subject. "In March I am going to England on a visit."

Alan's head snapped around. "What!"

"Yes. Mother arranged it. I am to spend six months with a cousin of hers."

"Are you serious, Van?" he demanded.

"Perfectly serious. Mother says Niall went to Paris and now it is my turn for a little . . . polishing."

"London!" Alan sounded horrified. "But what if there is a French landing?"

"If there is a French landing I shall come home."

He was looking very upset. "Van," he said, "you can't go away now. You know how I feel about you."

Van looked up into his troubled face. It was an honest face, she thought, and handsome too. "We've known each other since we were children," she began, but he interrupted her.

"I'm not talking about that! You were a child when I went away to Paris, yes, but you're not a child now. When I first saw you when I came back . . ." He broke off and then, very determinedly, he took her hands in his. "I love you, Van. I want you to marry me."

Van gazed into Alan's dear, familiar face. He had so many good qualities, she thought. She liked him very much. Why, then, did she not want to marry him? For she didn't—there was no disguising that fact from herself. She was suddenly very grateful she was going to England. If she stayed at home, she thought, she would probably find herself married to Alan Mac-Donald simply because she could think of no good reason to refuse him.

She smiled at him now and said softly, "Let's talk about that, Alan, when I return from England." And she disengaged her hands.

He frowned, frustrated, but no matter how much he argued, she would not change her mind.

3

Van sat on a gilt chair in the middle of the drawing room. The only sounds in the huge room were the crackling of the fire and the snip-snip of Frances' scissors as she cut her daughter's hair. The old sheet that had been spread under the chair was covered with locks of hair, strands of black and black-and-gray. There was no resident hairdresser at Creag an Fhithich and Frances always cut her family's hair. Van was the last in line today; Alasdair and Niall had already preceded her.

"There," Frances said at last. "I think all the ends are even." She stepped back, scissors in one hand, comb in the other, to regard her handiwork critically. Van's long hair streamed down her back and over her shoulders, a mantle of heavy black silk. Frances nodded decisively and Van immediately reached up to push her hair back away from her face. She stood up and stretched her back.

Frances was putting down her scissors when Van said abruptly, "I suppose I shall have to powder my hair when I go to England."

Frances looked at her daughter thoughtfully. "It's certainly the fashion," she said after a moment, "but I don't think it would suit you, darling. You're not a fair-skinned English girl. Powdering would only make your skin look sallow."

Van grinned. "It would make me look dark as a Gypsy, you mean."

"I mean that it would not enhance your beauty," Frances replied temperately. "Wear your hair *au naturel*. It will be more becoming."

"That will suit me fine," Van said instantly. "And as to my beauty . . ." She gave her mother a swift, ironic look that was the duplicate of one of her father's expressions.

Frances' blue eyes were steady on her daughter's face. "Don't you think you are beautiful, Van?"

"I? Beautiful? Of course not." Then, as Frances continued to look at her, she put a brief, reassuring hand on her mother's arm. "Don't worry, Mother. I realized long ago that I would never be a beauty like you. It doesn't distress me at all, I assure you."

"Don't you think Niall is handsome?" Frances asked slowly.

"Of course."

"You look very like Niall."

"But Niall is a boy, Mother. It's handsome to be dark. Girls are supposed to be fair."

"Must one be fair in order to be pretty?"

"Well, yes," Van answered in surprise. Then, "You are."

Frances stared at her daughter. "I have been thinking that I ought to tell you this, Van, so you will be prepared. It's true you aren't pretty. You're a great deal more than pretty, darling. You're beautiful. It's in your bones."

Van looked at her mother with affectionate amusement. "Mother, it isn't necessary to flatter me, I promise you. I don't at all mind not being pretty. I *like* looking like a MacIan."

Frances sighed. "Do you?"

"Yes." Van turned to look out the window. It had been raining all morning but now there was a distinct brightening over the mountains. "The weather's turning fine," she said. "I'm going out."

Frances gave her daughter a rueful look. "All right, darling. Just don't be late for tea."

As she watched her daughter's slender back disappear around the doorway screen Frances thought fervently: Thank God she is going to England.

She walked away from the hair-strewn sheet on the floor and went herself to the window where a few minutes ago Van had stood. She stared out at the loch. It was beautiful, yes, but—especially in winter—lonely. She was glad Van was going, true, but she would miss her daughter badly. She remembered, with a sudden ache, the years of her children's babyhoods . . . the feel of the little dark heads under her hands, the bliss of holding a sucking baby to her breast . . . she missed it sometimes so sharply it was like a physical stab of pain.

Frances drew a deep, unsteady breath. It was so hard to let go of one's children, she thought, but it had to be done. And she had Alasdair. She turned from the window and her eyes fell on a lock of gray-streaked hair. She smiled.

Alasdair was also thinking about Van's coming visit, but his mind was not running along the same lines as his wife's. The day before Van was due to leave, he called her into the room that served as his office for a talk. In this room Alasdair kept all the paperwork pertaining to his vast estate. Most of his land was rented out to tacksmen for cattle raising and farming, but the chief was the one who sold whatever they had managed to raise beyond what was needed for their own subsistence, and Alasdair kept meticulous records of all his dealings with French and Flemish merchants.

He was a devoted chief, Alasdair MacIan, Mac mhic Iain, and one who understood perfectly his position in life. He was of the same blood and name and descent as his people, and in the hierarchy of authority on earth he stood somewhere between them and God. The law of the central government had never penetrated beyond the Highland Line. In the glens of the Scottish Highlands, it was the chief who was the king.

Van admired her father more than anyone else she knew. Her mother and brother had her deepest love, but it was Alasdair's approval that she most desired.

He looked up now from his accounts as she entered, and gestured her to a chair. Alasdair was dressed in his usual daytime clothes of tartan trews and jacket. On the walls of the office hung a collection of broadswords and pistols. The Highlands had technically been disarmed after the last Jacobite rebellion, but the castle walls had defiantly retained their extensive armory of weapons and no government agent had objected. The rest of the clan had disarmed by pragmatically burying their weapons in convenient places so they would be ready when called for again.

"Your mother has set her heart on this visit of yours, Van," Alasdair said now, and there was a thin line between his well-marked black brows, "which is why I agreed to it. But I tell you frankly, I don't like it. Especially not now."

"Is there going to be a rising, Father?"

Two more lines bracketed Alasdair's mouth. "I don't know. The prince is eager to come but both Lochiel and I sent word that there will be little chance of success unless he can bring a French army with him. I don't know what is going to happen, Van, and I don't like the idea of you being so far away."

Van swallowed. "Do you want me to stay home, Father?"

"No." Van relaxed and Alasdair went on, "No, I promised your mother you should go, and go you will. But I want you to understand clearly that if there should be a French landing, you are to come home."

"Of course, Father," Van replied quickly.

"I will give you a letter to your mother's cousin to that effect."

Van nodded.

Alasdair's hard gray eyes scanned his daughter's face appraisingly. "Left to myself, I would not choose to send you," he repeated. "However, since you *are* going, it has occurred to me you might be useful to the cause."

Van's oddly light eyes widened in surprise. "How, Father?"

"If there is to be a successful rising, we need English help. There are many powerful Tory families in England but I fear that since the battle at Sheriffmuir in 1715, their Jacobitism has been steadily decaying. It is vitally important to the cause that their attachment to the Stuart family be reawakened." Van nodded. "This cousin of your mother's, for example," Alasdair went on slowly. "She comes from a family of steady Cavalier faith, as did your Mother, but I doubt the flame is burning so brightly as it once did. Perhaps you can be the means of rekindling it, my daughter."

Van's chin rose on her long, lovely neck. "I will do my best, Father."

"I have never been to London but I know Paris well

and I cannot imagine the social life differs greatly from one place to the other. Through Lady Linton you will have the opportunity to meet many of the people I am interested in knowing about."

There was a deep frown now between Alasdair's brows. "Take their temper, Van. You have a good brain—a better brain than Niall's, I think. I need to know the disposition of the English Tories. If the prince lands, will they join us? It is vitally important that we know where we stand in this matter."

A lovely warm color had flushed into Van's cheeks. "I understand, Father. I shall do my best."

Alasdair looked thoughtfully at his desk, picked up a paper knife, and began to turn it over in his hands. "You have a good brain, but you have very little experience of the world, Van, and your mother will not be there to guide you." Van's eyes were watching her father's slender fingers as they turned the knife over and over while he talked. "You have had very little experience of men." He looked up, his gray eyes suddenly narrow. "Be careful," he said. "Don't be taken in by fine clothes and soft words."

He was deadly serious. "Of course not, Father," Van said hastily.

"Do you like Alan MacDonald?"

Van moved infinitesimally back in her chair. "Yes," she said with reserve.

Alasdair sensed rather than saw her withdrawal. He stopped turning the knife and stared at his daughter in silence. She was a mystery to him, this girl-child of his. Niall he understood perfectly, but Van. . . . What would they make of her in England, with her beautiful face and her quiet intensity and her lack of sophistication? She lived such a secret life, Van did. Would anyone ever touch the deepest part of her?

Not Alan MacDonald. The thought came unbidden
and it was not welcome to him. He put the paper knife
down firmly. "Remember always who you are," he
told her, and he spoke now in Gaelic. "The Sassenach
will respect you because you are the daughter of an
earl. But you are more than that. You are a *chief's*
daughter, and you are Highland."

Her chin rose to the challenge and she answered in
the same language, "That thought is always in my
heart, Mac mhic Iain."

His hard gray eyes never wavered. "Go along to
your mother now. She wants to see you."

"Yes, Father," she replied, and obediently left the
room.

Van left the following morning as soon as the sky
began to lighten. Niall was to accompany her as far as
Edinburgh, and from there she would be escorted by
Alan Ruadh MacIan, Alan the Red, her father's foster
brother, and two of his sons. Frances had made arrangements with a cousin of Alasdair's in Edinburgh
to find a respectable woman to accompany Van as
well. Frances could just imagine the stir Van would
create when she arrived at the Lintons' country house
accompanied solely by three wild clansmen, two of whom
did not speak any English. But Alasdair was adamant
that his daughter be well-protected. Frances devoutly
prayed nothing would happen to provoke the body-
guards' quick tempers, and gave in.

Before she left, Van went to her mother's room to
say good-bye. Frances was sitting up in bed propped
against a pile of lace-edged pillows, her long brown
hair streaming over the fine woolen shawl around her
shoulders. She held out her arms and Van went to kiss
her.

How lovely mother always smelled. Van hugged Frances with unaccustomed fierceness. She would miss her so! Frances' arms loosened and Van stood up.

"I want you to remember one thing, darling," Frances said gravely. "I want you to remember that you are one-half English and that Katherine is as much your blood as any MacIan."

Van's lashes lifted in surprise.

"Will you promise me to remember that?" Frances asked.

"Yes, Mother."

"And try to judge people by their hearts, not by their politics!"

Van frowned. Whatever was her mother trying to say? But Frances smiled gaily and squeezed her hand. "Good-bye, darling. Enjoy yourself. And listen to the opera for me."

Saying good-bye to her father was easier. They were all on horseback in the courtyard—there was no way to get a carriage through the mountains—when Alasdair came out to bid his daughter farewell.

After issuing a few more instructions to Niall and to Alan Ruadh, he turned to Van. "Beannachd Leat," he said. "Blessings go with you, my daughter."

"Thank you, Father."

"Remember all I said yesterday."

"Yes, Father."

He nodded and Niall wheeled his pony and started out of the courtyard. Van's pony followed close behind. She looked up at the brightening sky as they started down the path and thought, with a flash of wry amusement, that her parents had given her totally contradictory admonitions.

They went through the mountains to Fort William,

one of the great forts built by General Wade to pacify
the Highlands after the last rising. From Fort William
they went south and east, through mountain passes
and across river ferries, stopping overnight at the house
of a MacDonald who was a friend of Lord Morar's.
They left the mountains the following day, coming
through Stirling, with its great castle guarding the gateway to the Highlands, past Bannockburn, where a
MacIan had fought with Robert the Bruce for Scotland's independence, across the Forth and into Edinburgh, ancient capital of Scotland and once home to
the Stuart kings.

In Edinburgh Niall saw to the transfer of Van's
baggage from the pack ponies to the coach Lord Morar
had hired for the trip to London. They stayed overnight with a cousin of her father's and there met the
middle-aged widow who was to chaperon Van. The
widow, Mrs. Robertson, was an Englishwoman who
had been visiting relatives in Edinburgh and who was
delighted by the prospect of a free trip home. The two
women were to ride in the coach, with Alan and his
two sons riding escort on horseback.

Niall kissed his sister before he handed her up into
the coach.

"You look splendid, Van," he said with genuine
admiration. "That new outfit makes you look a regular lady of fashion. You'll be the most beautiful girl in
London."

Van glanced down at her traveling dress of deep
green velvet. The material had come from France, but
it had been made by one of the castle seamstresses.

"I wish you were coming with me, Niall," she said
impulsively.

He grinned at her engagingly. "You are very well

able to take care of yourself, my sister. Only—do you not forget Alan."

"I am not likely to forget *any* of you," Van replied austerely. She was a little irritated. It seemed to her that her father and Niall were taking far too much for granted about Alan.

"Up with you, then," Niall said cheerfully, and handed her into the carriage, closing the door behind her.

"You have your pistol, Alan?" he asked his father's foster brother.

"Aye." Alan the Red, who was now more like Alan the Gray, uncarthed a weapon from the folds of his plaid and showed it to Niall.

"Good. But keep it hidden unless you need to use it. I don't have to remind *you* that the clans are supposedly disarmed."

"I will remember, Son of Alasdair. And we will guard the Lady Van with our lives."

Niall nodded and stepped back. The coachman slapped his reins and the team moved off. Van sat back and tried to get comfortable. It was a long way from Edinburgh to Kent in the south of England.

It was a week, in fact, before Van reached Staplehurst, principal seat of the Earls of Linton. The trip south had been tedious and uncomfortable but uneventful. They changed horses regularly at posting houses on the Great North Road and stayed overnight in a series of inns designed to accommodate travelers such as themselves. Alan and his sons, dressed in their tartan trews and great swathing plaids, created a stir wherever they stopped, but nothing occurred to provoke Alan to use his pistol.

They finally arrived at Staplehurst late in the afternoon of March 20. The setting sun lent a warm glow to the great golden stone house as they came up the drive. It was not the house, however, but the park that caught Van's attention. It stretched away all around them in vistas of lawn and ponds and waterfalls, all interspersed by groves of trees and wide avenues.

Van was impressed, although she would have died before she admitted it.

"My, my, my," her traveling companion, Mrs. Robertson, said admiringly. "So *this* is the famous Staplehurst park. The earl commissioned Capability Brown, a landscape architect, dear Lady Vanessa, to do it two years ago. It has been much talked about, I assure you."

"It's very pretty," Van said politely.

Mrs. Robertson stared at her in surprise and the coach pulled up in front of the house. A magnificently liveried servant came down the front steps and went authoritatively to the door of the coach, only to be virtually pushed out of the way by Alan Ruadh. "I will be opening the door for the daughter of Mac mhic Iain," Alan said haughtily, and proceeded to do so with dignity. Van repressed a smile at the look on the lackey's face.

"Thank you, Alan," she said to the clansmen in Gaelic as she stepped out of the coach.

"Vanessa, my dear," came a charmingly husky feminine voice, "is it really you at last?" And Van looked up to see her mother's cousin coming down the wide stairs.

"Lady Linton?" Van asked reservedly.

"Cousin Katherine, if you please." The countess had reached Van by now and took her hands into a warm, friendly clasp. "I am so delighted to meet you," she said, and smiled directly into Van's eyes.

Katherine Romney's own eyes were so dark a blue they were almost purple. She wore her hair powdered so Van could not tell what color it was, but her skin was very fair. She looked much younger than Van expected. Only the fine lines at the corners of her eyes and mouth gave away her age.

"I am happy to meet you also, Cousin Katherine," Van said composedly. "And may I present my traveling companion, Mrs. Cornelia Robertson." Mrs. Robertson blushed and curtsied and stammered, all of which the countess observed with serene good humor.

Donal Og spoke to his father in Gaelic and Lady Linton's violet eyes widened as they took in the sight of Van's escort.

"We will be leaving you, then, Lady Van," Alan said. "I will be telling Mac mhic Iain that you are safe."

"Are you really wishing to stay here?" Donal said in a rush to Van, speaking in the only language he knew. He looked around with ill-concealed doubt.

"I must," Van replied gravely. "It is the wish of Mac mhic Iain."

The three clansmen stepped back. If it was the wish of Mac mhic Iain, it must be done.

"Surely your . . . er . . . escort will stay the night?" Lady Linton asked. "They cannot start back north now. It will be dark soon."

"They would not wish to stay here," Van said simply. Then, to her father's loyal trio, "Beannachd Leat."

"Bennachd Leat," they replied with dignity, wheeled their horses, and were gone down the drive.

"Come into the house," Lady Linton said firmly. "I will show you to your room and then we shall have some tea."

The bedroom Lady Linton showed Van to was large and, to Van's eyes, extremely luxurious. Creag an Fhithich was filled with beautiful, priceless things, but her father's style of living had always tended toward the Spartan. About some things he was fussy; he would not drink any but the best claret, nor would he wear any shirts but those her mother exquisitely stitched for him out of the finest French cambric. But he did not believe in spoiling either himself or his children with an excess of creature comforts. The only one he spoiled in that fashion was his wife.

So the warm, comfortable, chintz-filled room, with a fire burning in the fireplace—in March! at this hour! —impressed Van greatly.

"Would you like a bath, Vanessa?" Lady Linton asked. "You have been traveling for so long, surely a nice hot bath would be refreshing."

A nice hot bath. Van looked at her hostess in wonder. They bathed frequently at Creag an Fhithich—her father thought it was good discipline—but only her mother rated hot water in the tub.

"That would be lovely," she murmured faintly.

A high-sided tin bathing tub was brought in, set in front of the fire, and filled with hot water. Van soaked luxuriously while a maid stood next to the tub holding a towel. Van didn't drag herself out until the water was almost tepid. She felt completely refreshed. A hot bath! she thought. No wonder her mother enjoyed them so.

Lady Linton was chatting pleasantly to Mrs. Robertson in the salon when Van arrived. She looked up, smiled warmly, and patted the sofa next to her. "Sit here by me, Vanessa. I want to hear all about your mother."

Van sat down rather stiffly and answered the countess's first questions with a good deal of reserve. But there was something about Lady Linton that reminded her of her mother. It was not her looks, but rather a warmth, a charm, a sense of genuinely caring about what you said and how you felt. She soon found herself relaxing and answering far more spontaneously. Mrs. Robertson, overwhelmed by her surroundings, was silent.

Katherine Romney, while skillfully setting Van at ease, was making some close observations of her own.

Vanessa's black hair was done very simply, in a coronet of braids on top of her head. Katherine would send her own hairdresser to the child in the morning, she decided. That severely simple fashion would not do at all.

Frances had said the child was not in the usual style, Katherine thought, and she most certainly was not. What Frances had not said was that Vanessa was beautiful. Her skin was dark, and against those eyes . . . The bone structure of her face was perfect. No wonder Frances had been anxious to get her out of that barbarian wilderness and into some decent society. The child was wearing an evening dress of deep burgundy silk that was beautifully made and showed off her small waist and long, lovely throat. Young girls usually wore pastels, but Frances had been right to dress Vanessa in burgundy. Frances' taste, Katherine remembered, had always been unerring.

There came a pause in the conversation and Katherine said, "Your mother desired that I choose you a wardrobe, Vanessa, but I don't see how London can better the dress you have on. It is lovely."

Van's long, narrow hand smoothed her silk lap. "Thank you. Mother had some clothes made for me at home, but she thought it would be easier to buy what I needed in England rather than have to lead a train of packhorses to Edinburgh."

Katherine arched a finely plucked eyebrow. "Packhorses?"

"You couldn't possibly get a carriage into Morar," Van replied unconcernedly.

"Oh," said Lady Linton, a little blankly. Then, "Tell me about Morar, Vanessa dear. Your mother thinks it beautiful, I know."

Van's great light eyes glowed and Katherine drew in her breath sharply. Her thoughts went, quite suddenly, to her son. Whatever was Edward going to think of this Scottish cousin of his?

After Katherine had heard all about the loch and the mountains and the sea, she introduced the subject that was on her mind. "My son the earl, your cousin Edward, was sorry not to be here to greet you, Vanessa. He was called to London unexpectedly, but he will be returning shortly."

Van smiled politely.

"And in the meantime"—Lady Linton smiled her lovely, warm smile—"You and I will have a chance to become better acquainted."

Van's own smile warmed a little in response. It was impossible not to like her mother's Cousin Katherine.

4

Lady Linton's hairdresser descended upon Van the following morning and took her in hand. First her long heavy tresses were washed and then attacked with the curling iron. Van's only stipulation was that she should not be powdered, and Lady Linton, who was present as an interested observer, agreed. "It would make you look sallow, Vanessa dear."

"That's what my mother said," Van replied.

The hairdresser went to work and Van sat quietly and allowed her to fuss as she pleased. As she watched in a mirror a series of long curls began to appear. Van stared curiously. "I did not think my hair would ever curl," she murmured. "It's so heavy and straight."

"Your hair, it is beautiful, Lady Vanessa," the hairdresser said. Then, in French she said to Lady Linton, "Mademoiselle does not look English."

"I am not English," Van replied in the same language. "I am a Scot."

The hairdresser looked delighted. "You speak very good French, my lady. You have traveled in France, perhaps?"

"No. My mother taught me French."

"Your mother always had a gift for languages," Lady Linton said and Van felt a stab of homesickness.

Her hair, when it was finished, looked lovely even

to Van's critical eyes. It was drawn back off her fore-head and fell in a profusion of ebony ringlets on her neck and shoulders. Van had refused the tiny lace-edged cap the hairdresser had tried to pin on her creation. In the Highlands there was an iron-clad rule that unmarried girls did not cover their hair. Both Lady Linton and the hairdresser had acquiesced grace-fully to her scruples and her hair was left unadorned save for a simple threading of ribbon.

After she was dressed in a day gown of fine green merino wool, Lady Linton took Van on a tour of the house. Mrs. Robertson had departed earlier in the Romney coach, full of gratitude and awe, so Katherine was alone with her guest.

Staplehurst was a much more formally laid-out house than Creag an Fhithich. Everything in the castle at home was come at by narrow spiral stairs or long winding passages. This English house had been added onto also, but the result was much more symmetrical than the rabbit warren of different levels and sizes that Van was used to at home.

Almost the entire ground floor of Staplehurst was occupied by living rooms. There were a dining room, drawing room and library, several smaller salons, and a great long gallery that was filled with pictures. On the ground floor as well was a state apartment of several bedrooms and dressing rooms, which had been occupied at times by both Queen Elizabeth and King James, Lady Linton told Van. A large conservatory led west from the dining room to the chapel, and concealed the huge service wing from the garden.

The second floor of the house was given over to bedrooms, with attendant dressing rooms and, in some cases, sitting rooms. The third floor held the nursery and the schoolroom, both still furnished and polished, although they had lain empty for many years.

"My son is planning an addition to the house," Lady Linton told Van as they finished their tour. "He has engaged William Kent to add a series of state reception rooms to the ground floor and some more bedrooms upstairs. It used to be that only family came to visit but in the past few years it has become more common for large house parties of people to gather at country homes for festivities and—of course—for politics. One needs different kinds of rooms to accommodate them all." Lady Linton smiled affectionately. "And Edward loves to build. The park has become quite famous, you know."

"It's lovely," Van said absently. Politics, she thought. This looked promising. Evidently that Romneys were still interested in politics.

"I have a letter for you from my father, Cousin Katherine," she said. "Would it be all right if I gave it to you now?"

Lady Linton looked surprised but she nodded. "Yes, of course, Vanessa. Go and fetch it and then come to the morning room."

The morning room was a pretty, very feminine room that the countess used as a combination office and sitting room. It was here that she attended to her correspondence, wrote out her invitations, her menus, and so on. She was sitting on a green silk sofa in front of the fire when Van returned with Lord Morar's letter. Van gave it to her, then went to sit in a high-backed velvet chair of the same green as the sofa.

There was silence in the room as Lady Linton read her letter. When finally she looked up, Van could not read her expression. "Your father seems to expect a French invasion," Lady Linton said thoughtfully.

"Yes." Van leaned a little forward. "Things look very promising, Cousin Katherine. The prince is most anxious to lead an expedition."

Lady Linton sighed. "Do you know, I had quite forgotten what a rabid Jacobite Morar is. Frances never speaks of it in her letters."

There was a startled pause. Then, "I don't think 'rabid' is the correct word," Van said. " 'Committed' is more appropriate."

"Perhaps." Lady Linton looked down at the letter once more. "Well, if there is a French invasion, Vanessa, be assured that I will see you get home safely." The violet eyes lifted to Van's face. "But I doubt there will be a French invasion, my dear. I doubt it very much."

Van frowned. It was Lady Linton's tone that warned her more than the words. "My mother thought you also were a Jacobite, Cousin Katherine," she said at last, carefully. "Was she wrong?"

Katherine Romney continued to look thoughtfully at the young face opposite her. "My father, like your mother's father, had Tory and High Church principles, certainly," she said at last.

Van was not liking the sound of this at all. "And you?" she asked bluntly. "Do you still hold to the faith of your father, Cousin Katherine? My mother has not forgotten her upbringing."

A flash of impatience flickered across Lady Linton's face. "Your mother has remained Jacobite because she is married to your father. I, on the contrary, married a man with very different principles." The violet eyes were faintly ironic. "Women, my dear Vanessa, tend to take on their husbands' politics, you know."

A fine excuse for betraying your king, Van thought

scornfully. But all she said was, "The Earl of Linton is not a Jacobite, then?"

"The Romneys have been Whigs for generations," Lady Linton said gently. "A Romney accompanied William of Orange when he came from Holland to accept the English throne. My son is a member of Lord Pelham's government. It was on government business that he was called to England."

Van was appalled. How could this have happened? She forced her voice to remain quiet. "I am quite sure my father did not know this."

Katherine Romney looked amused. "Considering this letter, I am quite certain also," she agreed. "But your mother did."

Dhé. Van's eyes opened wide.

"Oh yes." Lady Linton's eyes were half-humorous, half-rueful. "Frances certainly knew. The Romneys, my dear, are rather famous, you see. There is no question that Frances could be ignorant of their political affiliation."

Van was dumbfounded. "But why . . . ?"

"Because she wanted very much for you to have a chance to see something of the world outside your own hills." Lady Linton's voice was gentle. "Vanessa, dear, let us not allow politics to spoil your visit. Obviously your mother did not tell you that the Romneys are Whigs because she knew that if your father found out he would not allow you to come. And she wanted very much for you to come."

It must be so. Van remembered suddenly her mother's urging that she judge people by their hearts, not by their politics. Almost certainly she had known.

"Vanessa," Katherine said sympathetically, "it is not important, my dear. Believe me. It is not something we need ever discuss again. And should it hap-

pen that the prince lands with a French army, I promise
I will send you home." She got up and went over to
put a warm hand on Van's shoulder. "You have come
all this long way to enjoy yourself, my dear. Don't
disappoint your mother."

Van lifted her long, searching look to Lady Linton's
face. What Cousin Katherine did not know, she thought,
was that she had another sort of mission from her
father that still needed to be carried out. She forced
herself to smile. "No," she said. "I shouldn't want to
do that. Very well, Cousin Katherine. Between us,
we shall consider this subject closed."

Katherine squeezed her shoulder gently. "Good girl.
Now, would you like to play the harpsichord for me?"

"Of course," said Van courteously, and rose to her
feet.

Lady Linton planned to take Van to London as
soon as her wardrobe was extensive enough to allow
her to take part in the myriad events of the social
season. Consequently, Van found herself spending un-
told numbers of hours with dressmakers, who pinned
and snipped and hemmed like a hive of bees in full
activity.

She was not looking forward to the advent of her
cousin the earl. It was one thing to have to accept
Lady Linton graciously; after all, Lady Linton was her
mother's dear cousin and more a lapsed Jacobite than
a full-fledged Whig. But to have to be the guest of a
full-blooded Sassenach Whig! That stuck in Van's
throat. If it were not for the fact that she might be of
use to the cause in London, Van thought she would
certainly have gone home.

He came four days after Van's own arrival at
Staplehurst. Van and Lady Linton were sitting in the

drawing room waiting for dinner to be announced when the Linton butler, Fenton, came in to say, "His lordship has arrived, my lady. He just drove his horses down to the stable himself. Shall I tell Cook to put back dinner?"

Lady Linton's lovely face lit like a candle. "Yes, Fenton, do that, please." As the butler left the room she turned to Van. "I have no doubt at all my son will greet all his horses before he puts in an appearance before his mother. I hope you are not too hungry, Vanessa dear."

It was perfectly plain to Van that even had she been starving she was going to have to wait for the earl. "Of course not," she replied a little austerely, and listened with half an ear to Lady Linton's abstracted chatter. The countess clearly was not interested in Van's responses. All her attention was directed toward the door of the room.

At last it opened and both women stared at the tall male figure that filled the doorframe.

"Well, darling," Lady Linton said composedly. "And have you reacquainted yourself with the horses?"

The voice that replied was deep and clear and tinged with amusement. "You know me too well, Mama," and Edward Philip Henry George Anthony Romney, twenty-seven years old and Earl of Linton for the last five years, began to walk across the room.

Van had never wondered what he looked like and she felt the oddest tightening in her stomach as she watched him come. He was all Saxon: tall and fair and broad-shouldered. He was bareheaded and the rays of sunlight from the window struck sparks of gold from his neatly tied back hair. It did not take much imagination, Van thought, to picture a Viking's helm on that smoothly shining gilt head. He was the archetypical Sassenach and Van's spine was ramrod straight as she acknowledged Lady Linton's introduction.

"How do you do, cousin," the deep, beautifully timbred voice said easily. "My mother is so pleased to have a daughter-on-loan."

Van stared up into the bluest eyes she had ever seen, her face still and reserved. "How do you do, my lord," she answered in a voice she strove to make cool and distant. She removed her hand quickly from his grasp. "I am pleased to be here."

His eyes, impossibly, got ever bluer. "Did you have a pleasant journey?" he asked.

"Yes. Thank you." He was so big he blocked out her whole view of the room.

"François is holding dinner for you, darling," Lady Linton said, and he turned from Van to smile at his mother. It was a loving smile, a little amused and full of lazy sunshine.

"All right, Mama," he said. "I'll go and change."

Dinner was more than an hour late when the earl finally took his seat at the head of the polished rosewood dining-room table.

"It's a long trip from Scotland, cousin," he remarked genially to Van as liveried servants placed dishes on the table. "Was it very arduous?"

"Not arduous. Just tedious." Van forced herself to look at him. His blue gaze was directly on her face. There was no purple in his eyes, as there was in Lady Linton's, nor any gray, as in her mother's. They were completely and absolutely blue.

Sassenach eyes.

He raised his golden eyebrows. "And what have you been doing since your arrival?" His voice was perfectly courteous, but Van thought she detected a faint note of amusement in its dark depths. Her back stiffened.

"Getting fitted for clothes," she said. "Cousin."

Lady Linton added serenely, "Frances desired me to see to dear Vanessa's wardrobe, Edward. Just fancy, Vanessa says it is impossible to get a carriage in to her home."

"General Wade's roads don't go as far west as Morar," the earl replied calmly, and Van stared at him. Edward smiled at her, but not with his eyes. "Didn't you expect me to know where Morar is?" he asked.

"No. That is," Van amended hastily. "I hadn't thought of it."

"When Vanessa's wardrobe is completed we will leave for London," Lady Linton intervened. There was the faintest of lines between her lovely brows. For some unfathomable reason, her son and her guest did not appear to be getting along. "Did you look into engaging a music teacher, darling?" she asked now. "Frances was particularly anxious for Vanessa to receive some professional instruction while she is with us."

"Yes, I did, Mama," he replied impeturbably. Then, to Van, "You must play for me after dinner, cousin."

"Certainly," Van said stiffly. It was going to kill her, she thought, to be beholden to this . . . this Whig.

"How was the rest of your London visit?" Lady Linton asked her son. "What was that urgent summons about?"

He shrugged easily, his big shoulders moving smoothly under the blue velvet of his coat. "There were dispatches from Cumberland," he replied. He took a sip of burgundy and turned to Van. "The Duke of Cumberland is commanding a combined British, Dutch, Hanoverian, and Austrian force against the French," he said.

"I know." She paused and then added deliberately, "In Scotland we hear *all* the news from France. My brother, in fact, just recently returned from three years at the University of Paris."

"I see," said Edward, very softly. He looked over to his mother's face and smiled. "And have you planned every moment of Vanessa's visit for her, Mama?" he asked, his smile lazy and sweet, his blue eyes glinting. "Mama is in heaven at the thought of a daughter to take about," he added to Van. "She has been contacting all her old cronies and lining up invitations for months."

Van looked at Lady Linton, her eyes wide and startled.

"Edwards exaggerates," Katherine Romney said with dignity. Then, laughing, "But only a very little. My goodness, Vanessa, but this visit of yours is going to be fun!"

5

After dinner Edward insisted that Van play for him. She sat down at the harpsichord reluctantly, but soon the music absorbed her, as it always did. When she had finished she sat for a moment, hands in lap, back to her audience. Then she turned around.

His eyes were waiting for her. There was no amusement in them now; they were utterly and completely grave. "Herr Schmidt will not do for you at all," he said. "I will engage Martelli."

"Martelli!" Lady Linton said. "Do you think he would consider Vanessa as a pupil?"

"Yes," Edward replied matter-of-factly. "If I recommended her." His eyes had never left Van. "Do you know the Brandenburg Concertos?"

"Some of them," Van replied.

He nodded. "Play one, please," he said, and Van, automatically responding to his tone, turned back to the instrument.

She played for half an hour, sometimes stopping and correcting herself, but he never said a word. When she had finished he nodded and said, "I understand perfectly why your mother was so anxious for you to get further instruction." Van felt a flash of treacherous joy at his words and dropped her lashes to hide her emotion.

"Edward is a great music lover, Vanessa dear, so you can trust his word," Lady Linton put in. "And once we get to London he will be able to take you to a host of concerts—he's invited to every musical evening in London, you see—and to Vauxhall and to the opera as well. You will have a surfeit of music, my dear, I assure you."

Van's lashes lifted to reveal glowing eyes. "You can never have a surfeit of music, ma'am," she said a little breathlessly.

The earl didn't reply and after a moment he turned to his mother. "When do you plan to leave for London?" he asked.

"In about a week's time, I think," Lady Linton replied. "Vanessa is to attend the Duchess of Newcastle's ball on April 5."

He grinned. "The most important ball of the season, eh, Mama?"

"Well, it is certainly the ball that opens the season," Lady Linton returned imperturbably.

Van sat silently on her stool. The earl was standing now, leaning his big shoulders against the chimneypiece, looking at his mother with amused affection. The candles in the wall sconces illuminated the shining golden wing of his hair. His shoulders were enormous yet his waist and hips in the closely fitting satin breeches were narrow. He looked at Van. "Would you like to ride with me tomorrow morning, cousin?" he asked.

Van hesitated. She would actually like to spend as little time in his company as possible, but she could think of no excuse. "If the dressmakers don't need me?" she said to Lady Linton.

Edward had not missed her hesitation and his smile became sardonic. "I'm sure they can spare you for a morning," he said dryly.

"Of course they can," Lady Linton said.

"Very well," Van said, none too graciously. Then, hoping to shock him, "I'm afraid I've had none too much practice using a sidesaddle. At home I wear my brother's trews and ride astride."

Lady Linton looked scandalized. The earl, irritatingly, merely looked amused. "Did you bring your . . . ah . . . trews with you?" he inquired courteously.

"Of course not," Van snapped.

His blue eyes glinted. "Then you will have to ride sidesaddle, I'm afraid."

"Of course she will ride sidesaddle," Lady Linton said coldly. "Don't be ridiculous, Edward. Vanessa has a very lovely riding habit, I assure you."

"Mother insisted," Van said a little sourly. She really did not ride sidesaddle very well and she was not looking forward to making a fool of herself in front of the Earl of Linton.

"Don't worry, cousin," he said. "I won't let anything happen to you." His voice was sympathetic but there was a gleam of wicked laughter in his eyes.

Van's own eyes narrowed. Her palm itched to smash across that handsome, mocking face. She closed her fist and said austerely, "Thank you. I feel so much better." And at that he laughed out loud.

He was waiting in the hall the following morning and he raised a golden eyebrow as she came down the stairs. "This *is* a very nice habit, cousin," he said approvingly.

Van gave him a dark look. The habit Frances had had made for her was of a particularly becoming shade of green cloth. On her head Van wore a Scots bonnet of deep green velvet under which she had, as usual, simply bundled her hair. "Are the horses out front?" she asked in a clipped voice.

"No. I thought we'd walk down to the stables. Mama says you haven't been there yet."

"Well, let's get started than," Van said. She was in no mood to make polite conversation. He opened the door for her with unruffled courtesy and discoursed easily the entire way to the stables, seemingly oblivious of her monosyllabic answers. Van walked like a Highlander, with long, swift strides that ate up the ground; her green bonnet, she noted disgustedly, did not quite reach his shoulder. At that moment they came down a small rise of land and Van saw the stableyard.

The Staplehurst stables were magnificent. All of the buildings were of the same golden stone as the house; behind the barns and carriage houses stretched acres of fenced-in paddocks. Van stopped unconsciously and stared. None of this was visible from the house.

"I'm rather proud of my horses," Edward said at her elbow.

Van didn't reply but started to walk forward again. The stable at home was more a run-in shelter from the weather than anything else. The hardy Highland ponies they rode needed very little pampering.

A groom appeared out of nowhere. "Marcus is ready, as you requested, my lord. And Mallow. Shall I have them brought out?"

"Yes, Blackstone, thank you. Oh, and, Blackstone, this is Lady Vanessa MacIan. She is visiting my mother."

Blackstone ducked his head. "Morning, my lady."

"Good morning," Van returned.

"Did I tell you yesterday that I think I've got a buyer for Beau, Blackstone?"

The man looked suddenly alert. "No, my lord, you did not."

"Stanmore caught me at my club a few days ago. He's looking for a hunter. We'll have to get Beau out over fences a few times to get him in condition."

"Right, my lord."

There was the sound of hooves and Van turned to look at the two horses being brought out of the barn. She swallowed. They looked so big. The earl reached up to rub a dark bay forehead. "This is Marcus," he said.

Van had never seen a horse like Marcus before. His elegant head, with widely spaced, large, lustrous eyes and narrow, tapering nostrils, was set on an arched and powerful neck. His strongly sloped shoulders and muscled rear proclaimed sheer power, yet his legs were slender, even delicate-looking. He did not look as if he belonged to the same species as the shaggy, sturdy ponies Van had grown up with. He was magnificent, but Van thought she would much rather look at him than ride him.

"And this is Mallow," Edward went on. "He'll carry you very nicely."

Mallow was, mercifully, not so big as Marcus, nor so powerful-looking. He was a golden chestnut in color, with a dished, Arabian face and very soft, kind eyes. He was wearing a sidesaddle.

"Up you go," Edward said cheerfully and, before Van realized what was happening, his hands were around her waist and he was lifting her into the saddle. "How's the stirrup length?" he asked, and Van gave him a look of pure dislike. He had lifted her as easily as if she had been a child.

"Fine," she said, slipping her toe into the single stirrup iron.

Edward swung easily into his saddle and Van looked at

him nervously, expecting the great bay stallion to begin to dance around. Marcus stood rock-still, the flickering of his ears his only motion. "Ready?" Edward asked genially.

Van raised her chin. "Yes," she said. Marcus began to walk forward and Mallow followed.

They walked through the stableyard and along a road that led by the paddocks. Van stiffened in nervousness as the horses in the paddocks came to gallop alongside the fences, but neither Marcus nor Mallow stirred out of the steady, even, forward walk. As they entered a wide ride that led through a wood, Van began to relax.

"Feeling better?" Edward asked.

"Yes," Van answered shortly. Then, "I'm not accustomed to such large horses. At home I ride ponies."

"If you can ride a pony over rough ground, you'll have no trouble at all with my horses," Edward said calmly.

Van was beginning to think he was right.

"Let's trot, shall we?" said Edward, and before she could protest, the two horses moved forward.

It was like sitting on air. Van couldn't believe how comfortable Mallow was. She looked over at Marcus. The great stallion appeared to be floating, he was so light.

When they came down to a walk again Edward looked at her and, unbidden, Van's rare smile dawned. "They're marvelous," she said.

"Training a horse is like working on a piece of music," he said. "The end product must be smooth, light, effortless, but to get to that point takes a lot of hard work." The tone of his voice changed. "Speaking of music"—he was looking straight ahead now—"why didn't your parents send you to Paris to study? Why London?"

Van was silent, thrown off balance by the sudden change in topic and in tone.

He looked at her out of the side of his eyes, a flash of blue quickly withdrawn. "I take it from your none-too-veiled comments last night that you are still Jacobites in Morar?"

Van's face was still, her eyes veiled and wary. "Yes," she said. "We are."

"Then why not Paris?"

"My mother has no social contacts left in Paris," she replied carefully. "And your mother and she were like sisters when they were young."

His profile was unreadable. "I'm surprised your father let you come, into the lion's den, as it were."

Van looked straight ahead of her. "My father was under the impression that I would be visiting a Jacobite family." She paused and then added, "So was I."

There was a distinctly startled pause. Then he gave a short laugh. "Your mother was indeed anxious to get you away."

Van said a few Gaelic curses under her breath. Then a thought struck her. "How do you know my father is a Jacobite? Your mother had quite forgotten."

"My mother, bless her, is completely oblivious of politics. As your mother must be too, or she would never have arranged this visit. I thought it was suspicious the moment I heard about it."

Van's fine lips turned slightly down. "Suspicious?" she asked dangerously.

He stared at her, his blue eyes cold. "If not suspicious, than certainly odd."

"If you have such objections to my visit, then why

did you allow me to come?" she asked. Her chin had lifted in a gesture of perfectly unconscious arrogance.

"Because my mother was so pleased at the thought of having you," he replied grimly. "I was serious last night, you know. She has been planning for this visit for months."

Van's eyes fell to her own narrow hands on the reins. "Oh," she said.

"And if you do or say anything to upset or embarrass her," he continued evenly, "I will murder you, Vanessa."

Van's head jerked up. "I have no intention of embarrassing your mother!"

"Then you are really here just for social purposes?" He was pushing her relentlessly, his blue eyes cold and piercing.

Van's long lashes came down. "Of course," she said out of a suddenly constricted throat.

"It has nothing to do with the Chevalier's recent busy visits to France?"

"He is a prince, cousin, not a chevalier," she said defiantly.

"What he is," Edward returned grimly, "is a damn nuisance."

Van flung back her head. "He is the rightful heir to the throne!" she flared. "His father, King James, is our rightful king. The elector is nothing but a . . . a usurper."

"*King* George," he replied very deliberately, "is the duly chosen king of Great Britain."

"Chosen by whom?" Van shot back.

"Chosen by Parliament."

"Parliament doesn't have the right to choose a king," Van said fiercely. "That right is God's."

"And that, my dear Vanessa, is where we differ."

"Don't call me your dear Vanessa," Van snapped.

"It's true, you're not at all like a Vanessa," he agreed cordially. "However did you get the name?"

"It was my grandmother's," she replied reluctantly. Then, "At home they call me Van."

"Much more suitable," he agreed, and she glared at him. She did not want his approval.

"We differ in that I think the king should be responsible to Parliament and you think he should be responsible only to himself," Edward continued imperturbably. "It is the difference between an absolute monarchy and a constitutional monarchy. We in Britain want a constitutional monarchy, and so we have King George."

Van knew nothing of absolute versus constitutional monarchies. She knew only one thing. "King James has the right." He didn't reply and Van frowned in thought. He had not, she realized, answered her original question. "How did you know my father was a Jacobite?" she asked again.

"It's my business to know those things," he replied briefly.

Van's face was aloof and reserved. "You have a position in the government, I believe your mother said."

"Yes." He was riding bareheaded and a breeze blew up and stirred the thick golden hair at his forehead. He looked over at her austere, beautiful profile. "I know that the Chevalier has been in France. I know that there has been activity in the Highlands. I know about Murray of Broughton's visits."

Van felt a stab of fear. "My," she said with an effort at lightness, "I had no idea we were objects of such flattering interest."

"And I wondered very seriously, when my mother received Lady Morar's request, if perhaps you weren't

being sent south to contact English Jacobites," he
went on smoothly.

Van's heart began to pound. Her thin nostrils quivered. "And if I were?" she managed to ask.

The only sound for a long minute was the clip-clop
of the horses' hooves on the path. Finally Van could
stand it no longer and looked over at him. His gaze
was full upon her, lazy now, mocking. "Well, now, if
you were," he said softly, "then I should be most
happy to introduce you to whomever you desired to
see."

Van's hands involuntarily tightened on the reins and
Mallow stopped. Marcus halted too and the two riders
stared at each other, the air between them suddenly
dense with tension.

"Why would you do that?" Van asked slowly.

"Because nothing would please me more than to
have an accurate reading of the English temper sent to
Scotland," he replied. His eyes began to get very blue.
"You live in a fog of romantic dreams up there," he
said. "The Stuarts will never return to the throne of
England. England does not want them. And those
English Jacobites your father is so concerned about—oh,
they still make sentimental toasts to the 'king over the
water,' and all that rot, but if you think they will bestir
themselves to aid a rebellion, you are much mistaken."

Van's narrowed eyes glittered between their long
dark lashes. "I don't believe you."

"Whom do you want to see?" he asked coldly.
"Altop? Stowcroft? Marston? Darby?"

They were all names given to her by her father.
"Yes," Van said defiantly.

Marcus began to move forward and Gypsy followed.
"Very well," the earl said, "when we reach London I
shall arrange it."

Van's thoughts were a mass of alarmed confusion and she started when he reached over to put a hand on her arm. "My mother is to know nothing of this. And you and I are to be polite to each other. I will not have her pleasure spoiled by any Jacobite nonsense. Do you understand me, Van?"

Van's heart was thudding. For some reason, he could make her more furious than she ever remembered being in her life. "I understand you," she said through her teeth. "Edward."

"Good." Their eyes remained locked for a long minute and then he turned away. "Let's trot some more," he said abruptly, and the two horses moved forward in unison.

6

Edward spent the afternoon at the stables and Van spent the afternoon with the dressmakers. She and Lady Linton were alone at dinner.

"Edward sent word he was taking potluck over at the squire's," Lady Linton reported to Van with a smile. "He'll be back later in the evening."

Van thought that it would be fine with her if he never returned.

She was playing the harpsichord for Lady Linton when he finally came in at about eight o'clock, and for some reason, she, who wouldn't notice if the house burned down around her, was instantly aware of his presence. She finished the piece and then turned around on her stool, suddenly wary.

He gave her a sunny smile. "Lovely," he said approvingly.

"Yes, it is a great treat to have such grand music all to oneself," Lady Linton agreed. "Did the squire give you a good dinner, darling?"

"The usual." His blue eyes laughed at her. "Mutton."

"Oh, dear," the countess said comically. "He *is* so predictable."

"I'm hunting with him tomorrow morning," the earl said. "I want to get Beau out over some fences, and I want to get the squire and the rest of the local landowners turned up sweet for the Quarter Session."

Lady Linton turned to Van. "Edward is lord lieutenant for the county," she explained kindly, "and he has been trying to work with the landowners to develop a relief policy for the rural poor."

"I see," Van replied quietly. Then, "It didn't seem to me that poverty was much of a problem here in Kent. The tenents' houses I saw today all looked very prosperous."

The cottages of the Staplehurst tenants had in fact looked like palaces in comparison to the poor dwellings of sod and heather and stone that housed large numbers of MacIan clansmen.

"*Edward's* tenants are never in want," Lady Linton said proudly. "But not all landowners are as diligent or as clever as he."

"Nor as rich," Van put in dryly.

"It isn't merely a matter of money," Edward said, and his voice was very serious. "It's a matter of being open to new ideas. Most Englishmen farm the exact same way their great-great-grandfathers farmed. Agriculture will never progress until people are ready to use new inventions and new ideas."

"Such as?" Despite herself, Van was curious.

"Such as Jethro Tull's new seed drill. It sows seed in straight rows and makes weeding easier and more efficient. And all my own land is planted under Lord Townshend's crop-rotation plan. This eliminates the fallow year and allows you to bring more land into cultivation each year."

His eyes were brilliant. "Then there is the pedigree breeding of cattle," he began, but Lady Linton cut in.

"I don't think that is a proper topic to discuss with Vanessa, Edward."

Van stared at Lady Linton in surprise. "Why ever not?"

Edward grinned. "Young girls don't discuss breeding in mixed company," he said.

"Breeding *cattle?*" Van asked in astonishment, and Edward's grin broadened.

"It's time for the tea tray," Lady Linton said firmly, and rang the bell.

For the remainder of the week Edward and Van met only in the company of Lady Linton and were scrupulously polite to each other. Edward spent his days with his horses, his estate manager, and his tenants. Van was being bored into near-rebellion by the dressmakers and the constant talk of clothes and found herself increasingly resentful that the earl never even offered to let her ride again.

Then, on the day before they were to leave Kent for London, he told her to get her riding habit on and he'd take her out. Van's initial impulse was to refuse; his invitation had sounded remarkably like an order. But she was desperate to get outdoors and exercise, so she swallowed her temper and accepted.

"Just give me half an hour with Vanessa, darling," Lady Linton interposed. "The cream satin ball gown needs only one more fitting."

"Very well, Mama," Edward replied with resignation. He was already dressed for riding in a rust-colored coat and tan breeches that showed off his long, muscular legs.

"I'll meet you down at the stables," Van said.

His eyes just touched hers. "Very well," he said again. "I'll have one of the footmen escort you."

"I know my way, thank you," Van replied irritably.

He cocked a golden eyebrow and then nodded,

"Come along, Vanessa," Lady Linton said. "We don't want to keep Edward waiting too long."

An hour later Van arrived at the stables dressed in her green riding habit. One of the grooms immediately came over to her. "His lordship is riding Marcus in the paddock, my lady. I'll go tell him you're here."

"That won't be necessary," Van said. "I'll go." She could see a horse and rider circling the paddock immediately behind the carriage house and she moved in that direction.

Edward was riding Marcus in a large circle in one corner of the paddock. He was, as usual, bareheaded, and the April sun beat down on his bright hair and the richly shining dark bay coat of the stallion.

Van's throat began to ache strangely. The two of them were so beautiful, moved in such perfect harmony together. As she watched, Marcus turned his shoulder slightly and, still traveling forward in a soft, springy trot, began to cross his inside legs over in front of his outside ones.

Van's mouth dropped slightly open. She had never seen anything like that before. Then, smoothly and softly, with no perceptible movement on Edward's part, Marcus came back to trotting forward normally. As Van watched, he slowed the trot even more but came further off the ground at each step. It seemed, in fact, as if he hung in the air, the great, powerful stallion as light as a current of air himself.

Marcus came down to a walk and Edward leaned forward to pat his neck. Then he looked up and saw Van at the rail.

"Sorry," he said as he came up to her. "Have you been here long?"

"No." Van's great eyes were fixed on Marcus. "That was beautiful," she said, almost reverently.

"He's good," Edward agreed, patting the stallion again. He looked over Van's head. "Is Mallow ready?" he asked.

"Aye, my lord. She's coming."

"Good. Open the gate for me, please."

The groom hastened to do the earl's bidding and Edward and Marcus came out to stand by Van. She still could not get over how quiet the obviously highly bred horse was, how tractable.

"Here's Mallow now," Edward said, and Van let a groom give her a leg up into the saddle. She was much less tense this time and was able to sit relaxed and easy as the two horses walked out of the stableyard together.

Van filled her lungs with air. It felt so *good* to be outdoors.

"Beginning to feel a little caged?" the deep voice next to her inquired.

She shot him a sideways look. "I'm accustomed to spending a great deal of time out-of-doors."

He didn't reply and after a minute she asked, because she was intensely curious, "What was that you were doing with Marcus back in the paddock?"

His splendid profile was grave, unreadable. "Just some exercises," he replied.

"Can Mallow do them?" Van persisted.

He looked at her. "He can do the shoulder-in, but his *passage* is nothing at all like Marcus'."

"*Passage?*" she inquired.

"That slow, highly cadenced trot we were doing."

"Did you teach the horses to do those things?"

She got his profile again. "Yes."

Van was damned if she'd ask him any more questions. She directed her own gaze to the path in front of her and pretended she was alone.

"I'd better bring Mallow up to London for you," he said finally as they came out of the home woods onto one of the farm roads. "You'll want to do some riding in Hyde Park."

Van wasn't quite sure if her riding was up to London traffic, but she remembered the confinement of the last week and decided she'd rather look a fool outdoors than be relegated to the house all the time. "Thank you," she said expressionlessly. At that moment a dog erupted into the road in front of them, barking excitedly. Mallow began to dance around, but by this time Van was confident enough to sit calmly and tell him firmly to whoa. Marcus had his ears back but otherwise was quiet. A child dashed into the road after the dog and after a missed try or two finally grabbed it. Then he looked up at the earl and said guiltily, "I'm sorry, my lord."

Edward looked sternly at the tousle-haired youngster. Van judged the boy to be about seven, "You never even looked before you ran out into the road, Jem."

"S-sorry, my lord,'" the child repeated. He stared fearlessly up at Edward. "I didn't mean to hurt you or the lady."

"You are the one who would have been trampled," the earl replied emphatically. He looked then with distaste at the shabby ball of fur in the child's arms. "I hope you are keeping that mongrel away from my cattle."

"I am that, my lord." The boy's eyes began to sparkle. "Sam's ever so smart, my lord. I'm learning him all sorts of tricks."

"How delightful. Have you ever tried teaching him the trick of a bath?"

"Oh, yes, my lord," Jem replied blithely. "Only, he rolled in the pig's mud this morning."

At that Edward grinned. "He looks it. Get along with you, lad, back to your mother. The next time I come by, I'll expect to see those tricks."

The boy grinned back. "Yes, my lord!" Then he obediently raced to the house.

A reminiscent smiled lingered around the earl's mouth as the two horses started forward again. "I remember that age very well," he murmured nostalgically. "One never walked, one ran. And one's dog *always* seemed to be rolling in mud puddles."

Van thought for a minute and then her elegant nose wrinkled. "I think I'm *still* in that stage," she said doubtfully, and at that he threw back his golden head and roared.

"Do you raise cattle?" Van asked when his mirth had subsided.

"Yes. Beef is coming more and more into demand." He guided Marcus around a fallen branch and Van followed. "Cattle raising is one of the main occupations of the Highlands, I believe," he said to her over his shoulder.

"Yes. And we farm as well. The soil is rocky and hard, nothing like what you have here, but we plant corn. We fish. Mother has a huge kitchen garden filled with vegetables."

She came up alongside him again. "Do you sell your beef to the Lowlands?" he asked.

"No." Van's voice was cool and reserved. "We do all our trading out of Inverness. To France."

"Ah," he said very quietly. "Of course. To France."

The air between them, momentarily thawed by the incident with the dog, was frozen once more.

* * *

The following day they left for the Lintons' house in London. England's capital was the first large city Van had ever seen—Edinburgh was a mere village in comparison—and she was overwhelmed by its magnitude.

Linton House was a stately, sumptuous residence in the relatively new Grosvenor Square. Lady Linton informed Van that it had been built by her husband ten years previously. All the rooms were large and grand, either perfectly square or perfectly rectangular. Van thought of Creag an Fhithich, where no room resembled any other, and felt a stab of homesickness.

Edward disappeared for the evening and Van went to bed early, pleading fatigue from the trip. The following morning the earl brought Carlo Martelli to see her.

Van had dressed for the morning in a dress made of some soft apricot material and her hair was dressed loosely in long ringlets on the nape of her neck. She was running through some practice exercises when Edward arrived with the musician.

Signore Martelli was a slight, dark man whose large brown eyes regarded Van with an expression of kindly patience. "I have come to hear you," he announced, "because Lord Linton asked this of me. You wish to improve your performance, eh?"

"I wish to learn to play better," Van said.

"*Prego,*" the Italian replied. He walked to the harpsichord and looked through the music there. "This." He selected a sheet and placed it on the music rack. "Play that," he said.

Van swallowed nervously and her eyes went to Edward. He nodded to her once, gravely, and she went to the instrument and sat down. The Italian had chosen a piece by Handel that Van knew quite well.

At first the keys seemed strange under her fingers. She could feel how stiff her back was and her eyes followed the music in front of her with frantic attention. Gradually, however, the strangeness disappeared and the music took hold.

When she finished she felt that familiar moment of quiet deep within herself and then she turned around. Edward was not looking at her and Van could not quite bring herself to look at Signore Martelli.

"Play it again, please," the Italian said, and at that she did look. His eyes were directly on her, only now, instead of patient kindness they were filled with anticipation. "Again," he repeated softly, and Van turned back to the keyboard.

"You have a very great talent," the musician said when Van had finished her second rendition. "But I must ask you this—are you willing to work?"

"Oh, yes," Van breathed, her light eyes glowing.

"I mean work *hard*." The dark eyes looking at her were stern. "I will make you do it again and again and yet again, until you are ready to weep. Do you understand?"

Van's chin came up. "Yes," she said firmly. "I understand. And I am willing to work."

"Very well." The Italian turned to Edward. "I will come tomorrow morning at nine o'clock, my lord."

"Thank you, maestro," Edward replied. "You do Lady Vanessa a great honor."

"Yes," the musician returned superbly. Then, "I only come for you. Never did I expect to find this," and he gestured grandly toward Van. He turned to the door and Edward followed to escort him out. "Such a pity," Van heard the Italian saying, "that she is a lady."

"Why is it a pity that I am a lady?" Van asked Edward when he returned to the drawing-room.

He had not sat down but was standing at the chimneypiece, his shoulders comfortably propped against the marble. He was dressed in riding clothes and he slapped a whip thoughtfully against a polished boot as he regarded her. "I believe he feels a talent like yours should be shared with others, but the daughter of an earl can hardly go on the concert stage."

Van frowned. "I do want to get better," she said. "I want to be the best I can be. But not for others. I want it for myself."

He was regarding her with a strange look in his eyes. "I suppose that sounds selfish," Van said defensively.

"No," he replied. "Just rare. Most people require the approval of others." The whip in his hands had stilled.

"Thank you for bringing Signore Martelli." Van spoke with difficulty but it had to be said.

He smiled at her, his blue eyes suddenly full of that lazy sunshine he bestowed so generously on others and so seldom on her. "It was my pleasure," he replied. He straightened up, away from the chimneypiece. "I won't disturb you further, however. I know you have only begun to play."

Van's eyes followed him all the way to the door.

7

Van's first venture into English society came the following evening with the Duchess of Newcastle's ball. Van had never seen anything on the scale of this entertainment. First there was the crush of carriages on the street, where they had to wait in line for nearly half an hour before they reached the door of Newcastle House and could alight. Then there was the crowd of people in the great hall and on the stairs. The air was filled with the fragrances of conflicting perfumes and hair powders and the noise of more than a hundred people talking at once.

"My, what a crush," Lady Linton said next to Van. She sounded pleased. Van drew a deep breath and fought down a rising feeling of suffocation. Her eyes searched the crowd for Edward, who had been unceremoniously annexed at the door by an elderly man in an elaborate wig.

"Where *is* Edward?" Lady Linton asked, echoing Van's own thoughts. Her "Oh, good, there he is" came seconds after Van had spotted him herself.

He was crossing the room toward them as easily as if it had been empty. People seemed simply to fall away before him. Just so must the waters have parted for Moses, Van thought with a flash of mingled annoyance and admiration. To do him justice, it wasn't as if he seemed even to notice the effect his crossing created. He simply walked forward serenely, his unpowdered golden head inches higher than everyone else's, his shoulders in their elegant blue velvet coat inches wider. He reached Van and Lady Linton, smiled genially, and asked, "Shall we go upstairs?"

The duke and duchess were receiving their guests at the entrance to the ballroom. The duchess and Lady Linton fell into each other's arms and then Lady Linton presented Van.

"So," the duchess said, her blue-gray eyes looking Van up and down, "this is Vanessa."

"How do you do, your grace," Van murmured coolly. The duchess's eyes sparkled with approval. "She is perfect," she announced to Lady Linton. "The Ridley girl will have a rival this season." She nodded wisely at Lady Linton. "You were wise, Katherine, not to powder her hair." Van's hand was squeezed and then dropped. The duchess's whole face then lit up. "Ah, Linton. How good to see you here with your mama."

Van's face was wearing its most austere expression as they proceeded into the ballroom. She did not at all care for the way the duchess seemed to regard her as a dressed-up doll.

She was certainly dressed up, however, she thought as they came down the few steps that led to the ballroom. She was wearing her first formal ball gown, a creation of golden silk whose full skirts were spread wide by twin panniers. The gown's bodice was cut lower than anything Van had ever worn and ended in a point just below her waist. Her hair was dressed with golden roses, and high on her right cheek Lady Linton's dresser had placed a small black patch. Van had shrugged and let the woman do as she wished, not realizing how effectively the patch called attention to the blackness of her brows and lashes and the contrasting lightness of her eyes.

The ballroom was filled with people. Unconsciously, Van moved a step closer to Edward. He put his hand under her elbow and began to talk to her easily.

In two minutes they were surrounded by people wanting to be introduced.

When the music finally started up, Van was immensely relieved to find that she was to dance the first dance with Edward. As she walked out on the floor, her hand in his, she glanced up at his profile and said with a flash of wry amusement, "I never thought I'd be happy to see you!"

He threw her a mocking look. "Feeling a little overwhelmed?"

"Feeling smothered," she returned promptly. "Dhé, but there's a crowd of people here."

"There is. And they all want to meet you." He grinned. "Mama has surely been busy."

"I feel like some sort of an exhibit," Van said a little acidly.

"Not at all. You are a very beautiful young lady." Van was startled by the thrill of pleasure his words gave her. Did he really think her beautiful? A hint of steel came into his voice. "Just remember that, please, and don't start proselytizing about the bloody Stuarts."

Van glared up at him. "You don't have to give me a lecture on manners," she said through clenched teeth. He was such a condescending Sassenach bastard, she thought forcefully, and jerked her hand away from his to take her place in the line for the dance.

She remembered her dance with Edward very well, but the rest of her partners were a uniform blur. The one other person she did notice that evening was the extremely lovely girl whom Edward seemed to be spending so much time with.

"Who is the girl with Edward?" she asked Lady Linton during the one brief moment they were alone. Van had never learned the trick of obtaining information slyly. If she wanted to know something, she asked.

"That is Miss Caroline Ridley," Lady Linton replied promptly. "Isn't she lovely?"

Caroline Ridley's hair, also unpowdered, was almost as golden as Edward's. Her eyes, Van thought sourly, were probably blue. "Yes," she said. "Very lovely."

"It's about time Edward married," the countess said firmly. "He's had a number of years to enjoy himself, but now it's time for him to set up his nursery. He was twenty-seven this year."

Van stared at Lady Linton. "Does he *love* Miss Ridley?"

"Why shouldn't he?" the countess returned a little defensively. "She comes from an excellent family, is extremely beautiful and very charming. She appears to be a perfectly lovable girl to me."

Van was astonished by this point of view. "One doesn't love people simply because they are lovable, Cousin Katherine," she said.

Lady Linton stared at her son. "I don't see why not."

Why not? thought Van. Well, if what Lady Linton had just said were true, she, for instance, would love Alan MacDonald. Alan was also perfectly lovable. The fact was, however, that Van had scarcely spared him a thought since she left Scotland. Her thoughts at this point were interrupted by two young men who, it appeared, desired to be presented to her. Van repressed a sigh and forced herself to make polite conversation.

The following morning Signore Martelli arrived at nine o'clock and Van, who had not got to bed until three in the morning, was waiting for him. After her lesson she discovered that almost a roomful of flowers had arrived for her. The flowers were followed by a series of male callers, all of whom wished to take her driving in the park.

Van did go driving with Viscount Standish, principally because she discovered that he was the eldest son of the Marquis of Altop, one of the English Tory nobles her father had desired to know about.

It was a very depressing afternoon. "I am familiar with your family, Lord Standish," Van said almost as soon as they reached the park.

"You are?" The young viscount looked both surprised and pleased. "How is that, Lady Vanessa?"

"I believe your father and mine have the same principles," Van said meaningfully.

The viscount's slightly chubby face was puzzled. "Have our fathers met?"

"No," Van replied patiently, "but I understand Lord Altop supported a venture my father was very much involved in. I refer," she continued, as he still continued to look blank, "to the Jacobite rising of 1715."

"Oh, that!" The young man's brow cleared. "Yes, my father was all for the king over the water at one time."

"At one time," Van repeated. She frowned. "He does not then retain those sentiments?"

"Well, he ain't fond of the Hanovers, if that's what you mean. The thing is, you see, they serve a purpose. And it's Parliament that counts, when all's said and done." He looked at her, evidently keen to impress. "I've a seat in the House, you know."

"Then I take it the Standons of Altop are no longer interested in seeing a Stuart restoration?" Van said in an expressionless tone.

"Good God, no," the young man replied hastily. "The Stuarts would bring in the Catholics. And the French." Then, in an alarmed fashion, "I say, you aren't Catholic by any chance, are you, Lady Vanessa?"

Van's profile was aloof and still. "No. We are Episcopalians in Morar."

"That's all right, then," he replied cheerfully. He gave her an admiring glance. Van was looking extremely elegant in a pearl-gray driving outfit that emphasized the beauty of her dark coloring. "Are you still Jacobites up in Scotland?" he asked.

Van thought of a number of replies she would like to make to this vapid apostate, but she really did not wish to make things awkward for Lady Linton. So she forced herself to breathe slowly and to say only, very calmly, "Yes. We are still Jacobites in Scotland."

There was a moment of silence. Then he said heartily, "What did you think of the ball last night?"

Van replied pleasantly and by the time he drove her home Lord Standish was rambling away, as comfortable as he could be. Van, however, was not comfortable. And her mood of depression had not been helped by the sight of the Earl of Linton driving Miss Caroline Ridley behind his team of beautifully matched grays.

That evening they went to the opera. "Did you have a pleasant afternoon with Standish?" Edward asked Van as he settled a long velvet cloak around her shoulders.

Van's mouth set. "No. I did not."

His blue eyes glinted down at her, but as Lady Linton chose that moment to join them, he did not reply.

The opera that evening was to be *Samson* by Handel. "It's really an oratorio although it is performed at Covent Garden," Edward told Van as they took their seats in the Linton box. "It's based on Milton's *Samson Agonistes*. Do you know Milton?"

Van shook her head. "Is it the story of Samson and Delilah?"

He was looking around the half-empty house. "Not really. When the opera opens, Samson has already been betrayed by Delilah, and blinded and imprisoned by the Philistines. It's more of a character study, the revelation to Samson that he, despite his guilt and his suffering, is an instrument of God."

Van nodded slowly and then also looked around her. "Where is everyone?" she asked in surprise.

"*Samson* is rather serious for most people's tastes," Edward answered. He sounded perfectly affable. "There is no spectacle, not much action at all, really. The boxes will fill up, all right, but most of the people will come in later."

Van was horrified. "And miss half the opera?"

Lady Linton chuckled at her expression. "I assure you, Vanessa, Edward and I are always on time."

Indeed, Covent Garden was still half-empty when the orchestra sounded its first note. Van, however, did not notice. Nor did she notice the rustling and whispering as people slowly came in and took their seats. She was aware only of the stage, of the agonized suffering of the man who sang so magnificently, and of the man beside her whose concentration on the music was as intense as her own.

At the intermission a chattering collection of people filled their box. Van was intensely irritated. She did not want to talk to all these people. She wanted to be quiet.

Edward's hand touched her elbow. She knew it was he even before she turned her head. "Let's go for a walk," he said softly.

Van's look was grateful. "Oh, yes," she said, and he guided her along to a deserted hallway, where they walked slowly up and down, talking quietly about the music.

Van was quiet as well going home in the carriage. The concluding soprano aria, "Let the Bright Seraphim," where the singer's voice had vied with a trumpet in roulades, was still sounding triumphantly in her ears. Finally she turned to Edward, who was conversing easily with his mother.

"Do you have a copy of *Samson Agonistes?*" she asked. "Might I borrow it?"

"Of course. It would be my pleasure." And he gave her his rare, approving smile.

After her session with Signore Martelli the following morning, Edward asked her to come into the library with him. As Van walked in through the door the earl was holding for her, she realized there was someone else in the room.

"Lord Stowecroft," Edward said formally, "may I introduce Lady Vanessa MacIan."

"How do you do, my lord," Van said out of a suddenly dry throat. This stocky, pockmarked man was the single most important figure her father wanted to hear news of. She looked from him to Edward.

"I will leave you two alone," the earl said pleasantly. Then, to Lord Stowecroft, "Thank you for coming, sir."

The older man merely nodded, and as Edward turned and left the room, Van wet her suddenly dry lips.

"Linton said you wished to see me, Lady Vanessa," the earl said abruptly. "Do you have a message from Morar?"

"Yes," Van said. This man, she knew, *had* met her father—a long time ago, in France. "There is great hope of a French landing," Van said now, tensely. "My father wants to know what English support the prince can rely on."

"None," the Earl of Stowecroft said heavily. "Tell that to Morar. If the prince should land, he will get no help from England."

Van's face reflected her feelings. "My father thought—" she began, but the earl cut her off.

"I know what Morar thought. He thought he could count on me and on the other English nobles who have supported the Stuarts for all these years. Well, I would rather see a true-born Stuart on the throne than a German elector, but it is not going to happen, Lady Vanessa, and I'm damned if I'll ruin myself and my family striving for the impossible."

"It will not be impossible if the prince's friends prove true to him," Van said.

"It is impossible," the earl said bluntly. "It is too late. We might, perhaps, have succeeded in 1715, if we'd had the leadership. But now it's too late. This dynasty has occupied the throne for too long, Lady Vanessa. They won't be dislodged."

"If the prince can gather a French army—"

"Yes—that's just the trouble." The earl's heavy, pockmarked face was grim. "Do you think the English are going to welcome a prince who comes to them at the head of a *French* army? France is the hereditary enemy here, Lady Vanessa. I know you feel differently in Scotland, but here France is the enemy."

Van was silenced.

"Tell this to Morar," the Earl of Stowecroft said. "Tell him that England does not want a king who is beholden to France. And England does not want a king who is Catholic. And those of us who still feel differently are not foolhardy enough to set our heads up to be knocked off when such a venture ends, as it inevitably will, in defeat."

"You speak for yourself, of course," Van said, and he interrupted her once more.

"I speak for all of us. We've heard the rumors too. There is no English noble who will go out for the Stuarts, Lady Vanessa. Tell that to your father from me." His mouth tightened. "I should hate to see a good man like Morar get dragged down in a boy's wild venture."

"Unfortunately," Van said in a cold and contemptuous voice, "my father's loyalties are not so . . . adjustable."

The man flushed unbecomingly. "Oh, I can guess what you think of me," he said hardly, "but I've given you the truth."

Van's slender back was ramrod straight. "I will relay your words to my father."

"Good." He grunted. "I'll show myself out, then. Good day, Lady Vanessa."

"Good day, my lord." Van stood where she was until the door closed behind him; then she walked over to stare out the window at the garden behind the house. After a few minutes she heard the door open again and knew, without looking, who was there.

"Well," Edward said, "was your interview satisfactory?"

If he had a gloating look on his face, Van thought as she slowly turned around, she would smash him. But his eyes were not at all mocking. They were filled, in fact, with a cold blue light.

"I have the information I was asked to get," she replied.

"Well, I hope to God Morar has the sense to listen to it," he said viciously and, coming all the way into the room, he slammed his gloves down on a desk.

Van's fists clenched. "You almost sound as if you were afraid of us, my lord," she said tauntingly.

"Not afraid *of* you, afraid *for* you" was his disconcerting reply. He braced his hands on the desk and leaned a little forward. "If the clans rise for Charles Stuart, they will be signing their own death warrants."

Van could feel the pulse beating in her temple. "Why are *you* so opposed to the Stuarts?" she asked suddenly. "Are you afraid of France too?"

"We could handle France better than we could handle the Stuarts," came the grim reply. Van's lashes lifted and her eyes met his. "I have no liking at all for the Stuarts, Van," he said. "None. In fact, it would give me intense pleasure to hear that every last one of them had dropped off the face of the earth."

"Why?" Her lips moved, although barely any sound came out.

He gave a short, hard laugh. "Why? Because they are a selfish, arrogant, stupid, power-hungry family, that is why." He straightened up and began to walk around the room, his step long and quiet, a great golden beast loose in the room with her. "You, of course, have no notion of any of this. You have been brought up on legends of Stuart greatness." He paused in his pacing to stare at her. It seemed as if the cold, blue North Sea glittered in his eyes.

Viking, Van thought. Sassenach.

"Loyalty is a splendid thing, Van," he was saying. "But one must ask oneself: To what and to whom does one truly owe loyalty?"

Van rested her fingers on the back of a carved rosewood chair. "One owes loyalty to one's king," she replied.

"And if loyalty to one's king conflicts with loyalty to one's country?"

Van's fingers were white with pressure. "I don't understand what you mean," she said tautly.

"I mean that the king exists for the good of the country, the country does not exist for the good of the king. It is the country that comes first. The Hanovers understand that. The Stuarts do not."

This was not a point of view Van had heard before. Loyalty to the Stuarts had never been something one discussed at Morar. It was simply there, a fact of life, part of the very air one breathed. She had been brought up to believe that it was the simple duty of her father, her brother, her clan, of every man in Britain, to contribute to the restoration of the rightful king. What Edward was saying was disturbing.

"The Stuarts were good for the country," she said.

"Yes," he replied with irony, "they were such good rulers that we executed two of them and exiled two others." He ran an impatient hand through his hair and a few dislodged strands fell like golden thread across his forehead. "There is no such thing as the

Divine Right of Kings," he said. "This is the eighteenth century, not the Middle Ages."

Van released her chair so abruptly that it rocked. "Yes," she said acidly, "this is the eighteenth century and you consider yourself a great and progressive reformer. Well, government is not like agriculture, Edward. And what is new is not always what is best!"

"The problem, of course," he said bleakly, "is that in the Highlands you are still living in the Middle Ages."

Van walked out of the room.

8

Signore Martelli had spoken the truth when he said
he would make Van work. She spent two hours with
him in the morning and then another two or three
hours on her own, working on exercises, learning, in
the maestro's words, "to strip a piece down to its bare
bones and then put it back together again."

It was painstaking, tedious work. Van often longed
just to break out in an exuberance of sound, but she
did not. Nor did she complain. She worked.

"Lady Vanessa is a brilliant pupil," Carlo Martelli
said to Edward one morning when he met the earl in
the hallway of Linton House and Edward invited him
for some refreshment. "She covers what would ordi-
narily be four lessons in one. And she has the . . .
the dedication." The Italian sighed and sipped his wine.
"Such a pity she is a lady."

Edward looked amused. "Being a lady should not
stop her from giving concerts. They could not be pub-
lic, that's all."

Signore Martelli brightened. "That is so. A private
concert—a musical evening—in a home such as this
one . . ."

Edward stretched his long legs in front of him. "I
agree with you, maestro, that a talent like Lady

Vanessa's should be shared. She, however, will have to be persuaded of that."

The musician frowned. "It is odd. She has no desire to show herself off. None."

"My cousin had a rather solitary upbringing," the earl murmured. "It has left her more self-sufficient than most."

"Ah, yes. This castle she talks of with the unpronounceable name." Signore Martelli shuddered. "She sees no one of culture, the little one. No one save her mother. And yet she tells me they have paintings by Titian. In that barbaric wilderness! Titian!"

"They are civilized savages, the Earls of Morar," Edward said. "It's a feudal world up there, maestro. They are four hundred years behind the times."

"It's a mercy her mother had the sense to get her away," the Italian said.

Edward rubbed his head and looked rueful. "Yes," he replied doubtfully, "I suppose it is."

Lady Linton was enjoying herself tremendously and had begun, like any matchmaking mama, to dream dreams about Van's future. How lovely, she thought, if dear Vanessa should marry one of the half-dozen or so noble and eligible escorts who were so obviously attracted to her. She had initially had hopes that Edward might find Van appealing—she always had hopes for Edward. But lately she had given up on that idea. The two of them were scrupulously polite to each other but it didn't take a great deal of sensitivity to realize that they were at odds. The only thing that seemed to draw them together was music.

Oh, well. Lady Linton had great hopes of her son and Caroline Ridley. Edward was spending a great deal of time in her company of late. That Caroline was interested in Edward was not in question. Every marriageable girl in London was interested in Edward. With the exception, unfortunately, of Vanessa.

Such was the situation in the Linton household on the night of the Countess of Evesham's ball. The evening began much like any other, with Edward dancing with Caroline Ridley and Van dancing with her own collection of admirers. Neither Edward nor Van ever looked at each other, although both could have said instantly where the other was in the room at any given time.

The event that was to set this evening off from all its predecessors occurred at about eleven o'clock, when there came a stir at the doorway and Van looked up to behold a new arrival coming in. She was standing on the edge of the ballroom floor with Lady Linton and Sir Geoffrey Austen, and both of her companions were aware of the sudden stiffening of her slender body. "Dhia gleidh sinn!" (God in heaven) she said. Then, "What is *he* doing here?"

"Who?" Lady Linton replied in bewilderment. "Do you mean the Duke of Argyll, Vanessa?"

"Yes. The Duke of Argyll. What is he doing here?"

"Before her marriage, Lady Evesham was a Campbell," Sir Geoffrey put in helpfully.

"A Campbell!" Van's voice was full of loathing. "Why did you not tell me this?" she demanded fiercely of Lady Linton. "I would never have come here had I known."

"Why ever not?" Lady Linton asked, completely out of her depth at the sudden change in Van.

"The Campbells." Van looked as if she would have liked to spit. "They are the vultures of the Highlands," she said, "fattening themselves on the misfortunes of other clans."

As the three of them watched the object of Van's dislike, they saw Lady Evesham put a hand on his arm and begin to lead him around the room. Van stood like a flag, her black head high, her narrow nostrils white and pinched-looking. The duke came to a halt in front of her.

"Lady Vanessa," he said, without waiting for an introduction. "I would know you anywhere. You have a great look of your father."

Van's eyes glittered back at the man who was, unarguably, the most powerful man in Scotland, the chief of Clan Campbell and the MacIans' ancient foe. "I did not know the Countess of Evesham was a Campbell," she said.

The duke looked amused. He was a slender man in his sixties, elegantly dressed in a powdered wig and red velvet coat with a froth of immaculate lace at his throat. His eyes ran over Van's own finery. "I am surprised to find a daughter of Alasdair MacIan in London," he said slowly and thoughtfully. "What *are* you doing here, Lady Vanessa?"

Van switched to Gaelic. "That is no concern of yours, Mac Cailein Mor," she said through her teeth.

"Everything that happens in the Highlands is my concern," he returned in the same language. Lady Linton looked around worriedly. They were beginning to attract attention. She was relieved to see a tall blond head moving in their direction.

"*You* are not our king," said Van.

Argyll's eyes locked with hers. "What is Mac mhic Iain up to?" he demanded.

"Nothing that concerns Clan Campbell," Van returned, meeting his gaze with a burning look of her own.

Argyll's cold eyes narrowed in response. Lady Linton

swallowed and clutched at the arm of Sir Geoffrey for support. The entire veneer of civilization seemed to have slipped away and between Archibald Campbell, thirteenth earl and fourth duke of his line, and Lady Vanessa MacIan, there sizzled the pure hatred of centuries of clan warfare.

"Your grace." It was Edward's voice, calm and pleasant and faintly tinged with surprise. "How delightful to see you. You know Lady Vanessa, I see. She has been making a visit to my mother."

The duke's eyes stared at Edward in open surprise. "Morar's daughter is visiting *you?*"

"Yes," Edward said. His lazy blue gaze flicked around the room. "I'll call upon you tomorrow, Duke, if I may."

"Yes," Argyll said quickly. "Yes, Linton. Do that, please. I shall be at home all morning." The duke's eyes skated past Van's frozen face and bestowed an apologetic smile on Lady Linton. "My dear," he said to Lady Evesham, and the two of them moved on.

Van cursed him in Gaelic under her breath.

Edward put his hand on her bare upper arm. "I am taking my cousin for some refreshment," he said amiably to his mother and Lord Geoffrey.

"Yes, darling," Lady Linton said in relief. "That would be best."

Van opened her lips to protest and Edward's fingers dug into her flesh. "Come along, Van," he said very pleasantly. Too pleasantly. His face seemed perfectly composed but Van saw a muscle flicker once in the angle of his jaw. He began to walk her toward the supper room.

"I don't want any refreshment," Van said furiously.

"Good." He smiled across the room at the Duchess of Newcastle. They passed the supper-room door and continued on down the hall. Edward snatched a candle from a wall sconce, opened a door on his left, and almost dragged Van into a small anteroom. It was empty and dark save for the earl's single candle. He lit a candelabrum that stood on a side table and turned to face her.

Van rubbed her arm. "You didn't have to drag me," she muttered. The look on his face frightened her a little so she dropped her eyes to her arm. The imprint of his fingers was clearly marked in the smooth flesh.

"I want you out of Argyll's way," he said. "Another minute more and the whole ballroom would have been watching you."

Van flung up her head. "I don't care."

"Well, I do," he replied brutally. "You are my mother's guest and I don't want her involved in any unpleasant scenes. I've told you that before."

"I know." Van's voice now was low and trembling with anger. "You're always giving me orders. Well, I don't have to listen to you. You're not my brother!"

He laughed. Van's eyes widened in astonishment. It had been a sound of genuine amusement. "I've never felt in the least like your brother," he said, and then he was reaching out for her once more.

Van tried to back away, but he pulled her toward him ruthlessly, and before she realized what was happening, his mouth had come down on hers.

At first Van was shocked into immobility. She had had no warning at all that this was coming. His body was hard against hers, one of his hands behind her head forcing her face up to meet his kiss. She was stiff with shock and surprise. Then, as she raised her own hand to push him away, the quality of the kiss changed.

The hard, ravaging mouth softened, gentled, sought for a response from her.

A warm tide of feeling rose within Van. Her head stopped pressing against his fingers, relaxed, and then fell back gently against his shoulder. The hand she had raised to push him away curved possessively around his neck. Her lips opened under the sweet pressure of his. His body came further over hers and she was bent back in his arms.

The sound of voices in the hall outside the door brought them back to an awareness of their surroundings. Edward's mouth lifted from hers, although his hands stayed firmly on her back. They stared at each other in silence.

Then, "You shouldn't have done that," Van said. Her voice was woefully unsteady.

His hands dropped. "I didn't intend to." His voice was steadier than hers, his eyes as brilliant as sapphires in the flickering candlelight.

"We don't even *like* each other," Van said a little wildly.

His smile was mocking. "Liking has nothing to do with it."

Van ran her narrow hand nervously over her hair. She was beginning to feel frightened. What frightened her most, she realized, was the fact that she wanted very much to be back in his arms again.

He straightened a black curl. "There. You look all right now."

Van took a step backward. "I'm going back to the ballroom."

His face was perfectly serene. Only the unusual brilliance of his eyes indicated anything had happened to disturb him. "A good idea," he agreed. "I'll wait here for a few minutes."

Van gave him an uncertain look, turned, and fled the room.

Edward remained standing perfectly still for about a minute after she had gone. Then he turned, walked calmly to the window, and smashed his fist into the wall.

"Goddammit," he said in a low and vicious tone. "Goddammit all to hell," And he smashed his fist into the wall once more.

The incident in the anteroom all but banished her meeting with the Duke of Argyll from Van's mind. She played the scene with Edward over and over in her mind. On the surface they appeared to have gone back to their pre-anteroom relationship, but Van knew that something had changed between them. Or, at least, something had changed in her.

She was terribly, physically conscious of him all the time; conscious of the shape of his mouth, the strength of his hands, the width of his shoulders. It was horribly, shamefully clear to her that she was very attracted to Edward Romney. She would never have realized this if he hadn't kissed her.

She was furious with him for kissing her and precipitating this humiliating situation. All thoughts of Charles Edward Stuart were driven quite effectively from her mind.

It was a great relief when Edward went down to Staplehurst for a few days, ostensibly to check on his favorite mare, which was due to foal shortly. Van rather thought he was finding her presence as unsettling as she was finding his.

After all, as she had said on that infamous occasion, they didn't even like each other.

On May 11, 1745 the combined British, Dutch,

Hanoverian, and Austrian forces under the Duke of Cumberland were beaten by the French army at Fontenoy, in Flanders, making Marshal de Saxe virtually the master of all Belgium. Edward came posting back to London in haste to attend government meetings. The English, it seemed, had fought with great courage and gallantry but the superior numbers of the French had proved insurmountable.

London was in a furor over the battle. Van, who knew her father would be delighted by the French victory, found herself in something of a quandary. One of her constant admirers, Lord Bradford, had had a younger brother killed at Fontenoy, and one or two other of her acquaintances had lost friends or relatives as well. It was hard to rejoice in the face of their grief.

She was sitting at the harpsichord idly picking out a melody when Edward came in one afternoon after a meeting with Lord Pelham and his cabinet. She heard him hesitate in the hall before he came into the drawing room.

"All alone?" he asked. "Where are all your admirers?"

Van shrugged indifferently and continued to play with one hand. "At their clubs, I suppose."

He walked to the window and stood in the pool of sunshine slanting in through the glass.

"Do you know," Van said over the single soft chord her fingers were playing, "I never realized how much the English hate the French. At home we are so close to France. France is where my father and my brother were educated. It is where my parents met and where my grandfather is buried. We get our wine from France, and our books; our broadsword steel, Mechlin lace, velvet, silk, spices, shot, powder—all come from France. More ships from France call at Inverness than do ships from London." She moved the chord up an octave. "It's strange. I should be happy for a French victory."

He turned to look at her, the sun behind him rimming his hair as if with a halo. "I don't hate the French," he said. "In fact, one of the men I admire most in the world is French."

Van's fingers stilled. "Who is that?"

"François Robichon de Guérinière. He directs the king's stables in the Tuileries. It was he who taught me all I know about riding."

"How did you come to know him?" Van asked wonderingly.

"Before the war I went on the Grand Tour. I had read his *Ecole de Cavalerie,* and while I was in Paris I sought him out. He was very kind to me. You see, Van"—his face was very grave, very still—"because governments are at war, that does not mean people must hate each other. I disapprove of French policy. King Louis's adventurism must be restrained. That is why we are at war. But I don't hate the French people. I don't say *'français'* the way you say 'Sassenach.' "

Van's eyes dropped once more to the harpsichord keys. She began to pick out another chord.

After a minute he said, in quite a different tone of voice, "I understand from Lord Pelham that the king plans to make an appearance at the Grenville ball tomorrow night."

Van's head jerked up.

"I presume you do not care to be there to curtsy to him?" His eyes were as hard as his voice.

"I will never curtsy to the elector," Van said stiffly.

"Then we had all better go back to Staplehurst for a week. Mother will think up an excuse. It will look too obvious if we just don't attend. The Grenvilles would be offended."

Van pressed her lips together. "Very well." She gave him a scorching look. "Contrary to popular opinion, I do *not* wish to embarrass Cousin Katherine."

"I am glad to hear that," he replied smoothly. "I'll speak to Mama this evening."

Van began to play another chord and Edward strode out of the room.

9

"Of course we can go to Staplehurst, darling, if you think it best," Lady Linton said when Edward broached the subject to her. A tiny frown furrowed her smooth brow. "It's an awkward time, unfortunately, but I quite see your point about Vanessa and the king. If her encounter with the Duke of Argyll was any example of what to expect . . ." Lady Linton shuddered delicately.

"Why is it an awkward time?" Edward asked.

Lady Linton gave him a triumphant look. "Lord Bradford is going to make Vanessa an offer."

Edward's golden brows snapped together. "What?"

"Yes." Lady Linton looked very smug. "He came to see me this afternoon, in fact. Of course I told him that I was not Vanessa's guardian, nor were you, but if Vanessa wishes to marry him, I don't at all see why he shouldn't approach Morar."

"Mama, you must certainly have lost your wits." Edward's face was iron-hard. "You cannot possibly imagine that Morar will allow his daughter to marry a Sassenach? Granted, Bradford is a Tory, but he is not a Jacobite."

"Politics has nothing to do with it," Lady Linton said.

"On the contrary. Where Morar is concerned, politics has everything to do with it," came the grim reply.

"Well . . . perhaps where Morar is concerned," Lady Linton conceded. "But, my dear Edward, you are forgetting Frances."

Edward had been leaning on the back of a chair and now he came around the front of it to sit down. "What kind of a person *is* Lady Morar?" he asked.

His mother smiled at him. "Frances is a darling," she said warmly. "She was the sweetest, kindest, gentlest girl in the world. She was an only child, you know, and my aunt and uncle doted on her. My uncle was a scholarly man and he taught her far more than girls usually learn. Just fancy! He used to read her Virgil every evening." He raised a brow to indicate that he was suitably impressed. "Well," Lady Linton continued, "when she was nineteen they took her to Paris—for her education—and she met Alasdair MacIan."

Lady Linton sighed reminiscently.

"Go on," said Edward. His eyes had gotten very blue.

"Morar cannot possibly be more dismayed at the thought of his daughter marrying an Englishman than Uncle Henry was at the thought of Frances marrying Morar," Lady Linton said. "They carried Frances back to England immediately and forbade her ever to communicate with Morar again."

The golden brows rose once more. "Obviously they relented."

"They relented. It took a year." Lady Linton shook her elegantly coifed head. "No one thought Frances had it in her to be so unyielding. She did not defy her father, she simply was completely and overwhelmingly unhappy. It was quite clear that if she couldn't marry Morar she would never marry anyone." Lady Linton shrugged. "I know my uncle feared for her happiness

with a man like Morar, but he couldn't hold out against
Frances. He gave in and they were married. And I
believe it has been an exceedingly happy marriage,
too." Lady Linton gave her son a pleased smile. "How
delightful it will be to see Alasdair MacIan in precisely
the same situation as he put Uncle Henry!"

"Not precisely the same situation, Mama," Edward
said dryly. "Are you certain that Van cares for
Bradford?"

"No," returned Lady Linton sunnily, "but we shall
find out as soon as we return from Staplehurst."

Van found herself surprisingly glad to see Staplehurst
again. One forgot, she thought as the carriage came
up the drive through Capability Brown's famous
park, one forgot how truly beautiful it was.

Beside her Lady Linton sighed and expressed similar sentiments. "My, but it's always good to come
home. I adore London, of course, but Staplehurst is
. . . well, home." She turned to smile at Van. "I'm
glad Edward decided we should come down for a
week."

"I hope you're not just saying this to be polite,
ma'am," Van said ruefully. "I should be sorry to think
I had deprived you of any parties you were looking
forward to."

"Nonsense." Lady Linton laid a hand on Van's.
"There will be plenty of other parties, dear child."

Van looked back into Katherine Romney's smiling
eyes. What a genuinely lovely person her mother's
cousin was, she thought.

"You have been enjoying yourself, Vanessa, have
you not?" The violet eyes now looked a little anxious.

"Yes," Van returned truthfully. "I have been." She
caught sight of Edward's figure riding horseback next

to the carriage. "I wonder that Edward can bear to be parted from Miss Ridley for so long," she remarked to Lady Linton with careful unconcern.

"I suggested that we invite the Ridleys down with us for the week," Lady Linton replied a little despondently, "but Edward wouldn't hear of it. I hate to nag at him, Vanessa, but I do wish he would . . ."

Her voice trailed off and Van looked at her with affectionate amusement. "You never nag at him, ma'am. You think the sun rises and sets on that blond head of his."

Lady Linton laughed. "I know." She pressed her lips together. "But for all that, Vanessa, I do wish that he'd bestir himself and get married!"

Van settled into her old room at Staplehurst and it did feel, oddly enough, as if she too were coming home. Signore Martelli had parted from her with a long list of instructions, but Van decided she was going to take a rest from study for a while and simply play to please herself. The prospect of a whole week of unstructured time was delightful.

It rained the following day. An hour before dinner Van was curled up before the library fire reading when she heard Edward's step at the door. She had not seen him all day. The shoulders of his russet coat were wet and his hair was rain-darkened to a tawny bronze.

"Where were you?" she asked.

He came over to the fire and held out his hands. "At the stables. Cora looks as if she's going to foal very soon."

"Why are you so worried about her?"

He frowned. "I don't know. She's never had any trouble before. There's just something about the way she looks . . ."

Van put a marker in her book and set it down on the table. "What are you reading today?" he asked.

Her eyes were still on the book. "*Joseph Andrews* by Mr. Fielding."

He looked at her averted face, at the beautiful line of brow and cheekbones. "Do you like it?" His voice sounded strange to his own ears. "I thought it was a very funny parody of Richardson's *Pamela*," he said more firmly.

Her face flashed suddenly from gravity into smiling. "Wasn't she a dreadful hypocrite? I had a tremendous argument with Lord Bradford about that book." She looked directly at him. "I didn't think she was virtuous at all. She didn't love that man. She only wanted to get him to marry her."

He stared at her for a long moment in silence, at the narrow, dark, fine-boned face with the great light eyes. "Did *you* think she was virtuous, Edward?" she asked.

The atmosphere in the room was too close, too airless. He was finding it difficult to breathe properly. "No," he said. "No, I did not. I thought she was a clever little schemer."

Van looked pleased. "Precisely my feeling."

He had to get out of this room. "I'm going to go change for dinner," he said, his voice harsher than usual, and he forced himself to walk to the door with long and deliberate steps. He could feel her eyes on him. Up in his bedroom he refused the ministrations of his valet and simply stood for a long time at his window, staring out.

In the end he did not go down to dinner at all. He received a message from Blackstone that Cora was going into labor and, rather grimly thankful, the earl returned to the barn to spend the evening with his mare.

*   *   *

When Edward still had not returned to the house by eleven o'clock, Lady Linton went to bed. "He is most likely passing a brandy bottle around," she said to Van with affectionate resignation. "Cora's foals are special to him." She yawned and stood up. "Are you coming, Vanessa dear?"

"I'd like to finish my chapter, if you don't mind, Cousin Katherine."

"Of course not." Lady Linton kissed Van's cheek. "I'll see you in the morning, my dear child."

"Good night, ma'am." Van watched Lady Linton leave the room and then turned back to her book, but for some reason the hilarious adventures of Joseph Andrews could not hold her attention. Outside, the rain was still coming down steadily. She had a premonition that something was wrong at the stable.

He came in at twelve-thirty. Van heard his voice in the hall talking to the night footman who had let him in. Robert would tell him she was still up. She put her book down and looked worriedly at the drawing-room door.

She knew something had gone wrong the moment she saw him. His hair and coat were soaked with rain, his boots caked with mud. "Edward, you're drenched!" Van stood up. "Come over here by the fire." Then, as he hesitated in the doorway, she went over to him, put a hand on his soaked sleeve, and guided him to the chair placed closest to the chimneypiece. She pushed him into the chair and he looked up at her, his blue eyes clouded with pain.

"She died," he said.

Van's heart ached for him. "Oh, Edward. I'm so sorry." She began to unbutton his jacket. "Come, you must get out of this wet coat. It's soaked through. However did you get so wet?"

"I walked back from the stables." He let her slide the jacket off his shoulders. There was blood as well as water on the sleeves. His shirt was wet as well. Van went to add another log to the fire.

As the flames blazed up she turned to look at him. "What happened?"

He was staring down at his muddy boots. His shirt was open at the neck and the firelight glimmered on the strong, smooth column of his throat. "The foal was in the wrong position," he said in a strange, dull voice. "We couldn't get it rotated. She was trying so hard that we couldn't turn him. One of his legs was caught." He leaned forward and pressed his knuckles against his eyes. "She just couldn't get him out," he said, his voice muffled. "Christ. It went on so long."

Van's throat hurt with the tears she was trying to suppress. She left the fire and came over to stand beside him. "I'm so sorry," she repeated, feeling how woefully inadequate the words were.

His fists tightened and the motion set the muscles rippling along his arms and shoulders. The wet shirt was clinging to his skin. Van drew her breath in sharply. "I had a feeling about this foal," he was saying. "I just had a feeling."

"There was nothing you could have done," she said. "Edward." She knelt so she could see his face. "You tried," she said. "There was nothing more you could have done."

He dropped his hands away from his face. The heat of the fire had begun to dry his hair and the loosened strands that slanted across his forehead were turning a coppery gold. She continued to kneel beside him, her face very close to his. She scarcely saw his hands move to reach for her, and then his mouth was coming down on hers, crushing, urgent, merciless. Van flung her arms around his neck. She felt his body rock-hard against hers, his strong arms lifting her up. It was a savage, searing kiss, one that should have frightened a girl of Van's inexperience. What she felt running hot through her veins, however, was not fear, but desire.

His mouth left her lips and moved to her throat, her breasts. She could feel the fire of his kisses through the silk fabric of her blue gown. She slid her fingers into his disordered wet hair. "Edward," she whispered in a shaking voice. "Edward."

She felt his entire body tense. He pulled away from her a little and lifted his head. If taking her would ease his pain, Van thought, she wouldn't stop him. He read the thought in her eyes and drew a deep, shuddering breath. "Van," he said in an unrecognizable voice, "this is not a good idea."

She didn't reply and, without another word, he set her away from him, stood up, and walked to the far side of the room. Van ran her fingers through her disordered curls and sat back on her heels.

"I can't bear to see you so unhappy," she said in a small and wavering voice.

He was breathing as if he had been running, but he had got his voice under control. "Is this true?"

She ran her tongue around suddenly dry lips. "Yes."

There was a very long silence. Van found herself listening to the tick-tocking of the clock in the corner. A log fell on the fire, sending up a spray of sparks.

"We don't even like each other," he said at last. There was a look about his mouth she had never seen before, not even for his mother. Van's heart began to pound.

"Viking," she whispered. "Sassenach."

At that he crossed the floor back toward where she was still kneeling. When he reached her he held out his hands and drew her to her feet. Then he bent his head and kissed her again.

It was not so frantic this time, but long and slow and remarkably thorough. Van melted to him, answered to him, her body pliant and yielding against his. When finally he raised his head, she found herself trembling. He held her close against him and she leaned her cheek against his wet, warm shoulder. His back felt so strong against the palms of her hands. She closed her eyes.

"That settles it then," he said in a deep voice. "You'll marry *me*."

Van's eyes flew open. "Marry you?" she said, clearly startled. Then, as his words registered, she stared at him out of wide and frightened eyes. "I can't marry you, Edward. My father would never allow it."

The eyes that met hers was burningly intense. "I'm not interested in your father," he said. "At the moment I am only interested in you. Do *you* want to marry me, Van?"

His eyes were so blue. She said, on an audibly caught breath, "Yes. Oh, yes, Edward. I do want to marry you!"

That look was back about his mouth again. "Van," he said. "The most honest woman in the world."

Her whole body was aching for the feel of his hands. She forced herself to move away from him and ask, "Why do you say that?"

He smiled, that beautiful tender look still about his mouth. "You never pretend," he said. "Not even to yourself. That time I kissed you at the Evesham ball— any other woman would have blamed it on me. But not you."

"But, Edward," said Van, "I kissed you back."

He laughed and the fireplace flames danced in his

brilliant eyes. "You see what I mean?" he said. "You admit it."

Van gave him a long, considering look. "You sound as if that sort of thing has happened to you before."

He chuckled. "As it happens, I don't make a practice of kissing girls in anterooms."

"Well, I should hope not!" she said forcefully, and he chuckled again.

"I have been trying so hard not to think about that kiss," Van said.

"I have been trying so hard not to do it again," he returned with amusement. Then, a serious look coming over his face, "But it was not until this afternoon that I realized how much I loved you."

She gazed up at him out of wondering eyes. "This afternoon?"

"Mmm. When you said you couldn't abide Richardson's Pamela. I knew then. I had known for a long time, of course, but I wouldn't let myself know I knew." He smiled faintly. "If that makes sense?"

Van smiled up at him tenderly. "It makes perfect sense. I have been telling myself that my feeling for you was only a physical attraction."

His eyes began to dance. "Well, there *is* that, of course."

She ignored him. "But tonight, when you were so hurt, *I* hurt too."

He cupped her face in strong, gentle hands. She gazed up at him, her eyes full of trouble. "Edward," she whispered, "I cannot marry you without my father's permission."

He sighed. "I know, sweetheart. I know." He kissed her forehead and dropped his hands. "We'll get his permission."

She looked at him doubtfully. How was she to ex-

plain her father to a man like Edward? "He is not very
. . . flexible, you see," she began. Her narrow, sensitive lips quivered faintly. "He is never going to understand my wishing to marry a Sassenach!"

"If I understand correctly, he married one himself,"
he said dryly. "Sit down, sweetheart, and let's talk this
out."

Obediently she moved to the sofa he had indicated.
Then, when they were seated side by side, "Dhé!
What if there is a French landing?"

"There won't be a French landing," he said calmly
and convincingly. "The French are far too busy consolidating their gains on the Continent. Perhaps, if
Louis XIV were still king, he would send an army for
the Stuarts. But this king won't. He proved his lack of
interest when he gave in to English demands and
forced the Pre . . . ah, James to move his court from
France to Rome."

Van believed him. They had been waiting since 1715
for the French to send an army, she thought. Why
should it happen now?

"But, Edward, my father still thinks there is a good
possibility the French will come."

"What does your mother think of all this?" he asked.

"Of the possibility of a French landing?" Van thought,
her brow furrowed. "Mother never says very much
about it," she answered at last, slowly.

"Would your mother object to our marrying?"

Van thought of how her mother had deliberately
deceived her father about the Linton political affilia-
tions. "No. I don't think she would object."

"Well, then, I suggest that you write to your mother
while I write to your father. From what I gather,
Morar took your mother from parents who were fully
as unhappy about him as he is likely to be about me."

Van gave a sudden deep chuckle.

"We won't make any mention of my political party," Edward said dryly.

She looked at him, suddenly somber. "I will never curtsy to the elector, Edward."

He was equally serious in reply. "I would never ask you to." He raised her hands to his mouth and kissed her fingers and then her palms. "I think you had better go on up to bed."

She closed her fists over his kiss, as if to hold it safe. "Good night," she said softly. "M'eudail."

They stared at each other. "You and I," he said at last, and the familiar amusement was back in his voice. "Who would have ever thought it?"

Van rose to her feet. "Well, I know someone who is going to be delighted," she informed him. "Your mother. She has been praying for years for you to get married!"

He began to laugh, and after a light, proprietary touch on the top of his now-dry gilt hair, she went upstairs and got into bed.

Lady Linton was more than delighted; she was ecstatic. As Van finished her letter to her mother, she found herself wishing that her own parents would react to the news with such wholehearted approval. Her mother very well might, but there was no disguising from herself the fact that her father was going to be furious.

She wouldn't think about it, she decided, after she had given her letter to Edward to be franked and posted. There was nothing else she could do, so she might as well stop fretting and enjoy the time she had with Edward. The time seemed even more precious because of the half-buried fear of her father's reply.

It was astonishing, Van often found herself thinking, how brilliant and beautiful life could be when you did even the smallest, most trivial thing with the one you loved.

A thought similar to this came to her one afternoon as she leaned against the paddock fence and watched Edward work Marcus. As always, the grace of the huge stallion, the complete harmony between horse and rider, brought an ache in her throat. Then Marcus began to come down the center line of the paddock toward her at a slow canter. As Van watched, he began to change leads at every step. Her eyes widened with sheer astonishment.

"What was that?" she asked Edward when they had halted in front of her. "It looked as if he were dancing!"

"Flying changes of lead on every step," he replied. "It's difficult to do." His blue eyes laughed at her and he grinned like a schoolboy. Van's heart turned over. "We were showing off for you," he said.

"It was beautiful." Her voice was very soft. "Can you do it again?"

"Of course," he replied cockily, and turning Marcus to the diagonal line of the paddock, he proceeded to do so.

Van drew a deep breath. This is happiness, she thought. Standing here, with the sun on my head, and Edward and Marcus showing off for me. No matter what may happen, this is a moment I will always have. Nothing can take it away from me.

The spring weather was beautiful and for the week they were at Staplehurst they were almost always outdoors. One afternoon Edward took Van fishing at a small secluded lake a few miles from the house.

"I know it's nothing to compare to Loch Morar," he said to her, "but I spent a great many happy childhood days at this lake."

They had finished fishing and were picnicking on some cold meat and fruit Edward had brought along with them. Van's white teeth bit into a perfect peach from the Staplehurst greenhouse and she looked thoughtfully around the small, glassy lake on whose shores they were so comfortable reclining.

"It's very pretty here," she said, and meant it, "But, no, it's nothing like Loch Morar."

"What is Morar like?" he asked, his deep voice curiously quiet.

"Morar is beautiful," Van answered. "The loch is surrounded by mountains." She looked around. "Nothing is green, as it is here. It's all jagged cliffs and purple heather, and the sky, on a clear day, is blue as cobalt. When you look in the waters of the loch you can see the mountains as if in a mirror." She rested her chin on her up-drawn knees. "At the end of the loch is the sea." Her eyes were focused ahead, on something quite different from the placid waters of Staplehurst's little lake "When you look across the sound, you can see the Cuillens of Skye."

He was leaning up on one elbow, gazing at her averted face. When he didn't answer, she turned to look at him. His long body was stretched comfortably on the grass, his eyes half-closed against the brightness of the sun.

"You can see the loch from your home?" he asked.

"Yes. From two sides of the castle, at any rate. The other two sides look out only on the mountains." She smiled at him. "Mother called it the most beautiful place in the world. I think she's right."

He smiled back almost imperceptibly, and putting his hand on her wrist, levered her back until she was lying beside him on the grass. She looked up into his eyes, now so close to hers. "It's nothing at all like Kent," she said softly.

The smile had completely left his face. It was serious, concentrated, intent. "You have your mother in you," he said, and his low voice held a note that Van could feel in her stomach. "Her music, her intellectual curiosity. But the fire and the passion—*they* are from Morar. You're the perfect mixture, Van. Sassenach and Celt. Did you know that?"

She didn't answer. Her eyes were locked on his mouth, which was coming closer to hers, and closer still. . . . She stretched her body all along the length of his, her arms around his neck, her breasts crushed against the hard wall of his chest. When his tongue came into her mouth she shuddered a little and arched up against him. His hand moved on her back, her waist.

It was agony when she felt him pull away from her. "Almighty God," he said. "This is a very dangerous activity for the open air."

Van lay back on the grass where he had left her and stared at him. He had opened the neck of his shirt earlier against the heat and she could see a pulse beating wildly in the hollow of his throat. He was so beautiful, so strong. She wanted to see him without his shirt, wanted to run her hands along the smooth skin that covered the hard muscles she knew were there in his back and arms and shoulders.

Dhé, thought Van a little wildly. I never knew I was such a wanton woman.

Her hair was disheveled, her mouth a little swollen from his kisses. Her eyelids looked heavy. "If we don't get out of here immediately," Edward said, "I won't answer for the consequences." He ran a hand over his own sun-bright hair. "Get *up*, Van," he said, almost irritably. And she moved to obey him.

On the way home they went by the paddock, where Marcus was turned out with one of the mares. Edward stopped the trap he was driving.

"I thought Marcus was always turned out by himself," Van said, puzzled.

"It's time Aurora was bred," Edward replied. He was staring at the two horses in the paddock.

Van looked too. Stallion and mare were galloping around, the mare seemingly trying to avoid him but unable to do so. He nipped her flanks and herded her from one end of the paddock to the other until, finally, he had her cornered. At that point, the mare gave up.

Van stared at the spectacle before her with a pounding heart. She had seen dogs mating before, but it had never been anything like this—powerful, primitive, grand. The mare, once caught, had been totally receptive. As Marcus slid out and brought his forelegs back to the ground, Van's eyes flew to the man beside her. He glanced at her face very briefly and started the trap forward. "A good one," was all he said. Van clasped her hands together in her lap to conceal their trembling.

Two days later they all went back to London to await word from the Earl of Morar.

10

Spring had come to the Highlands as well. Frances MacIan sniffed the air with pleasure as she bent over a bed of daffodils in the walled garden Alasdair had built for her some years ago. She finished her gardening and walked slowly back to the house, gazing around her with intense appreciation for the sun-bathed landscape of mountain and loch. All of the hardships of her life in the highlands had always been mitigated by this great natural beauty among which she lived.

She came into her own small sitting room, stripping off her gloves and throwing them down on a table. It was a moment before her eye spotted the letter on her writing desk. Frances recognized the signature of the Earl of Linton on the frank and smiled with pleasure. Van had been rather dilatory about writing recently. Frances took the letter over to the window and opened it.

She read it through completely three times. Then she folded it and stared blindly out at the mountains that loomed so closely behind the castle.

Van and the Earl of Linton. Frances couldn't believe it. The thought, of course, had crossed her mind once or twice, idly, speculatively, but she had never considered it at all seriously.

Good God, Frances thought distractedly, what was Alasdair going to say?

She looked down at the letter once more. "I know you will all find it difficult to believe," Van had written. "But I love him, Mother. I love him—and where he is, that is where I want to be also. You, I think, will understand that."

Frances let out her breath and began to pace the room, her brow furrowed. If Van felt like that, then she must marry Linton. In fact, Frances thought ruefully, were it not for Alasdair, she would be delighted by such news. Van was far more suited to be the Countess of Linton than she was to be Lady MacDonald of Lochaber. Of course, Alasdair would never see that.

Alasdair. It all came back to Alasdair. He would be furious at this news. Furious at Van and furious at her. Frances shivered. In all their married life she had never had anything from Alasdair but tenderness and love. How could she possibly oppose him on this matter of Van's marriage?

She would have to. She knew, unerringly, that his instinct would be to demand Van's immediate return home. Her daughter was counting on her for help. Van's letter had made that clear.

Van had said that Linton had written to Alasdair. God in heaven, Frances thought with cold horror, what if Alasdair also found out that Linton was a Whig? Van had to know, although she had never written a word on the subject. Everyone in Britain knew of the Romneys, Frances thought a little wildly, everyone except the chiefs of the Western Highlands, to whom the English nobility were as alien as Turks.

Alasdair had gone to Achnacarry a few days ago on one of his endless conferences about the mythical French invasion they were all so anxiously awaiting. Of course, there would be no French invasion. Frances knew that and it seemed as if reality was finally penetrating into the glens of the Highlands as well. The King of France was not interested in restoring the Stuarts to the throne of Britain.

Her husband would be home tomorrow. All her married life, Frances had looked forward eagerly to his returns; it was an odd and frightening feeling to find herself dreading seeing him again.

He arrived the following evening. At this time of year the light reversed itself and instead of the endless nights of winter there were apparently endless days. It was perfectly bright when the Earl of Morar arrived home at nine o'clock on a chill June evening. He sought his wife out immediately.

"How are you, m'eudail?" he asked, bending to kiss her mouth.

"Very well," she replied. They were alone. Niall was visiting in Lochaber for the week.

Alasdair began to unfasten the shoulder brooch of his plaid. "It's good to be home," he said, his gray eyes devouring her with a sort of hunger—hunger for peace, for respite. "I'm so weary of listening to promises." He tossed his plaid on a chair and sat down in his favorite chair. His dark head, so distinctive and arresting, was outlined against its high back.

"The French are not coming," he said, an expression of brooding bitterness on his face. "Say what the prince will, there will be no French landing in Scotland."

"Oh, darling," Frances said out of an aching throat. His whole life had been dedicated to this cause. She herself was only glad to see it ended, but her heart was torn for him. And now, on top of this, to give him the news about Van!

Perhaps she should wait. Let him relax, take her to

bed, then tomorrow . . . She looked at his face and knew she could not do that. He would be angry enough, but if she withheld the news from him it would be worse.

"Alasdair," she said steadily, "a letter came for you yesterday. From the Earl of Linton. I think you should read it." She got up and went over to the mantelpiece where she had propped it. She put it into his outstretched hand.

There was a very long silence. Finally he looked up. "Do you know what this contains?" he demanded. His black brows were drawn almost together.

"Yes. I had a letter from Van."

His mouth was thin and hard. "Let me see it."

"It's in my desk," she replied. "I'll go and get it."

He was rereading Linton's letter when she came back into the drawing room. He stretched out an imperative hand, his eyes still on the sheet in front of him. Frances gave him his daughter's letter and sat down once again. She stared blindly at the fire.

He cursed in Gaelic, long and fluently. Then he looked at his wife. "This is what has come of sending her to England," he said harshly. "I should never have let you talk me into it."

Frances swallowed. "It isn't so very terrible, darling," she began, but he cut her off.

"Not so very terrible! My daughter and a Sassenach!" His eyes narrowed. "I hope you do not expect me to allow this . . . this *mésalliance*, Frances? Van is to come home immediately."

Frances forced herself to sustain that hard gaze. "Why, Alasdair? You read her letter. She loves him."

"She thinks she loves him, you mean." He threw the letter down contemptuously on the table beside him. "We sent her away with no one of her own to be a companion to her, to advise her. She was lonely, of course. And this Linton took advantage of the situation." His voice was as hard and as cold as his face. "I'm disappointed in Van," he said, "but I blame myself more than I blame her. I knew I should not have sent her."

"No," Frances disagreed strongly, "we were right to send her, Alasdair. She was not lonely. She's had a wonderful time. Her letters have been full of all her activities: parties, dances, music lessons, concerts, opera."

He made a curt gesture of dismissal. "She would never tell you she was lonely. She knew how much *you* wanted her to go. Van loves you too much to want to disappoint you." He got to his feet, his movements at age fifty as lithe and quick as those of a man twenty years younger. "She will come home," he repeated. "I will communicate that to Linton and to her in no uncertain terms."

"No." Frances spoke very quietly, but the effect of her words was instantaneous. He swung around to stare at her. Her blue eyes were deadly serious. "Van is my daughter too, Alasdair, and I say she should marry Edward Romney. She loves him."

There was a flicker of surprise in his gray eyes. Never, in all the years of their marriage, had she seriously opposed him. "I know what it means, Alasdair, to fall in love with a man one's parents disapprove of. I know what it means to face the heartbreak of giving him up, the anguish of defying one's father." She took a step closer to him. "Don't you remember, darling?" Her voice quivered for the first time. "After all, *you* married a Sassenach."

There was a white line around his mouth. "That was not the same thing."

"Not for you. I was the one who had to come to your world. Well, your daughter is a woman and she too will have to go to the world of her husband."

"She will marry Alan MacDonald and stay in the Highlands."

"The same way my father wanted me to marry Charles Trusdale and stay in England?"

Alasdair's black brows were straight above his shadowed eyes and his lips pressed together before he answered at last, "There can be no comparison between you and me and Van and the Earl of Linton."

"Why not?" Frances pressed him relentlessly. "She is *our* daughter, Alasdair. God knows, she should be capable of loving a man!"

He turned on his heel and left the room.

Frances stayed up for a long time, until the fire had nearly burned to ash, before she finally went upstairs to their room. Alasdair was in bed asleep. Frances had earlier sent all the servants to bed, so she undressed alone in the chill evening air and, leaving her hair unbrushed, climbed into bed beside Alasdair. She was cold and normally she would have curled up next to his warm back for comfort and warmth, but tonight she could not do that. She had put a wedge between them as effectively as if she had in fact built a physical wall.

She had won her point. She had known that the minute he left the room. He had not had an answer for her. He would not dash off a letter tomorrow demanding Van's instant return.

She had won. Would he ever forgive her?

Alasdair said nothing to her the following day about Van, nor the day after that either. Frances too held her tongue. He had not written to Linton one way or the other; she must be content with that for the moment.

He had understood her point of comparison. He didn't like it, but she had forced him to see it and, because he was so essentially a just man, he could not ignore it. The Earl of Linton wanted to steal his daughter in much the same way he had stolen his own wife more than twenty years ago. The way he looked at Frances made her think, very bleakly, that at the moment Alasdair was regretting his choice.

Niall came home and was told the news. He sought out Frances in her sitting room after his interview with Alasdair in the study.

"Mother," he demanded imperatively as he came in the door. "What is all this Father has been telling me about Van and that Sassenach Linton? Surely she can't seriously wish to marry him?"

"Yes, Niall," Frances replied calmly, "I'm afraid she does."

"But what has gotten into her?" Niall sounded more bewildered than angry. "This Linton has nothing to do with us. He is a Sassenach. A Whig. An enemy."

Frances felt a thrill of fear. "What do you know about Linton's politics?"

"I know they are all Whigs down there in England," he returned fiercely. "You saw Van's letters to Father. They will none of them stir a finger to restore their rightful king to his throne. I wouldn't soil my hands by taking a sip of water from any of them—no, not if I were dying of thirst! And for Van to wish to marry one! Van!"

Frances had known this was going to be difficult. Niall and Van were much closer than the ordinary brother and sister. They had spent the greatest part of their childhood with only each other for companionship. They had shared the same tutor. They had never been separated until Niall went to Paris at the age of eighteen. Frances looked at her son and said gently, "What does the heart understand of politics, Niall? She loves him."

"She can't."

"I think Van is the best judge of that."

"What of Alan?" he demanded furiously. "I thought she and Alan would marry. He loves her."

"Well, Van does not love him."

Niall stared at his mother. His face, for once, had lost all of its youthful exuberence. He looked uncannily like his father. "You can't let her do this. She will listen to you, Mother. Write and tell her to come home. I will go and fetch her myself."

Frances' heart ached for him, but she shook her head. "No, Niall. I will not tell her to come home. If she loves the Earl of Linton, and I believe she does, then she should marry him."

"If she does," Niall said, his mouth thin and straight-lipped, "then she is no longer my sister." And he flung himself out of the room.

The following week was the worst time Frances had ever lived through. Worse, even, than that horrible year when she had set her will against her father to win her love. Well, she had won him. She had trampled her parents' love and concern into the dust under her feet and she had prevailed. She supposed she couldn't complain that after twenty-four years of happiness she was being called on to pay the piper.

She had no doubt that Alasdair and Niall were wrong and she was right. Men, when it came to hearts other than their own, were so blind. Niall was worse than Alasdair. Alasdair, at least, had some understanding of why she was acting as she was.

He said to her one evening as they were seated in front of the drawing-room fire, "I will write to Linton and give him my permission, if that is what you wish." His gray eyes on her were hard and accusing. "I will not write to Van. Since she has chosen to cut herself off from Morar, so be it."

His look was like a blow at her heart. "Just because she has chosen another way of life doesn't mean she has cut her ties with us, Alasdair. The place you grew up in, the people you spent your childhood with, they are always home to you. No matter where Van goes, Morar will be home. And she will never forget you and me, or these mountains and lochs and skies and seas. We are all a part of her, forever."

"Has Morar ever been home to you, Frances?" There was no softness about his mouth. "You went away from your childhood place as surely as Van will."

Her fair skin was faintly flushed by the heat from the fire, her neck and shoulders lovely in the low-cut bodice of her evening dress. Her blue eyes on his were large and filled with longing. "*You* are home to me," she said softly.

His eyes fell away from her gaze. He stood up. "I have some work to do in the study," he said. And left.

She had a nightmare that night, a terrible, frightening nightmare. She dreamed that Alasdair had died. She woke to the sound of his voice.

"Frances. Frances. Wake up. You're dreaming. It's all right. You're safe. Wake up."

Her eyes opened and he was there, his worried face

bending over hers. She could see him clearly in the slanting moonlight coming in through the open window.

"Oh, Alasdair!" She threw her arms around his neck and held him convulsively. She was trembling all over.

"What were you dreaming, heart of my heart, to frighten you so?" His voice was soft and gentle, a voice she had not heard in weeks. "Shh, now. Shh." This as she began to weep. "It's all right." His hand gently stroked her long brown hair away from her forehead. "You're safe."

"I dreamed I lost you." Her voice was muffled against his chest.

"Frances."

There was a new note in his voice now and she looked up. "Frances," he said again, and then he kissed her.

The relief that flooded through her at the touch of his mouth was overwhelming. It was all right. It was over. He was hers again. Her lips opened under the urgent pressure of his and her hands moved up and down his lean, muscled back. It had been unendurable, to be shut out from him like that. His body was coming over hers and she welcomed him with utter joy.

11

Both the Earl of Linton and the Earl of Morar were correct in their assessment of the French king's unwillingness to assist in a Stuart restoration. What neither earl had reckoned on, however, was the determination of the Stuart heir, Prince Charles Edward. On July 5 he boarded the ship *Du Teillay* with scarcely more than a dozen men and set sail for Scotland to win his destiny.

The word was brought to Morar by a MacDonald from the Western Isles: the prince had landed on Eriskay two days previously. He was sailing for Moidart, where he expected to meet with all his loyal followers.

"He has come alone," Alasdair told his wife and his son as they sat up in the late-night sunshine of July. "Atholl and Aeneas MacDonald are with him, and some few Irish officers. He has no army." Alasdair's face was bleak. "Folly!" he said forcefully.

Niall leapt to his feet. "It's not folly, Father. It's grand! We don't need the French. The clans alone can put King James back on his throne."

His parents ignored him. "What will happen, Alasdair?" Frances asked tensely.

"I do not know. Under these circumstances, Clanranald will never come out. Nor will MacDonald of Sleat or Macleod of Macleod. They made it very clear they would raise their clans only if the prince came with a French army."

"*You* made that clear as well," Frances said. Her long, musician's fingers were cramping, she had them clenched together so tightly.

A flicker of annoyance passed over his brow. "I know."

She didn't back off. This was too important. "Lochiel also. It's madness to think that the clans, armed only with pistols and broadswords, can rise against an established government!"

"You talk like a Sassenach, Mother," Niall said with contempt.

Alasdair's eyes locked with his son's. "Do not ever use that tone of voice to your mother again."

Niall's eyes were the first to fall. "Sorry, Mother," he muttered.

"I will have to see him," Alasdair said to Frances. "Perhaps he has promises of assistance we do not know about."

Frances did not think so but she deemed it best to remain silent. Alasdair's own good sense would prevail, she thought. Dedicated he was, certainly, but he was not blind. He would never raise the clan unless there was an army at his back.

Alasdair and Niall set off for their rendezvous with Charles Edward in the company of Donald Cameron of Lochiel. Morar and Lochiel were the decision makers as to whether the rebellion would take place or not, and they both knew it. Morar could put more than a thousand MacIans into the field, Lochiel about nine hundred Camerons. If the MacIans and the Camerons went out, then many of the small clans would follow. If Morar and Lochiel stayed home, there would be no rebellion.

The small frigate *Du Teillay* was anchored in Loch Nan Uamh, and as the three men with their tail of followers rode down the hill to the water's edge, the sun, under cloud cover all morning, came out. Niall turned to his father, his white teeth flashing. "A good omen, Father."

Alasdair did not reply.

They were greeted by the Jacobite Duke of Atholl, who had been in exile with the Stuarts since the rising of 1715. A sort of tent had been erected upon the deck of the ship and Alasdair and Lochiel were seated.

"Have you promise of an army?" Alasdair asked Atholl.

"No promise," the older man replied serenely. "The prince has come alone, trusting to the loyalty of his good Highlanders."

Alasdair frowned. "I believe we made it plain, Atholl, that a rising had no chance of success without an army. I suggest that you go back to France and wait for a more auspicious opportunity."

Behind him Alasdair could hear his son's sharply indrawn breath. At that moment a young man came out on deck.

He was tall and fair, clean-limbed and handsome. He wore a plain black coat and cambric shirt. All of the men rose instinctively to their feet.

"Your royal highness," said the Duke of Atholl, "may I present the Earl of Morar and Cameron of Lochiel."

The young man gave the two older men an extraordinarily charming smile. "How happy I am to meet two of my father's firmest friends," he said.

Alasdair stared at the tall, handsome youngster before him and felt his heart swell within his breast. After all these years, he thought, with deep emotion, a Stuart was back on Scottish soil.

"Your royal highness," Lochiel was saying beside him, "you must go home. Without a French army there is no hope for a successful rising."

Charles Edward's hair was a fair, reddish color, but his eyes were brown. He looked now, deliberately, from Alasdair to Lochiel. Then he said, "I am come home, sir. And I will entertain no notion at all of returning to France."

There was a moment of tense silence and then the prince's eyes discovered Niall standing behind his father. Niall's dark face was blazing, his fists opening and closing in the effort to remain silent.

"Niall MacIan," Charles Edward said. "Will *you* not assist me?"

"That I will," returned Niall fiercely. "Though not another man in the Highlands should draw a sword, my prince, I am ready to die for you!"

The two young men stared at each other for a moment; then both pairs of eyes, light and dark, turned to the faces of the two older men on whose response their fates would hang.

"I will not return," Charles Edward said firmly. "In a few days' time, with the few friends I have, I will erect the royal standard and proclaim to the people of Britain that Charles Stuart is come over to claim the crown of his ancestors, to win it, or to perish in the attempt. Morar and Lochiel may stay at home if they will, and learn from the newspapers the fate of their prince."

It was too much for Donald Cameron. "No," he replied. "I'll share the fate of my prince; and so shall every man over whom nature or fortune has given me power."

They all turned to Alasdair. His face was grave but there was a faint glow in his eyes as he looked at Charles Edward. "I will raise the clan," he said.

Frances could not believe her ears when Alasdair told her what he had done. "You cannot be serious," she said incredulously. "You said yourself that it was folly, that without the French there was no hope of success."

"I don't know, Frances." She had been in bed when he returned and now he went to the window, threw it open, and looked up at the still-luminous sky. He turned back to her. "He is all Stuart," he said. "With a prince like this to lead us, I believe we can do anything."

"To lead you?" She leaned toward him, her hair streaming over her shoulders. "Alasdair, this boy is scarcely older than Niall. He has never seen a battle-field. He has no idea of what he is asking you to do. He has no right to ask this of you!"

"He is my prince," he returned, and now there was an undercurrent of steel in his voice. "He has the right to ask me for anything he chooses."

"Not your life," she flung back at him. "Dear God, Alasdair, the clans don't even have artillery."

"Yes," he said. "Even my life."

She thrust her hair away from her face. "*I* have some small stake in your life, I believe." For the first time there was bitterness in her voice.

"Frances." His voice was low but the steel was even more evident. "Do not try to come between me and my duty."

"Your duty. Alasdair, your duty is to your family and your clan. You cannot ask over one thousand men to throw their lives away for a dream, a fantasy!"

Alasdair stood there facing her, feet apart, his arresting dark head poised in the fashion of an animal when it scents danger. "A dream?" he said.

"Yes, a dream. You read Van's letters. There is no hope the Stuarts will regain the British throne—not even with a French army behind them."

He was looking at her as if he had never seen her before. "I never knew you felt this way."

"Alasdair." She was frantic to reach him. Couldn't he see the disaster he was bringing down on them all? "*Think*, darling. You are much too clever not to see the probable outcome of all this."

"No," he said, his voice hard and cold. "It's you who are the clever one. For all these years you have been letting me think you were one with me on this."

He was looking at her as if she revolted him. Her palms felt suddenly clammy. "I *was* with you," she said. "Then. But now is different."

"The cause has not changed. It is as just today as it was twenty years ago."

"There is more involved here than the justice of the cause!"

"For you, perhaps. Not for me." He walked to the bedroom door. "I will send the fiery cross around tomorrow to raise the clan. And Niall is leaving in the morning for England to bring Van home."

He closed the door behind him and she was alone.

Word of Charles Edward's landing reached London three days after Alasdair's meeting with the prince. Edward and Van were preparing to go for a drive in the park when a messenger came to Linton House with a summons from the prime minister. Edward read the brief letter and looked up at her. All the good humor had vanished from his face.

Van was instantly alarmed. "What has happened?"

"I'm afraid I can't take you driving." His face was white under its coat of summer tan. "Van," he said, and stopped.

She stepped closer to him. "For God's sake, Edward, what is it? You're frightening me."

"Charles Edward has landed in Scotland," he said bleakly.

"Dhia gleidh sinn," said Van, and sat abruptly in the nearest chair.

"I quite agree." He sounded bitter.

Her eyes clung to his. "Has he brought an army?"

"I don't think so. He can't have. An army could not have sailed without our knowing it." He crumpled the letter in his hand. "Van, I must go. Pelham wants to hold a meeting of the government immediately. I shall find out there exactly what is happening."

Her eyes were wide and curiously blank-looking. She nodded. "Yes. Go. You must go."

He hesitated, then came over to her chair and kissed her quick and hard on the mouth before he went out.

Van sat for a long time, staring blindly into space, her mind scarcely working at all. All she felt at present was a terrible sense of foreboding. Finally she got to her feet and went into the drawing room to the harpsichord. She sat down at the instrument and let her fingers pick out a single chord over and over. As always, this simple exercise freed her mind. The suffocating sense of fear receded and she was able to think.

The prince had landed. Alone. What would her father do?

The answer was immediate and certain. Her father's entire life had been dedicated to the Stuart cause. To him, it was sacred. If his prince called upon him, he would go.

They had heard nothing from Morar since she and

Edward had written almost a month ago. Van had begun to think that perhaps her father might countenance their marriage after all. The fact that he had not ordered her home immediately was a very auspicious sign.

But . . . now, everything was different. The prince was here, upon Scottish soil.

There was no way out of it. She would have to go home.

Edward's meeting with the prime minister and other government ministers went on until late in the night. One of the government's chief Scottish advisers, Duncan Forbes of Culloden, was present and it was his evaluation of the situation that most interested Edward.

"My understanding is that neither Clanranald nor Macleod will lift a finger in this matter," Forbes told the half-dozen men Lord Pelham had called upon to decide the government's course of action.

"Just how many fighting men can the chiefs put into the field?" Edward asked grimly.

"I would say that the total fighting strength of the Highlands does not number less than thirty thousand men, my lord. Of course, this includes the Campbells, who will most certainly come out for the government. The Sutherlands will remain loyal to us as well."

Edward's blue eyes were cold. "How many men are likely to follow the pretender, Forbes? Clanranald and Macleod are neutral, you say. So—how much of an army is that extremely irritating young man likely to raise?"

"That depends, my lord," came the deliberate reply. "If Morar and Lochiel go out, perhaps half the others will follow."

Every eye in the room was on Edward's face. He

and Van had made no formal engagement announcement, but these last few weeks in London had made clear to all the *ton* that such an announcement would certainly be forthcoming.

Edward's blue eyes, hard as diamonds, flicked once around the council. His face showed absolutely no emotion. "And if Morar and Lochiel stay out of it?"

"It cannot go forward without Morar and Lochiel." Forbes was positive. "They are the leaders."

"What if one goes out and the other does not?" Lord Pelham asked abruptly.

"I do not think that will happen. They will act in concert."

"What do *you* think is going to happen, Forbes?" Edward's deep voice was forcibly calm.

"I have met both men," Duncan Forbes of Culloden returned slowly, "but I know Morar better." His eyes went from face to face around the table and stopped at the Earl of Linton's. "He is a man from another world, another time. His sense of honor is sacred to him. If that honor is in question, I do not think that he will count the cost." Duncan Forbes paused and then said quietly, "I think Morar will go out."

Edward's face was brutally composed but Forbes, watching him closely, saw a muscle jump in his jaw. Then Edward said very grimly, "Well, gentlemen, it looks as if we have a rebellion on our hands."

Edward came home through the dimly lit streets of London with murder in his heart. He longed with a savagery that would have put him right at home among any clansmen, to have Charles Stuart's neck between his fingers. And the emotion that fueled his anger was mainly fear.

He was not afraid of the rebellion succeeding. It

might be a little chancy at first, for most of England's army was across the channel, but the ultimate outcome would be success for the government.

It would be disaster for the Highlands. He had sensed that in the council meeting tonight. The government was tired of Jacobite plots, tired of chiefs who lived as a law unto themselves, tired of having what they considered an uncivilized tribal society only four hundred miles from London. Another rebellion would serve as a perfect excuse to crush the Highlands once and for all.

This was not a solution Edward would ever have favored, but the situation now held far more than political significance for him.

He could not let Van go back.

A pulse was throbbing in his temple as he walked from the stable around to the front door of Linton House. How to keep her out of it? Keep her safe. Keep her with him.

He let himself in with a latchkey. The candles were lit in the hall against his return. He took a candlestick and went along to the library, where he sat behind a desk containing the law cases he had been studying earlier in the day. As lord lieutenant he functioned as chief justice of the peace for his county. He decided he needed a glass of wine.

He drank a bottle of claret slowly and abstractedly, his mind on only one thing—the girl asleep upstairs.

How to keep her? How to keep her?

Finally he rose, picked up his candle once again, and climbed the stairs to the bedroom floor. He opened Van's door without knocking and closed it again behind him. She stirred in the big bed at the sound.

"Van." He came into the room until he was standing at the foot of her bed. "Van," he said again, his voice low but authoritative.

She pushed herself up on her elbow and blinked. Then she saw him at the foot of the bed. "Edward!" she said in astonishment. "What are you doing here?"

"I thought perhaps you'd want to know what happened tonight."

She sat up. Her long hair streamed over her shoulders and down her back, a shining mantle of black silk. The throat that rose above the round neck of her thin cotton nightdress was so slender . . . her body was slender too, but the feel of it against his was so soft. To take off that nightdress, to have her naked beneath him . . . to be inside of her . . .

"Edward?" Her voice seemed to come from very far away. "What happened?"

He fought to get a grip on himself. "There is no French army." His voice was harsh. "The prince is depending upon the clans to come out for him."

She had drawn her knees up under the bedclothes and now she bowed her head down upon them. "What is the government going to do?" she asked in a muffled voice.

"We have issued a reward for his capture."

At that her head snapped up. "Dhé. He is not a criminal, Edward!"

"In my opinion, he's worse," came the bitter reply. He walked around to the side of the bed and put his candle down on a table. He looked down into her upturned face.

"Van," he said.

Van had no question at all about what she saw looking at her out of Edward's eyes. Desire. Hungry, intense, stark. Desire.

In that split second as they looked into each other's eyes, Van realized the decision was hers. He had not come in here to tell her about the meeting. She could send him away, however. No matter how he looked, Edward was far too civilized a man to use force on a woman.

Why now? she wondered. When he had exercised such restraint all these weeks, why now?

The answer came in a flash of intuition. He was afraid of losing her. He was afraid of losing her and this was the way he had chosen to bind her to him.

He couldn't do that, of course. But at least she would have the memory of this to hold on to. So she looked fearlessly into those burning eyes and said, "I love you." He bent and his mouth locked on hers.

A tidal wave of desire flooded through her at the touch of his mouth. She clung to him and after a minute he pressed her back onto the pillows, his body following hers, coming down on top of her, hard, strong, urgent.

The tidal wave swelled. She moved her hands up and down on his shoulders. Her mouth was open to him, her body rejoiced in the powerful weight of his. He pulled away from her and she almost cried out with dismay.

But he was only stripping off his coat. She watched as he threw it to the floor, followed quickly by the rest of his clothes. He stood for a moment then, looking down at her, and she looked back out of dark and smoky eyes.

He was so beautiful as he stood there, beautiful with the potent and powerful beauty of a stallion. For a brief moment a picture of Marcus and the mare flashed into her mind. She began to tremble.

How she wanted him, longed for him. When finally he came into her the pain was as nothing compared to the great waves of pleasure that rolled through her with his movement. She clung to him, to the strength of him, the power. And then the night splintered into the shattering white light of pure sensation.

As they lay together, his arms still around her, his golden head pillowed on her breast, for the first time Van felt fear. She ran her fingers caressingly through his hair. It clung to her fingers, thick and gilt-colored in the candlelight. He kissed her breast and pushed himself up on his elbow to look down at her.

"I had wanted to be so gentle," he said. "I'm sorry, my love. Did I hurt you?"

She gazed at the great muscled shoulders, the broad expanse of chest. She had not wanted gentleness from him tonight. "No," she said. "You didn't hurt me."

He kissed her tenderly and then gathered her into the crook of his arm. She lay with her head pillowed in the slightly damp hollow of his shoulder and tried to beat back her fear.

He had done this to bind her to him, and he had succeeded. She would leave him still—she had no choice about that. But she was his as surely as if he had put his brand upon her.

She closed her eyes and listened to the beat of his heart against her ear. He murmured something to her and she half-smiled. Fool, she thought to herself achingly. Oh, Van, you fool. You have made everything so much worse for yourself.

And the worst part was, she would do it all again.

12

Edward left her before dawn and Van finally went to sleep. She awoke late, for her, and had chocolate and bread and butter in bed before she dressed for the day. A note from Edward had come in with her breakfast tray telling her he had been summoned to a meeting with the king and would see her when he returned to Grosvenor Square.

Van sat at the harpsichord and picked out, one-handed, the MacIan battle song. It was one of the most famous in the Highlands, having been composed a hundred years earlier by the great piper Patrick Mor Mac Crimmon. It sounded strange on the harpsichord and Van imagined the notes as they sounded on the pipes, wild and heart-lifting, ringing out their challenge to mountain and sea and sky: Buaidh no Bas! Buaidh no Bas! Victory or Death! Victory or Death!

Edward had gone to see the king. Nothing else could have made clearer to her the impossibility of her present situation. This was not a fight she could stand aloof from, not when those she loved were so deeply—and divisively—involved.

She was still at the harpsichord when Niall knocked at the front door. He had made it from Morar in four days, galloping the whole way, changing horses at every posting stop, scarcely stopping to sleep. Van swung around on her stool, eyes wide with shock, when Fenton announced behind her, "Lord MacIan."

"Niall!" said Van, and jumped to her feet. "Whatever are *you* doing here?"

He looked her up and down before he replied. She had put on a thin mauve-colored dress that morning and her hair was worn in a mass of loose ringlets threaded through with a pink ribbon. She looked lovelier than Niall had ever seen her. His mouth set in a hard line. "Father sent me to bring you home," he said baldly.

"I see." Van returned his look. He wore a brown riding coat and breeches and his boots were covered with dust from the road. "Father has raised the clan, then?"

"Yes." He came a few steps closer to her. "Did you doubt that he would?"

"No." Her face was grave. "No, I did not doubt it."

"The standard is to be raised at Glenfinnan in two weeks' time. I must be there. We must leave immediately." His eyes, the same color as hers although not so large, bored into her. "This business between you and Linton is over, Van."

She was so still, so intensely still. He frowned a little and said, louder, "Van. Did you hear me, Van?"

Her eyes were on him but he did not think she saw him. Her voice, however, was steady. "Yes, I heard you, Niall. Do you have a coach or are we traveling by horse?"

He felt an immense rush of relief. He was not sure what he would have done if she refused to come with him.

"Would you mind traveling on horseback? It's faster."

"No," Van said, and for the first time since he had come in, he smiled.

"Good girl."

"Vanessa dear," came Lady Linton's voice from the door. "Fenton tells me your brother is here."

"Yes, Cousin Katherine. May I present my brother, Niall, Lord MacIan. Niall, this is Mother's cousin, Lady Linton."

Niall bowed slightly. "Ma'am," he said stiffly.

Katherine Romney raised her lovely violet eyes to his face and smiled. "My, how alike you and Vanessa are."

Niall's face was not friendly. "We resemble our father," he said, and deliberately stressed the last word.

Lady Linton looked at Van.

"I am very sorry, Cousin Katherine, but I must leave for Scotland immediately. My father sent Niall to escort me. He has raised the clan for Prince Charles."

"Oh, my dear God." Katherine Romney's cheeks were pale.

"I'm sorry," Van repeated. She made an indecisive gesture. "There is nothing I can do."

"Someone ought to give Morar a good shake," Lady Linton said furiously. "What can he be thinking of?"

"He is thinking of his prince, ma'am." Niall's voice was insufferably arrogant.

Lady Linton was not intimidated. She stared at his splendid-looking young face and her blue eyes flashed. "Well, he ought to be thinking of his daughter. And of his wife. How will Frances bear up when she sees her husband lose his head to the executioner's ax?"

Niall was staring at his mother's cousin as if she were some strange sort of insect. Then he turned to his sister. "Are you coming, Van?"

"I must go and put on riding clothes."

"Riding clothes?" Lady Linton asked sharply.

"Niall has horses, ma'am," Van said gently. "And he wishes to leave immediately."

"But Edward . . ." said his mother in great distress.

"Edward is with the king."

"The *elector*," Niall said fiercely.

Van ignored him. "I must pack a few things into a small bag, ma'am. Come upstairs and assist me." She put a hand on Lady Linton's arm and began to walk her to the door. She threw Niall a cool look over her shoulder. "I will be about half an hour. Wait here."

Twenty minutes later, as Niall was pacing the length of the drawing room, the refreshments brought by Fenton untouched on the side table, the door opened and the Earl of Linton walked in.

"MacIan," he said from the doorway. Then, as Niall swung around to face him, "I'm Linton."

Niall's eyes narrowed as he took in the look of this Sassenach who had tried to steal his sister. Edward came further into the room and threw something down on a chair. He said nothing further, just looked at Niall out of intensely blue eyes.

The hostility in the room was so strong the air seemed to crackle. Niall's eyes narrowed almost to slits. "I have come to take my sister home," he said between his teeth to the big blond Viking in front of him.

Something flickered in the earl's hard blue eyes. "Morar has gone out, then?"

"He has gone out."

"The goddamn fool," Edward said, very softly but with extreme violence.

"It's you who are the fool, Linton, to think you would be allowed to lay a hand on my sister!" Niall flared.

Van was coming in the doorway as he spoke and at

his words she stopped dead, her eyes flying to Edward. The earl's clear-cut features were iron-hard. He did not look at her. "Your sister," he said to Niall, "is perfectly capable of speaking for herself." And at last he turned.

Van felt as if she were being cleaved in two. He was so angry, she thought, but his anger was not hot like Niall's. His blue eyes were hard on her face.

"Your father is making a great mistake," he said.

"Perhaps. I do not know." She was trembling. "Edward." Her eyes were lifted to him. "Don't you see? It is precisely because he comes alone and trusts himself to us that we must follow him. And he has the right!"

His eyes were blue ice. "You are leaving, then?"

This was anguish, to part from him like this, in front of others. But to be alone would be no better. Worse, perhaps. She gripped her hands hard to conceal their tremors. "I must."

"Edward." It was Lady Linton's voice, full of distress. "He is taking Vanessa on horseback! All that long way!"

The blue eyes took in her riding habit, then went to Niall. "You will take my carriage," he said. "It is well sprung. Send it back when you get to Edinburgh."

Niall flung up his head. "I'll take nothing of yours, Sassenach!"

Edward was ice to Niall's fire. "I am not offering it for you, MacIan, but for your sister. A week in the saddle is too much for her."

Niall looked as if he were going to refuse again but Van said, "Thank you, Edward," and stared at her brother.

Edward rang a bell and said to the footman who appeared almost instantly, "Have the carriage sent around immediately." Then he turned to Van. "Do not expect England to follow Scotland's example."

"I know." Her voice was faintly breathless. "But England and Scotland were two different countries with two different kings for centuries. Why should they not be so again?"

He did not reply and Lady Linton said urgently, "Vanessa, you are to tell your mother that she has friends in the Lintons. If ever she—or you—should have need of us, we are here."

"Thank you, Cousin Katherine," Van said unsteadily. "You have been so very kind to me."

"Dear child." The countess embraced her warmly.

"The carriage is at the front door, my lord," said a footman.

"Come along, Van," Niall said crisply, and Van looked for the last time at Edward.

"Good-bye, Van," he said. Then, meaningfully, "If you need me, you know where to find me."

The pain in her heart was so great it was difficult to breathe. "Good-bye." Her lips formed the word, although no sound came out. Then Niall had her arm and was ushering her out to the hall. When she was in the carriage she looked once more toward the house. The countess was standing on the front steps waving. Of Edward there was no sign.

They were on the outskirts of London when Niall turned to his sister. "How could you have wanted to marry him? A Sassenach. And he was talking to the elector! How could you, Van?"

He was outraged, furious, and, under it all, bewildered and hurt.

Van's face was as remote as the moon. "I do not

wish to discuss Edward with you, Niall," she said, and turned her head to look out the window.

Niall had never seen his sister look like that. "Van," he said urgently, and put his hand on her arm.

"I have left him," she said over her shoulder. "That should make you and Father happy. I do not wish to discuss him again." And she removed her arm from her brother's grasp.

They rode in silence for quite a long time. Then Van turned back to him. "What has been happening at home?" she asked composedly. "Did you have any warning of the prince's coming?"

Thankfully, Niall began to tell her all that had occurred in the Highlands these last few weeks.

They arrived home to find the clan preparing for war. It was a relatively simple matter. Clansmen pulled broadswords from the sod where they had been hidden since the Disarming Acts. They dug up Lochaber axes and steel dirks. They primed muskets and dags. The piper composed a new song to be played in honor of the Prince:

> O Thèarlaich mhic Sheumais, mhic Sheumais, mhic Thèarlaich Leat shuiblainn gu h-eutrons 'n am éighlich bhith màrsad . . .

Angus Mor was playing it as Van and Niall came riding into the courtyard of Creag an Fhithich.

Alasdair was not at home and Morag told Van that the countess was in her sitting room, which was at the back of the house, where she would not have seen their arrival. Van went up to the familiar room and stopped at the door to look at her mother. Frances was alone, sitting in a blue velvet chair, her hands idle in her lap, her face abstracted and serious. Then she looked up and saw her daughter.

"Oh, my darling." Her voice was so gentle, so full of love. "I am so sorry. So very, very sorry." And she held out her arms.

Kneeling before her mother, Van felt the touch of Frances' hand on her cheek, her mother's lips on her hair. She closed her eyes against the agony in her heart. Oh, the comfort, the understanding, the peace of Mother.

Van pressed her cheek against her mother's soft breast. "I love him so much, Mother. But I couldn't stay. Even if Niall hadn't come, I would have come home."

"I know, darling."

Van pulled away and sat back on her heels. "Was Father angry with me?"

"A little. But he had agreed to the marriage before . . . before this."

Something flickered behind Van's eyes. "He agreed?"

"Yes."

Van straightened up. "Perhaps it will be all right, then, Mother. If the prince can take and hold Scotland, we may be two countries again instead of one. And once peace is restored, Edward and I can be married."

Frances did not have the heart to discourage her. She reached out and brushed a stray curl off her daughter's cheek. "Perhaps, darling. You may very well be right."

Her reward was the life that seemed to come back into Van's eyes.

Alasdair wasted no reproaches on Van. He simply

held her two hands in his and said, in Gaelic, "It is good to have you home, my daughter."

"It is good to be home at such a time, Mac mhic Iain," she replied.

He gestured her to a chair. "Your reports on the English Jacobites were not encouraging." His black brows formed almost a straight line across his dark gray eyes.

"I spoke to most of the men you wished me to see, Father. They would smile to see King James on the throne, but they will not lift a finger to put him there." Van's face was somber. "Father, I hope you do not think that what I am about to say is disloyal, but I feel I must say it for I feel it is true."

He was completely attentive. "What is it, Van?

"England does not want the Stuarts, Father. They are afraid of a Catholic king and they are afraid of France."

Alasdair's face was stern. "The Stuarts are England's rightful rulers, Van."

"Yes, I know that. But the English do not. The English think they have the right to choose their king, and they do not choose King James."

He frowned. "Are you quoting the Earl of Linton to me?"

She kept her face expressionless. "Not just the Earl of Linton, Father."

"The common people—"

"No," Van interrupted him, and he frowned even harder. "I am sorry, Father, but the common people will not risk their lives for the sake of one dynasty as opposed to another. It is simply not that important to them."

He made a sound indicative of contempt and Van leaned forward. "Be honest, Father. You are fighting for the Stuarts, but the clansmen who follow you are fighting for Mac mhic Iain and for no other man, king or prince, that exists in this world."

His gray eyes met and held hers. She was right and he knew it.

"You are saying then that we can expect no help at all from England?"

"None." She flung up her head in a proud gesture. "It is *we* who want the prince, *we* who are true to the Stuarts. We can give him Scotland. Why should he not be content with that?"

Alasdair looked at his daughter's face and his hard gray eyes began to glow. "Why not, indeed, my daughter?" He began to smile. "The Act of Union has always left a bad taste in my mouth."

Van awoke early on the nineteenth of August to the sound of the piper who was pacing back and forth in front of the castle with a stately tread. The notes of his tribute to the prince filled the morning air:

> Oh, Charles, son of James, son of James, son of Charles,
> With you I'd go gladly when the call sounds for marching . . .

Van hastily got out of bed.

Niall had scarcely slept at all. Today was the day the prince would raise the standard. The chosen place was a narrow valley at the end of Loch Shiel, Glenfinnan by name. There on this day were to gather the MacIans, the Camerons under Lochiel, the MacDonalds of Keppoch and Lochaber, and assorted other clans from the surrounding area. Today the clans would officially announce that they were in arms against the usurper king who sat on the British throne.

Alasdair was attired in the full panoply of his rank when he came punctiliously to bid his wife farewell. For the last few weeks they had spoken to each other with cool courtesy when it was necessary to communicate, and that was all. Frances had not forgiven him for raising the clan and he had not forgiven her for opposing him.

Frances was sitting up in bed when he came into the room. He wore the kilt today, not the trews, and at his waist hung a dirk and wrought-steel pistol. The rest of his weapons consisted of a broadsword, which dangled by his side, and a target which hung upon his shoulder. His bonnet was decorated with an eagle's feather, the sign of a chief. He looked barbaric, magnificent, and tough as nails.

"I will be saying good-bye to you," he said formally.

"Good-bye, Alasdair," she replied. "Godspeed."

He kissed her cheek, a kiss cold as a knife, and then was gone.

Gone to what? Frances though bitterly as she lay back and stared at the canopy over her. Gone to rebellion, to battle, to ultimate disaster.

He knew that. He *had* to know that. He was much too astute not to understand what he was doing. And yet, the prince had called, and so he went.

She could forgive such a reaction in Niall, but not in Alasdair. A grown man should be more flexible, able to change and revise his thinking with the times. But not Alasdair. Oh, never Alasdair. He would bring them all to utter desolation, but he would have remained true.

She could see him now in her mind's eye, marching at the head of his clan, head up, frown between his eyes. She felt such fear for him. She felt such fear for

them all. With a heavy heart she pushed back the
covers and got out of bed.

The prince and a small party of followers were already at Glenfinnan when the MacIans arrived, marching in two long lines, led by their chief and their piper.
Niall's heart swelled as his clansmen filed into the glen
and his father went to give allegiance to his prince.
Then came the sound of the Camerons' battle song:
"Clanna nan con, Thigibh an so, thigibh and so . . ."
"Sons of the dogs, come hither, come hither and you
shall have flesh." Lochiel's men also were pouring
down the hillside. Soon the little glen was filled with
clansmen and the aging Duke of Atholl, one of the
staunchest of veteran Jocobites, unfurled the prince's
red-white-and-blue standard. Charles Edward then
stepped forward to speak.

Niall was perfectly happy. There in that rocky glen,
looking out toward the loch, the sea, and the Western
Isles, was gathered the last feudal army ever to assemble on British soil. Niall looked around at the brilliant
tartan colors, the bonnets and feathers, the flash of
sun on sword and pistol. The prince finished speaking
and a great roar rose to the heavens. The Rebellion of
1745 had begun.

II

Scotland and England, September 1745–April 1746

The Year of Charlie

13

The ancient palace of Holyrood was ablaze with light on the evening of September 18. For years the traditional home of the kings of Scotland had lain empty of royalty, serving only as a garrison for English troops. But on this glorious evening the palace of Scotland's hereditary kings was once again occupied by its rightful owner. The day before, with pipes skirling and tartans swinging, Prince Charles Edward Stuart had entered Edinburgh and taken up residence in the palace of his ancestors.

Torches were flickering along the length of the Canongate as Frances and Van drove their carriage toward the palace where the prince was giving a reception and ball for his loyal adherents. All of Edinburgh lay at his feet. All, that is, except the English garrison still holding the castle at the other end of the Royal Mile. Tonight, however, it was possible to forget that stubborn spot of resistance and rejoice in the ease with which the prince and the clans had conquered all opposition up till now.

Van's face was lit with excitement as she and Frances alighted at the blazing door of the palace and began to make their way along the long dark halls and passages that led to the audience chamber and state reception gallery where the ball was being held. The halls were filled with people, and Van looked around her for a familiar face.

"Your father said he would be waiting for us," Frances said as they reached the door of the reception gallery. Alasdair had been in a conference with Lord George Murray and the prince that afternoon when his wife and daughter arrived in Edinburgh, and they had not yet seen him. The two women paused in the doorway and while Frances searched the crowd for her husband, Van eagerly tried to find the prince.

She spied him almost immediately, at the far end of the gallery, a tall handsome young man in Highland dress. He was unmistakably royal, she thought as she watched the smiling ease with which Charles Stuart was talking to a man she did not know. Van's eyes went from the prince to circle the room, and her heart swelled with emotion. Here they were, in Edinburgh, in the Palace of Holyrood. A Stuart once again in his proper place. And the clans had done it unaided. Van's chin came up a little and she too began to look for her father.

Frances saw him first. Alasdair's back was to the door and he appeared to be deep in conversation with a tall, haughty-looking man she recognized as Lord George Murray, the Duke of Atholl's brother, who had been named commander of the Jacobite army. Frances looked at the back of her husband's head and almost instantly he turned and saw them.

Van's eyes glowed with pride as she watched her father coming toward them across the crowded floor. He wore a red velvet coat and dress kilt and his unpowdered hair was tied back in a queue with a velvet ribbon. A large diamond pin adorned the fine lace at his throat. He stopped before them and spoke to his wife.

"I am sorry you had to come alone. I could not get away earlier."

His voice was formal, his gray eyes cool. Some of the brightness left Van's eyes. She had been aware ever since her return home that something was wrong between her father and her mother. She had hoped, after the clans had had such a signal success in the taking of Edinburgh, that the coolness between her parents would have dissipated. Alasdair looked from his wife to his daughter and his expression became less stern.

"Can you introduce us to the prince, Father?" Van asked.

"I am looking forward to doing so," he replied and his look at her became positively approving. Van was aware that she was looking her best this night, in an ivory taffeta ball gown with a silk tartan sash that crossed her breast from shoulder to waist. Her only ornaments were the heirloom pearls she wore at her throat and her ears. She looked very well, she knew, but still she was not half as beautiful as her mother. Frances' dress was more sophisticated than Van's simple taffeta, a blue satin that was cut over her shoulders and breast. The close-textured, pearly skin it revealed was as soft and resilient as a young girl's. Frances was beautiful indeed, but Alasdair's eyes as he looked at her held none of their old accustomed glow. They were hard, ironic almost. He offered his wife his arm and they began to cross the floor toward the gallery where the prince was receiving his guests.

Van felt her heart begin to accelerate as they approached the young man whose praises had been sung in her ears ever since she could remember. Here was the Stuart himself, Scotland's lawful ruler, her father's dedicated vision in the flesh.

He was tall and his hair was a light reddish-brown and his complexion was fair. On his breast shone the star of the Order of St. Andrew. He looked up as Alasdair approached him.

Her father bowed respectfully. "Your royal highness, may I present my wife, Lady Morar, and my daughter, Lady Vanessa."

The prince smiled and held out his hand. "Lady Morar. I am delighted to meet the lady of one of my most loyal adherents."

Frances curtsied gracefully. "Thank you, your royal highness."

Charles then turned to Van. "I would know your parentage anywhere, Lady Vanessa," he said. "You wear it on your face." His brown eyes smiled at her in frank admiration. "It takes no master of ceremonies, you see, to introduce a MacIan to a Stuart."

Van smiled radiantly back and sank into a deep curtsy. "This is a great moment for us all, your royal highness."

"Indeed it is." He raised her to her feet and turned courteously to include Alasdair in the circle of his attention. They stayed talking for almost five minutes before the prince's attention was claimed by someone else.

"I can quite see why everyone is wild over him," Frances said as they walked slowly down the gallery. "He is extremely charming."

"He is a prince in every imaginable way," Alasdair said.

"He is a Stuart," said Van, and her father smiled at her.

"He is indeed, my daughter."

Van looked once again around the room. "Where is Niall?" she asked.

"He will be here," her father returned. Then, "Ah. I see Alan MacDonald." He gave Van a swift sideways look before saying to the approaching young man, "How are you, Alan? A splendid evening, is it not?"

"It is that, sir." Alan's hair, reddish like the prince's, only darker, was covered by powder. He wore a dark green coat that made his hazel eyes look greener than usual. "I was hoping you would dance with me, Van."

She smiled. "Certainly. If it is all right with you, Mother?"

"Go right ahead, darling, and enjoy yourself."

"I've hardly seen you since you came home from England," Alan said to Van as they took their places for the dance.

"You've been busy," she said with an approving smile. Alan was looking splendid tonight, she thought. He and a company of Lochaber MacDonalds had taken a small garrison of English troops and made them prisoners a few weeks ago. Niall had been very proud of his friend's exploit. Van grinned at him. "Isn't this exciting, Alan? Did you ever believe we would be dancing together in Holyrood Palace?"

"Of course I believed it." He smiled back at her. "You are looking beautiful tonight," he said. "You are the most beautiful girl in the room."

This was not a conversation Van wished to pursue. She shook her head. "No. My mother is."

At that he laughed. "Certainly, your mother is beautiful," he agreed.

At that moment the music started up and they were forced to break off talk and bow to each other. As the dance finished Alan said, "Come and sit by me for a while. I want to talk to you."

Van agreed and they found seats along the wall. "I missed you while you were in England," Alan said when they were sitting side by side on small velvet-covered gilt chairs. "You seemed to be gone a very long time."

Van looked at him, a slight frown between her black brows. Surely Niall had told him about Edward, she thought. But Alan's face, filled with tenderness, warned her suddenly that her brother had said nothing. Anger flared in her heart. Damn Niall, she thought. He might at least have spared her having to tell Alan herself.

She looked away from Alan's face to the brightly lit ballroom. The dancers swirled gracefully and she thought of her reply. What was she to tell him? That she was going to marry the Earl of Linton? But she was not going to marry the Earl of Linton. Perhaps for now it would be best to say nothing.

"A great deal certainly happened in my absence," she prevaricated.

"Aye." He followed her lead. "Everything happened so quickly, it seemed. We raised the standard and the Sassenach ran for Inverness. We marched to Edinburgh with very little opposition."

"Are the English still in Inverness?" Van asked curiously.

"No." Alan's look was surprised. "Did not your father tell you? The English army is at Dunbar. We will be marching out to meet them the day after next."

Van felt her heart jolt. "No." Her mouth was dry. "I did not know. We did not see Father this afternoon." She wet her lips with her tongue. "Does this mean that there will be a battle, Alan?" she asked.

"Aye." He looked pleased at the prospect.

Van's hand went to her throat. "Dear God."

"Now, Van, do not be fretting yourself." She stared into hazel eyes which were clear and full of confidence. "The noise of the pipes alone will frighten the Sassenach back to England," he said reassuringly.

He was not in the least afraid, Van thought. Suddenly she was filled with admiration for him, and pride too. He was a Highlander. The blood stirred in her own veins. "But the English are professionals," she said, echoing words she had heard before. "They have artillery and cavalry."

"They will not stand against the clans," he replied and, against all logic, Van was swayed by his sublime confidence. After all, she thought, the right was on their side. She smiled at him and felt him take her hand into his.

"We must talk, Van," he said softly. "After the battle."

She drew a long, uneven breath. "Aye," she said. "After the battle."

"Alan MacDonald." A young man in a blue tartan kilt was bowing before them. "I demand that you introduce me to Lady Vanessa," the stranger said with mock truculence.

Alan frowned and Van gave him a sympathetically amused smile. Reluctantly Alan presented the newcomer to her and Van politely accepted Donald Stewart's invitation to dance. The floor was filled with couples. On the eve of battle the mood of the ball was wildly gay, a mood that Van found infectious. When Donald Stewart said something to her, she laughed and answered and, catching sight of Alan over her partner's shoulder, she sent him a particularly beautiful smile.

Frances and Alasdair stood together and watched

Van move onto the floor with Alan. Then Frances glanced up at her husband's profile. "Has anyone told Alan about the Earl of Linton?" she asked.

"No." Alasdair still did not look at her. "If Van wishes him to know, she can tell him herself."

Frances compressed her lips but did not reply. The music began and the couples on the floor bowed to each other.

"Where *is* Niall?" Frances asked. She had not seen her son since she arrived in Edinburgh early that afternoon.

His voice was impatient. "Edinburgh has many interests for a young man, Frances. He will be here."

Frances' hands closed hard on the delicate fan she was holding. This was how he had been for the last two months. He had shut her out completely. Her own anger had long since given way to bitter hurt. How could he be this way? After all they had been to each other. The love they had shared. It seemed now he could scarcely bear to look at her. She felt tears sting behind her eyes and angrily blinked them back.

"There is Niall now," Alasdair said beside her, and her eyes went to the door.

Her son was standing on the threshold of the gallery. Charles Stuart might be an impressive young man, Frances thought with a surge of maternal pride, but Niall's young male splendor was stunning. Almost every female eye in the room was on him as, poised and arrogant, he stood in the doorway and surveyed the scene before him.

"Cocky young beggar," Alasdair said. He sounded amused.

Frances smiled. "He looks like a youthful sultan inspecting a rather unpromising consignment of harem girls," she said, and her husband laughed.

Niall's eyes stopped suddenly. Then, with scarcely a glance to left or to right, he stared purposefully around the floor. Frances watched with intense curiosity as her son came up beside a small, delicate-looking girl in a pink gown. From halfway across the room it was evident how her small face lit up when he spoke to her.

"Who is that?" Frances asked her husband.

"A cousin of Lochiel's. Jean Cameron. Niall met her at Achnacarry about a month ago."

Frances frowned slightly. "Is he interested?"

"I don't know, Frances. He only saw the girl that once. We've been busy since, as you know." Across the room they saw their son give Jean Cameron his most devastating smile. "He certainly seems interested," Alasdair said dryly. He put a hand on her elbow. "Shall we go meet her?"

"Yes," said Frances, and allowed him to guide her expertly through the crowd.

Niall was pleased to see his mother and immediately introduced her to the girl at his side.

"Are you staying with Lady Lochiel?" Frances asked kindly.

"Yes." Jean's big brown eyes shone. "Isn't it wonderful, Lady Morar?" and she gestured with a small graceful hand toward the prince.

Frances smiled. "It certainly is."

"I see Van is dancing with Alan." Niall's voice held a distinct note of complacence and Frances gave him a sharp look. His attention, however, was no longer on his sister. "May I have the next dance with you, Miss Cameron?" he asked with his most beguiling smile.

"I should be happy to dance with you, Lord MacIan," Jean replied shyly, and Niall took her hand into his.

The present dance was not yet ended and Niall stood with his parents, watching Van dance with Alan, Jean's hand held firmly in his own. Frances saw the girl make one move to withdraw it, but her son's hand only tightened its grip. Faint color stained Jean's cheeks.

Finally the dance was over and couples began forming on the floor for the next set. Frances frowned a little as she watched Niall and Jean take their places. "He could hurt that child badly," she said to Alasdair. "He had better be serious."

"She's a pretty little thing," he returned thoughtfully. "And Lochiel's cousin." He stared at his son for a moment in silence. Then, "It would be wise for Niall to marry." He seemed to be speaking more to himself than to her. "We must make certain Morar has an heir."

Frances felt a cold hand close around her heart. She spoke with great difficulty. "Is there going to be more fighting?"

"General Cope has landed at Dunbar with an army. We are marching to meet him on Saturday."

Frances' hands were icy. An army. So far there had been a series of skirmishes, but the Highlanders had not yet had to face an organized army in battle. Her fingers closed tensely on her husband's arm, feeling its hardness through the softness of velvet and lace. For a moment the room seemed to swim before her eyes.

"Frances!" His voice was sharp. Then his hand was on her waist. "Come over here and sit down." She followed, blindly, the pressure of his hand and found herself shortly in a gilt chair along the wall. He was standing in front of her, shielding her from the view of the room.

"For God's sake." His voice was not gentle. "Get hold of yourself. This is no place for the vapors."

"I am all right." She was very pale, however. Her heartbeat was more rapid than usual. A battle, she thought. She looked around the gallery, at all the brilliantly garbed, high-spirited men who thronged the room. In two days' time some, at least, of this vital company would be dead.

Not Alasdair! she thought frantically. Not Niall!

"We can beat Cope, Frances." His voice was quieter, less impatient. "There is no need to be so frightened."

"I'm sorry." She tried valiantly to rally. "It was just so sudden. I did not realize there was an army that close to Edinburgh." She stood up. "I am all right now, Alasdair."

He looked at her searchingly, then nodded. "Come," he said. "I wish to talk to Lord Ogilvy."

She rested her hand lightly on his arm and moved with him in the direction of the prince.

"Is it true there is going to be a battle?" Jean Cameron asked Niall as the dance ended and they walked together in the direction of Lady Lochiel.

"Yes." Niall's light eyes glowed. He grinned at her. "The Sassenach are about to get a taste of how a Highlander fights."

Her eyes were great dark pools of feeling. "I will pray for your safety," she said.

"Will you, m'eudail? That will be nice."

Her eyes dropped at the endearment and a flush colored the delicate heart-shaped face. She was so small, so fragile-looking. She made him feel he wanted to protect her, take care of her. It was not an emotion he was familiar with. His feelings for all the previous women in his life had been purely carnal.

"I like you in that pink dress," he said, and her eyes flew upward again. They were approaching Lady Lochiel now. He bent to say into her ear, "Wear that dress at the first ball after the battle, and I'll dance with you."

Jean stared up into his face. Once more he gave her his beguiling grin. There was something so confidently godlike in his look, his smile. It was impossible to believe that anything could happen to him. She smiled back, her heart in her eyes. "I will wear the dress, my lord. And hold you to your promise."

His eyes glinted but before he could reply they were at Lady Lochiel's side. "How are you, Niall?" Lochiel's wife greeted him pleasantly. "And how are the MacIans faring these days?"

He answered her politely, but his thoughts remained on the small, quiet girl at his side.

The ball concluded when the orchestra fell silent and a single musician, a harper, moved onto the floor. This was Rory Dall, one of the last great harpers of the Western Highlands. He ran his fingers briefly over the strings of the small Scottish harp he carried and said, in Gaelic, "This is my song for Teàrlaic mhic Sheumais," with a bow to the prince, "and for the raising of the standard at Glenfinnan." He plucked the strings once again and then began to sing in Gaelic:

> There is mist on the mountain, and night on the
>   vale
> But more dark is the sleep of the sons of the Gael.
> A stranger commanded—it sank on the land,
> It has frozen each heart, and benumb'd every hand.
>
> The dirk and the target lie sordid with dust,.

The bloodless claymore is but redden'd with rust;
On the hill or the glen if a gun should appear,
It is only to war with the heath-cock or deer.

But the dark hours of night and of slumber are
    past,
The morn on our mountains is dawning at last;
Glenaladale's peaks are illumed with the rays,
And the streams of Glenfinnan leap bright in the
    blaze.

Ye sons of the strong, when that dawning shall
    break
Need the harp of the aged remind you to wake?
That dawn never beam'd on your forefathers' eye
But it roused each high chieftain to vanquish or die.

Let the clan of MacIan, whose offspring have given
Such heroes to earth and such martyrs to heaven,
Follow Morar, your chief, with the pipe's mighty
    swell
Till far Corryarrick resound to the knell!

True son of Sir Evan, undaunted Lochiel,
Place thy targe on thy shoulder and burnish thy
    steel!
Stern son of Lord Kenneth, high chief of Kintail,
Let the stag in thy standard bound wild in the
    gale!

Oh, sprung from the kings who in Islay kept state,
Proud chiefs of Clanranald, Glengarry, and Sleat!
Combine like three streams from one mountain of
    snow,
And resistless in union rush down on the foe!

May the race of Clan Gillean, the fearless and free,
Remember Glenlivat, Harlaw, and Dundee!
MacNeil of the Islands, and Moy of the Lake,
For honor, for freedom, for vengeance awake!

'Tis the summons of heroes for conquest or death,
When the banners are blazing on mountain and
 heath:
They call to the dirk, the claymore, and the targe,
To the march and the muster, the line and the
 charge.

Be the sword of each Chieftain like Finn's in his ire!
May the blood through his veins flow like currents
 of fire!
Burst the base foreign yoke as your sires did of
 yore,
Or die like your sires, and endure it no more!

The silence in the long gallery was profound. Not
for the first time that evening Van felt her blood thrill
through her veins. They would beat the Sassenach, she
was sure of it. And after they had set the prince firmly
on his throne, England would have to acquiesce to an
independent Scotland. She looked up at her father's
stern profile and her own chin rose with pride.

"Come," her father said to her mother, "it is time
to be going."

As the great room slowly emptied, the orchestra
played yet another Jacobite song, this one with English words:

An' Charlie he's my darling, my darling, my darling,
Charlie he's my darling, the young Chevalier

14

Edinburgh in 1745 was still very much a medieval city. The main street, the High Street, was built on the ridge of land that ran from the heights of the castle on one end down to the Palace of Holyrood on the other. The distance from castle to palace was approximately one mile, so the street that connected the two—called the Canongate on the east side of the city wall, the High Street on the west—was known as the Royal Mile.

Frances and Van were staying at the house of a cousin of Alasdair's located in one of the narrow wynds that went off from the High Street and on down to the Nor' Loch that lay at the foot of the ridge. Alasdair's cousin was not in residence at present, so Frances and Van had the house to themselves. Alasdair had moved his clothes in, but they were almost the only sign of his residence. Niall did not even keep his clothes there. From Alasdair's short reply to her question, Frances gathered that her son had a mistress in the town.

Frances awoke a few minutes before dawn on Saturday morning to find Alasdair asleep beside her in the bed. He had come in so late she had not even heard him. The window was open, as usual, and the pale light of very early morning was creeping into the room. Frances sat up in bed and looked at her husband.

His back was to her, his head resting on his arm, his hard, chiseled profile visible in the light from the window. He looked younger as he lay there asleep, but she thought he also looked very tired.

Frances clasped her arms around her knees and laid her head on them, her long brown hair spilling down over the coverlet in a shining, silken fall. Her hands were gripped so tightly the knuckles showed white.

He was going into battle today and the two of them were still at odds. There was nothing more she could do; she had made every overture of reconciliation she could think of. He would not be placated.

She thought it was his own doubts that stood in their way. If he had been truly confident of success, then he would have been able to forgive her her doubt. Then he could have afforded to be magnanimous, generous, forgiving; he would have been right.

He was worried. Even with the victories they had had, the triumphant entry into Edinburgh, he was worried. And he could not share that worry with her. She had declared herself opposed to his cause and so he had put her outside his trust. She was the enemy for him, a living reminder of all his own most private fears. And he was all she had.

He stirred. His lashes lifted and he assessed the time from the light at the window. Then he rolled over onto his back and saw her. For a brief moment something flashed in his eyes; then the shutters came down. "What are you doing awake at this hour, Frances?"

She swallowed. "I don't know. I just woke up."

"You should have awakened me," he said. "It's getting late." And he swung out of bed and went to the wardrobe.

Frances watched him in silence as he stripped and dressed. He would be marching at the head of his clan, not riding, and so he put on the kilt. "We have as many men as Cope," he said as he fastened the brooch that held his plaid on his shoulder. "This battle we should win."

"Where is Niall?" Frances asked.

"He bedded down with the clan last night. They are encamped with the rest of the army in the King's Park." His teeth showed in a quick, hard smile. "I am too old a dog to sleep on the ground when a bed is available."

He was fully dressed now and he came over to stand beside the bed. "Do not worry, Frances. I will see you soon enough."

She raised her arms, not caring if he rejected her, aware only of her own fear and need. "Oh, Alasdair. Take care of yourself. Please take care of yourself."

His arms came around her, hard and crushing. He kissed her once, fiercely, burningly, then he let her go. Without another word, he turned and left the room.

If Alasdair felt some doubts on that morning of September 20, Niall felt none. He went among the men of his clan, all air and fire, supremely confident, totally unafraid. He saw before him only the glorious prospect of complete victory; the possible alternative of a soldier's grave scarcely crossed his mind.

The Highlanders were quartered on the rolling ground that lay behind Holyrood Palace and, as each clan's piper sounded forth, the army gathered into marching order and prepared to set forth. Alasdair had Niall beside him and his foster brother and piper behind him as the MacIans swung out onto the road that took them under the green height of Arthur's Seat and eastward toward the sea.

The sun was going down when the Highlanders re-

ceived word they were within a mile of the English
army. The prince immediately gave the order for the
clans to get off the low coast road they had been
following and take the heights that commanded the
plain which stretched between the villages of Prestonpans and Cockenzie. As the clansmen formed into
battle lines on the hill, the van of Sir John Cope's
army appeared from among the trees on the far side of
the plain.

"Cope wants to hold the level ground between us
and the sea," Alasdair said to Niall as the two of them
watched from their hillside position.

Niall could see plainly the squadrons of dragoons
forming opposite them. There was only about a half-
mile between them and the enemy army. Behind him
Alan Ruadh was arranging the line in their own battle
formation. Similar maneuvers were going on all over
the hillside.

"There is the artillery," Alasdair said quietly.

Niall watched with burning eyes as the field pieces
were brought up, placed before the dragoons, and
pointed up against the heights. Then came three or
four regiments of infantry marching in open column,
their fixed bayonets showing like successive hedges of
steel, and their arms flashing like lightning as, at a
given signal, they all wheeled up, and were placed in
direct opposition to the Highlanders. Then a second
train of artillery, with another regiment of horse, formed
on the left flank of the infantry, the whole line facing
southward.

Niall's hand tightened convulsively on the Lochaber
ax that hung at his belt. His lips drew back over his
teeth. He whirled to look at the hundreds of MacIans
massed behind him.

"Buaich no Bas!" (Victory or Death) he cried out to their ranks.

"Buaich no Bas!" they roared back.

The English below heard them and shouted defiance toward the hill. A cannon went off. Alasdair laid a hand on his son's arm.

"Be quiet!" he ordered. His straight black brows were almost meeting over his arrogant, high-bridged nose. "I do not like the ground."

"What do you mean, Father?" Niall asked. "We are almost on top of them."

"The ground is marshy," Alasdair said shortly. "And look at that ditch, Niall. It will slow our charge fatally. The artillery would get us before we could ever reach them." He turned and shot an order to Alan Ruadh before he turned back to Niall. "Never mistake the ability of the saighdearan dearg, my son."

Niall looked down at the row upon row of English "red soldiers" with a somber face.

"I am going to see the prince and Lord George," Alasdair said. "You may come with me if you wish."

The result of Alasdair's interview with the prince and the commander-in-chief was that some men were sent out to scour the neighborhood for a man to guide them across the marsh. The Highlanders withheld their attack and darkness fell. One of the prince's scouts returned with a local man, Robert Anderson of Whitburgh, who said he knew a secret path through the marsh. At midnight Alasdair and Niall wrapped themselves in their plaids and lay down on the cold hard ground to sleep.

They were wakened after scarcely three hours had passed. The night was heavy and dark with mist. In eerie silence the clans formed into line and crossed the marsh behind their leaders and Robert Anderson. It was still dark as they moved into battle formation, ready at the first light of dawn to fall upon the unsuspecting English.

But even the rising sun did not dissipate the thick white fog the Scots call a haar that shrouded the plain that morning. The English soldiers awakened to its dreariness with annoyed resignation. It was just the sort of weather one could expect in this uncivilized country, where men went unbreeched and spoke a barbaric language and fought with axes. The veterans of Fontenoy, secure in their artillery and their cavalry, did not anticipate much trouble in dealing with the primitive clansmen on the hill.

The mist was just lifting when there came the sound of shots, then a shout of alarm, and then, terrifyingly, the war cries of the clans as they rose from more than two thousand throats. Before the English veterans knew what had happened, like hunters in quest of their prey, the Highlanders were on them. There was no chance to use the artillery. The cavalry horses ran mad with fear. As the English lines broke and tried to flee to their rear, they ran into the long stone wall about twelve feet high that was immediately behind them. The despised broadswords and Lochaber axes did murderous damage. In less than fifteen minutes the English army was routed, and in some cases, cut to pieces. General Cope with a remnant of men fled to Berwick-on-Tweed.

The English left five hundred dead on the field at Prestonpans and nine hundred wounded. The Highlanders' total casualties amounted to one hundred. On Sunday, September 21, 1745, Prince Charles Edward Stuart was the undisputed master of all Scotland.

*   *   *

Van and Frances waited tensely in Edinburgh for news of the battle. As the morning dragged on, Van felt herself becoming more and more uncertain. No one could be braver than their men, certainly, but they were not professionals. The English army had fought wars before, had fought in Europe in the wars against France. She thought of her father, of Niall. Of Alan.

Only once during the long course of that morning did the picture of a blue-eyed man intrude on her thoughts. And her feelings toward him were not kindly. Edward was risking nothing in this fight, she thought. He was not out there on the battlefield. He was back in London, riding his horses. On the Sunday morning that the battle of Prestonpans was fought, London and Staplehurst and Edward Romney seemed very far away from her, seemed another world, a world that had nothing to do with her or with Frances or with the men they loved who were risking their lives that day for their beloved cause.

Early in the afternoon, as Van and Frances were sitting in the small parlor of their house, the sound of bagpipes came swirling up the High Street. They looked at each other and both ran for the door at the same time. Down on the street they followed the crowd that was moving quickly toward the Netherbow Port, the gate in the city wall that had been erected in 1513 after the defeat by England at Flodden. On the other side of the Netherbow Port was the Canongate and the sloping road to Holyrood Palace.

Van recognized the badge in the Highlanders' bonnets as soon as the first man came through the gate. She clutched her mother's arm. "It's the Camerons, Mother!"

It was indeed the Camerons, and above them flew

the colors they had captured only hours earlier from General Cope's dragoons. The air the pipers played was an old and favorite Jacobite song: "The King Shall Enjoy His Own Again."

"We won, Mother!" Van's face blazed with exultation. "I can scarcely believe it! We did it! We beat the English! We won!"

Frances' face reflected none of her daughter's joy. In fact it was rather pale. "I wonder what the casualties were," she said.

"I'm sure Father and Niall are fine," Van responded bracingly. Her mother looked very white and she put an arm about Frances' shoulders. The pipes were skirling as more and more Camerons poured in through the city gates. "We'll ask one of the officers for news of them," she said to Frances, and began to scan the ranks for a familiar face. She was not at all afraid. She was certain her men were safe. The jubilant faces of the Camerons told her it was a solid victory. We won! We won! We won! she thought as, arm around her mother, she guided her toward Hector Cameron, who would certainly have news of the MacIans.

They did not see Alasdair that day but they got the news of his safety from Niall, who arrived at his mother's doorstep some hours after the Camerons' entry half-carrying a wounded Alan MacDonald.

"The musket shot passed right through his arm, Mother," Niall said after he had got Alan into bed. "One of the doctors cleaned and bandaged it. You'll take care of him, won't you? Lady Lochaber is not in Edinburgh."

Frances smiled down into Alan's pain-filled face and spoke reassuringly. "Of course we'll take care of you, Alan." She put a cool hand on his forehead. "But you should not have tried to come back to Edinburgh so soon."

"I told him that," Niall said beside her. "The prince is staying at Pinkie House for the night. But he insisted."

Van had gone to her mother's room for some laudanum and now she came back into the bedroom with a bottle and a spoon in her hand. "Insisted or not, you should not have let him," she said to Niall as she handed the medicine to Frances. Then she looked at Alan. Poor boy, she thought. His eyes were heavy with pain. She put her hand against his cheek. "You're a fool, Alan MacDonald." Her voice was gentle.

Behind her back, Niall smiled with satisfaction.

Alan tried to speak lightly. "I did not want to die without seeing you again."

Van frowned fiercely. "You are not going to die." She looked at her brother, and his face grew instantly grave. "I just might kill Niall, however."

"He seemed perfectly fine at Prestonpans," Niall said defensively. "And we came on horseback." He grinned. "There were plenty of fine English horses to be had after the battle."

"Out of here, everyone," Frances said firmly. "I am going to give Alan something to make him sleep."

"I knew you'd know what to do, Mother," Niall said gratefully as she herded them out the door.

He wanted to go seek out Jean Cameron, but his mother and sister would not let him go until he had told them all about the battle.

"The dawn attack was Father's idea," he said proudly. "They did not know we were coming until we were on them."

Van stared at him in awe. "Did you kill a lot of them?" she asked.

"Hundreds. And many were wounded. The field

looked like a slaughterhouse." Niall looked pleased. "The axes did their work well."

Frances looked at her son with a mixture of horror and resignation. She could not blame him for being so bloodthirsty, she thought. Killing was what he had been brought up to do, what his training and his tradition had geared him for. He had been weaned on songs of battle and slaughter, had got his first gun when he was five, shot his first stag when he was nine. Killing was the activity for which he had been most intensively trained; she supposed she could not blame him if he enjoyed it.

Van's regard had changed from awe to faint amusement. "You sound as if you liked it," she said.

He grinned, a boy's grin. "I did," he replied simply. "Now, if you don't mind, I'm off to see Jeannie Cameron."

As Van watched her brother leave the room, the image of Edward once again crossed her mind. He and Niall—there could not be two more different men. Niall would never understand Edward, she thought. Niall thought with his heart. And it was thinking with the heart that had brought them this far. Looking at their cause with Edward's eyes, intelligently, dispassionately, one would have said they hadn't a chance of success, yet here they were in Edinburgh, and the clans had just soundly defeated the greatest army in the world. It was Niall who was right, she thought fiercely. Niall and Alan and her father—those who held to their loyalty and their honor, not those who followed the path of prudence.

She was vaguely aware that she was being unfair to Edward, that his actions were as firmly based on principle as were those of her father and Niall, but she did not want to see that just now. She wanted to rejoice in this victory and feel pride in her cause and not think of Edward at all. It confused her to think of him. And it hurt. Better by far to live in the present and not think too much of anything else.

"I'll give you a list of things to get from the apothecary, darling," Frances was saying. "Alan's arm will have to be dressed again."

Van raised her chin and stiffened her spine. "Yes, Mother. I'll go right away." And she followed Frances into the parlor.

15

Prince Charles returned to Edinburgh and sent another message to old General Guest, the commander of Edinburgh Castle, demanding its surrender. General Guest replied as previously that the prince could take his terms of surrender and go to hell. And so, as the prince and his chiefs and generals continued to reside at Holyrood and fight over what their next course of action should be, the English presence remained intact in the form of the bulk of Edinburgh Castle towering over the town.

In London there was also discussion as to the road the prince would take next. "Will he invade England?" Lord Pelham asked the Earl of Linton as they sat together in the prime minister's office early on the morning of October 6.

"He will be a fool if he does so," Edward replied equably. "His only chance of success is to make this a national war, denounce the union, and pit Scotland against England in the cause of Scottish independence. A national Scottish war would almost certainly gain aid from France."

"Great God." Lord Pelham visibly shuddered at the thought. "Do you think that is what the pretender will do, Linton?"

Edward's blue eyes glinted. "It is what *I* should do if I were in his place, but I doubt if the pretender will show such restraint. If he is like all the Stuarts, he will overreach himself." Edward raised a golden eyebrow. "I think he will invade."

Very slowly Lord Pelham nodded. "Yes. I think you are right." The prime minister closed his fist upon the table. "I shall send Marshal Wade to Newcastle."

"That would block any invasion by way of Edinburgh," Edward agreed.

"Very well." Lord Pelham stretched his shoulders. "I shall get a messenger off to General Guest with that information. It is essential Guest hold Edinburgh Castle."

"You don't need a messenger," Edward said. "I'll go to Edinburgh for you."

The prime minister stared. "You?"

"I have some business to attend to in the city," the earl replied blandly.

Lord Pelham had an idea just what that business was, but didn't dare to ask further. "Very well," he agreed after a moment. "You will stay at the castle, of course. There is not exactly a welcome sign hanging out for Whigs in Edinburgh these days."

Edward laughed ruefully and went home to make preparations for a journey to Scotland.

At the very moment that Edward was speaking to Lord Pelham, Van was having a similar conversation with her father. "What will we do now, Father?" she asked Alasdair as she caught him leaving the house after coming home to change his clothes. They saw very little of her father these days; he was almost always at Holyrood Palace.

"That matter is under almost constant discussion, my daughter," he replied a little grimly.

"What do *you* think we should do?" Van asked.

He looked at her consideringly, then evidently decided to answer, for he sat down on the stiff, uncomfortable parlor sofa and gestured her to a chair opposite him. "The prince is for invading England," he said, "and the chiefs are for staying in Scotland and consolidating our position here. The more successful we are in the north, the more support we will attract. Glenbucket has come in, and Mackinnon of Mackinnon. And Cluny MacPherson. There will be more if we continue to hold Edinburgh."

"The English will send more armies against you," said Van.

"I know that well. But if we are Scotland against England, I think the French will come to our assistance."

Van looked at her father somberly. He was looking tired these days, she thought. The victory at Prestonpans had not given him the confidence it had given to Alan and to Niall. "Why does the prince wish to invade?" she asked.

"It is his right. His father is King of England as well as of Scotland. Which is true enough, but to invade England we need more than the clans. And your reports, Van, do not lead me to have much hope in the English rising to join us."

"I do not think they will, Father."

He nodded. "So we are better off staying in Scotland and waiting for France."

Van smoothed her skirt. "The war is a long way from being over, isn't it, Father?" she asked in a low voice.

"A long way, my daughter," he agreed. "Prestonpans was but the first step on a weary road."

She raised her head and looked directly at him, light green-gray eyes into darker gray. "Will we win?"

"If I did not think we could win, I would not have gone out," he replied. "But we can do just so much on our own. We need the French."

Van sat on for a long time in the parlor after Alasdair had gone back to the palace, her mind contemplating soberly and chillingly the prospects before them. As her father had said, it all depended on the French. If the Scots invaded England without French aid, the English would never rise to join them. The clans alone could not hold England.

If they stayed in Scotland they had a better chance of success. But if, as Alasdair suggested, they made this a national war—Scotland against England—and the French came in, still there would be no quick resolution. Van had been in England long enough to know that the English would never allow a bastion of French influence to sit peacefully on their northern border. They would fight to the death to keep Scotland.

The gulf between her and Edward had never seemed so great. There would be no quick or easy solution to this war, no peaceful mending of the breach between her country and his. In fact, it was entirely possible that she might never see him again.

She tried, unsuccessfully, to stifle the pain that ripped through her at that thought.

Van sat at Alan's bedside, her eyes on his sleeping face. His wound had become inflamed shortly after his arrival in Edinburgh and he had been very ill with fever. Van and Frances had taken turns sitting with him for the first week of his illness, but for the past few days he had been much better, and Van had become more his companion than his nurse.

Alan's head moved restlessly on its pillow and Van's expression became more alert. After a moment his lashes lifted and his hazel eyes found her. She smiled. "Would you like a drink?" she asked.

"Aye." He pushed himself up on his pillows and accepted the glass she handed him. "You do not need to be spending all your time with me, Van," he said when he had handed the empty glass back to her. "I am much better, thanks to you and to Lady Morar. I feel guilty keeping you from your own activities. Is there not a ball at the palace this night?"

"Aye." She put the glass back on the night table and went to draw the curtains more closely around the windows. She turned back to face him. "I have no wish to be dancing at the palace, Alan," she told him. "Besides, with you ill, whom would I dance with?"

"You would not lack for partners, Van." His green-gold eyes were intent upon her face.

"Perhaps. I don't know. I don't care." She came back to resume her seat at his beside. "Mother is just as happy as I to stay home. Father does nothing but huddle in corners with the chiefs and Lord George Murray, and Niall has no thought for anyone but Jean Cameron, so we are really quite deserted at these affairs. You give us a good excuse not to have to go."

"I am glad, then, I was not wounded in vain," he retorted. Their eyes met and they both laughed.

He settled himself against his pillows. "Tell me about Niall and Jean Cameron."

Van, however, was beginning to frown. Alan had the redhead's fair skin, but right now she thought he looked as white as his pillow cover. She hoped his fever had not come back. She got up and put a competent hand on his forehead. He was cool. He smiled at her in faint amusement as she sat down again. "Well, he certainly seems to be pursuing her," she said, continuing the conversation imperturbably. "At least I imagine that's where he's spending his time. We don't see much of him here."

"Niall has always had a flirt," Alan said comfortably. "I wouldn't refine too much upon it. Although Jean is not just in his usual style."

"Oh?" Van leaned a little forward. "And what *is* his usual style, Alan?"

But he only grinned and shook his head. "I'm telling nothing."

"Never mind." Van's voice was dry. "I can imagine. I've met his current mistress, and to judge by her, he likes an older, fleshier type than Jean."

Alan sat up so abruptly he jarred his wound. "How the devil did you meet Alison?" he asked, wincing.

"I saw them by chance in the Grassmarket the other day." Her eyes glinted wickedly. "I made Niall introduce me. He was furious."

"I can imagine," Alan replied feelingly.

"She's almost as old as Mother. And not as pretty."

"Niall's known Alison for a long time," Alan said defensively. "She's more a good friend than anything else."

Van's fine lips curled. "I'm sure she is."

Alan looked around the room and his eye fell on the book of plays they had been reading. "Aren't you going to finish reading *Tamburlaine* to me?" he asked hastily. "It was just getting interesting."

"Not as interesting as this conversation," she replied. Then, as he set his jaw and looked stubborn, she laughed. "All right," and she picked up the red leather-bound volume, took out the marker, gave one more amused glance at Alan, and began to read.

The course of Niall's love affair with Jean Cameron was not running as smoothly as he was accustomed to. He complained of this fact to Alan and Van when he came the following day to make a brief visit to his friend.

"Lady Lochiel is as good as a prison guard," he told them resentfully when Alan asked him how Jean was doing. "It's fine that Lochiel became Jean's guardian when her father died last year, but Lady Lochiel is overdoing her role as chaperon."

"How is she overdoing it?" Van asked curiously.

"I asked Jean to go on a picnic with me to Arthur's Seat," he said indignantly, "and she acted as if I were not to be trusted with a gently reared young lady."

Van was beginning to find him funny. "Well, brother dear, you must admit you don't have the world's finest reputation when it comes to the ladies."

He looked at her as if he could not believe his ears. "What is wrong with my reputation?" he demanded. "I'll have you know, I've never raped anyone in my life."

"Niall!" Alan was slightly scandalized by the way Niall was talking to his sister, but Van never blinked.

"Congratulations," she said cordially.

"I'd never hurt a hair of Jeannie's head," Niall said.

"I'm sure you wouldn't. But look at it from Lady Lochiel's point of view, Niall. Here you are, fresh from your Paris conquests"—she raised a hand as he started to protest, and continued ruthlessly—"living with your Edinburgh mistress, and courting innocent little Jean Cameron. Of course Lady Lochiel doesn't trust you. She assumes the first thing you'll do when you get Jean alone is kiss her."

It was, of course, exactly what he was planning to do.

Van and Alan looked at him, looked at each other, and began to laugh.

Niall stared at his brogues, frowning thoughtfully and ignoring their mirth. "I think I'll move back home," he said after they had fallen quiet.

Van and Alan looked at each other once more.

"Good idea," Alan said in an unsteady voice.

Niall rose to his feet. "I have been thinking of it anyway," he told them loftily. Then, to their disbelieving faces, "Be damned to you both." He grinned good-naturedly. "See you tomorrow, Alan."

He was in the hall when Van caught up with him. "Are you really going to move back home?" she asked.

"Aye." He looked at her in the light of the open door and said impulsively, "Why don't you ride out with me this afternoon, Van? You are looking rather peaked. Do you good to get some fresh air for a change."

She gave him a grateful smile. "I'd love to."

"Good. Change your clothes and I'll be back in an hour with the horses."

They rode out past the army encampment and along toward Arthur's Seat, both of them dressed in trews and plaids, both of them glad to be away from the city.

Niall spoke first. "Alan is looking that much better," he said.

Van smiled faintly. "Aye. Mother says he may even get up tomorrow."

"Good. That means he should be ready to join us when we march for England."

Van stared. "March for England?" she echoed. "When was it decided to march for England?"

He shrugged slightly. "It has not precisely been decided yet. Father and the chiefs are against it. But I think we will march. The prince wants to."

"I know that," Van replied slowly. "Father told me so. But the chiefs may prevail."

"I don't think so." Niall stopped his horse and looked at her. "What else did Father say?"

"That the success of everything depends still upon the French."

"I don't agree, Van," Niall said positively. "I think the clans can carry the day on their own."

"In Scotland, maybe," Van returned somberly. "But not if you invade England, Niall." Her lashes lifted and she looked at him fearlessly. "The English do not want a Stuart. If you think otherwise, my brother, you delude yourself."

"The Whigs do not want him, you mean," Niall retorted quickly. "The Earl of Linton does not want him. But there are plenty of squires and yeomen throughout the country who are loyal to their true king. *They* will rise to join us. You will see."

"The Earl of Linton has nothing but dislike and contempt for the Stuarts," Van said tonelessly. "He, and others like him, will never rest content with a Stuart on the English throne. And he is a powerful man, Niall. A very powerful man." Her lashes had dropped once more to cover her eyes. "I do not think there will ever be a Stuart restoration in England."

Niall stared at her guarded face. He said suddenly, with savage anger, "Dhé, Van, how could you have wanted to marry him?"

She did not answer and her silence only goaded him into further speech. "He is a Sassenach," Niall said. "Dhé, he even looks like a Viking!"

For some reason that word, a word she had so often called him herself, brought Edward to her mind as he had not been for quite some time. For a brief moment she had a vision of him as he had looked that day at Staplehurst, riding Marcus in the sunshine, showing off for her, he had said. She saw his blue eyes, so full of tenderness and amusement. She heard his voice. The king, he had said, must be responsible to the people. Her throat ached. And, out of an impulse of loyalty toward her lost love, she answered, "We did not like being saddled with a king we did not want. I do not think we should turn around now and do the same thing to the English. Let the prince stay here in Scotland, where he is welcome."

Niall's fingers tightened on his reins and his horse backed. Niall stopped him with a curse, and forced him up to Van's side once more. "You don't still have hopes in Linton's direction, do you?" he said. Then, "Stand, damn you!" The horse sidled and laid back its ears.

"Stop bullying him, Niall," Van said sharply. "You're the one at fault, not the horse. Leave his mouth alone."

"Do you love him still?" Niall asked. His voice was hard. It was the first time they had spoken of Edward Romney since he had brought her home from England.

"The heart is not so easily ruled," Van replied, and her own voice sounded a little muffled. "It does not always respond as one would wish." She looked over at her brother, wanting him to understand a little. "If you knew Edward, Niall, you would understand."

"Never!" His head went up. "Never will I understand how you could have wished to marry a Sassenach!"

Niall could be such a pighead. "Well," she said acidly, "Father did."

There was silence. Niall had never been able to win an argument with her. He tried another tack. "What about Alan, whom you have been caring for so tenderly?"

She answered steadily. "I care for Alan in the same way you do—as a dear friend."

"You will break his heart."

"I don't think so."

"Yes," he said fiercely. "You will."

"There would be little chance of that if you had had the decency to tell him about Edward!" Van returned hotly. "But you never said a word, did you? If he gets hurt, it will be just as much your fault as it is mine, Niall MacIan."

They stared at each other in mutual anger. Then Niall pushed his bonnet back on his head. His temper was always like the summer lightning—bright and furious and quickly over. "I don't want to quarrel with you, Van," he said in a milder voice.

She raised an elegant black eyebrow. "You have a strange way of showing it." But her voice was now softer as well. They began to move their horses forward once again. They rode in silence for several minutes before Van brought up the subject she had really wanted to discuss with him. "I'm glad you're moving home," she said soberly. "I think it will help Mother."

He looked startled. "Help Mother? What do you mean, Van?"

"Mother is in trouble," she said. "Haven't you noticed how thin she has become?"

He had been too full of his own concerns to pay much attention to his mother. He felt guilty and asked gruffly, "What is the matter with her?"

Van was staring between her horse's ears, a frown on her face. "I think there is something wrong between her and Father. In fact, I *know* there is something wrong. Father is angry with her."

"Father? Angry with *Mother*?" He was dumbfounded.

"Yes. I don't know why, but I can tell by the tone of his voice. You know how it used to change when he talked to Mother?" He nodded. "Well, it doesn't anymore."

Niall thought. "She did not want him to raise the clan."

Van sighed. "Whatever it is, she is making herself ill over it. And it isn't good for her to be confined to that house all day, either."

"I'll get her out, Van," Niall said repentantly. "You should have told me sooner. I'll get hold of a carriage and take her driving."

"You haven't been around much to discuss anything with," Van said dryly.

"I know. I know. I'm sorry. I will rectify the matter immediately. You may expect me and my baggage tomorrow morning."

Van smiled at him. Having Niall around would be good for her, too. "Race you to the edge of the park," she said.

"Done!"

And, with a drumming of hooves, they both were off.

The following day Niall escorted his mother and his

sister to church. Since he had not been inside the Episcopalian church on the High Street since he was eighteen years old, his arrival caused something of a stir among the faithful who knew him. His face was grave and composed as he took his seat on the aisle beside Van. He did not betray by the flicker of an eyelash that he knew Jean Cameron was seated right across the aisle from him.

Jean was painfully conscious of his much-too-handsome person in such close proximity to her. She murmured responses automatically, her mind not on the service at all. Then, when Lady Lochiel stopped to speak to Lady Morar after church, Niall came up to her with his sister on his arm.

Jean looked shyly up into Vanessa's beautiful, fearless face and answered her questions in a low, sweet voice.

"Look, Van," Niall said suddenly. "It's Master Armstrong."

John Armstrong was a finicky, precise man of about thirty-five whom Frances had employed some ten years previously to try to teach her children. They had not taken to each other and after a month in Morar, Master Armstrong had returned to Edinburgh. Van looked now at the man's profile and said something under her breath to Niall. They both laughed.

"I beg your pardon, Miss Cameron," Van said contritely. Then, giving her brother a sideways glance, she added, "Perhaps Lady Lochiel would allow you to join us for dinner this afternoon?"

As Jean blushed a little and said she would certainly ask, Niall gave Van a grateful look.

Jean came to dinner and when they returned to the parlor afterward, Alan came downstairs to join the company. Alasdair was not here; he was dining with the prince.

Van and Frances and Alan watched Niall being charming to their shyly lovely guest. Jean's pale brown hair was unpowdered, and she was quietly dressed in a slate-blue frock. The only jewelry she wore was a small gold locket on a chain about her throat. Her large brown eyes regarded Niall with unabashed adoration.

How could he resist her? Van thought with a trace of amusement. She looked at him as if he were God.

After Niall had left to escort Jean home, the three people remaining in the room looked at each other in amazement. "I do believe he is really serious," said Van.

"Aye." Alan shook his head. "She's a pretty thing," he offered. "Reminds me of a little woodland deer."

Van leaned back in her chair. "But whoever would have pictured Niall with a little woodland deer?"

Frances was more perceptive. "Perhaps she is what he needs. His voice is more gentle when he speaks to her. Kinder." It was a note Frances herself recognized very well. Tears stung behind her eyes and she stared at the teapot. Stop it, she told herself firmly. You are worse than a baby.

"Your hour of freedom is over, Alan MacDonald," she heard Van saying. She spoke to Alan exactly as if he had been Niall. "Upstairs with you now. After a rest you can come down again."

"I'm fine," Alan protested. "Do not banish me so soon, Van. I'm that sick of my bedroom."

"Well . . ." Van turned to Frances. "What do you think, Mother?"

"I see no reason why Alan can't remain down here for a while longer," Frances said composedly.

Alan grinned. "There you are, Van. Now, what about a game of chess?"

"Oh, all right. You stay right there and I'll get the board."

Frances watched Alan's eyes as they followed Van out of the room. She sighed. How much simpler life would be, she thought, if only Van loved Alan instead of the Earl of Linton.

Niall looked at the brown head that just topped his shoulder and smiled a little. A cold wind was blowing up the street and Jean seemed to shiver. "Come," he said, "let us get out of the wind for a minute," and he pulled her into the doorway of a shop. Edinburgh on a Sunday afternoon was quiet as a churchyard. There was no one on the street but the two of them. Niall turned so his back was toward the street and looked down into her upturned face.

"Jeannie," he said. "I have been trying for so long to get you to myself."

Her big brown eyes widened in surprise. Her lips parted. "You have?"

"I have." His voice was deeper than usual. He cupped her face in his hands and held it. "Kiss me, Jeannie," he murmured, and bent his handsome head.

Her mouth was soft as a petal under his. She smelled like flowers. He raised his head and looked down into her wondering eyes and knew that he could never hurt this girl, never do anything that would dishonor her. He picked up her hand and held it to his mouth.

"Such a cold little hand, m'eudail," he said. "Will you give it to me?"

"Oh, Niall." It was the first time she had used his given name and he thought it had never sounded sweeter.

"My little love." Her hand was tight within his own warm grasp. "Will you, Jeannie? Will you marry me?"

"Yes," she said on a trembling note, and he kissed her again.

The betrothal of Niall MacIan and Jean Cameron was accorded almost universal approval by all interested family and friends. Alasdair, in particular, was pleased. Jean was by no means a great match for the future Earl of Morar, but she was acceptable and she was at hand. Alasdair wanted the wedding to take place immediately.

When his father told him this, Niall was more than willing. "I don't know if the women will agree, though," he said ruefully. "I never knew such a fuss could be made about so simple a thing as two people being married."

"The women will agree," Alasdair said. He looked at his son. "I think we will be marching for England, Niall, and I want you wedded and bedded before we leave."

Niall's face blazed. "Has the decision finally been made then, Father?"

"Not finally, no. But the prince, as you know, desires it and now Lord George Murray has been brought to agree."

"We have delayed too long as it is," Niall said.

"I agree that we must make a decision. I think we will be marching in a week."

"Dhé! Can I be married in so short a time?"

"You can and you will," said Alasdair grimly. "I will speak to the prince about standing up for you. *That* will get the women moving."

Niall grinned. "It will that." He looked at his father

curiously. "I know why I am anxious, Father, but why are you?"

Alasdair gazed back at his son for a moment in silence. Unbearable even to contemplate this splendid young manhood going down to the grave. His voice when finally he spoke was harsh. "We are at war, my son. It will be well to make sure Morar has an heir."

Niall's gray-green eyes never wavered. "Ah," he said on a long note of revelation. "So that is it." He grinned like a schoolboy. "Well, Father, I promise to do my best!"

Alasdair gripped his son's arm. "I'm sure you will, my son. I'm sure you will."

16

Van was going over her wardrode with Frances, trying to pick out a dress to wear to Niall's wedding, when the message came. At first she was puzzled, wondering who could be writing to her, but when she opened the note and read it, all the color drained from her face.

"What is it, Van?" Frances asked in quick concern. "Sit down, darling. You have gone quite pale."

Van did not reply but read the note through again. Her head felt curiously light. Edward. Here in Edinburgh. And he wanted to see her. Dhé! She could not quite take it in.

"Van!" Dimly, through the sudden pounding of her heart, she heard her mother's voice. She looked up into Frances' worried blue eyes.

Thank God she was with the one person she could tell. "It's from Edward, Mother," she said. "He's here in Edinburgh and he wants to see me."

Frances' eyes enlarged noticeably. "Edward?" she said faintly. "Edward Romney?"

"Yes."

"Dear heavens."

"Yes," Van said again. She made an attempt to calm her breathing. "He wants me to reply by the same messenger. I am to name the place." She stared at Frances. "Dhé, Mother, where am I to meet him? Not here, with Father and Niall in and out all the time and Alan in the parlor for most of the day."

"Do you want to see him, darling?" Frances asked.

Did she want to see him? There was no point in it, really. No point in going over past arguments, in stirring up the pain once more. No point at all. "Yes," she said. "I want to see him."

Frances nodded and looked out the window. "He's in the castle, I take it."

"Yes. He arrived yesterday."

"It really isn't safe for him to come into the city." But Frances spoke absently, as if her mind were not on her words.

"No one knows him, Mother," Van said. "And he isn't a soldier. He's not in uniform or anything."

"Lady Balwhinnie's," said Frances.

"Yes," Van returned thoughtfully. "But do you think she will agree?"

"I'll invite her here for dinner and cards. You can wait in her house while she is gone. She needn't know why."

Lady Balwhinnie was an elderly Lowland widow whom Frances had known for years. "I'll think of some excuse for leaving you there," Frances continued. "Her house is rather near the Netherbow Port, but it can't be helped. I really cannot think of any other location, darling."

"Lady Balwhinnie's will be fine," Van replied a little breathlessly, and went to write a reply for the messenger.

It was early evening when Van sat in the small back parlor of Lady Balwhinnie's house and waited for Edward to arrive. Her hands were clasped tightly in her lap and her mind was filled with conflicting thoughts. It was foolish of her to have agreed to see him, she knew. What had been between them before was over now. It had been over the moment Charles Edward Stuart landed in Scotland. Surely he understood that. Surely he was not hoping that she had changed her mind. . . . There was a soft knock at the front door and Van raced into the hall. She opened the door quickly and almost pulled him inside the house.

"You can get that hunted look off your face, Van," he said with slow amusement. "No one is following me."

She had not been prepared for what the sight of him, what the sound of his voice, would do to her. He towered over her in the hallway; she had forgotten just how big he was. "Come into the parlor," she said abruptly, and led the way into the small back room. As she went to close the door behind him, he took off his hat and tossed it onto a chair. The sight of that bright head, suddenly revealed, hit her like a blow in the stomach. She could feel herself beginning to shake. She forced her voice to calmness and asked, "What are you doing in Edinburgh, Edward?"

He looked at her. How could she have forgotten how blue his eyes were? "Officially," he answered, "I brought messages to General Guest at the castle. Unofficially"—his eyes held hers captive—"I came to see you."

She held her own eyes steady. "If you came to take me back with you, then you have made a trip for nothing."

"I did not come to take you back." He sounded impatient, even annoyed. "I came to assure myself that you were all right."

Van frowned in bewilderment and then realized what

it was he meant. Color flushed into her cheeks. "I am all right," she said. "You told me to get word to you if I were not." She was not quite meeting his eyes. "I understood you."

"You may have understood me," he said grimly, "but I was not so certain you would heed me."

Van looked at the ground. "The occasion did not arise."

"I am relieved to hear it." He watched her downcast face. "I did it to hold you, you know, but not in that way. Conceited of me, wasn't it, to think you'd stay just because I took you to bed?"

Van's hair was gathered high into a knot on the back of her head, from which a few long curls had been allowed to fall. The line of her cheek and jaw were clear to him and he saw distinctly the quiver that flickered along both. She did not answer, could not answer. This was torture, she thought. She should never have agreed to meet him, should have kept him as a memory. The living flesh and blood of him was playing havoc with her heart. There was a long silence and she finally raised her eyes to his face. She could see pain in the lines of his mouth. "Edward," she said. Then, "You almost succeeded."

She was not quite sure who made the first move, but quite suddenly she was in his arms, her own arms locked about his waist, her cheek pressed against his heart. She could hear it thudding through his coat.

"I should have known that nothing could bind you against your will." His voice was muffled by her hair. "My God, Van, I have been so afraid. I had visions of you being pregnant and forced to marry someone else."

"No," she said. "No."

"Van." His hand was under her chin, pushing it upward. She obeyed the pressure of his fingers and their mouths met. His kiss was hard and fierce and demanding and she answered it involuntarily, all her senses responding to the remembered power of his touch. After a moment he began to move her toward the sofa. Her feet were swinging off the ground and she did not care. She made a soft sound, deep in her throat. It was that small, infinitely sensual sound that brought Edward to his senses.

"Christ, Van. This won't do at all." His voice was deep and profoundly shaken. He set her on her feet, not on the sofa as he had intended, and backed away. "I came to make sure you were safe," he said, "not to put you in jeopardy again."

Van sat abruptly on the sofa and watched as he crossed to the window. She was as shaken as he had sounded. If he had not put a halt to it, she would have . . . She closed her eyes. Dhé. She should never have come here. She opened her eyes and saw him outlined against the window.

"Edward!" she said sharply. "Get away from that window. Someone may see you."

He shrugged but moved obediently to stand against the wall. Van tried to regain some semblance of composure. "What messages did you bring to General Guest?" she asked. "Or is that privileged information?"

"It's information your people will have shortly enough," he replied. His face was in the shadow; she could not read his expression. "General Guest, of course, is not to surrender the castle." He took a few steps toward her. "Field Marshal Wade is at Newcastle with a newly raised force of fourteen thousand men." Van forbade her face to change expression. "And four thousand cavalry," he added.

The Highland army, at its full strength, would not number more than seven thousand. Van felt fear clutch her throat. She scanned his face, visible now in the light of the fire. "Have you recalled all your troops from France?" she asked.

"Not yet." His eyes were very grave. "The Duke of Cumberland is returning with that army. He will be in England shortly."

God in heaven. Van swallowed and said bravely, "We smashed General Cope at Prestonpans. My brother said your troops could not stand against Highlanders."

"Perhaps not, if the numbers are even." His reply was gentle but implacable. "But the numbers will not be even the next time, Van. And you won't always have the advantage of a surprise attack."

She would not let him see how frightened she was. She jumped to her feet and went to poke at the fire. "You're making excuses," she said defiantly. "The fact of the matter is that we have taken Scotland. We broke your army at Prestonpans." She gave the logs a vicious jab. "If your English army invades the Lowlands, it will produce the same effect on Scots as you are always telling me a French army would produce on the English. The Lowlands have not forgotten Flodden and Pinkie, Edward. The Act of Union is new. England was Scotland's enemy for centuries, remember."

"And is the prince planning to remain in Scotland, then?" His voice was uninflected but Van turned to look at him through suddenly narrowed eyes.

"Surely you don't expect me to answer that question," she said after a moment.

"No, I suppose not." He lifted an ironic golden eyebrow. "But I'll tell you this, sweetheart. Charles Stuart is not going to be satisfied with just the crown of Scotland. I would bet you anything on that."

Van's narrow nostrils quivered. "Charles Stuart is *my* prince," she said in a hard voice, "and I don't like the way you talk about him."

"All right." He put his hands into the pockets of his coat and bent his head a little. There was little doubt in his mind as to the outcome of this rebellion, but he could not tell her what he thought. She would not listen. She was afraid to listen, he realized, because in her heart of hearts, she knew too.

"All right," he repeated. "Let's not talk about politics. Let's talk about us."

"There is no 'us' to talk about," she replied steadily. "You are a Whig and I am a Jacobite, and that is a gulf we cannot bridge."

"Not now, perhaps," he began, but she interrupted. "Not ever! You must understand that, Edward. You must . . ." She swallowed, then continued with determination, "You must forget about me." She made an effort to smile. "You know how anxious Cousin Katherine is for you to marry and to have a son. You must do that. Don't let me hold you back."

"Ah." His eyes were intensely blue. "You are releasing me from any . . . er . . . obligations I might have toward you. Is that it?"

"Yes," she said. "That is it."

"And you? Do you wish me to release you in like fashion? Is there perhaps some fine Highland lad whom you wish to wed?"

Van thought of Alan and his merry grin and his tender green-gold eyes. "No," she said. "There is not." But she could not quite meet Edward's eyes.

There was a pause. Then he said very softly, "There had better not be." Her eyes jerked up to his face. She had never heard that note in his voice before. She stared at him warily, but the dangerous undercurrent that had been in his voice was not apparent on his face. Suddenly he smiled. "I don't mind waiting for you, sweetheart," he said, and now his voice was very tender. "Who knows, perhaps someday you will be a subject of King James of Scotland and I of King George of England and we can be wed with the blessing of both our monarchs and all our relatives."

Van said nothing and he reached out and took her hands into his. "I must go," he said, and raised her palms to his mouth.

She might never see him again. The ache in her chest was unbearable. "Don't do anything rash," he said sternly, and bent to kiss her, quick and hard, on the mouth. He dropped her hands and picked up his hat.

Van's hands clenched and she hid them in the folds of her skirt. She was very pale. "I won't say good-bye." He was at the parlor door. "Think of me sometimes," he said, and gave her the ghost of his old smile. Then he was gone. She could hear the front door close firmly behind him. She was alone.

She sat down and stared blindly into the fire. An acute and anguished sense of loss engulfed her. This was worse than the last time, she thought. She did not think that she could bear it.

Frances got her home with a minimum of fuss. She was not required to talk or to explain, for which she was vaguely grateful. Once home, she went right to her room and got into bed. She lay awake the whole night, dry-eyed, staring sightlessly at the crack in the ceiling over her head.

It was Frances, remembering the desolate look in her daughter's eyes, who cried.

Two days later, Niall MacIan was married in the Episcopalian church on the High Street. The prince stood up for him and Van was maid of honor for Jean. The wedding had turned into a major occasion in the capital's social life and the church was crowded as Jean, on the arm of Lochiel, came down the aisle to join Niall at the altar.

Van listened to her brother's voice as he made his responses, and tried desperately to keep her composure. This might have been she and Edward, she thought. If only . . .

It had made it so much worse, seeing him again, and yet she was not sorry she had done it. That one brief moment in his arms, the sight of him . . . It had been worth it.

Niall was putting the ring on Jean's finger now. Her small face gazed up at him adoringly.

Van had laughed at Jean once, she thought, for looking at Niall as if he were a god. She must look at Edward in the same way. The thought brought the faintest of smiles to her mouth. Her feeling for Edward had not changed, nor, apparently, had his for her.

Don't do anything rash, he had said. Like what? Like marry Alan? Her eyes went to the stalwart redheaded figure who was seated just across from her. She could not marry Alan, not when she felt as she did about another man. Next to her she saw her mother suddenly bow her head, and she reached over to put a comforting hand over Frances' as it lay on the front of the bench.

Frances sat on the front bench between Alasdair and Van and remembered her own wedding so many years ago. They had been married in her parish church. It was the first and the only time Alasdair had ever set foot in England, that time when he came south to wed her and take her away. Her parents, having given in, had tried to put a good face on it, but it was clear they did not like either Alasdair or the marriage.

"You have chosen him, Frances." Her mother's words to her on the eve of her wedding came back to her now over the years. "You have gone against everyone who loves you, who is concerned for you, and have chosen this man. Remember that when things are hard. He is what you wanted."

At the altar Niall was putting a ring on Jean's finger.

Some things had been hard for her, Frances thought as she watched her son at the altar. It had not been easy adjusting to life in the Highlands. She had grieved that she could bear only two children. But through it all, there had always been Alasdair's love to help and to support her.

She had lived so much more intensely, so much more passionately than ever she had dreamed possible. Her family had thought her buried in the Highlands, but her life had been so much richer than most. It was because of Alasdair, because of the bright flame in him, that her own life had been so vital. She looked at his hand, resting lightly on the bench in front of him. Alasdair . . . proud, courageous, generous, ruthless, obstinate, passionate. Alasdair.

Pain caught suddenly at her heart and she bowed her head to hide her face. Next to her Van reached out and put a comforting hand over hers.

17

All the MacIans went to spend the evening at Lochiel's, tactfully leaving the newly married couple alone. There was no time for a traditional honeymoon. In two days' time they were leaving for England.

It was a strange feeling for Niall as he went up the stairs toward the bedroom where his young wife was waiting for him. Niall had had his first sexual experience when he was even younger than Jean, sixteen in fact. He had come to Edinburgh with his father, but Alasdair had been busy and had left his son to entertain himself. Niall had been looking at the gravestones in Greyfriars churchyard when he met Alison Scott. She was fifteen years older than he, a widow, and she had taken him home with her that afternoon.

Alison was uncomplicatedly sexual and their relationship had always been based on a pure and mutual lust. There had been women in France, as well, all of them as frankly bent on pleasure as he. But now it was Jeannie waiting for him in that big bed in his room. He couldn't come at her like a bull. He would hurt and frighten her. He drew a deep, steadying breath and opened the door.

She was sitting up against the pillows, her soft hair falling like rain down her back. She wore a white nightdress with little pearl buttons. He went over to stand beside the bed. He was still dressed in shirt and kilt, although the shirt was open at the throat. He sat down next to her.

"Jeannie," he said. He touched the delicate line of her cheek. She was so beautiful.

She gazed up at him. Her eyes had dilated into great brown peat pools full of reflected light from the fire. She rested her cheek against his fingers.

"Are you afraid?" he asked softly.

"Of you?" She shook her head. "No." But he thought he saw a flicker in her eyes.

He cradled her face in his hands. "I think it hurts the first time."

"That's all right." Her voice was a small whisper. He leaned forward to kiss her and her arms came up around his neck.

His young male body was instantly aroused, but he disciplined himself sternly. He held her and touched her and caressed her and all the time he fought a battle with himself. When finally he had her naked beneath him he thought it had been worth it. She was reaching for him, wanting him, and there was no trace at all of fear.

He entered slowly, carefully, but, inevitably, he had to hurt her. When she cried out and tried to pull away, he held her with hard hands and gave his straining body its own release.

"I'm sorry, m'eudail," he said contritely as they lay together. "I'm sorry I hurt you. But it couldn't be helped."

She nestled against him in a trusting movement that caused his heart to swell. "I love you," she whispered.

He kissed the top of her hair. "I love you too."

Later in the evening Van returned home with her

mother, father, and Alan. As she moved toward the stairs to go to her bedroom, Alan said, "Van, may I talk to you for a moment?"

She was worn out emotionally from the last few days, from seeing Edward again, from the wedding. She opened her mouth to plead fatigue, looked into Alan's face, and said instead, "Of course. If it is all right with you, Father?"

"I think we may safely leave you alone with Alan," Alasdair replied gravely. He and her mother went on up the stairs and Van sat down on the hard sofa and folded her hands in her lap. She could not avoid this interview forever. It would be best to get it over with now, she thought.

The room was cold. There was no fire in the chimney. Alan's face was shadowed; his gold-flecked green eyes watched her steadily. "Before you left for England I asked you a question," he began. "You said we would talk about it when you returned." He smiled a little wryly. "You have been back for some time, Van, but we have had very little opportunity to discuss anything between us."

She looked down at her folded, ringless hands, then up again. "We have been almost constantly together these last weeks," she reminded him.

He made an impatient gesture. "A man does not like to be flat on his back when he asks a girl to marry him." He crossed the room and dropped to one knee in front of her. "You know that is what I wanted to say."

She nodded. This was even more painful than she had imagined. "Alan," she said in a constricted voice, "I never meant to hurt you."

He seemed to stop breathing. Their faces were almost on a level with each other and she could clearly see his eyes. "Does that mean no?" he asked carefully.

"Niall should have told you," she said. "When I was in England, I was going to marry the Earl of Linton."

The green eyes widened. "The Earl of Linton," he repeated. "The man you were visiting?"

Her own eyes fell. "I was visiting his mother."

Slowly he rose to his feet and looked down at her for a moment before he went to lean his shoulders against the chimneypiece. "And are you still going to marry him?"

She did not look up. "No. He is a Whig, Alan. I cannot marry him now."

She heard the faint release of his breath. "You're right," he said. "Niall should have told me. *You* should have told me."

At that she looked up. "I know." Her light eyes were shadowed but they met his unflinchingly. "It was cowardice on my part, I suppose. As I said earlier, I did not want to hurt you."

"I love you, Van," he said tightly.

"I love you too," she replied, "but not in the way you want me to, Alan."

"What happened in England?" he asked abruptly. Van drew a breath. He deserved to know, she supposed. And so she told him about Edward, but she did not tell him of the earl's recent visit to Edinburgh.

"Under the circumstances, I could not possibly stay in England, of course," she concluded. "So I came home with Niall." She had been staring into the empty grate while she was speaking, and now she looked up into his face. It had lightened considerably during the last few minutes.

Alan's thoughts matched his face. Van was a loyal Jacobite to the very marrow of her bones. She would never marry the Earl of Linton now, he thought. Blood, training, conscience, everything in her was against such a match. The chances were she would never see Linton again.

She had said she cared for him. That was a start. And he was here, while Linton was not. She was looking at him, her lovely face was somber. He smiled and crossed the room to sit next to her on the sofa. He took her hands into his and bent his head to kiss them. She remembered Edward's bright head bent over them only two days ago. "My poor little love," Alan said softly. "What a time you have been having."

It was not what she had expected. To her horror, Van felt her eyes fill with tears. Alan was so kind, so good. She did not deserve such kindness from him. "I'm sorry, Alan," she said in an unsteady voice.

"Do not fret yourself over me," he replied. He smiled down at her. "I am willing to give you all the time you want, m'eudail. I have not given up hope, you see. With you, I am prepared to be very patient."

Van looked up into his hazel eyes. I don't mind waiting, Edward had said. She would never feel for Alan what she felt for Edward. But he was going into England in a few days, into what might be mortal danger. She could not tell him that now. And he was very dear to her. These last weeks had forged a bond between them that had not been there before. So she smiled back at him and said, "I am not ready to marry anyone right now, Alan."

He leaned down and kissed her forehead. "I understand." She was close enough to him to sense the change in him and, being no longer innocent, she knew what it meant. But he made no move to pull her into his arms. Instead he said, "Go on up to bed, Van. It's cold down here."

He was so good, Van thought again. She didn't deserve him. She stood up and said good night and went upstairs. It was of Alan she was thinking that night as she finally fell asleep.

On November 3, 1745, the army of Charles Edward Stuart marched out of Edinburgh and along the road that led past Arthur's Seat to the village of Dalkeith. At Dalkeith they split into two columns, the main part of the army heading southwest, toward Cumberland, while a picked number of regiments under the dukes of Perth and Atholl followed the more direct southern route toward Newcastle. The purpose of the two dukes' command was to decoy Marshal Wade, still at New-castle with a very large army, into remaining there.

Niall was in high spirits as he marched beside his father at the head of his clan. Brought up since birth to believe in the rightness of his cause, he looked forward with soaring confidence to the successful ac-complishment of all his dreams. Every step he took brought him closer to London, and he whistled the clan's battle song under his breath as he strode along.

Alasdair was silent. They passed through the hills of the border country, through Lauder, Kelso, and Jed-burgh, and at every mile a few more clansmen slipped away and headed home. The Highlanders, as Alasdair had known, did not want to enter England. By the time the border was reached, more than a thousand clansmen had melted away.

The River Tweed ran between the two countries, and as the army halted briefly on its banks, Niall turned to his father. "The Rubicon!" he said, teeth flashing in his dark face. His eyes blazed with laughter and he drew his sword and waded in. As he reached the other side, he turned back toward Scotland and saluted.

The army was silent, but as each man stepped into the river he drew his sword and, as he reached the other side, whirled to the left to once more face Scotland.

They reached the English border capital of Carlisle and on November 17 the town surrendered to them. The Jacobite army at Carlisle numbered about five thousand foot and five hundred horse. The prince entered the city mounted on a white stallion with a procession of a hundred pipers to precede him. No one from Carlisle joined the prince's standard.

Charles was not daunted. He was quite sure that large numbers of recruits would join him in Preston and Manchester. It was common knowledge that those towns were sympathetic to the Jacobite cause. The army continued its march southward.

Three recruits joined them at Preston. At Manchester, where the Jacobite leadership had been hoping for fifteen hundred recruits, two hundred signed up.

Niall was undaunted. The lack of recruits only confirmed his feelings about the Sassenach. They had no faith, no courage. When word came that the Duke of Cumberland was in the vicinity with a government army of 2,200 horse and 8,250 foot, Lord George Murray deftly maneuvered so the king's son thought the Highland army was heading for Wales. Cumberland hastily moved his own army west and left the way to Derby open. On the clansmen came, to Derby, one hundred and fifty miles from their destination of London.

In London there was panic. People withdrew their money from the banks. The royal yacht was ordered prepared to evacuate George II and his family if it should prove necessary. The populace, terrified they would be descended upon by a ravaging army of savage Highlanders, began to assemble a citizens' army to defend the capital.

The Earl of Linton, meeting with other members of the government, was extremely short-tempered.

"There is no cause for all this alarm," he said irritably as discussion flowed on what were the proper measures to take.

"Well, I'm glad you can be sanguine, Linton," Lord Newcastle snapped. "The rest of us, however, cannot feel easy knowing there is an army of barbarians virtually at our front gates."

"Barbarians?" Edward raised a golden eyebrow. "They are the most well-behaved army imaginable, my lord. There has been no looting in any of the cities they have occupied, no rape, no murder. These ridiculous rumors that Highlanders eat babies are simply that—ridiculous rumors."

"The London populace does not know that," said Lord Pelham. "The newspapers say that the Highlanders are monsters with claws for hands."

"I heard today that they have dogs trained to tear a man to pieces," said a man down the table.

Edward looked sardonic. "Quite frankly, I think the rabble army that is assembling at Finchley is far more dangerous than the Jacobites," he said. "Good God, every rogue and vagabond in the city has joined it!"

"I know," Pelham said gloomily. "But both Wade and Cumberland are too far away to protect us. What are we to do?"

"Nothing," Edward said calmly.

"Nothing?" They stared at him in stunned horror.

"Nothing. Let them take London, although I agree the king must be got away. There are five thousand of them, my lords. Five thousand clansmen who will shortly be extremely homesick. Marshal Wade's and the Duke of Cumberland's armies are six times their size. The pretender will not maintain his tenure here for long."

"I don't know . . ." said Lord Newcastle.

"What if the French should send an army to assist the pretender?" It was the prime minister, Lord Pelham, speaking.

Edward looked soberly around the table. "The French worry me more than the clans. It is the French we cannot allow to reach London. If they should land, they must be beaten back. It is on the Channel that our closest watch should be kept. On the Channel and on the French coast."

"The navy is patrolling, my lord," he was assured by Lord Newcastle. "But I cannot agree with you in this matter of turning London over to the pretender!"

"Nor I. Nor I. Nor I," came from voices all around the table.

Despite Edward's protest, it was agreed to call up the militias of London and Middlesex and to keep the rabble at Finchley in arms. Double watches were to be posted at all the city gates.

Edward was very gloomy as he walked back to Linton House late that night. It was clear to him that the populace weren't the only ones panicking before the Highland threat. The government was genuinely frightened as well.

"When we finally get the upper hand, and we will," he said out loud as he stood looking into the fire that was burning in his bedroom chimney, "God help poor Scotland."

He lay awake for a long time trying to decide if it would be worse for the Highlanders to retreat or to advance. Either way, he foresaw nothing but disaster. They should have stayed in Scotland. "But I knew he wouldn't," Edward muttered. "The bastard. I knew he would want it all."

It was almost dawn before he finally got to sleep.

At Derby the Highland High Command decided on retreat. The prince protested. He wanted to continue on to London, which he was certain would open its gates to welcome him, but Lord George Murray and the chiefs voted to return. Faced with such unified opposition, the prince acquiesced. On Friday morning, December 6, the Jacobite army began its retreat to Scotland.

Niall was outraged. "How can you do this, Father?" he cried to Alasdair in stunned protest. "You are leading the prince back like a dog on a string! He wants to go on. We *should* go on. We are but one hundred and fifty miles from London!"

"Yes," Alasdair returned grimly. "And there are two large armies under Wade and Cumberland dogging our tracks. There is no sign of a French invasion. And—most of all—there has been no Jacobite uprising among the English."

Niall's eyes flashed. "We don't need them!"

"Yes we do," Alasdair contradicted him. "Think, my son. Suppose we do get to London. Suppose we take London. Then what are we to do? Garrison it indefinitely with the clans? They will not tolerate that. They are not a professional army. Dhé. They will all want to be going home for the spring planting!"

Niall stared at his father mutinously. "Once we have shown what we can do, others will join us."

"Do not count on it." His father's voice was flat. "We got no support from the northwestern counties, which we were told abounded with wealthy squires and hardy yeomen devoted to the cause. Where were those wealthy Tories, Niall?"

Niall's nostrils flared.

"In every town where we have proclaimed King James, the reaction has been the same," Alasdair continued relentlessly. "The mob stands and listens, heartless, stupefied, dull. Van had the right of it. England does not want the Stuarts."

"Well, what are we to do then?" Niall asked despairingly.

"Return to Scotland, where we can join with Lord John Drummond. He has brought us some French troops—not an army, but still . . ." Alasdair straightened his back and forced himself to smile. "All is not lost, Niall." He put a brief hand on his son's shoulder. "Take heart. In Scotland we are on our own ground. We will prevail."

Niall tried to smile back. "We came so close, Father."

"I know." Alasdair looked around at the encamped army behind them. "I know, my son." His voice was unusually gentle. "Get some sleep, Niall. We march early tomorrow morning."

As he watched Niall move off, Alasdair's face settled into very grim lines. This retreat—they had had no alternative. But he knew in his bones that it was the beginning of the end for them all.

18

All throughout early December, in particularly vile winter weather, the Highland army retraced its steps northward. The Duke of Cumberland set out in pursuit, and at Clifton, in the north of England, his advance guard finally caught up with the Jacobite rear guard. There was a brief skirmish in which the government forces got much the worse beating, and Cumberland gave up trying to pursue the returning Highlanders.

On December 20, 1745, the Jacobite army reentered Scotland.

Van, Frances, and Jean remained in Edinburgh throughout November and December, living from one report to the next on the progress of their army.

Van hated the waiting. "I wish I were a man!" she raged to her mother. "I was not made for sitting at home."

"Thank God you are not a man," Frances retorted quickly. "It's enough that I have your father and brother to worry about without adding you to the list."

"I'm sorry, Mother." Van put a hand on Frances' arm.

Frances smiled at her. "I know this is hard on you, darling. It's hard on all of us. They are so far away

. . . so vulnerable . . ." Her voice died away and Van's hand tightened.

"There has not been a shot fired, Mother," she said bracingly. "And they have made it to Derby!" She grinned at Frances, trying to instill confidence and hope. "Next year at this time, we will all be dancing at St. James's."

Then came news of the retreat. Frances decided to remove to the vicinity of Glasgow, where she expected the army to land in Scotland. She found accommodations for herself and the girls at an inn on the northern outskirts of the city and so was one of the first to know when the main body of the Jacobite army reached Glasgow on Christmas Day. She sent a servant to find and deliver a note to either Alasdair or Niall.

Niall came first, bringing a gust of air and a breath of life and energy into the room with him.

"Niall!" Jean cried and jumped to her feet.

He laughed. "Jeannie!" And, under the interested eyes of his mother and his sister, he kissed her thoroughly.

Jean emerged from his embrace breathless and flushed.

"You look splendid, darling," Frances said. "How is your father?"

"Father is fine, Mother. He was with Lord George when I got your message." He grinned down at his wife. "I didn't wait for him."

Jean's small face was beautiful. "We have been so worried," she said softly. "Everything seemed to be going so well . . . then we heard of the retreat . . ."

Niall's face darkened. "The prince did not want to retreat. Lord George and the chiefs forced him to it."

"Sit down, darling," Frances said gently, "and tell us about it."

Niall sat on an old sofa and pulled Jean down to sit beside him. He kept her hand in his on his lap. "There was no English rising," he said, and his eyes locked with Van's for a minute. "You had the right of it. The Sassenach did not move."

She looked back at his severe face. "I would have been glad to be proven wrong," she said quietly.

After a minute his face relaxed. He turned to his mother. "There was no help from England and no help from France and we had two large English armies coming after us, so the chiefs deemed it wisest to return to Scotland and make our stand on friendly ground. Although it seems that Glasgow"—he scowled at the name—"is scarcely less Whiggish than England. Damn Lowlanders."

"Well, I'm glad you're back," Frances said firmly. "I know your father was against the invasion from the first. You will all be much safer here in Scotland."

"Yes," said Jean fervently, and gazed up into his face.

Van said nothing.

Shortly thereafter Frances sent Niall and Jean upstairs to "spend some time together," as she tactfully put it, and she and Van remained in the private parlor she had hired and discussed what Niall had told them. Frances was emphatic in her belief that the clans had been right to return to Scotland. Van was not so certain.

"Would you have ordered the retreat if the decision had been yours?" she asked Niall later as a table was being set up in the parlor for dinner to be served. She was standing next to him by the window, a little distance away from Frances and Jean. She kept her voice low.

He answered in the same tone and without hesitation. "No. No. If it had been up to me, I'd have gone on. We were only one hundred and fifty miles from London." He smiled a little ruefully. "I have no sensible reasons for such a choice, I fear. Things certainly did look very discouraging. But, Dhé! We were almost to London, Van! I'd have gone for it."

Van looked up into her brother's burning eyes and felt, in her heart, that he was right. She trusted Niall's instinct in this more than she did her father's caution. She said nothing, however, but asked him the question that had been on her mind since his return. "How is Alan? Is he all right?"

Niall nodded. "Alan is fine. He feels as I do about the retreat, but we are only young hotheads according to Father and the chiefs." Her brother shrugged. "Well, we haven't lost a battle yet. Lord George soundly thrashed Cumberland's advance guard at Clifton." He grinned at her. "Alan will tell you all about it himself. He is not yet in Glasgow, but I expect he will be here by tomorrow."

Jean came up to join them and he draped an arm around his wife's shoulders. "I'm starved," he said. "When is dinner?"

"Right now," said Frances as the first servant bearing a steaming dish came in the door.

Dinner was very gay, with Niall recounting every amusing incident he could recall to make them laugh. Of his listeners, however, only Jean was as happy as she seemed to be. Van was uneasy, although she gamely strove to catch the mood of optimism her brother was so gallantly spreading. And Frances, even as she listened and responded to her son's talk, had one eye always on the door. It opened once, to admit a servant with a note for Niall. Of Alasdair there was no sign.

"Come outdoors for a walk with me," Niall said to his wife after they had eaten. "You are looking pale, m'eudail."

"I have not liked to go out too frequently," Jean said softly. "Glasgow, as you mentioned earlier, is very much a Whig town."

"You'll be safe with me," Niall said confidently. Then, to his sister, "You too, Van. You must be needing some air."

Van hesitated, looking toward Frances.

"Come along," Niall said sharply, and she looked at him to find him frowning at her meaningfully.

"Oh," she said. "Yes. I'd love some air. I'll go get my cloak too."

She left the room and Niall smiled at Frances. "I'd invite you as well, Mother, but I imagine you want to wait here for Father."

Frances smiled back a little mistily. "Thank you, darling. You are very thoughtful."

He kissed the top of her head. "Marriage has been good for me," he said teasingly, and as soon as Jean and Van returned, he herded them deftly out the door.

The room was very quiet after they had gone. Frances sat on the old sofa, her hands idly crossed in her lap, her eyes fixed abstractedly on the door. After a few minutes there came the sound of a step in the passage outside. Frances' hands tensed. The door opened and Alasdair was standing there.

Her heart began to slam. She did not leap up as Jean had done, but stayed in her seat, her eyes scanning his face. She said his name.

He gave her a sober smile. "Here's a Christmas present you did not expect, Frances," he said, and came across the room.

He moved like a man who was very tired, not just muscle-tired but soul-tired. He did not touch her but sat in the hard chair that was placed opposite the sofa on the other side of the fire. "You have all the news from Niall, I suppose."

She tried to answer, failed to make any sound, and tried again. "Yes," she managed to say this time. Then, "I thank God you are all home."

He was looking at the fire, not at her. He was trying to keep his face expressionless but she, who knew him so well, could read the pain on it. "Not all," he said harshly. "We left a garrison at Carlisle."

Frances did not understand. "To hold the city?"

"They cannot possibly hold the city against Cumberland. They will be taken. And executed."

Frances was appalled. "But why leave them there then?"

"The prince wanted to make a show of force, not to abandon England completely. Of course, he has every intention of returning."

"But he won't?" Her voice was scarcely a whisper.

"He won't." At last he turned to look at her. "You were right, Frances. The clans alone cannot topple an established government. And there is no sign of help from England or France." She made an involuntary motion toward him and stilled it. His gray eyes were dark and shadowed. "But, you see, the damnable thing is, if it were all to do again, I would do the same. That is why I cannot ask you to forgive me."

"Oh, darling." Her heart rose in her chest with grief for him. "There is nothing I could not forgive you. If you don't know that by now . . ."

Her voice trailed off because he had left his chair in a kind of a lunge and was coming toward her. Then he was next to her on the sofa and she was in his arms.

His kiss was full of hunger.

She clung to him as one drowning might cling to a safety device thrown out just before he has gone down for the last time.

"There is so much for you to forgive me," he said in her ear when his embrace finally loosened a little. He rested his cheek against her hair. "I don't know what got into me, Frances." His voice sounded bewildered. "It was as if I had a hard knot of anger inside of me and I could not see or hear around it. I was like a stone. I knew I was making you unhappy, but I could not seem to help myself." He laughed shakily. "A fine excuse, I know."

"When you looked at me, you saw all your own doubts." Her arms were holding him close to her.

"Yes." His voice was very low. "Yes, I suppose that is true."

"Alasdair." She drew a deep breath and closed her eyes briefly. She had to say this right. "It does not matter what happened in England, what will happen here in Scotland. You are my husband, and where you go, I go. Your honor is my honor, your cause, my cause. You are in this to the end, I know that, and I am with you."

There was a long pause. Then he said in a low and shaken voice, "I don't deserve that."

She made an effort at lightness. "Well, that's what you've got." She took his face between her long, slender fingers and looked up into his eyes. "Just don't ever put me . . . outside like that again." Her voice was almost inaudible. "I don't think I could bear it."

"Never." He was looking deep into her eyes. "You

are the very heart in me, Frances. When I put you out, I became a stranger even to myself. There is no real life for me without you."

"I love you." She ran a forefinger along the line of his high cheekbone.

"I don't know why. I have never known why. Scarcely a day has gone by since we married that I did not look at you and wonder at the miracle that had given you to me." He put his hand over hers, then turned his face to kiss her fingers. "Come upstairs with me, Frances," he said. "Come upstairs."

It was as if nothing had changed, Frances thought, as though the last desolate months had never happened. He was hers once again. His thin, hard hands were so achingly familiar, the lean, muscled strength of his body so well known to hers.

Her body had always answered to the call of his, but this time was more fiercely passionate than any she could remember from the past. He wanted her with such a single-minded intensity, needed her with such an overwhelming need. Frances' profoundly feminine nature responded deeply to his urgency, abandoning without reserve all her own prodigious sweetness to the hard, driving manhood that needed it so desperately.

He held her for a long time afterward, not saying anything. Then, "When I married you I wanted to buy the sun and the moon to lay them at your feet. I wanted to give you the world to hold in your lovely white hands. And I have only given you grief."

"That's not true," she said strongly. She raised up a little on an elbow and stared down into his sober face. "Never say that, Alasdair. Never think it. It's not true."

"Is it not?" His voice was soft.

"No." She bent to put her mouth on his. "I have had everything in life I ever wanted," she said and kissed him. His arms reached up to pull her down and after a minute he rolled so that she was once again beneath him.

"I thought you looked tired when you first came in," Frances said later, a hint of laughter in her voice. "You seem to have recovered."

"You are a tonic, mo chridhe," he said in return.

She snuggled her head against his shoulder. "You timed your entrance well. The children had just gone out."

"I know." His voice was amused. "I sent Niall a note and told him to get himself and the girls away for a few hours."

Frances sat up and stared down at him. "You didn't!"

He grinned and for a moment looked almost as young as Niall. "I did. The people at the inn told me you were at dinner and I wanted to see you first, alone. So I sent in a note to Niall."

"So *that* was the note the servant brought in." She gave her husband an admiring look. "How clever of you, Alasdair."

"Thank you, m'eudail."

Frances laughed. "Niall told me marriage had made him more sensitive. I should have known he was not as sensitive as that." She sobered. "I think Jean may be with child. She has been sick every morning for the past week."

He looked absolutely delighted. "Good for Niall!" he said heartily.

"Good for Jean." Frances' tone was decidedly dry.

"Good for both of them."

"Don't say anything to Niall, Alasdair. Jean will want to tell him herself."

"All right." He yawned and stretched and sat up. "The children will be back by now. Perhaps we ought to go downstairs."

"Yes. Niall couldn't keep the girls out for too long. It's cold."

"The cold won't hurt them," he said imperturbably as he began to dress.

Frances looked at him and smiled, her eyes misty with a sudden surge of love.

19

The Highland retreat had dramatically changed the mood in London. If the government was not yet triumphant, still it clearly felt that now triumph was in its future. Even the news of the Highland victory at the Battle of Falkirk on January 17 did not dampen English spirits. The Highlanders had defeated General Hawley, but the Duke of Cumberland, with his great army of regulars from France, was inexorably closing in on the pretender and the rebellious clans.

Edward got more detailed news of the Battle of Falkirk from the Duke of Argyll, who had received firsthand reports from some Campbell participants.

"Hawley evidently thought that the Highlanders would never stand up under a cavalry charge," the Campbell chief told Edward as they sat together at their club one afternoon. "He sent his cavalry, some seven hundred and fifty strong, straight in to attack the Highlanders' right wing." The duke lifted an eyebrow at Edward. "Where the MacIans were," he added a little dryly.

Edward's eyes narrowed to mere slits of blue. "And?" he prompted.

"The clans held their fire until the horses were almost on them—a very shrewd tactic. But then Lord George Murray was commanding the right wing, and

Lord George has a good military brain. The cavalry is well-trained, however, and they did not break under fire but continued to come on." The duke paused dramatically. "Hawley's plan was to trample the clansmen underfoot."

Edward sighed. "What happened next?"

The Campbell smiled slightly. "Hawley forgot about the dirks," he said. "The Highlanders simply lay on the ground, drew their dirks, and stabbed the horses in their bellies. The cavalry broke and ran for Edinburgh."

Edward was frowning. "But if it was such a rout, why didn't the pretender's army follow up their advantage? They could have retaken Edinburgh."

The duke looked cynical. "Dissension among the leadership, Linton. The pretender and Lord George Murray don't see eye to eye."

"The Highland army cannot afford to disagree among themselves," Edward said bluntly.

The duke looked pleased. "No, they cannot. At the moment the pretender is engaged in besieging Stirling Castle, a futile enterprise, I fear. The clans will never tolerate such tedious work. If he doesn't look out, half the pretender's army will be slipping off home to their glens."

Edward and the duke had another glass of wine together and then Edward walked slowly home to Linton House. He went around to the stables before he entered the house, however, and snapped at a groom who was sitting around doing nothing and set him to polishing an already-polished harness. Then he inspected the stalls and complained that the bedding wasn't deep enough. Two grooms jumped to fetch wheelbarrows and more straw.

When the earl finally moved toward the house, there

was a general sigh of relief throughout the stable area. "I never seen his lordship so out of temper," one groom remarked to another as they forked straw into the offending stalls. "Something must have happened. Be best if we all keep busy until he calms down." His companion agreed fervently and both men went to get more straw.

The staff at the house was not faring much better than the grooms, and when the earl finally locked himself into the library, there was a universal letting out of breaths. Inside the closed doors Edward was sitting at his desk, a rather formidable frown on his face as he went through a pile of papers.

He was feeling helpless and it was not a feeling he was accustomed to. Images of Van danced through his mind and he knew that with every passing day she was getting farther and farther away from him. They had met last in the glow of Charles's triumphant occupation of Edinburgh. They had met as equals. The next time they met, one of them would be the victor and one the vanquished, and he knew beyond the shadow of a doubt which one would be which. He prayed to God that at least her father and her brother would not be killed. As it was, she would have enough to hold against him.

Edward gave up all pretext of reading the papers on his desk and stared grimly into the fire. He could not even write Van a letter, he thought bitterly. He had no idea where she was.

Van was at Stirling. Alasdair had sent for the women when he realized they were going to be stuck in the town for weeks trying to take Stirling Castle. He was as convinced as the Duke of Argyll of the fruitlessness of such a siege, but Lord George Murray had been overruled by the prince and consequently the Highland army was in Stirling.

The city, traditionally the gateway to the Highlands, was full of excitement when Van, Frances, and Jean arrived. Lord Strathallen had recently joined the prince with a regiment of Frasers, MacKenzies and Farquarsons. And, more interestingly, Lady Mackintosh had arrived, leading a contingent of four hundred Mackintoshes for the prince. Her husband, the chief, Mackintosh of Mackintosh, had previously come out for the government.

"Dhé," said Van with a laugh when she was told that piece of news. "That was courageous of her. But I would not like to live in that marriage!"

Frances thought of how implacable Alasdair had been at the merest mention of opposition to his decision, and shuddered.

"I cannot imagine how she ever brought herself to do it," Jean said, gazing with big eyes at Niall. She added hastily, "Although of course I am glad that she did."

The laughter had died out of Van's face. "We all do what we have to do," she said in a hard, abrupt voice. Jean looked bewildered and Frances compassionate. Niall took his wife's small hand in his own comforting grasp.

Of the three women gathered in the room with him, only his sister had it in her to do as Lady Mackintosh had done, he thought. His mother and his wife were too gentle, too feminine, ever to stand alone so defiantly. They would follow their husbands' lead, in war as well as in peace.

Van was different. Van might love a man, but that would not stop her from going the road she herself deemed right. He looked at his sister's proud face. It was not that she was unfeminine, though. She was just . . . Van.

Jean's fingers curled within his. The man who loved
Van would never feel for her the overwhelming pro-
tectiveness he felt for Jeannie, he thought. Or the
intense possessiveness. Van was too strong a spirit to
be loved like that. Niall had a brief vision of the Earl
of Linton's splendidly tall figure and hard blue eyes. A
man very different from himself, was Edward Romney. Niall looked into Jean's great brown eyes and
smiled. He loved his sister, but he decidedly preferred
marriage to someone like his Jeannie.

Alan was in Stirling as well and he came to see Van
the day after she arrived in the city. They had had
only a few brief hours together in Glasgow before he
had had to leave for Lochaber, so Van was delighted
to see him when he called at her mother's lodgings in
the Stirling High Street. When he asked her to ride
out with him for the afternoon, she accepted with
alacrity.

They went to Bannockburn, the field where Scotland had won its independence from England five
hundred years since.

"Impossible to imagine this peaceful place as the
scene of a bloody battle," Van murmured. They had
dismounted and were standing on the winter-hard
ground, their horses' reins in their gloved hands. There
was no one else in sight. The cold January wind whipped
their plaids but, true Highlanders that they were, Van
and Alan ignored the weather.

"The Bruce had six thousand men, Van," Alan
said. "Six thousand Scots against the King of England's twenty thousand. And we won."

Van stared up at the boy beside her. Alan's jaw was
set—hard. Not a boy, she thought. Not any longer the
boy she had grown up with. Alan was a man now. As

was Niall. And she—God knew the heart she carried was no longer that of a carefree young girl.

Alan was looking around him with narrowed eyes. "We won because our cause was just," he said. "On this field we became our own country, with our own king." The eyes that met hers were slits of green. "We will do it again, Van. I know we will do it."

His face was grim, dedicated. For all its youth, it most definitely was not a boy's face anymore. These last months had changed Alan. If he had been like this before . . . If she had not met Edward . . .

"Alan." Her voice was not quite steady. "You have the heart for it, of that I have no doubt. But . . ." He was the first person she had said this to. "What if we should lose?"

"If we should lose . . ." His reddish hair was blowing in the wind. "Then we will have the Sassenach in our glens once more. The chiefs will have to flee to France. They will take away our arms and our pride and our dignity." His lips smiled. "A good reason to win, is it not?"

"Aye." She too looked around the field. Pride flooded through her, pride in the men of her blood who risked so much in the face of such an enemy. "I wish I were a man!" she said fiercely. "Do you know how hard it is to sit and wait?"

"Ah, Van." There was a new note in his voice. "Do not ever wish that, m'eudail. There is no man who knows you who would have you other than you are."

She lifted suddenly shadowed eyes to his face. "Alan . . ." she began uncertainly.

He gave her a warm smile, with his eyes as well as his mouth. "Do not worry yourself over me. If I still keep some hopes over you, that is entirely my own affair."

She laughed, and the guilty feeling vanished. He was the dearest man. "Is that true?" she retorted.

He looked down into her beautiful face. It was the first time all day that he had seen her smile. Her great light eyes were regarding him with undisguised affection.

Aye, Alan thought as he playfully pushed her bonnet down more firmly on her head. I can wait. She said something, ducked her head, and laughed again. The Earl of Linton was a long way away, he thought comfortably, and on the wrong side. All he needed was a little patience. Patience would come hard, but the prize was worth the effort. More than worth it. He grinned and said, "Come along. Your mother invited me for dinner and I do not want to be late."

"I'm starving," Van agreed. Then, wonderingly, "It's the first time in weeks I've been hungry."

"You need more fresh air," he replied easily. He gave her a sidelong look and there was the faintest trace of a satisfied smile in his eyes. He took her hand into his own as they walked toward the horses and her fingers curled intimately around his. They made it back to Stirling in time for dinner.

The chiefs advised Charles Edward to disband the army for the winter. Many of the clansmen were sick, most had not seen wives or children for months, all hated the dreariness of laying futile siege to Stirling Castle. The men had fought long and faithfully for their prince, Alasdair argued. They needed time to rest and recover.

Charles Edward was horrified at the suggestion. "My God! Have I lived to see this?" he exclaimed, and absolutely refused to disband the army.

The result was exactly as Alasdair had foreseen. By the end of January nearly half of the army had deserted.

On January 31 the Duke of Cumberland reached Edinburgh, where he replaced Hawley as commander-in-chief of the government forces.

The prince gave up his siege of Stirling Castle and marched north to Inverness, which surrendered to him without a struggle. The castle, called Fort George and a symbol of English rule, was gleefully blown up by the Highlanders. Charles Edward and his followers settled into the town, the traditional capital of the Highlands, and made themselves comfortable.

The social scene in Inverness soon became reminiscent of the prince's first glorious occupation of Edinburgh. There were dances and receptions and social gatherings of all sorts. But the mood in Inverness was different from the mood in Edinburgh, Van thought. The high-hearted excitement had gone. The Duke of Cumberland was in winter quarters in Aberdeen, and with the spring would come what might be the decisive confrontation between the Jacobite and English armies. Van often felt as if they were people dancing and laughing and talking on the edge of a smoldering volcano.

She spent all of February and most of March in the company of Alan MacDonald. It was to Alan alone that she was able to open her heart and talk about the fears that weighed on it. Niall had gone south with Lochiel to try to take the two English fortresses of Fort Augustus and Fort William, so he was not around. Nor could she talk to her father. He was as worried as she, Van thought, but he was putting so much effort into keeping her mother happy that she had not the heart to put any more strain on him. For almost the first time in her memory she could not talk to her mother. Frances was looking like a girl again, her blue eyes unshadowed, her brow smooth and serene. Van could not intrude between her father and her mother now. And Jean was carrying a baby and looking forward happily to Niall's return. Van was extremely thankful for Alan those long weeks in Inverness.

Alan was not unmindful of the problems that beset the prince's army, but still he felt that, given a fair battle, the Highland army would prove the victors. It gave Van heart just to be with him. She said as much one evening as they were talking together at a reception at the home of the Dowager Lady Mackintosh, where the prince was residing during his sojourn in Inverness.

Alan looked at her soberly. "I am glad to hear that." He hesitated, then went on. "I am leaving tomorrow, Van, for Lochaber."

Van felt her heart sink. She had become very dependent upon Alan these last weeks. He was a shield between her and her own thoughts—a shield between her and Edward. "Why?" she asked.

"To recruit," he responded briefly. She needed to ask no more. Desertions had been heavy this winter, and with the coming spring the Highland army had to increase its strength. A number of chiefs had gone home to raise more clansmen to the standard.

"I see." She looked up at him and made herself smile. "I shall miss you."

He did not smile back. "Will you, m'eudail?" His voice was as grave as his face.

Van felt a flash of fear. She had been living each day as it came this winter, trying desperately not to look ahead, and even more desperately not to look behind. She had found Alan useful in this struggle, and so she had used him. But what had it meant to him?

His eyes were very green as he looked down at her.

He was looking splendid himself tonight, in his dress kilt and his velvet jacket. He wore his hair unpowdered and it glinted richly auburn under the sconce that hung above them. She did not just find him useful, Van admitted to herself. There was more between them than that.

"I said I would be patient," he was going on, "and I have been trying to be. But, Dhé, Van, it is hard going!"

"Alan . . ." She searched his face. "I care for you, you know that. But I don't know if it is enough."

He took her hands and drew her closer to him. Their faces were very near. They might have been alone in the crowded room for all the notice they took of those around them. "Let me be the one to worry about that," he said.

The temptation to give in to him was tremendous. Edward was so far away now. In her mind she had given him up. Yet still she hesitated. Don't do anything rash, he had said to her. Marrying Alan was exactly the thing he had been cautioning her against; she knew that well. But they were at war, and Alan might be killed. . . . "I need a little more time, Alan," she said breathlessly. "I don't know." She made a resolve. "When you come back to Inverness, I'll answer you then."

His eyes began to turn from green to gold. He was the closest he had ever been to getting what he wanted, and he knew it. He was not fool enough to push her now. "All right, m'eudail," he said gently. "I can wait until then."

Van lay awake for a long time that night, turning over in her mind what had passed between her and Alan. She was not sure she would be doing the right thing to marry him. She did not love him at all in the

way she had loved Edward. What she felt for Alan
was deep affection and respect. She did not ache for
him to take her into his arms, the way she did every
time Edward looked at her. But she and Edward were
finished. Would it not be easier for her to bear that if
she were not alone, if she had someone else to care for
and live for? She could make a life with Alan. She
could stand by him and help him and bear his children
and find some measure of contentment with him. But
would that be enough for Alan? He loved her more
than she did him; she knew that well enough. Would
it be fair to saddle him with a marriage in which he
would be the one doing most of the giving?

"Let me be the one to worry about that," he had said.

She went to sleep still not knowing what it was that
she should do.

The months they spent in Inverness were a time of
great happiness for Frances. Alasdair had refused a
chance to join Lochiel's expedition to the Great Glen
and she knew he had done so only because he wanted
to be with her. After so many months of desolation, it
was almost unbearably sweet to have him again.

February passed and March was almost over. Frances and Alasdair sat together in the narrow parlor of
their house on Church Street one evening listening to
the wind rattle the shutters and smiling at each other
whenever their eyes chanced to meet. Frances was
doing some embroidery and Alasdair was reading a
book. They had sent Jean and Van off alone to the
prince's reception this evening and elected to remain
home together.

Alasdair closed his book and stretched. "I'm sorry
we don't have a harpsichord here," he said when she
looked at him. "I would like to hear you play again,
mo chridhe."

Her fingers stilled. The way he had said that . . . "When this is all over, I'll play for you every day," she said with an effort at lightness.

He did not reply and, almost fearfully, she looked into his face. It was very quiet, very calm. He saw her look and smiled reassuringly. "That will be nice."

"Alasdair." She put down her embroidery. They had not spoken of the future all this winter. Deliberately she had not talked of it, thought of it. But now she asked steadily, "What is going to happen to us all?"

He shook his head. "I do not know, Frances." His gray eyes on hers were clear and peaceful. "If we fail at this enterprise, we may well have to go to France."

She went to sit beside him on the sofa. "I don't mind that," she said, her head resting comfortably against his shoulder. "I don't care where I go, as long as I have you."

He touched his cheek to her hair. After a minute Frances closed her eyes. The beat of his heart against her cheek was so comforting. "What time is it?" she murmured finally. "Van and Jean should be home soon."

She could feel his chest expand under her cheek. He drew another deep breath and then said the words that effectively destroyed all her peace. "I have been thinking, Frances, that we should get Jean away to France now."

She felt herself go rigid. "What do you mean?" she demanded.

He answered carefully. "It is as I said before: I do not know what is going to happen. It would be well to safeguard the heir." He paused. Then, even more carefully, "Perhaps you would accompany her, m'eudail."

"No." Frances sat up. "No," she said again, flatly, definitely. "I will go to France only if you go too."

Their eyes met. Then, "All right," he said quietly.

Frances' eyes were strained-looking but she spoke softly. "Is it really necessary to send Jean, Alasdair?"

"It would be . . . wise," came the cautious reply.

She wet her lips. "Send Van with her, then."

"No." His negative was as strong as hers had been. "No. I want Van with you."

Dear God. I must be calm, Frances thought frantically, I must not let him see how frightened I am.

"I doubt that Jean will want to go," she managed to get out.

"I will speak to Niall when he returns to Inverness." Alasdair frowned thoughtfully. "She can go to Lochiel's brother, John Cameron of Fassefern. He is in France and he will look after her."

"Yes," said Frances in an unsteady voice, "you must discuss this matter with Niall."

The girls came in and she made a tremendous effort to behave normally, to hide from them and from Alasdair the terror that had suddenly filled her heart. It was not until she was lying awake next to her sleeping husband that she allowed her mind to dwell upon his words.

He had told her so much more than he had ever meant to.

He wanted to hear her play the harpsichord because he did not think he would ever have the opportunity to hear her again.

He wanted Van to stay with her.

He wanted Jean safely in France.

He was afraid he and Niall were going to be killed.

Dear God. Dear God. Dear God.

She was so cold.

It won't happen, she thought. It *can't* happen.

But she knew that it could.

She pressed closer to Alasdair's warm back and laid her hand and cheek against it to try to draw from him the courage and the strength she knew she would need in order to face the future.

Fort Augustus fell to the Highlanders but after a full month of siege Fort William still held out. At the beginning of April Lochiel raised the siege and returned to Inverness.

Niall was delighted to be finished with siege work. Cumberland's army was showing signs of getting ready to move out of winter quarters in Aberdeen and Niall was looking forward to some real action. Consequently, his interview with his father came as a severe shock.

"You've made arrangements to send Jeannie to France?" Niall repeated, bewildered and beginning to get angry. "She said nothing of this to me!"

"She doesn't know," Alasdair returned calmly. "I have made arrangements but I waited for you to come back before speaking to her. Of course I would not do anything final until I consulted with you, Niall."

Niall was slightly mollified but still bewildered. "If you are worried about her safety in Inverness, then we can send her to Morar, Father. She will be safe there."

"If we lose this upcoming battle, my son," Alasdair said somberly, "nowhere in Scotland will be safe."

Niall's black brows met in almost a straight line. "We won't lose, Father. We've always beaten them before."

"We have lost a great number of men, Niall. We are at least two thousand men under strength right now."

"The Sassenach are afraid of us," Niall insisted.

"These troops with Cumberland are hardened veterans fresh from the French war. And they have had several months of drilling in how to withstand a Highland charge."

Niall had never heard his father sound so negative. "You are too gloomy, Father," he said abruptly.

"Perhaps. I hope so. But it would be well for us to safeguard the heir. Do you wish your ghost to see strangers in Morar, my son?"

Niall's head came up quickly. "No. Of course not!"

"Well, then, send Jean to France. Lady Lochiel has found someone to accompany her. She will go to Fassefern; he will take care of her."

Niall's lips were thin. "Why can't Mother go with her?"

"Your mother has refused to leave."

"Well, Van then."

Alasdair spoke patiently. "Niall, I cannot leave your mother here alone to face what she will face. Van must stay with her. And, too, *someone* must be here to look after the clan back in Morar."

Niall stared into his father's eyes and realized, with deep shock, that Alasdair expected to die.

"Father . . ." His face was white. "Is it that bad?"

"There is no money, Niall," came the measured reply. "The gold from France was captured by English ships on March 25. I am reduced to paying my men with meal, and that is short as well. Hay of Restalrig has replaced Murray of Broughton as secretary and he is not competent." Alasdair's gray eyes were clear and steady. "I do not know what will happen," he said, "but it is best to be prepared."

"I see," said Niall. He cleared his throat. "Very well, I'll tell Jean she must go to France."

Alasdair smiled wearily. "That will be best, Niall. For Jean, for the bairn, for us all."

Jean did not want to go.

"You must go, m'eudail," Niall said patiently. "If

we should lose this battle, the Sassenach will take
Inverness. You would not be safe. The Duchess of
Perth and the Countess of Strathallen were both seized
in their houses and carried as prisoners to Edinburgh.
The same could happen to you. There is a warrant out
for both Father and me on the charge of high treason.
As my wife you too are implicated."

"Your mother and Van are staying." Jean's eyes
were filled with tears. "Why must *I* be the one to go?"

He cupped her small face in his hands. "Because
you carry the heir, Jeannie. You are the one we cannot risk." He gave her a twisted smile. "Father said to
me, 'Do you wish your ghost to find strangers in
Morar?' " She stifled a sob. "I could not rest in peace
if that were to happen, Jeannie."

She sobbed again and he put his arm around her
shoulders. "Jeannie," he said, "please. Do this for
me. Let me go out to fight easy in my mind that you
and the bairn are safe."

She shivered against his arm and then, leaning her
body along his, she turned into him and reached her
arms around his waist. "All . . . all right, Niall." Her
voice was scarcely coherent. "I will go to France."

20

Jean took ship for France on April 12, the very day the Duke of Cumberland's army crossed the River Spey. The Duke of Perth and Lord John Drummond, who had been assigned to cover all the Spey crossings, brought the news to Inverness.

Alasdair told Frances and Van late in the evening of the thirteenth. "The prince has summoned the army to march tomorrow," he said. "We have come to the crisis point. If we can beat Cumberland, we will put heart into our troops and take the heart from theirs."

Van's slender, high-cheekboned face looked somber. "The Macphersons are not here, Father. Nor a great number of MacDonalds."

Alasdair looked at her from under his brows. "Lochaber and Alan rode in a few hours ago," he said.

Van felt fear catch in the back of her throat. So Alan had made it back in time for the battle. He would be happy, but she would much prefer to see him safe. This was not the time to fight the English: the Highland army was undermanned—even she knew that. "He said he would come to see you tonight," her father was going on, and Van nodded and took a deep breath.

"Father, wouldn't it be best to retreat? Postpone this battle until you are at full strength?"

Alasdair cast a quick glance out of the corner of his eye at his wife. Retreat had been his own counsel, but, as usual, the prince's Irish officers had prevailed. Frances was white as a ghost. He turned back to his daughter. "The prince has given his orders. We are to rendezvous tomorrow at Culloden House." He held Van's eyes and went on carefully, "Should we loose this battle, Van, Niall and I may have to flee for our lives. Do not worry about us. We can take to the heather well enough. But you and your mother must leave Inverness immediately. Go to Morar. There must be someone there for our people."

Van met his eyes and then nodded slowly. "Aye, Father. Be sure we will not remain in Inverness to greet the Sassenach. I have no wish to join the Duchess of Perth and Lady Strathallen in prison."

Thank God for Van's cool brain, he thought. "If things become impossible"—he stared at her meaningfully—"you must join Jean in France."

Almighty God, thought Van as his meaning struck her. Her throat was dry. He was looking at her as if he wanted an answer, and she managed to say, "I understand, Father. Do not worry. I will take care of Mother for you."

He smiled at her. "Thank you, Van."

Frances said absolutely nothing.

There came a knock on the front door and Alan MacDonald was announced. Alasdair took Frances up to bed and left his daughter alone with the young clansman.

There was silence in the room after the older couple had left. It had been raining lightly and there was the glint of moisture on Alan's face and hair and shoulders. He unpinned the brooch on his shoulder and let his plaid fall to a chair.

Finally Van spoke. "I wish I could say I'm glad to see you." Her face was thin and strained-looking. "I know the prince needs your men. But . . . oh, Alan, I would rather you were still safely in Lochaber!"

"You don't mean that," he said soothingly as he came across the room toward her.

"Aye. I mean it all right." She smiled up at him a little unsteadily. "I did not nurse you back to health from one battle only to see you throw your life away in another."

He reached out and smoothed a stray curl off her cheek. "You are too pessimistic, m'eudail. No English troops have yet withstood a Highland charge. I think we will win this battle."

She felt as if a strong hand were squeezing her lungs and her heart. "I have just been talking to Father." Her eyes closed briefly and then she looked up at him once again. "He thinks he is going to die," she said.

"Oh, Van." He put his hands on her shoulders and drew her against him. She went willingly, glad for the comfort of his strong arms. "I cannot pretend that there will be no deaths," he said over her head. "But remember this: we all go out to this battle because we wish to."

He was so dedicated. So brave. She did not have it in her to feel as he did. She pressed a little more closely against him and shivered.

"Do you remember what you said when last we met?" His head was bent close to hers, his voice very close to her ear.

She remembered well, and until now she had not known what it was that she would answer him. Standing here now, so close to him, the both of them so

near to the edge of defeat and death, her little fears
and concerns seemed infinitely trivial. If she could
make him happy, why should she hesitate? "Aye," she
said strongly. "I will marry you, Alan."

His grip on her tightened for a moment before he
put her away so he could look down into her face. "Do
you mean that?" he asked a little unsteadily.

"Aye. I mean it." She smiled at him and when he
reached out for her again she raised her face.

He kissed her passionately and Van put her arms
around him and held him tightly. His touch awoke no
sexual feeling in her, only an endless tolling sorrow for
the warm flesh so close to her own that tomorrow
might be cold and still.

It was Alan who stepped away first. His eyes were
golden, his breath coming hard. "I love you," he said
in Gaelic.

"Ailein, Ailein, Ailein," she replied in the same
language, "I love you too." And she did, if not in
quite the way he wanted.

He looked down at her, his eyes devouring her face.
Then, reluctantly, "I cannot stay, Van. There is much
to be done before the morning.

She nodded, unable to speak.

"I wish we had a minister here right now," he said
with barely concealed violence.

She would have to tell him about Edward, she
thought. She could not marry him without telling him
the truth of that. But not now. "After the battle there
will be time enough," she said, and hoped devoutly
that she spoke the truth.

She sat for a long time after Alan had left, staring
sightlessly into the fire. She had sent her men into
battle before, but this, she knew, was different. This
time they would not all be coming back. She sat on

until her brother arrived home, thinking and planning, trying to foresee all the possibilities.

Niall was surprised to see her still up. He yawned and sat down on the sofa across from her, lounging on his spine.

"Dhé," he said. "What a day this has been."

Van had been thinking very hard for the last hour. "Niall," she said to her brother now, "if you have to take to the heather, remember the cave at the head of the loch."

He sat up, his attention arrested. The cave Van referred to was one they had found as children. It was carved into the rock of the mountain and screened from view by a waterfall. To their knowledge, no one else knew of it. "If the worst befalls," she continued steadily, "I will take Mother home to Morar. I can get provision out to the cave by boat."

Two pairs of darkly lashed light eyes met and held. "I will remember that, my sister."

"Niall . . ." Her voice was not as steady as she had hoped it would be. She took a deep breath and tried again. "Father thinks he is going to die," she said for the second time that night.

Like Alan, he made no attempt to allay her fears; they were Highland and took premonitions very seriously. "I will do my best to bring him back, Van," he said at last.

"Dhé." Van's face was stark. "What will Mother do should anything befall Father?"

"Mother is stronger than you think," Niall said firmly.

Van's fine lips thinned and set. "I wish to God the prince had never come."

"You don't mean that," Niall replied, as Alan had before. "Nor would Father agree with you. He is our prince, and if we must die for him, then that is our privilege."

He meant every word of it.

Van smiled a little bitterly. "Women regard these matters differently from men," she said, and for the first time realized that this was true.

He held out his hand. "Come and sit next to me," he said. "We are both of us lonely this night, I think."

She changed her seat and he put his arm around her shoulder. They sat for a long time in silence, until the fire burned out, the two similar black heads close together, the two fine-boned dark faces quiet and very grave.

There was no peace for Frances that night. Alasdair's lovemaking had been long and slow and lingering, as if he wanted to touch and memorize every part of her, as if he knew he would never touch her like this again. As if he knew he were saying good-bye.

The worst anguish of all was her own helplessness. There was nothing she could do to stop him. But I cannot live without you, her heart cried out to him silently. Alasdair, I cannot. I cannot.

He murmured to her, and called her love names, and the anguish rose even higher in her heart.

He went to sleep and she lay awake and stared at the partially open window. She tried not to be restless; he needed his sleep this night. Finally she could bear lying motionless no more and got out of the bed.

He woke a few minutes later, sensing her absence. He looked around and saw her standing in front of the window in the darkness, her head pressed against the glass.

"Frances," he said. "Do not."

She heard his voice, heard the pleading in it. She

wiped the tears from her face with her fingers before she turned around. She could not let go now. She could not let him leave with his mind full of fear for her.

"I'm all right," she said shakily. "I will be all right."

"Come back to bed, m'eudail. It's cold."

She crawled in next to his warmth and lay against the hard strength of his body. His arms enfolded her.

He spoke over her head. "Frances. In the future it may be necessary for you to remember you are English. You have family with some . . . influence. You may find it necessary to call upon them."

She knew, without asking, that he did not mean she would need help for him.

"I will remember, Alasdair." She drew a deep breath. "And Van and I will take care of the clan."

He held her closer. "That's my brave girl."

"Go to sleep, darling," she said softly. "You need your rest." And a few minutess later, still holding her in his arms, he did.

The town of Inverness awoke the following morning to the sound of drums and pipes calling the army to muster. Alasdair and Niall were on foot at the head of the MacIans, not far behind the prince, who rode at the head of his army on a gray gelding. Frances and Van watched silently from the sidelines as the column swung to the east, out of Inverness and toward Duncan Forbes's empty house of Culloden, which was their destination.

Niall marched beside his father, his spirits rising with every step. The sound of his own battle song on the pipes filled his heart with joyous anticipation. They had prevailed against the Sassenach before. They would do so again tomorrow.

Alasdair spent several hours seeing his clan quartered in the park of Duncan Forbes's fine house. Patiently he went from man to man, calling each by name and speaking a heartening word.

"Mac mhic Iain, Mac mhic Iain," he was greeted on every side by smiling faces. It was late in the afternoon when he finally went up to Culloden House to meet with the prince and his council of advisers. Lord George Murray was just arriving as well. He had stayed in Inverness to bring up the men who had been quartered in the neighborhood of the town. He and Alasdair went into the meeting together.

Niall remained with the clan, talking to Alan Ruadh and his sons, waiting for the food to be distributed.

Alasdair returned to his men with a deep, hard line carved between his brows. "Father," Niall asked apprehensively, "what happened?"

"That damn fool O'Sullivan has chosen the moor as our battleground," Alasdair replied. "No one, of course, thought fit to consult Lord George on this trifling matter."

Niall stared at his father. "We would do better if we had some hills," he said.

Alasdair cursed. "Any Highlander could tell you that. Lord George wants to take up our ground on the other side of the Nairn water. The ground there is hilly and boggy. The Sassenach could not effectively use their cannon or horse."

"Dhé!" said Niall. "And did the prince agree?"

"The prince is no longer listening to Lord George or to the chiefs," Alasdair snapped. "We are to fight on the moor."

Niall pulled his plaid close around him. It was cold and he was hungry. "When are the provisions coming up, Father?"

Alasdair looked bleak. "There are no provisions. Hay of Restalrig neglected to bring the food wagons from Inverness."

Niall stared in disbelief.

Alasdair straightened his own plaid. "Lord George has given command of the battle to the prince. He himself will command the right wing. We are to fight next to him, then the Camerons and the Appin Stewarts. The MacDonalds are to have the left."

"By tradition the MacDonalds have always had the right," said Niall blankly.

"Not tomorrow," Alasdair replied wearily. "Well, there is food for you and me at Culloden House. The rest of the clan is to be issued a biscuit a man."

Niall cursed in Gaelic, soft and long.

"Aye," said his father. "I quite agree."

The following morning, April 15, the whole army marched up the braeside to Culloden Moor, a flat plain at the northwestern edge of the much larger stretch of rough upland country known as Drummossie Moor. The army was drawn up in battle order and was reviewed by the prince, who was pleased by the spirit of his men.

The clansmen who stood on Culloden Moor that morning, wearing the traditional plaids of their hills and following, in feudal fashion, the orders of their chiefs, had eaten only one biscuit in the last twenty-four hours. They stood, unwavering, in battle formation, their faces to the northeast, their eyes searching the heather for the first sign of Cumberland's infantry.

Cumberland did not come. By eleven o'clock Lord George learned that it was the duke's twenty-fifth birthday and he had decided to stay at Nairn to celebrate. There would be no battle that day. The prince grandly told his men that they might refresh themselves with sleep "or otherwise." But there was no "otherwise." John Hay of Restalrig had still not brought up the food from Inverness.

The chiefs, the generals, the prince, and his Irish advisers held a meeting. Alasdair and Lochiel counseled retreat.

"This is no field for the clans," Alasdair said forcefully. "They have no stomach to stand waiting as they are waiting now. And with empty bellies too!"

"The food will be got!" Hay said hysterically.

"When, for God's sake?" demanded Lord George.

"I will not retreat," the prince said flatly. "You made me retreat from Derby and all has gone wrong since then. I will not retreat now."

"Very well," said Lord George heavily. "If that is so, then I am willing to lead a surprise attack on Cumberland's camp at Nairn."

The prince leapt at the suggestion. After some discussion, Alasdair and the chiefs concurred. It was to be a night attack. The clans were to march at dusk that day, pass around the town of Nairn, and fall upon the Sassenach soldiers in the darkness. As Alasdair remarked sourly to Lochiel, "Anything is better than standing on that moor as canon fodder."

The march to Nairn began at dusk. For as long as he lived, Niall was to have nightmares about that night march. To begin with, it was found that a third of the men had slipped away to Inverness in order to seek food. Time was lost while a futile attempt was made to round them up, and the march did not commence until nearly eight o'clock.

Lord George Murray was in a black mood. Niall, watching, saw the prince put an arm around his shoulders, but Lord George merely took off his bonnet, bowed coldly, and said nothing in reply to the prince's words. Lord George then took his place in the van of the army and the march began.

The MacIans were in the front along with Lord George's Athollmen, the Camerons, and the Appin Stewarts. Their guides were the officers of Clan Mackintosh, whose country this was, but the ground through which they passed was treacherous—boggy and full of quagmires. It was dark, foggy, and cold, and all along the way exhausted men threw themselves onto the heather and refused to move further. The gap between the van under Lord George and the rear under the prince widened.

A halt was called and in the darkness, while tired and hungry men struggled to collect themselves, Lord George and O'Sullivan argued bitterly. Niall listened in a kind of daze. This can't be happening, he thought. The night was eerie with fog. The very ground seemed to shift and move under his feet. It was four more miles to Nairn.

Next to him Niall heard his father's voice, speaking with such familiar acidity that he was, unaccountably, heartened. "If we are to make Nairn before dawn," said Alasdair, "we had best stop arguing and get the army moving forward."

But when the first light began to streak the sky, the Highlanders were not yet at Nairn. In the distance Niall could hear the English drums beating the call to order. A surprise attack was impossible. The army was ordered to retreat. In the growing light, the exhausted, starving clansmen retraced their steps to Culloden House, where they fell in their tracks to sleep. There was still no food.

Two hours later the pipes sounded to call the men into position once more on Culloden Moor.

Niall had had no sleep at all, nor had Alasdair. When they marched back to the moor the army left some thousand men asleep where they had fallen; nothing, not even the rant of their clans shrilled on the pipes, had been able to wake them. In spite of this, behind Niall and Alasdair, to the left of the Athollmen in the line of battle, stood some five hundred MacIans.

The army that faced the Duke of Cumberland on the sixteenth was in considerably poorer condition than it had been twenty-four hours earlier. The men had made a night march of nearly twenty miles and consequently had had no sleep. For two days they had subsisted on a ration of a biscuit and water. They had lost almost two thousand of their number to desertion and exhaustion. The French adviser to the prince, the Marquis d'Eguilles, wrote that morning to the French king: "In vain I represented to the prince that he was still without half his army; that the greater part of those who had returned had no longer any targets; that they were all worn out with fatigue; and that for two days many of them had not eaten at all." In spite of the French ambassador's advice to retreat, the clans that morning stayed in position on Culloden Moor.

Niall stood beside his father and watched the English lines form. Snow was falling. Once Cumberland had his cannon placed, he began to cannonade the Highland line.

The cannon fire went on and on. The prince, waiting for Cumberland to initiate the attack, rode up and down among his troops encouraging them.

The deadly round shot went on. "For God's sake, Father," Niall cried to Alasdair, "when are we going to charge?" Men were falling all around him.

Alasdair stood among his dying MacIans, sword and

pistol in hand. There was both anguish and anger on his face. "Go to Lord George, Niall! Tell him I cannot hold my men longer."

Niall ran hard until he reached Lord George, who was seated on his horse among his Athollmen looking like a thundercloud. Niall repeated his father's message.

"I will send to the prince and ask if he wants me to charge," Lord George snapped immediately. "Get back to your position, MacIan."

Niall had scarcely returned to Alasdair's side when the order came to charge.

Alasdair turned to his men and screamed the war cry of the clan: "Buaidh no Bas! Buaidh no Bas!" And, raising his sword, he began to run forward. Without a moment's hesitation, the men of his clan followed their chief.

Lord George and the Athollmen were to their left, Lochiel and the Camerons to their right. The entire right wing of the Highland army came on in a surge of tartan and pipes, and broke through Cumberland's first line.

Niall fought to keep his shoulder next to his father's. The fighting was fierce and Lord George's command found itself pressed between their own center line and a wall on their right flank. The quarters were so tight that Niall could hardly use his sword. They kept going forward, climbing over their own dead as they penetrated the ranks of Barrel's regiment.

It was not until much later that Niall was to learn what had happened to the left wing of the Highland army. It received orders at last from the prince to charge, just as the right had, but the MacDonalds, angry and sullen that their traditional position on the right had been taken from them, refused to advance.

The Duke of Perth, commanding the left wing, vainly

urged them on. "Claymore! Claymore!" he shouted. "Convert the left into the right. Behave with your usual valor and henceforth my name is MacDonald!"

The battle wavered before them. In anguish Mac-Donald of Keppoch called out, "Mo Dhia, an do threig Clann mo chinnidhmi?" (My God, have the children of my clan abandoned me?) He rushed forward, pistol in one hand and drawn sword in the other. He was shot down immediately and the clan, which had begun to move forward slowly, halted.

Niall and Alasdair were deep inside the enemy lines when the English began to reform behind them. Men were falling all around them, from musket shot in front of them and bayonets behind. In ones and twos and then in groups, the Highlanders began to fall back.

Still Alasdair pressed forward with Niall at his side. It was a soldier from Sempill's regiment who fired the shot that hit the Earl of Morar in the breast.

Niall dropped to his knees beside his wounded father. Alasdair's eyes were open and he looked at his son. "I'll get you away, Father," Niall said urgently. "Can you put your arm around my shoulder?"

Alasdair shook his head. His voice was perfectly clear although very low. "Niall," he said, "comma leat misse, mas toil leat do bleatha thoir 'n arrigh dhuit fhein!" (Niall, do not think of me, take care of yourself if you value your life.)

Niall looked around him wildly and a man of his clan came to his side. Together they lifted Alasdair in his plaid and began to retreat from the field.

The battlefield was in chaos, with the Highland army now in full retreat. Niall carried the body of his wounded father further and further away from the enemy lines, away from the moor, his eyes straight ahead of him, his exhausted legs trembling with effort.

He turned at the sound of his name and saw a wounded MacIan clansman leaning on the shoulder of his own son. "Is it Mac mhic Iain?" the man asked sorrowfully.

"Yes," Niall replied. "He has been wounded. We are trying to get him to a place of safety."

The man removed his own arm from around the neck of his son. "Go to Mac mhic Iain," he said sternly. Then, as the boy hesitated, "Your first duty is not to your father but to your chief. Go." And the boy came and took up a piece of the plaid on which they were carrying Alasdair.

On and on Niall and his two clansmen went, Niall in front, the two men behind, Alasdair's body slung in its plaid between them. Toward Balrain they came upon a little barn. "Inside!" Niall called, and they carried Morar in and placed him on the ground. Niall bent to his father and found he was dead.

Outside came the thunder of hooves and then the sound of English voices. A party of dragoons in pursuit of fleeing clansmen had found the barn. Niall drew his sword and motioned the two MacIans to do the same. The three men ranged themselves between the door and the body of their chief and prepared to die with him.

There came another shout and then the clink of steel as troopers once more mounted their horses. The sound of hooves and then silence. The dragoons had been called away.

Niall sheathed his sword and turned back to his father. Alasdair's chest was covered in blood, but his face was peaceful.

"I cannot just leave him here for the Sassenach to find," Niall cried despairingly.

"Mac mhic Iain." It was one of the clansmen speaking. Niall looked at him in bewilderment before he realized it was he who was being addressed. "Mac mhic Iain," the man said again, "burn the barn."

Niall looked around him. It was quiet in the small barn now. Peaceful. Fire. "Yes," he said. "We will send him out cleanly, with fire. There will be nothing of him for the Sassenach to defile."

They built a funeral pyre out of straw for Alasdair Niall Hector Donald MacIan, Earl of Morar, Mac mhic Iain, and set it afire. Then the three of them took to their heels and ran for their very lives.

21

Van knew as soon as the first of the fleeing Highlanders reached Inverness that the ax she had been dreading for so long had fallen at last. The army was beaten. She remembered her promise to her father and told her mother to make ready to leave.

Frances did not want to go.

"If we stay, Mother, we will be made prisoners," Van said relentlessly. "That will not help Father or Niall at all."

"I cannot leave until I know what has happened to them!" Frances cried wildly.

"I know," Van replied. "I know." She had studied her maps diligently and now she said, "We shall remove to Beauly for the moment, Mother. We should be able to get further news there. But I promised Father I would get you out of Inverness!"

Frances finally acquiesced and with the two clansmen whom Alasdair had left for their protection, the two women rode west out of Inverness only half an hour before the Duke of Cumberland entered the town. Cumberland immediately appropriated the house recently occupied by the prince—"my cousin Charles," as the duke called him. The prince's former hostess, the dowager Lady Mackintosh, was made a prisoner.

Cumberland ordered that no quarter was to be given

to the defeated Jacobites. All those who had taken up arms for the prince were to be regarded as traitors and outside the law.

Orders were issued that no one was allowed to go near the wounded rebels, who still lay on the battlefield entwined with the already dead.

The pursuing army had sabered pretty well everyone they saw during the pursuit, whether they were innocent bystanders or Jacobite soldiers, yet there were still enough prisoners to fill the jail at Inverness to overflowing.

Orders were given that the wounded prisoners were to be offered no medical assistance. Two doctors with the prince's army, also prisoners, asked for permission to treat the wounded about them. They received no permission and their instruments and medicines were confiscated. They did their best with their unaided hands.

It was three days before Cumberland allowed anyone on the field of battle and then he sent detachments of soldiers to kill all those who were still alive.

The duke had come north with a sanction from his father the king "to do whatever is necessary for the suppressing of this unnatural rebellion." He was going to do his duty.

News came to Frances and Van at Beauly that the prince had got away. Lord George Murray was also known to be safe.

Several Camerons fleeing through Beauly reported seeing Niall carrying his father off the field. There was no word of Alan.

"If I thought they were lying on that bloody field I would go to the duke myself and beg to be allowed to look for them," Frances said despairingly.

"The clan would not have left Father or Niall wounded on the field, Mother," Van replied. "Not so long as there was a man of them left to carry them away. If they are lying on that field, they are dead."

Frances' face was white and set. "I think your father is dead, Van. I can feel it."

"Mother." Van's nostrils were pinched-looking. "I think we should go to Morar. If they are alive they will look for us there. Or they will send us word."

"Yes," Frances said dully. "Yes. And I promised your father I would be there for the clan."

So they went southward, down the Great Glen, only a day in advance of companies of Cumberland's soldiers who were bringing his ultimatums to the towns of the Highlands:

All arms were to be surrendered, under penalty of hanging;

Information was to be laid against hidden rebels, under penalty of hanging;

The young pretender was to be surrendered, under penalty of hanging. . . .

It was at Fort Augustus, still in ruins from the work of Lochiel the previous month, that Van and Frances first heard that the prince was ahead of them. He had been through Fort Augustus the day before.

From Fort Augustus the two MacIan women turned west, toward Loch Arkaig, where they stayed the night at Lochiel's house of Achnacarry. Lady Lochiel was in residence, although she spoke of taking the children to a cottage in the hills the following day.

"I fear the English will be here looking for Donald," she told Frances and Van. "I do not want to be made a prisoner."

Lochiel was alive, she told them, but injured in both

ankles. He had been carried off the field by his clansmen.

She too had heard that Niall was seen carrying Morar off the field. She knew nothing more of their fates.

The prince had been through Loch Arkaig the previous day.

"Who is with him?" Van asked.

"Just three men," Lady Lochiel replied. "They stayed at Cameron of Glen Pean's cottage, so that is how I know. I believe they were heading for Morar."

"Morar is inaccessible enough to shelter him for a while," Van said grimly. And the following morning she and Frances, with their two MacIan escorts, turned westward once more, toward the braes of their own country.

Niall was making for Morar also. After the battle he and his two companions had gone to Ruthven to join Lord George Murray. Lord George, however, was understandably bitter about the way the battle had been conducted and furious at the incompetence of both O'Sullivan and Hay of Restalrig. He told Niall he was resigning his commission and would not order his men to remuster. He was going to send a message to the prince to recommend that he return to France.

Consequently, when Niall set out for Morar he was a day behind the prince and only hours ahead of his mother and Van.

Charles Edward spent the day of April 20 in Morar, sleeping in a clansman's cottage. That night, under a moon four days from the full, he walked to Borrodale on the north shore of Loch nan Uamh.

It was early in the afternoon of the twenty-first when Niall arrived at Creag an Fhithich.

The old men and the women servants were still

there. They broke into terrible keening when they heard that Mac mhic Iain was dead. Niall was wandering around the rooms like a lost ghost when he looked out a window and saw Van and Frances coming wearily up the drive.

Frances knew the moment she saw her son standing alone in the doorway that Alasdair was dead.

Niall told them about the battle as they sat in Frances' small sitting room with the fire burning in the chimneypiece. His voice was low and he did not look at his mother. He could not bear to see her eyes.

"I could not leave his body for the Sassenach," he finished at last. There was deep bitterness in his voice. "He would have been a likely trophy for them."

"Cumberland would not allow anyone on the battlefield to search for their men." Van's voice was as bitter as his had been. "He posted guards, Niall, to keep the families away. You did well by Father. He would have been left there to rot."

At that Frances cried out.

Van put a hand on her mother's arm. "I'm sorry, Mother."

Frances didn't answer, just stared ahead of her with dazed-looking eyes and set face. Van looked at Niall but he only shook his head uncertainly.

"I think you should rest, Mother," Van said softly. "It's been a long, hard journey. You're exhausted. Go up to bed for a while."

"Yes," said Frances. It was the first word she had spoken since Niall had told her Alasdair was dead. She rose from her chair slowly and painfully, like an old woman, Van thought.

"Shall I come up with you?" Van asked.

"What?" Frances paused and looked at her.

"Shall I come with you?" Van repeated.

"Oh. No, darling. No. I shall be all right." She clutched her plaid around her shoulders as if she were very cold, and left the room.

Their bedroom was so cold. Frances stood in the doorway for a full minute before she could bring herself to go in. Then, as she paused, uncertain, by the foot of the bed, Morag came in to light the fire.

The room was warmer with the fire going, and more cheerful, but nothing would ever fill its emptiness again.

Alasdair was dead.

She had feared it for so long, lived for so long with the possibility of this moment, that she had thought herself prepared. She had been wrong.

He was dead. Niall had burned his body on the battlefield. She would never see him again.

She could not believe it.

She looked slowly around the room and clutched the plaid even closer to her breast.

Her whole life had been spent within the circle of Alasdair's arms. How was she to go on without him? What would she do? How would she live? After a moment she found herself walking like a sleepwalker to the wardrobe that held his clothing. She opened the door, took out one of the shirts she herself had made for him, and slowly raised it to her face.

Anguish struck her like a blow in the stomach, and she sat down on the small blue chair and wept.

Downstairs in the sitting room Niall and Van talked quietly.

"Have you news of Alan?" was the first thing Van said after Frances had gone upstairs.

"I think he is safe. Lochaber was wounded and taken off the field; I believe Alan got away also."

Niall looked at her somberly. "Alan fought," he said. "Both Lochaber and Alan. They did not hang back with the rest of the MacDonalds. Someone at Ruthven told me he had seen Alan and some men of Lochaber leaving the field after the English overwhelmed us. That is all I know, Van."

Van nodded without any other reply.

"Father had the right of it," Niall said. "This whole enterprise should not have been undertaken without French help. But, even so, we came so close, Van! If it had not been for that damn night march, if there had been food, if the prince had chosen other ground . . ."

"But he did not," Van said wearily. Then, "You must get away to France, Niall."

"Aye. I must get to Jeannie. She will be fretting for news of me."

"Where is the prince now?" Van asked.

"Angus has told me he is in Borrodale. Young Clanranald and Elcho are to join him there."

"You must join him also," Van said. "The French will send a ship to take him off. It is your only chance of escape, Niall."

"Yes." He looked at her gravely. "I do not know how long you and mother will be safe here, Van. But how are you to get ship for France?"

"I will post watchers," Van said. "If the English come I will take Mother to the cave. I'll get blankets and food out there tomorrow."

Niall looked around him. "They may burn Creag an Fhithich," he said.

"I'll get some of the pictures down to the cave too. And we'll bury the silver."

For the first time since the battle Niall smiled. "Father would be proud of you."

Van's eyes were wide. "I cannot believe he is gone," she said. "I keep expecting to hear his step at the door."

"I know," said Niall. "Somehow I always thought Father was immortal." He rubbed his forehead in a tired gesture. "There was nothing I could do, Van," he went on a little desperately. "I was right next to him when the shot hit him."

Van went over to where he was sitting and, standing in front of him, she put her hands on his shoulders. "He told me to save myself," Niall said in a muffled voice. He put his arms around her waist and pressed his face against her breast.

Van's heart ached with grief, for him and for her father. "You did well by him, Niall," she repeated, and felt him shudder under her hands.

"He was in the front," he said. "He was always in the front."

"He was Mac mhic Iain." Van's voice was slightly muffled.

"Aye." Niall dropped his arms and Van stepped back. "He was a chief." He drew a deep, sobbing breath. "Van, I am Mac mhic Iain now."

"There is nothing you can do here in Morar, Niall," she said in answer to his unspoken question. "You must go to France. Father did that once, after Sheriffmuir. There will be an Act of Indemnity one day, and then you can come home. But you have a wife in France, and a bairn soon too. Go with the prince. I will do all I can here in Morar."

He looked up at her out of darkened eyes. His shirt was filthy and he had not shaved in days. "If it becomes necessary," he said hesitantly, "could you not send to Linton?"

Van's face closed. "Go get a bath and a shave," she

said. "You are not likely to get another for quite some time."

Niall left Creag an Fhithich under cover of darkness to walk over the hills to Borrodale to join the prince. After he had gone, Van sat down at the harpsichord. It was the first time she had been near an instrument since last September, when they had left Morar to join the prince in Edinburgh.

Seven months, Van thought. Seven months, and the whole world had changed.

She began to play, but after only a few notes she stopped. All her life, music had been the great healer for her; it was frightening to realize that it could not help her now. She sat for a long time looking at her still fingers on the keys. It seemed as if there were no music left in her at all.

Seven months.

Edward was lost to her. Father was dead. Niall and Alan were in hiding.

Seven months.

For the first time since she was eight years old, Van bowed her head and cried.

The news of the victory at Culloden was brought from Inverness to London in eight days' time. Church bells rang in thanksgiving. The Duke of Cumberland was toasted in every household. Civilized society had been saved from the savage Highland menace.

The government met and had only words of praise for the Duke of Cumberland and his work. Edward sat in stony silence and listened to the advice that was offered to the prime minister on how to deal with the Highlands.

"Starve the country by your ships, put a price on the

heads of the chiefs, and let the duke put all to the fire and the sword," said Lord Newcastle.

The Duke of Richmond agreed. "I own I had rather the duke should destroy the rebels than that they should lay down their arms. The dread example of a great many of them being put to the sword, and I hope a great many of them hanged, may strike a terror in them and keep them quiet."

"We have been at war with France for years," Edward said quietly, "and we have never behaved in the fashion you are presently advocating. May I remind you, gentlemen, that we are a Christian country living in a civilized century."

"That is precisely it, Linton," Lord Newcastle said in a hard voice. "The Highlanders are not civilized. They must be dealt with as the savages they are."

"What you are advising is wholly outside the recognized rules of war," Edward said sharply. "If you turn Cumberland's army loose on the Highlands, it is not merely the rebels who were in arms who will suffer."

"We all know you have a weakness for Highlanders, Linton," someone down the table said acidly.

The prime minister, Lord Pelham, spoke. "The clans have shown themselves to be the only available reservoir for a Jacobite army. It is our duty to see to it that they never rise for a Stuart again."

Lady Linton was waiting in the drawing room of Linton House when Edward arrived home.

"What happened, darling?" she asked when he was standing in front of the chimneypiece facing her.

"It's as I thought. They were terrified by that invasion. They want vengeance." His eyes were burning with a cold blue light.

Lady Linton clasped her hands together tightly. He

frightened her when he looked like this. "What will you do?" she asked.

"I resigned from the government, of course. I spoke to Pelham after the meeting." His lips were tight. "In a nutshell, they are giving Cumberland carte blanche to do what he will."

"What of Morar? Do you know, Edward? And Niall?"

"There are few details, except that the prince escaped. Damn him. The battle was a rout. The rebels had upwards of two thousand killed."

"Dear God," Lady Linton breathed. "Edward, what of Frances and Van? Will they at least be safe?"

"No one will be safe, Mother," came the grim reply.

"But what can we do?"

Edward looked at her. His blue eyes glittered. "Tomorrow at dawn," he said, "I ride north for Scotland."

III
May–October 1746

From the lone shieling of the misty island
Mountains divide us, and the waste of seas—
Yet still the blood is strong, the heart is Highland
And we in dreams behold the Hebrides.
                    —David Macbeth Moir,
                        The Canadian Boat Song

22

Niall discovered the prince in a small cottage not far from Borrodale House. With him were several of his Irish officers and young Clanranald and Lord Elcho. When Niall arrived he found the group in the midst of a strategy discussion.

The prince greeted Niall warmly and pressed him to join the loyal gathering in front of the smoky fire of the small cottage. Charles, it seemed, had resolved to try to return to France. "I am of little use to you on this side of the water," he told Niall. "In France, however, I can certainly engage the French court either to assist us effectually and powerfully, or at least to procure you such terms as you would not obtain otherwise. My presence there, I flatter myself, will have more effect to bring this sooner to a determination than anybody else."

It never even crossed Niall's mind that the prince might be flattering himself. "Aye," he agreed wholeheartedly. "And the French are certain to send a ship for your royal highness."

"That is what we were discussing before you arrived," Lord Elcho said. "I also think that the French will send a ship to take off his highness. And what is more, I think they will send it to Arisaig, where they landed him a year ago."

The stubborn look they had all learned to recognize crossed Charles's face. "I do not agree, Elcho. Arisaig is too obvious and too unprotected. I think we will all stand a better chance of escaping if we cross over to Skye or the Outer Isles."

For three days Charles Stuart and his loyal followers stayed in Borrodale debating their future course. The prince's final decision was aided by two events. The first was the arrival in Borrodale of Donald MacLeod of Skye, an old man of nearly seventy years of age. Donald was a seaman and had access to a boat. The other event was a rumor, to which Cumberland listened, that the prince had already escaped and was hiding on faraway St. Kilda. Accordingly, Cumberland ordered the fleet to St. Kilda to investigate, and the Long Island—that is, all the Outer Isles from Barra to the Butt of Lewis—was left unguarded.

At nightfall on April 26, Prince Charles Edward Stuart, fleeing for his life, left the mainland of Scotland for the Outer Isles. With him were his Irish officers; Donald MacLeod, his pilot; and Niall MacIan.

On May 3, two French frigates landed in Loch nan Uamh to rescue the prince. Learning that they had missed him, they instead took off the Duke of Perth, Lord John Drummond, and Lord Elcho. After a brief confrontation with a British naval contingent, the French ships returned home without their royal quarry.

Edward rode from London directly to Inverness. He wished to speak to the Duke of Cumberland personally before he rode to Morar.

The reality of Inverness was worse than he had imagined. The prison was packed and every time he passed it Edward could hear pitiful voices crying out for water. The prisoners who could not fit into the prison were being held on ships in the firth, packed together like cattle, with nothing to lie upon but the stones and earth of the ballast. There was no medical treatment available and little food or water.

Edward was granted an interview with the duke in Lady Mackintosh's house, which still served as the commander-in-chief's headquarters.

"Well, Linton," the duke said in exaggerated surprise when Edward was bowing before him. "What brings you into this unhappy part of the world?"

Edward looked at the king's son and made a heroic effort to refrain from speaking his mind on the subject of this "unhappy part of the world."

The Duke of Cumberland was not nearly as handsome as his cousin Charles. He was dressed, as befitted his role of commander-in-chief, in a magnificent scarlet frock coat with blue lapels edged with gold, but he was undeniably fat. His heavy face above the white foam of lace at his throat was very red, in contrast to the white curls of his wig. His dark eyes protruded noticeably and just now they were staring at Edward with unveiled suspicion.

"Your royal highness," Edward said respectfully, "I have come to beg you for a favor."

The protuberant black eyes glittered. "Oh? And what is that, my lord?"

"I wish to secure from you the safety of the Earl of Morar's tenants and property," Edward answered calmly, his blue eyes very steady.

The duke laughed. "The Earl of Morar is a proscribed traitor, my lord, and the king's enemy. His land as well as his head are forfeit to the crown." Edward did not reply and Cumberland added curiously, "The old earl is dead, did you know that? Killed at Culloden."

Edward's grave, attentive expression did not change. "I did not know. And the son?"

"Running for his life, like my cousin Charles."

"Is there any news of the young pretender, your highness?" Edward asked, and Cumberland slammed his fat, powerful hand down on the table behind which he was seated.

"He is believed to be in the Outer Isles," he answered angrily. "The navy is patrolling the Minches but we can get no word of him. I have offered thirty thousand pounds for his capture. It is my hope that one of these miserable wretches of clansmen will give evidence against him."

"It would certainly be in their interest to do so," Edward replied. "The Stuart pretender has brought nothing but sorrow and grief to those who support him."

Cumberland grunted. "And I am here, Linton, to make very sure that no one in this benighted country ever supports him again." His bulging black eyes glittered at Edward. "And that includes the Earl of Morar," he added coldly. "I shall do to Morar exactly what I did to Lovat's estate of Castle Dounie last week—pull it down stone by stone and lay the glen waste from the loch to the hills."

A muscle flickered along the line of Edward's jaw. When he spoke, however, his voice was quiet and respectful. "Have you sent men to Morar yet, your royal highness?"

"No." The duke leaned back in his chair and the wood creaked in protest. "Tomorrow I am sending three battalions of foot to Fort Augustus," he went on. "From there we will carry fire and sword throughout the whole of the Great Glen. Then we will move west." The duke's face was a shade more red than usual. "I mean to stamp out this Jacobite disease for good, Linton."

Edward went down on his knees. "As your royal highness knows," he said softly, "the Romney family has never supported the House of Stuart. My grandfather was one of those who escorted William of Orange to England, and since then the Earls of Linton have ever been among Hanover's chief supporters in Parliament."

"I am aware of all this." The fat red face of the king's son was unmoved. "Why do you want Morar, Linton?"

"I wish to marry Morar's daughter, your royal highness. I wish to save her home for her"—one golden eyebrow rose slightly—"for a wedding present," he finished. He bowed his bright head. "I beg this from you as a personal favor, your royal highness. A personal favor to your good and loyal subject."

The duke did not ask him to rise. "Morar's daughter," he said.

"Yes, your highness." Edward raised his eyes to the duke's face. "I love her, you see."

The fat red face was hard. It was evident the duke did not like being put in the position Edward was putting him in. "Morar was one of the worst of the traitors," he said. "It was his decision to join that made the rebellion possible."

"He has had his punishment, your highness," Edward replied soberly. "He is dead."

"The son is not dead." The duke stared grimly at the man on his knees before him. "I will not extend my protection to Morar's son."

The blue eyes before him were perfectly steady. "I understand, your highness."

"Have you spoken to the government about this matter?" Cumberland demanded abruptly.

"Yes, your highness. Lord Pelham has agreed to accept my surety for the loyalty of Morar and its people to his majesty King George—provided, of course, that this is acceptable to you."

There was a long hard silence. If Edward were finding his position uncomfortable, he gave no sign of it. "I cannot allow my cousin Charles to escape," the duke said at last.

"If it were ever in my power to capture Charles Stuart, I should do so unhesitatingly," Edward replied. "It would be best for everyone in this entire kingdom were he dead."

"Very well." The duke looked suddenly annoyed. "Get up, man, for God's sake. You can ride south tomorrow with the battalions going to Fort Augustus."

Edward's eyes were brilliant as he rose easily to his feet. "Thank you, your royal highness," he said. "You are very kind."

On the following morning, three battalions of the King's Foot, Cumberland's advance party, marched south halfway down the Great Glen to Fort Augustus. Edward accompanied them, and all during the long ride which took them along the shores of Loch Ness, he saw not one single human soul. The only native living creatures in sight were the red deer on the brae and the eagle on the mountain wall.

The weather was chill and cold, more like February than May, Edward thought.

At Fort Augustus he parted company with the English army and, with a MacDonald guide and one other essential companion, he struck west toward Loch Arkaig and the braes of Morar.

They buried the silver from Creag an Fhithich down near the shores of the loch. They carefully wrapped the most valuable paintings from the castle—the

Giorgione, the Titians, the Veroneses—and brought them out to the cave in the mountains Van and Niall had discovered as children. Frances also put together a box of the most important family papers, and this too they buried.

The men of the clan who had survived Culloden began to trickle home to Morar. Frances and Van rode around the hills and the braes that were home to so many MacIans and left word that if the "red soldiers" were seen, the men were to take to the heather.

"English soldiers will not molest women and children," Frances said. And she believed that until word began to filter through to Morar of what was happening in the area around Inverness.

"They are burning the cottages and driving off the cattle," Lachlan MacIan told Frances and Van. He had been injured in the battle but had managed to crawl off the field and a kind MacIntosh family had taken him in. "The hills are full of women and children who have nowhere to go and nothing to eat."

"Dear God in heaven," said Frances, truly appalled.

Van looked grimly determined. "Is there nowhere we can hide some of the cattle?" she asked Lachlan.

"The English are everywhere," came the somber reply. "And where they do not go, there are the Campbells."

"The Campbells," Van said with loathing.

"Aye. But the Campbells are better than the Sassenach, Lady Van. They are enemies but they are still Highland. They do not rape women."

"Rape?" Frances said faintly.

"Aye." A look of extreme anguish crossed Lachlan's face. "I saw it happen once. God help me, I was skulking in the heather high up on the hill when the soldiers came to the MacIntosh's cottage. They burned the house and then they raped Mrs. MacIntosh. Five of them. Her children were watching."

Van had not known it was possible to feel such anger. "You are right, Lachlan," she said in a low and trembling voice. "They are worse than Campbells. They are worse than the lowest vermin that crawl upon the earth. I would like to take a knife and personally geld every one of them."

"Van!" Frances was very pale. "Evidently it is not enough that the men hide from the soldiers. The women too must take to the hills. And the children."

"Aye. But if they burn our homes and drive off our cattle, what will we do, my lady?" Lachlan asked despairingly. "We will starve."

"We will think of something," Frances said with more confidence than she felt.

"Think of what, Mother?" Van asked after Lachlan had gone.

Frances closed her eyes briefly. "I don't know, Van." She pressed her hands to her face. "Your father would know what to do. We must try to think like him."

Van's face was bleak. "We are the conquered, Mother, and the Sassenach are the conquerors. I don't think even Father could change that. We are at their mercy. And may their souls burn in hell for all eternity for what they are doing to this country!"

The following day Van was oiling the few guns left at Creag an Fhithich when a clansman brought her the news that a party had been seen coming over the mountains toward Morar.

Van felt fear clutch her throat, but she managed to speak calmly. "Soldiers?" she asked.

"Na," came the reply. "There are three of them only, and one is a Highlander. The other two are dressed like Sassenach."

Van frowned. "Just three men only?"

"Aye, Lady Van. Only the three. Angus and I made certain of that."

Van was confused. She did not know if she ought to give the signal to hide or not. Three men hardly sounded dangerous, but suppose Donald and Angus were wrong and they were an advance party of some sort.

"You're sure none of them was in uniform?"

"Aye. One wore the trews and the other two were dressed like Sassenach gentlemen."

Van made up her mind. "How were they traveling? Where are they likely to be now?"

"They should be at the top of the loch by now, my lady. They had but two ponies."

Van took one of the guns she had been oiling and stuck it in her belt. She herself was wearing trews, as she had been out all morning. The other gun she handed to Donald MacIan, the man who had brought her the news. "I'll come with you," she said, "and see for myself."

Van, Donald, and Angus rowed most of the way up Loch Morar and then beached the boat and took to the hills. Van was as swift and as surefooted as the two men as they moved through the heather, coming ever closer to the route the strange trio was following. Finally they reached the point for which they were aiming, the pass where the rough mountain path came down to the shores of the loch. The three lay down in the heather and waited.

The day had been cold and overcast all morning but now a few rays of sun burned through the clouds. Van lay perfectly still, her eyes on the spot where the three men should appear.

They waited in silence for almost half an hour.

"One of the Sassenach is old," Donald murmured in her ear. "They are going slowly."

Van nodded but her puzzlement only increased. What on earth would an elderly English civilian be doing in the mountains of Morar?

"Look!" Angus hissed, and there, at last, coming along the rocky mountain path, was the mysterious trio. The Highlander was in front, leading a pony. Behind him, also walking, came another man dressed in a brown riding coat, breeches, and high boots. He was leading a pony on which sat the third man of the party. The Englishman on foot looked very big in contrast to the Highland guide.

As they came out of the mountains and had their first view of the loch, the entire party paused in instinctive tribute to the stunning beauty of the lake in its mountain setting. Just then the sun came out, and the deep still waters of the loch sparkled and threw back the reflection of the mountains that towered around it on three sides.

The sun was warm on Van's back and as she watched, the big Englishman removed his hat to let the sun's rays beat directly on his head. His uncovered hair was as bright as the sun whose warmth he was enjoying, and Van's heart knew him even before he looked up and she saw his face.

All her apparatus for breathing seemed to shut down. Edward. Her lips moved but no sound came out. The blood suddenly surged in her ears. Her heart was hammering in her chest. Edward. Here in Morar. She stood up and her knees shook.

"Come," she said over her shoulder to Donald and Angus. "Follow me."

23

He saw her coming through the knee-deep heather and he seemed to go very still. Van stopped when she was ten feet away from him; Angus and Donald halted behind her. She could feel her pulse beating in her head. She had never expected to see him here.

His eyes were bluer than the cobalt sky.

Van spoke first, her voice hard with the feelings she was trying to suppress. "What are you doing here?"

He didn't answer at first, just stood there looking at her with those impossibly blue eyes. Then, calmly, almost conversationally, "How are you, Van?"

The deep tones of his voice shook her almost as profoundly as the sight of him had done. "As well as can be expected," she answered shortly. Her breathing was still not normal. She made a great effort to steady it. Then, "What are you doing here?" she asked again.

"I came to see you, of course." Pause. "I came to help."

"Help?" Her laugh was hard, ironic. "And how do you plan to do that, my lord?"

He stood there holding the pony's reins and regarding her almost thoughtfully. Her slender body was braced and taut; her eyes glittered with hostility. He had not expected their meeting to be easy, but he had not quite expected this hard opposition either.

He smiled at her, his most disarming smile, the one full of lazy sunshine, and said, "If you would be kind enough to conduct us to a place of shelter, I will tell you." He gestured toward the clansman. "Lady Vanessa, this is Colin MacDonald, who has been kind enough to serve as our guide." He turned a little to the man on the pony. "And this the Reverend Mr. Drummond." The blue eyes returned to Van's face. "Mr. Drummond is elderly and has found the trip to be a hardship," he added softly.

Van's eyes narrowed as she took in the figure of the man on the pony. He was white-haired and thin and he certainly did look extremely weary. She had no idea what he was doing traveling with Edward, but she supposed she would find out soon enough. "I have a boat not far from here, sir," she said in a softer voice than any she had yet used. "From there it is but a short row down the loch to my home. I'm sure my mother will make you welcome."

The old man gave her an extraordinarily sweet smile. "Thank you, Lady Vanessa." His accent was unmistakably Scots.

Van shot Edward a sharp, puzzled look before she said, in a clipped voice, "If you will follow me?"

He put his hat back on over his bright locks, raised the pony's reins a trifle, and replied composedly, "Certainly."

They walked in silence, Van and her two clansmen in the front, then Edward leading the minister's pony, then Colin MacDonald. The only sound was Van's occasional warning to Edward to watch out for an obstacle in the path.

At the first sight of the small boat, Edward said,

"Van, you and I and Mr. Drummond will go by boat. Colin can take the ponies if your two men will be good enough to show him the way."

Van gave him a hostile look. They were precisely the arrangements she had had in mind, but she did not like this easy assumption of command. "Very well, my lord," she said. The emphasis on his title was sarcastic and deliberate.

Edward made no move to touch her as she got nimbly into the boat, but he virtually lifted the elderly Mr. Drummond into his seat. Then Edward himself got in and picked up the oars. He pushed off expertly and began to row, smoothly and powerfully pulling the small boat through the shining waters of the loch.

"You told me that Morar was beautiful," he remarked easily to Van as his head lifted to look about him, "but one has to see it to truly comprehend."

"Yes," Van responded tersely. His knees were almost touching hers and she was angry at the effect his closeness was having on her. She turned to Mr. Drummond. "Did you come from Edinburgh, sir?"

"No, Lady Vanessa." The old man's eyes were a very light, very clear blue. "We came from Inverness."

Inverness! Van's eyes flew to Edward. "What were you doing in Inverness?" she asked breathlessly.

"I do not wish to discuss Inverness with you, Van, while I am rowing a boat." His voice was perfectly pleasant. "Let us wait until we reach Creag an Fhithich, shall we?"

There was a long, tense pause. Then, "All right," she agreed tightly.

"I have never been in this part of the Highlands before," Mr. Drummond remarked. "I am from Inverness, myself, Lady Vanessa."

"It is not an easy trip from Inverness to Morar,

unless you go by sea," Van replied. She looked at Edward. "Did you walk the whole way?"

He shook his head. "I abandoned my horse at Loch Arkaig. He could not handle the rough terrain." He rested on his oars for a moment and looked at her. "I could not precisely see myself on a pony," he said humorously.

Her eyes fell. Her hands, hidden by the folds of her plaid, clenched. "No," she managed to say. "No, one cannot see you on a pony."

They came around a small promontory and saw the castle. Mr. Drummond gave an exclamation and Edward stopped rowing for a minute in order to look.

He could not imagine anything more different from Staplehurst. His home was the epitome of civilization: gracious, balanced, with stretching manicured lawns and artfully landscaped fountains and lakes and waterfalls. It was the result of a highly developed culture, created for living on the grand scale, full of elegance and harmony and comfort.

Creag an Fhithich was the product of a totally different kind of spirit. It was stunningly beautiful, but utterly opposed to everything he had created at Staplehurst.

He and Alasdair MacIan, he realized, would not have had a thought in common.

He looked from the castle to the face of Alasdair's daughter. His plan for saving Morar and winning Van now seemed far more fraught with obstacles than he had previously anticipated. "It is magnificent," he said soberly.

"Aye," said Van. "You can beach the boat over there." She pointed, and following her instructions, he brought the boat to shore.

The front hall of the castle was a depressing room paneled in dark oak. Van spoke in Gaelic to a servant and then said, to the two men with her, "Mother is in the drawing room. Follow me." She led them up a set of narrow spiral stairs whose walls were covered with nails where once decorations had hung. Glancing around to see if Mr. Drummond were all right, Van caught Edward's eyes on the now-naked walls.

"The walls used to be hung with swords, claymores, broadswords, and dirks," she said flatly. Edward did not reply, but continued to follow her up the stairs, which curved upward in the traditional clockwise direction, he noticed. Stairs in old fortresses were always built thus so that a defender would have the benefit of the free right-handed swing of his sword arm against a mounting attacker.

At the top of the stairs was a set of large double doors. Van opened them and led the two men into a very large, very lovely room. A woman was seated at the far side of the room, near the largest fireplace Edward had ever seen. She put down her sewing as they entered, and Edward heard Van say, "Mother, may I introduce the Earl of Linton."

Edward smiled at Frances MacIan and saw her lovely face light with warmth at the sound of his name. "You look very like your father," she told him as he bent over her outstretched hand. Then, with a slight catch in her voice, "I am so very glad to see you, Edward!"

Much gladder than her daughter, Edward thought ruefully as he turned to present the Reverend Mr. Drummond.

"Mr. Drummond!" Frances cried, surprised. "Whatever are you doing here?"

"Do you know Mr. Drummond, Mother?" Van asked bewilderedly.

"Of course I know Mr. Drummond." Frances was

on her feet. "My dear sir, you did not make that terrible journey on foot?"

"No, no, Lady Morar. His lordship was kind enough to lead my pony the whole way," the elderly man reassured Frances. He took her hands. "May I tell you how very sorry I am about your husband?"

"Thank you," Frances replied in a low voice. Then, with the genuine concern that was so large a part of her charm, "You look exhausted, Mr. Drummond. Would you like to be shown to your bedchamber to rest?"

The clergyman replied gratefully that he would, and Frances summoned Morag to perform this chore. "The blue bedroom, Morag. And then bring tea to the drawing room, please."

The door shut behind Morag and the three of them were alone. Frances smiled at Edward. "And how is your mother?" she asked.

"Very well, Lady Morar," he replied courteously. "But concerned about you."

"Dhé!" said Van, leaping to her feet. "This is not a London reception! For God's sake, Edward, what were you doing in Inverness?"

It was the first time she had said his name. He looked at her slender, vibrant figure outlined against the fire. The narrow stem of her waist and the slim lines of her hips and long legs were clearly visible in the close-fitting tartan trews. The long black braid that fell across her shoulder was as thick as his arm. She was looking at him as if he were an enemy.

"I went to see the Duke of Cumberland," he said calmly.

"Cumberland!" said Frances. Her voice trembled with loathing and fear.

Something flared in Van's eyes. "Were you bringing him messages from London?"

"No." She was still and taut as an animal at bay. "No," he went on, "I am no longer connected to the government, Van. I resigned my position after Culloden."

Her lips parted slightly but she did not reply.

It was Frances who spoke. "You are aware, then, Edward, of what has been happening in the Highlands?"

"Yes." He turned to the Earl of Morar's widow. "It is a policy that has been dictated from London, Lady Morar. I spoke against it, but no one would listen. England is going to make very sure that the Highlands never rise for a Stuart again."

"Disarm us, then!" Frances cried passionately. "That is fair, after what has happened. But to take vengeance on women and children! Did you know that women and children are being burned out of their homes and sent to roam the hills? In this weather! With no food and no shelter! My God, Edward, England has never made war on women and children."

He regarded her with compassion. "It was the invasion, Lady Morar. England was terrified. The king was ready to flee to Hanover." He looked back at Van. "The measure of our vengeance," he said slowly, "is the measure of our fear."

"Niall was right then," Van said. "The retreat was a mistake. They should have gone on."

Morag brought the tea tray in and Frances began to pour. Edward accepted a cup from her hands, sipped it, and then put the cup down on a rosewood side table. He looked into the fire and said very quietly, "Where is Niall?"

He sensed rather than saw the look that passed between Frances and Van. They did not answer.

"He must be got away to France," Edward continued as if he had noticed nothing amiss. "I can arrange for a boat to take him out of Loch Morar if you wish."

There was dead silence. Then Frances spoke, her voice trembling. "*Thank you*, Edward. You are very good. But he is not in Morar at present."

Edward looked at her. "Can you get word to him?"

Frances shook her head. She looked unspeakably distressed. "He is somewhere in the Outer Isles," she said. "With the prince."

He heard the sharp sound of Van's indrawn breath. He turned his head to look at her. "Cumberland knows the prince is in the Outer Isles," he said slowly. "The hunt is up in earnest now. The seas around Skye and the Long Isle will soon be full of navy ships, if they are not there already."

"Oh, my God." It was Frances' low voice.

Van stared back at him, and her light eyes were full of challenge. "How would you get Niall away?" she said.

"I have a yacht." Her eyes widened slightly and he went on, "The *Sea Queen* was not ready to sail when I left London, but I left orders for it to be brought to Morar as soon as possible."

"The navy would stop and search it," Van said breathlessly.

"Not if I were aboard." His golden brows rose slightly. He had never looked more like a prince himself.

"Perhaps we could get word to Niall," Frances said suddenly.

"I can get him away for you," Edward replied. "But if he is taken there will be little I can do. He is a traitor under the law and the mood at court is not for leniency. I have some influence, but . . ."

"Yes," said Frances. She was very pale. "I understand." She drew a long, unsteady breath. Her hands were tightly clasped in her lap. They had met for the first time only minutes ago, but they spoke in the low, quiet tones of intimacy. They were both acutely conscious of Van's taut, silent figure, although neither of them looked at her. "Will the soldiers be coming to Morar?" Frances asked.

"Cumberland just sent three battalions to occupy Fort Augustus. They have orders to do to Locaber what has been done to Inverness. After Lochaber they will be in Morar."

"Dear God." Frances looked at him pleadingly. "Edward, if they drive off our cattle, the clan will starve."

In answer he looked from Frances to Van. "You asked before what I was doing in Inverness," he said to her.

Her light eyes were bright and wary. "Aye."

"I went to see Cumberland with a plan to save Morar."

The light eyes narrowed. "And what is that?"

"Marry me," he said simply. "Marry me and the duke will regard Morar as loyal to the crown. There will be no punishment exacted here. The clan will be safe."

Van's whole body seemed to quiver. Beside him he could hear the sharp intake of Frances' breath. "There will be an Act of Indemnity one day," Edward went on, "and when it comes, Niall can resume the title. Until then, Morar will be safe under my protection."

"And Cumberland agreed to this?" It was Frances' voice.

"Yes." He still looked at Van, who had said nothing. "Van?" he asked. His voice was very soft, very deep. Van looked at her mother.

Frances rose to her feet. "This is something for you two to discuss privately," she said. Then, to Van, "I'll be in my sitting room, darling, if you should want me." She moved soundlessly across the Persian carpet to the big double doors. They closed behind her with audible finality.

Edward and Van were alone.

24

They stood facing each other, separated by only six feet of space. Once he had been all the world to her, Van thought. Once all she had wanted out of life was to marry him. But that was before.

"Sweetheart." His voice was deep, caressing. "Don't look at me like that. We are not enemies, you and I."

Dhé. How she remembered that voice. Her nostrils flared and she straightened her already straight shoulders. "Perhaps not," she replied. "But too much blood lies between us, Edward. Too much has happened for us ever to be to each other what once we were."

His eyes kindled. "I don't believe that."

"It is true." Her voice was steady but he could hear the effort it was for her to keep it so. "My father died at Culloden. Do you know that?"

"I know that. And I am deeply sorry, sweetheart. But he knew what he risked when he went into this rebellion."

Color flushed into her face. "It is not Culloden!" she cried passionately. "You are right. That was a battle and they all knew what they risked. Father and Niall killed English soldiers, I know that well enough. It was *after* the battle, Edward." For the first time the still, frozen look had lifted from her face. It was aflame now with anger and contempt. "Did you know that

Cumberland would not let anyone go on the field to help the wounded or claim the dead? He posted guards, Edward, to keep us away! That is not war. That is something else altogether. We *always* gave medical aid to our wounded prisoners."

His eyes were very blue in his white face. "I know, Van."

"And now they are after us like beasts of prey. Murder. Plunder. Rape. Starvation. This is not merely the pursuit of rebels who were in arms against the government. This is extermination."

"I told you," he said. "The government is going to make very sure Scotland will never rise for the Stuarts again."

She took a step toward him. Her eyes were narrow and glittering. "You always told me that cruelty would never work on an animal. That you would only drive him into opposition. Does it work, then, on people?"

That reached him, as nothing else had. His own eyes blazed. "Christ, Van! Do you think I approve of what is being done here?"

She sustained that blue blaze for fully half a minute before she said, almost unwillingly, "No. I suppose not."

"You *suppose* not?"

"Well, then, why don't you do something about it?" she cried. "You are important enough. The government always listens to you."

"They are not listening to me now." There was a cold stillness in his voice that made her shiver. "I did my best, but it was no good. So I resigned."

"How noble of you," she said.

There was silence.

Van let out her breath. "All right, I'm sorry I said that," she flung at his grim white face. "But don't you see, Edward, how impossible a marriage would be between us now?"

"Come here and kiss me," he said. "Kiss me and then tell me that marriage between us is impossible."

"No!" she cried sharply, almost shrilly. She turned and walked away to the window and stood staring out at the loch. She was breathing rapidly. He saw the rise and fall of her breasts, the long slim line of her body, and his mouth hardened.

Van looked blindly out the window and tried to get a hold on her emotions. She could not marry Edward. It was impossible. Alan. She tried to think of Alan, whom she had heard was a prisoner now in Fort Augustus. She shook her head.

"If you do not marry me," he said, "I do not see how I can protect Morar."

Her head swung around. "There must be some other way," she said breathlessly.

"Not that I know of." His eyes moved to her throat, her breasts, to her waist and her hips. She felt the dark blood begin to throb in her veins. It was what frightened her most of all, this perilous attraction he had for her. Even now, with her country falling in ruins about her, she had only to look at his mouth to remember the feel of it on her mouth, on her body. She forced her voice to steadiness. "If I marry you," she said, "it will only be for Morar."

He was coming toward the window, his hair bright as a Viking's helmet in the light of the sun. He was so big. He stopped in front of her and placed his hands on her waist. "Then marry me for Morar," he said, and bent his head to hers.

It was as if a hood came down upon her mind. Her body arched up against his and her arms went up to circle his neck. The thick rope of her hair swung down past her waist, brushing against his hands as they slid caressingly along her hips. Her lips opened under the pressure of his. His body was so strong against hers.

He raised his head and looked down into her face. His eyes were narrow and brilliantly blue. "Marry me," he said imperatively.

"Yes," Van breathed, and he kissed her again.

Van closed her eyes and pressed her cheek into the hollow of his shoulder. It would be so easy to give in to him, she thought. So easy to lose herself in the physical bond that undeniably existed between them. But it was not as simple as that. He might not be an enemy, but he was still a Sassenach. A Sassenach and a Whig.

"Did you mean what you said before about helping Niall to escape?" she murmured.

She felt his lips in her hair. "Yes."

She filled her lungs with air, straightened her spine, and stepped away from him. "I can get word to Niall, I suppose," she said steadily, "but I know already that he will refuse to abandon the prince."

He looked down at her, his face very grave. "Then I cannot help him," he said.

"Edward." They were no longer touching, although they were still very close. "Edward," she said again, softly, pleadingly, "could you not help the prince to escape as well?"

His face changed and she knew, even before he spoke, what his answer would be. "No," he said flatly, coldly, finally. "No, I will not assist the prince. I will get Niall away because he is your brother, but I will have nothing to do with Charles Stuart, Van. Nothing."

Still she persisted. "But why, Edward? He is no longer a danger to England. Surely you can see that."

His eyes were as hard and cold as his voice. "He is a

danger to *Scotland*, Van, not to England. To help him escape is to inevitably bring more pain and suffering on the people of this poor country. For as long as he lives, Charles Stuart will be a center of intrigue and of trouble. There will be more plots, more schemes, and more good men will throw away their lives for this worthless prince. It would be far better for everyone if he were caught and executed. Then there would be an end to all this plotting, and Scotland could start to build her future on realities, not on tarnished dreams."

Part of Van knew that he was right, that his was the voice of reason. She herself over the last months had grown more and more disillusioned with the prince and the Stuart cause. If Niall had spoken thus to her, she would have accepted it. But she could not accept such words from Edward, who had ventured nothing in this conflict, who was an outsider, an Englishman, a Whig.

"I do not think my father felt he was throwing away his life," she said stiffly. "He gave his life for his prince and his true king. There are worse ways of dying."

"I have never been an admirer of lost causes," he answered shortly.

"Well, we in the north are not so cool and so calculating as you," she cried, goaded into anger. "We follow our hearts—and our loyalty, once given, is sacred. The poorest clansman who fought at Culloden would not betray the prince—no, not for all the gold in the elector's coffers!"

"That is probably true." He looked down on her from his great height. "And that is precisely why the government is coming down so hard on the Highlands. If they cannot change you, then they will break you." His mouth was a grim straight line. "And that is also why it would be best for the Highlands if the prince were captured. The government's vengeance would then be directed at its proper object, and the Highland way of life might survive."

Her hands clenched at her sides. "You speak of expedience. I speak of loyalty."

"Loyalty is a reciprocal arrangement, Van," he replied. The coldness had left his face and he looked very sober, sober and tired. "How loyal has Charles Stuart been to Scotland? Do you remember the plan you outlined to me when last we met? That the prince should declare his father King of Scotland? That he should forget England and hold Scotland alone? That he should call once more on the 'auld alliance' with France?"

Van's eyes dropped from his face to his chest. "Yes," she said in a low voice, "I remember."

He caught her off guard with his next question. "Was your father in favor of invading England?"

Her eyes flew upward for a brief, revealing moment. "I thought not," he said.

She turned away from him sharply and went to stand by the teapot. "Sweetheart." He spoke to her back and his voice was very soft. "Let us have done with raking over the past. We are in agreement at least on the present, that the government's actions in Scotland are unpardonable, are against all the recognized rules of war, and that we want to do what we can to help the innocent victims of this . . . this policy of extermination."

He meant what he said. She remembered what she had thought when Niall told her about Prestonpans, that she had thought Edward would never enjoy the bloodshed of battle as Niall had. She remembered Edward's infinite patience with his horses, his kindness, his concern for his tenants and his dependents. He had resigned his government position over this policy toward Scotland.

But the gulf was still there between them, the gulf between a man who had lost nothing and a girl who had lost all, the gulf between conqueror and conquered. It was not something she could forget.

He was, however, Morar's only chance for survival. She turned to face him and forced a smile. "I wondered why you were traveling with Mr. Drummond. Is he going to perform our marriage ceremony?"

"Yes." He smiled back, her favorite smile, the one that made him look like a boy. "Fortunately, he seemed to be devoted to your mother. He made the trip for her sake, not for mine."

"Perhaps he will be able to comfort her," Van said. She did not sound as if she placed much trust in this possibility.

"You are quite sure that your father is dead?" he asked gently.

"Oh yes." She looked at him out of shadowed eyes. "Niall carried him off the field. He burned his body in a small barn they found, so at least he was not left to rot until Cumberland ordered the bodies dumped into the mass graves."

"Christ," he said. "Van, I am so sorry."

"It is Mother who is suffering most. And I think, now, that it is going to be worse for her. You see, we have been so busy and so worried trying to save what we could here in Morar that there has not been much time for grief. But now, if we are truly safe . . ." She gestured. "The loss is going to strike her hard," she said. "Mother and Father—they did not have just an ordinary marriage."

There was a little silence; then he said quietly, "She must be wondering what we two have decided."

"That is so." Van made a motion of tucking her shirt into her trews. "Shall we go to see her?"

"You go," he said. "I will wait here."

"All right." She rang the bell. "I'll have Morag take you to your room," she said. "Are you hungry?"

"Starving," he replied instantly.

Her eyes smiled for the first time all day. "We'll feed you then, my lord. In an hour in the dining room? I'll have Fergus come and get you."

"An hour," he agreed.

Van waited until Morag appeared before she went up the stairs to see Frances.

"Well, darling?" her mother said gently as Van entered the small sitting room and sat down in silence.

"I shall marry him, of course." Van's voice was curiously flat and devoid of expression. "What other choice is there?"

Frances scanned her daughter's face. "I thought you loved him, Van."

"I did. But there is too much between us now for things to ever be as once they were."

"Darling, it is not fair to blame Edward for something over which he has no power."

"I know that." Van's thin hands moved restlessly in her lap. "But one cannot control what one feels, Mother. And I feel that there is blood between us. Father's blood," she added somberly, and looked to see her mother's reaction.

Frances waited a moment before she spoke. Then, quietly and deliberately, "Almost the last thing your father said to me before he marched for Culloden was that I should remember that I am English." Van's eyes widened. "I think he knew what would happen, Van. He knew and he told me to call upon my English relations in time of need." Frances held her daughter's eyes steadily. "Your father would not object now to your marrying the Earl of Linton. Of that I am quite certain."

Van's face relaxed very slightly. Then, after a moment, "You must write a letter for Niall. Lachlan will be able to find him."

"Yes. Yes, I will do that immediately." Frances, however, knew her son very well. "Van, I do not think he will leave the prince. Is it possible that Edward might . . . ?" Her voice trailed off at the bleak look on Van's face.

"Edward has informed me that he will have nothing to do with helping the prince to escape."

"Well, darling," Frances sighed. "One can hardly blame him. Indeed, it is something that he has agreed to help Niall."

"I wonder if he informed Cumberland about his yacht," Van said ironically.

Frances shook her head. "You heard him. He was not given Niall's life. He is probably endangering his own position by agreeing to get Niall away. If it were discovered, I am sure he would be in trouble."

"I wonder," said Van, "if we could slip the prince aboard the yacht without Edward's knowing."

The two women looked at each other. It was Frances who finally said no. "If Edward were not going to be on board, perhaps we could get away with it. But not if he is to be present himself. He is too shrewd not to spot the prince immediately. His accent would give him away, if nothing else."

"I suppose that is so." Van felt as if a weight had rolled off her chest at her mother's words. The possibility of smuggling the prince away on Edward's yacht had been in her mind ever since he had mentioned the boat. To do that, she thought, would be such a betrayal of Edward's trust . . . the relief that she would not have to do such a thing was enormous.

"The French will send a ship for the prince," she said stoutly. "I am sure of it."

"Well, I hope to God they do it soon." Frances shivered. "Edward said the Minch would soon be crawling with navy ships looking for them."

Van stood up. "I told Morag we would have dinner at four, Mother, if that is all right with you."

"That will be fine, darling. Did Edward and Mr. Drummond have any baggage?"

"Yes. It is coming on one of the ponies. I must go and make arrangements to have it sent to their rooms." She bent down to kiss Frances' cheek and then was gone.

Van's wedding was a very simple affair, celebrated in the drawing room of Creag an Fhithich on a cold and rainy May afternoon. The rooms of the castle had been restored to their original state since Edward's arrival. The silver had been dug up, and Donal Og had removed all the pictures from their hiding place in the cave and they once again hung on the castle walls in their accustomed places. Van had been very careful not to take Edward to the cave; it would be well, she thought, to keep its location secret from him. Just in case.

It was not a happy feeling, this sense that she could not trust him all the way, this knowledge that he was wrong to trust her. Divided loyalties were keeping her from him now just as surely as they had on the day she left Linton House to ride north with Niall.

Frances had tried to talk with her on the eve before her marriage, but as soon as Van realized that her mother was attempting to prepare her for her wedding night, she had stopped her. After all that had happened, she thought, there was little point in pretending to an innocence she no longer had.

"It's all right, Mother," she had said. "I know." She was sitting up in bed and Frances was seated on its edge, looking earnestly into her daughter's face. Van gave her mother a rueful smile. "The least of my concerns over this marriage is the fact that tomorrow night Edward will be sleeping in this bed with me."

Frances' blue eyes widened. "Van. Have you two . . . ?"

"Yes."

"Oh." Frances was clearly startled.

Van laughed and reached out to cover her mother's hand with her own. "Don't look so horrified," she said. Her face sobered. "If it were just that, Mother. If only it were just that."

She thought of that conversation now as she sat at the dining-room table over the dinner the cook had specially prepared for her wedding party. There was beef from their own herd and fish from the loch and Frances had ordered some of Alasdair's finest wine to be served. Edward was seated at the head of the table with Van at his right while Frances sat at the foot with Mr. Drummond next to her.

Edward in her father's seat. It was so strange. Everything about today had felt so strange. She looked down at the ring on her finger and then up to the man beside her.

He was talking to Frances across the length of the table, talking humorously, charmingly, trying, Van realized abruptly, to take her mother's mind off the fact that he was sitting in her husband's place. And he seemed to be succeeding. Frances was smiling and the tense white look she had been wearing lately had relaxed. Edward finished talking and Frances actually laughed.

Edward glanced sideways at her and smiled faintly, his lids half-hiding his very blues eyes. "You are looking very beautiful," he murmured as Frances turned to say something to Mr. Drummond.

Van was wearing the ivory taffeta gown she had worn her first night at Holyrood Palace. She told him now, "I was wearing this the first time I met the prince."

Her voice had been challenging but he refused to be ruffled. He lifted his lids to look at her directly and there was laughter at the corners of his mouth. "I'm sure he found you beautiful too," he said, and the gravity of his voice was at odds with his eyes.

She wanted desperately to be in his arms. There was no way of hiding that knowledge from herself with sharp words; nor was she fooling him. For all the generous charm he was directing at her mother, Van knew where his real attention lay. It lay with her. As hers was with him. She knew that both of them were only waiting for the moment when they could close her bedroom door behind them and be alone.

25

The rain was falling steadily, beating hard as pellets against the windows of Van's room when she and Edward entered together. Edward went to the window. "What a night," he said as he stared at the rain-lashed landscape. Van imagined the scene he was regarding: the wind-whipped loch, the lowering mountains. He closed the curtain and turned to look at her.

"May is usually the loveliest month in Morar," she said. And it was. The sun was brilliant this time of year and the dense thickets of rhododendrons that covered the steep hills glowed with an almost tropical brightness. The glittering white beaches shone against the tumbled sea. The long evenings were usually calm and sweet and honey-colored with the slowly fading sun. But this year . . .

"The prince is having fugitive's weather this spring," she said. "It may not be comfortable, but it makes pursuit the more difficult."

He came across to her and, putting one hand under her chin, he raised her face to look at him. "Shall we call a truce?" His voice was very deep and very soft.

"All right." She was perfectly still, allowing her chin to rest in his fingers without resistance. He lifted his other hand and began to remove the pins from her hair. Van watched his intent face as he went about his task, watched his mouth. When the last pin was out and her hair was tumbling down around her shoulders he looked back at her face. He grinned. "It may not be a hairdresser's delight, but this is the way I like it best."

Her heart turned over inside her breast at that look. He slid his hands into the hair he had just loosened and bent his head to kiss her. Desire, instant, intense, painful, stabbed through her at the touch of his mouth. They left their clothes in a heap on the floor and fell together onto the bed.

There was no pain this time, only intense, stunning sensation. She was shocked by its sheer primitive power, shocked and a little frightened.

"Christ, sweetheart." His voice was still slightly breathless. He shifted until he had her cradled in his arms. "Things between us never seem to go as I plan."

The thudding of his heart against her cheek was beginning to slow. "It's . . . a little frightening," she murmured.

"Yes." His voice above her head was perfectly sober. "It is." And she felt oddly grateful that he too was disturbed and overwhelmed by the powerful need that drew them so urgently together.

Slowly he began to rub her back. Van relaxed against him, soft and warm and trusting. After a while his hand moved to the small of her back. Van sighed. He kissed the top of her head. "Let's take it slowly this time," he murmured, and she felt the ripples of desire stir deep within her.

He wooed her with hands and voice and mouth. She turned to him, a flower turning and opening to the heat and light of the sun. He was bright and powerful and she was warm and flushed from his caresses. He sank into her slowly and easily. Her eyes closed and she breathed deeply. From without came the sound of the rain drumming mercilessly against the window. Van drifted off to sleep on a flood of rich peace and satisfaction.

She woke in the morning to find him still asleep beside her. He was lying on his stomach, his face hidden by the loose golden hair that fanned across his cheek. His shoulders and upper arms were visible above the quilt and Van stared at the massive muscles that were usually hidden under his beautifully made coats, at the thick bright hair that was usually confined so neatly by its black ribbon. Lying there in her bed, he seemed to her another being altogether, mystic, potent, godlike. Then he rolled over and opened his eyes and became Edward once again.

On the day his sister was married, Niall MacIan narrowly missed being captured by a British man-of-war. The prince's party was desperately trying to move southward down the Long Island, to Benbecula, where they hoped to get a boat to Skye. Their stay in the Outer Isles so far had been fraught with danger and discomfort. They had spent the last week or so sheltering in a wretched hut on the small desert island of Iubhard, hiding from the English frigates which had returned from St. Kilda and were cruising off the shore of Harris.

On Van's wedding day the prince's boat was spotted north of Rodel Point, the most southern tip of Harris, and they only escaped capture by steering into the shoal water near Rodel, where the larger man-of-war could not follow. Niall had scarcely breathed a sigh of relief, however, before they ran into another English frigate, this time near Lochmaddy on North Uist. It was only by spending the night at sea, rowing steadily

and quietly southward, that they managed to escape.
The heavy rain and wind caught them as they reached
Loch Uskavagh in Benbecula, and there they sheltered in a poor bothy, existing on seabirds and fish. It
was three days before they could land on the mainland
of Benbecula. MacDonald of Clanranald directed them
to shelter in Corradale, in South Uist, where they took
up residence in a tenant's cottage that looked like a
palace compared to their most recent habitations. They
remained in Corradale for three weeks and it was
there that Lachlan found Niall with his mother's letter.

Niall was not present when Lachlan arrived at the
cottage, escorted by a few local MacDonalds who had
been helping to supply the prince's party with bread
and meal. The hills around Corradale were teeming
with game and the prince and Niall kept the party well
supplied with grouse and with deer. Niall was out
hunting with Charles when Lachlan arrived. They returned to the cottage, laughing and in good spirits, to
find Lachlan eating and drinking in front of the cottage fire.

"Mac mhic Iain," Lachlan said, leaping to his feet.
Then he acknowledged the prince. "I have brought
you a letter," Lachlan announced, and produced Frances' missive. Niall took it eagerly and, excusing himself, went a little apart from the others to read. At the
first line he went rigid with shock.

"My dearest son," Frances had written. "On May
10 your sister will be married to the Earl of Linton."
Involuntarily Niall looked up from his letter and over
to the corner of the cottage where the prince was now
seated talking to O'Sullivan. Charles was dressed as a
Highlander, in a suit of tartan brought to him by
Clanranald, and he was busy lengthening a clay pipe

with the quill of a seabird's feather while he talked. The prince had become adept in the simple things of Highland life during the weeks since Culloden. Niall turned and left the cottage in order to be completely alone with his disturbing letter. He did not want anyone to be reading his face.

Outside, he leaned his shoulders against the cottage walls and opened the letter once more. "I do not know if you realize how hard the Duke of Cumberland has come down upon the Highlands," his mother's words continued. "His soldiers have been burning cottages and driving off cattle all around Inverness and the Great Glen. There is starvation and rape and murder wherever they go. Van and I were helpless to do aught to protect the clan, Niall. We were just waiting here, helpless, until the soldiers came. Then Edward arrived.

"Niall, he extracted a promise from Cumberland that the lands and the people of Morar would not be touched if Van would marry him. And there is more. Edward has sent for his yacht and he engages to take you to France.

"He is doing all of this because he loves Van. But he is still an Englishman. He will not help the prince to escape, Niall, only you.

"Darling, think of Jean. How lonely and frightened she must be by herself in France. You have a duty to her now. You have more than discharged your duty to the prince.

"Come home to Morar, my son. My heart is so heavy with fear for your safety. Please allow your sister's husband to convey you to France.

"Van has enclosed a note for you as well.

"I pray I shall see you soon. Your loving mother, Frances MacIan."

Niall unfolded Van's letter slowly, a frown drawing his black brows into a straight line above his intent eyes. His sister's letter was shorter than his mother's. "We cannot possibly smuggle the prince aboard the yacht. Edward plans to be on board personally and he would check any companions you might have very carefully. Morar should be relatively safe from English patrols. I have not told Edward about the cave. Let me know if you need help. Van."

As Niall finished his sister's letter the frown lifted from his brow and a smile crept slowly across his face. He might have known he could trust Van, he thought.

He was not impervious to his mother's words about Jean. His wife had been much on his mind, particularly these last calm days in Corradale. But he could not desert his prince. Should they be unsuccessful in picking up a ship here in the western isles, and be forced to return to the mainland, Charles would desperately need his services as a guide. And there was the cave, where they might shelter, protected by Van and her unknowing husband.

No. When and if he returned to Morar, he would have the prince with him. In the meanwhile, he had a letter to write to his mother.

Frances sat by the window of her sitting room, holding Niall's letter and staring out at Edward's yacht, which was anchored in the loch.

She had known he would not take the chance to escape. He was just like his father.

Alasdair.

Unbearable to think that just two months ago she had had him. And now . . . The tears began to course down her face. She could not seem to stop crying these days. Alone here in her sitting room, alone in her bed at night, the knife edge of grief would overwhelm her. And once she started to cry, she could not seem to stop.

Van's presence was the only thing that helped the pain at all. Without Van it would have been absolute desolation. Van knew how she felt. Van mourned for him too.

She looked down at the letter in her lap and tried to stop her weeping. Niall wanted his mother to go to France to be with his wife. The baby was due in August and he was worried to death about Jean being alone.

Oh, but she did not want to go! She did not want to leave this place where she had passed her life with Alasdair. She did not want to leave her daughter.

Frances stood up and went slowly up the stairs to her bedroom, where she splashed cold water on her red, swollen eyes. Her window looked toward the head of the glen and from it she could see her son-in-law approaching the castle. Edward had been spending his days visiting the clan holdings, assessing what would be needed in the way of food for the future. There had been little planted this spring, with the men away at war. With Edward was Alasdair's foster brother, Alan Ruadh, who had been acting as the earl's interpreter.

Frances stared out the window at the distant bright head of her son-in-law. Edward had been kindness itself to her, never seeming to grudge his wife's attendance upon her mother.

I take Van away from him too much, Frances thought. There was a clansman running up the path toward Edward, and Frances watched as he spoke to the earl, his hands gesturing with Celtic grace. Edward waited patiently while Alan Ruadh interpreted.

Van should be doing this with him, Frances thought suddenly. She should be with her husband, not with me. I have been too selfish in my grief. I have been thinking only of myself.

I must go to France.

The thought brought pain, but she closed her fingers on the curtains and straightened her back. It was right that she go, she told herself sternly. Van must be left free to make her marriage. I have been wrong to cling to her so, Frances thought. I have been wrong to burden Van's young heart with my grief. Niall is right. It is Jean who needs me now. It is time that Edward and Van were left alone.

Frances told Edward and Van about Niall's letter while they were having tea in the drawing room that evening. There were four of them, as Mr. Drummond was still at Creag an Fhithich.

"Niall refuses to leave the prince," Frances said to Edward. "He feels that is where his duty still lies."

There was a flash of what looked like impatience in the very blue eyes of her daughter's husband. Then he shrugged his big shoulders. "That is his decision," he said coolly, and began to butter a slice of bread.

Frances continued steadily. "However, he has asked that I go to France to be with his wife. She is expecting a child, as I believe you know. Would it be possible, Edward, for your yacht to take me instead of Niall?"

He looked up from his bread and, for a brief revealing minute, she saw what was in his mind. Then his face was a mask of perfect courtesy. "My yacht is at your disposal, Frances, of course. But are you sure you wish to leave us?"

"Yes." She smiled at him. "It is time for me to go,"

she said gently, and he knew that she had seen his relief at her decision.

He grinned at her, exactly like a small boy caught stealing goodies from the kitchen. He had more charm than any man she had ever known, Frances thought, as, irresistibly, she smiled back.

"Jean will be perfectly fine without you, Mother." Van's voice was hard, her thin face angry. "I'm quite sure Fassefern has provided for her. You don't want to leave Creag an Fhithich, you know you don't."

"But I do," Frances said firmly. "And what is more, darling, it is what your father would have wished of me. Jean carries the heir to Morar. You know how important that was to him."

Van's light eyes looked doubtful. "Are you certain . . . ?"

"Quite certain." Frances' tone was final. She turned back to Edward. "We can sail through the Moray Firth and return Mr. Drummond to Inverness on the way."

Mr. Drummond, who was beginning to feel as if he were to be immured forever in Morar, was obviously delighted.

The conversation flowed and as Van listened to her mother's plans she began to think that perhaps it would really be good for Frances to get away.

About one thing Frances was adamant. She did not want Edward's escort. "It is not necessary," she said. "I am not one of the people the government is interested in apprehending. You may give me a letter, in case the boat is stopped. But really, Edward, no one is going to arrest the Earl of Linton's mother-in-law."

"You can't be sure, Mother," Van said worriedly.

"Well, if I am arrested I will send you word and Edward can come and rescue me." Frances' humorous

tone and smiling eyes seemed to reassure Van, and for
the first time since the topic had been introduced, her
face relaxed into a smile.

"A change of scene will be good for her, you know,"
Edward said to Van as they were undressing for bed
that night. "And it will be good for her to feel needed.
There are too many memories here in Morar just at
present."

"Perhaps you are right." Van, seated in a velvet-
covered chair before the fire, bent forward to remove
her stockings. She wore only her chemise, and her
shining hair was streaming over the flawless skin of
her shoulders and breasts.

Frances had read Edward correctly. He *was* glad she
was leaving Creag an Fhithich. Not because he did not
like her—he did, very much. But he felt strongly that
there was a barrier between him and his wife and he
thought that Frances was a part of it. Every time Van
looked at her mother, she remembered her father's
death. With Frances gone, perhaps the resistance he
felt in Van would melt.

The physical attraction between them was stronger
than ever. At night, in his arms, she was every man's
erotic dream come true. But it was not enough for him
that they could set the night ablaze with passion. He
wanted what they had had in the days of their brief
engagement, before the prince had landed. He wanted
that oneness, that deep sense of communion between
two hearts and two minds, that touching of spirits.

They had not recovered that since their marriage.
Van's body was his, but the rest of herself she held
aloof.

She did not play the harpsichord anymore.

He had to be patient, he told himself. She had been

through a terrible time; he could not expect her to forget so quickly.

Van straightened up. In the light of the fire her hair shone blue, not brown. She gave him a shadowy smile. "You have been very good to us, Edward. Thank you for letting Mother use your yacht."

A dark storm rose within him. He did not want her gratitude. She was within his reach and he stretched out an arm to pull her toward him. He kissed her throat, her shoulders, her breasts, then swung her up into his arms and carried her to the bed, where he could assert their union in the only way he could find, where their marriage was deep and personal, where the particularities of selfhood were submerged in the great primal darkness of physical love.

26

It was raining when Van awoke, the drops beating hard against the windowpane. Poor Mother, she thought immediately. Frances had left for France on Edward's yacht the previous day.

Van lay on her back and looked at the empty chimney. Someone would be in shortly to make up the fire. Edward did not believe in living like a Spartan. He was asleep next to her now, his big body very warm beside hers under the quilts.

Poor Mother, Van thought again. I hope the sea is not too rough.

Van had not wanted Frances to leave, and when the graceful white-sailed yacht had sailed out of Loch Morar yesterday, she had felt fear cramp within her stomach. She had been hiding behind Frances for weeks, and now she was alone.

She turned her head slowly and looked at the man she had been hiding from. He was lying on his side, his face relaxed and very young-looking within its tangle of golden hair. He wanted her to forget what was happening to the Highlands, to forget and to love him as completely as once she had. But she could not forget. She *would* not forget.

He had put her in a position in which she had had no choice but to marry him. He had virtually forced her to marry him. It was unfair of him to expect anything from her but dutiful compliance.

The fact that she gave him far more than dutiful compliance in bed rankled her pride, but she was helpless before the physical attraction he had for her.

But that was all it was, she thought defiantly. Physical attraction. The girl who had once loved him had died with the clans at Culloden. Nothing between them could ever be as it had been before.

Van was doing an inventory of her mother's medical supplies early that afternoon when Lachlan came to find her. An escaped prisoner from Fort Augustus had taken refuge in his father's cottage and wanted to see Van. The fugitive was Alan MacDonald.

The rain was still falling heavily when Van, wearing trews and wrapped in a plaid, took one of the ponies and rode out to the distant glen that was home to Rory MacIan, Lachlan's father. The path took her through the mountains, up steep and rocky slopes that only a sure-footed Highland pony could handle. Her plaid was soaked by the time she arrived at the small cottage—really scarcely more than a hut—where Alan was sheltering. Rory met her at the door.

"He is sitting by the fire, my lady," the old man told her courteously, and Van walked slowly into the smoky room.

He must know she had married Edward. The last time they had met she had promised to marry him. Van looked at him somberly through the smoke of the fire and waited for him to speak first.

He said nothing. The red in his hair was bright in the light of the fire. The beard on his unshaven face was red as well. His face, however, was so thin as to look almost cadaverous. Van's eyes widened. "God in heaven, Alan. You look like a skeleton! What has happened to you?"

"I'm all right," he replied. "Dirty, but otherwise fine." There was a pause; then he said, deliberately, "And how are you?"

Van swallowed. "I'm married," she said baldly.

There was no flicker of expression on his face. "So I have heard. To the Earl of Linton."

"Aye." Van could not keep looking at that still face. "He came to Morar a month ago," she said to the fire. Her voice was quiet, toneless. "He had a promise from Cumberland that Morar would not be touched if I should wed him. Under the circumstances, I had no choice."

She heard him let out his breath. "And was it only for that?" he asked. "Did you marry him only for Morar, Van? You loved him once."

Her eyes met his once more. She said deliberately, "I married him only for Morar."

The guarded expression in his eyes lifted and the gold blazed into life. "Oh, Van," he said, and held out his arms. Van went into them and began to cry. "Do not distress yourself so, m'eudail," he said.

"You look awful," she wept into his shoulder.

"Don't you like me with a beard?" His voice was deliberately light and she could feel the tenseness in his body. She fought for composure, dropped her arms, and stepped away from him.

"I'm getting you all wet." She gave him an unsteady smile and began to unfasten the broach that held her plaid.

Old Rory appeared to take it from her and spread it on a chair before the smoky fire to dry. Then he set a chair for Van, and with a grateful smile she seated herself. Alan sat down as well and Van regarded him worriedly. "Has Rory fed you?" she asked. "You look so thin."

"Aye. Rory fed me fine."

She leaned a little forward in her chair. "Alan, tell me what happened. Lachlan said you were a prisoner at Fort Augustus and escaped."

"Aye," he said again.

"But how did you escape, Alan?" she asked wonderingly. "No one has escaped from Fort Augustus before."

"I did not escape from Fort Augustus itself," he began. "A platoon of soldiers was escorting me to Glasgow for trial, and I escaped on the road." He turned to find her regarding him out of huge eyes. "An old woman near Invergarry slipped me a dirk. I cut the ropes at my wrists and escaped through the mountains."

"Taking you for trial!" Van repeated in horror. "I had no idea, Alan. I thought you would simply be held, not . . ." She broke off, shivering, knowing what the result of such a trial would have been. "I would have asked Edward to intercede for you if I had known," she said.

"I don't need the Earl of Linton, thank you." Alan's voice was harsh.

"But, Alan, you would have been executed!"

"I know that fine, Van. That's why I was so keen to escape."

"Thank God for that old woman," Van said fervently.

He grinned and for the first time resembled the Alan she remembered.

"Alan, what is happening?" she asked urgently. "We are so isolated here in Morar that I hear virtually nothing. There have been no soldiers here at all."

"Well, you can thank God for that, Van." His voice

was harsh and bitter. "Fort Augustus is an armed camp, filled with cattle and ponies that have been driven in from all over the Highlands. Badenoch and Lochaber are deserts. The hills are filled with starving women and children." Van's hands were pressed to her mouth. "They burned Achnacarry, did you know that?" Alan asked.

Her hands dropped. "No. Lochiel?"

"Lochiel is safe. He was hidden in a cave above Loch Arkaig when the soldiers came. And Lady Lochiel and the bairns are safe as well. But Achnacarry—you know what a lovely house it was, Van."

"Aye." Her voice was scarcely audible.

"They burned everything. All Lochiel's fine chairs and tables, all his cabinets. They pulled the fruit garden to pieces and laid it waste. The summerhouse was burned as well. There is nothing left. Nothing."

"Barbarians," Van said with loathing.

"Aye," Alan agreed. "They are no better than the Vikings they were a thousand years ago."

Vikings. Unbidden, a picture flashed before Van's mind of a tall, blond, blue-eyed man. Viking. She closed her eyes to blot the picture out, but still it stayed.

"Van," she heard Alan saying urgently, "they are looking for Niall."

Her eyes flew open, all thought of Edward instantly banished. "What do you mean?" she asked tensely.

"The English particularly want to capture Niall. He is the Earl of Morar now, and his trial would make a fine show for the government. They knew I was a friend of his and they questioned me closely."

Van's black brows were drawn together, her eyes blazing like a tiger's. "What do you mean—they questioned you closely? They did not torture you, Alan?"

He smiled at her reassuringly. "No. Nothing so terrible as torture, Van. They did not feed me, that is all."

"Dhé! That is why you are so thin!"

"Aye. But they had to feed me finally to make sure I could stand the journey to Glasgow. It was not so terrible, Van. Don't look like that, m'eudail."

Van felt herself shaking with rage and with fear. "Where is Niall?" she heard Alan asking, and she answered unsteadily, "He is with the prince."

Alan's breath whistled in a sudden intake of air. "Van, the narrow seas between the Long Island and Skye are filled with English ships, all searching for the prince."

"I know," Van said wretchedly. "Dear God, Alan, I know."

They sat in grim silence, each of them contemplating the ugly picture of Niall and the prince in English hands. It was Van who spoke first. "You will be safe here in Morar, Alan. Stay here, please. I will bring you some of Father's clothes. And food. You must put some weight back on."

"And what of your husband?" The words were spoken quietly, deliberately. A shadow came across Van's face. "Edward does not need to know that you are here," she said, and he felt a surge of fierce joy within him. It was true, then, what she had said. She did not love this Earl of Linton.

It was late when Van returned to the castle. She had missed both dinner and tea. She would tell Edward she had been to visit a sick tenant. He would understand. It was the sort of thing his mother did all the time.

Her plaid was drenched through once again when

she reached the castle and rain was dripping from her eyelashes and her nose. Morag told her Edward was in her father's office and she decided to put on dry clothes and do her hair before she had to face him. She was standing in front of her bedroom fire, dressed in a red velvet robe and drying her hair, when the door opened and her husband was there.

He closed the door behind him, came into the room, and stood regarding her in silence. He was wearing evening clothes and the lace at this throat was immaculate, the blue velvet of his coat fresh and uncreased. The silence went on. Van put down her towel and said, "I'm sorry I wasn't here for tea. I had to go visit one of the tenants who was sick."

"Oh?" His voice was perfectly pleasant. It was the chill look in his eyes that was making her nervous. "And who was ill?" he asked.

Van's heart stopped. She had not thought of singling out any tenant in particular. "Ah . . . Maire, Fergus Roy's wife," she said. Her own calm voice was belied by the pounding of her heart.

"That is strange." The cold blue eyes held hers remorselessly. "I saw Fergus only today, and he made no mention of a sick wife."

Van said nothing, only stood there with her streaming wet hair and her slim hands clutching together the folds of her robe.

"If you are going to lie to me, Van, you will have to do better than this." The cutting, contemptuous edge in his voice brought color to her cheeks.

She flung up her head. "Very well, then. You tell me where I have been."

"To see some wretched fugitive who has found his way to Morar, I should imagine."

Damn him. Van glared at him. "Yes, my lord conqueror," she answered mockingly. The effect of her sarcasm, however, was marred by her shaking voice. "I have been seeing to an old friend who has just escaped from the attentions of your countrymen at Fort Augustus. Where they starved him, my lord, in order to obtain news of the whereabouts of my brother!" Her voice had risen. "He brought wonderful news of Badenoch and Lochaber, where the women and children are starving in the hills while their cattle are driven to Fort Augustus to be sold into England." Her mouth was shaking now too and she pressed her lips together to try to regain the control of herself she knew was fast slipping away.

Edward did not answer, only crossed over to the window and stood there for a little, his back to his wife. But Van did not think he was seeing the dark loch or hearing the heavy drumming of the cold rain. She waited with hammering heart for him to answer her.

His reply was completely unexpected. "I am leaving tomorrow for Inverary." He spoke over his shoulder. "Alan Ruadh is going with me."

Van stared at his back in stunned surprise. "Inverary!" she said in a voice full of shock and horror. Inverary was the main seat of the chief of Clan Campbell, the Duke of Argyll.

"Yes." He turned to look at her. "I believe the duke is in residence and I wish to speak to him."

"You cannot!" She spoke instantly, unthinkingly. "The Campbells are as bad as the Sassenach, Edward. You cannot possibly have anything to say to Mac Cailein Mhor."

"Oh, but I do." His voice was gentle. His eyes were cold. He was very angry. Well, what did he expect? Van thought defiantly. He had forced her into this marriage. He was just going to have to put up with what he got. She could not imagine what he was going to discuss with the Duke of Argyll, but she was damned if she'd ask him now.

"You seem to have made quite an admirer out of Alan Ruadh," she said, and even to her own ears she sounded sullen.

"He knows *I* have the best interests of the clan at heart." The emphasis on the pronoun was faint but unmistakable.

Van stalked to the table where she kept her toilet articles, opened a drawer, and took out a hairbrush. Silently she began to brush out her wet hair. Temper quivered in every line of her body.

Edward walked to the door. "You must be hungry," he said. "I'll have Morag bring you some food."

After he had gone, Van threw her hairbrush across the room.

He came to bed very late that night. Van pretended to be asleep and he made no move to awaken her. His deep, slow breathing told her he had gone to sleep long before she herself fell into a fretful, restless slumber.

Edward and Alan Ruadh left before seven the following morning. He kissed Van's cheek courteously before he departed and she went to the window to watch him and Alan walking down the drive. Edward was wearing buckskin breeches and boots and his russet riding coat. He should have taken a plaid, Van thought. There was nothing like a plaid to protect you from the Highland weather. She could have given him one of her father's. A plaid was about the only thing of Alasdair's that would fit him.

She straightened her spine. If he caught cold on his

way to Inverary, it would serve him right, she thought fiercely. And her father's clothes would fit Alan. She would bring him a kilt and some clean shirts that morning.

The day after Edward had left for Inverary, word came to the prince and Niall in Corradale that they would have to leave that hitherto safe refuge. General Campbell of Mamore had just sailed into the waters around the Uists with a squadron of ships and he had landed a regiment of three hundred local militia, MacLeods, on Benbecula. The hunt was up in earnest and it was coming nearer.

On June 5 the prince's party left Corradale and sailed to the little island of Ouia, where they remained for a few days while they desperately tried to determine where it was safe to go. At last Niall and the prince left the others on Ouia and tried for Rossinish, to see if they could get further news. From Rossinish they began to move cautiously southward.

The hills were crawling with militia and the lochs and inlets were filled with hostile ships. The only thing that saved the fugitives was the underground network of loyal well-wishers, who appeared with magical regularity to warn them of troops on the next hill or ships in the loch.

"We must get off the Long Island," Niall said desperately to Charles as they sheltered from a gale in what was no more than a cleft in the rocks above Loch Boisdale. "We must get across to Skye."

There had been fifteen enemy sails in the loch when Charles and Niall had deserted their own boat to take to the land. The weather, miserable though it was to be out in, was in reality a blessing. When the gale had finally blown itself out, a local man appeared with the news that a party of militia was but one mile away. The man, a schoolmaster named Neil MacEachain, volunteered to lead the prince and Niall to Ormacett on the west side of South Uist. There, he told them, he knew someone who could assist the prince to escape from the island. The someone was a woman and her name was Flora MacDonald.

27

Alan was much safer in Morar than Niall and the prince were on the Long Island, but he too was looking for ways to escape.

"I must get a ship to France," he told Van a week after his arrival. "I cannot hide here in Morar forever."

"It isn't safe for you, Alan," Van said wretchedly. "And I don't know where to tell you to go."

"I'll go north, toward Skye," he returned. "The French must know the prince is in the Isles. There is a good chance of a ship in the Sound of Sleat."

"I wish you would stay here." Van looked at him worriedly. He had put on weight this past week, and he was clean and shaved once more. Why could he not stay in Morar?

"I am of no use to anyone skulking here in Rory's cottage," he answered when she expressed this sentiment. "And I may well be a danger to you when your husband returns. He will not like it, if you continue to shelter a government fugitive."

Van said nothing.

"I must go." They were walking together in a field of heather about a quarter of a mile from Rory MacIan's cottage. It was one of the rare days that June when the sun was actually shining. Alan stopped now and Van stopped also, "I must go," he repeated. "And you must stay here with your husband." His face was unutterably bleak.

"Alan." Van made a gesture with her hands and dropped her eyes. She could not bear to see him look so.

"It is not thus that I dreamed once of you and me," he said.

"I know." Her head was bent, her voice muffled. "I am so sorry, Alan."

"It is not your fault."

She looked up, her thin nostrils flaring. "When will you go?"

"Tonight." He forced a smile at her expression. "I will be all right, Van. I'm a dandy hand for skulking in the heather."

She laughed shakily. "The birthright of a Highlander."

"Aye." His mouth was smiling but his eyes were grave.

She drew a long breath. "I think you will be safe, so long as the prince is still in the Isles. The hunt is concentrated there."

"Aye. If the luck is with us, we will all get a ship together."

"Oh, God, Alan, I hope so!"

At that he reached out and took her hands. "I know I have no right to ask this of you, Van," he said intensely. "But will you kiss me good-bye?"

"Of course I will, Alan," she said immediately, and raised her face to his.

She knew, as soon as he touched her, that she had made a mistake. He kissed her passionately, intensely, with the hunger of a man long denied water who is finally brought to drink. And she felt nothing.

She smiled bravely when he stepped away from her.

"May God keep you in the palm of his hand," she said.

"Farewell," he answered. "My love." And she turned and walked away, walked over the mountains and did not look back.

She saw Alan Ruadh as she came by the vegetable garden. Edward was back.

She did not want to see him. She was afraid to see him. She went straight to her room and, thankfully, found it empty. She wished she could lock the door. Morag told her the earl was out, however, and she thought she was safe for a while.

She would change her clothes, she thought. She would change her clothes and after she had composed herself, she would go to sit in the drawing room. That was the best place to meet him.

She almost made it. One of the housemaids was fastening the hooks on her dress when the door opened and Edward came into the bedroom. Her head jerked up like a startled colt's and she stared at him out of dilated eyes. She could say nothing.

"Aren't you going to welcome me home?" His voice was pleasant but distinctly cool.

"Welcome home," she said. Her heart was plunging; she felt close to fainting. She made a tremendous effort and added, "I hope the weather did not catch you out too badly."

He shrugged and leaned his shoulders against the wall by the window. He was looking at the housemaid, not at her.

"Thank you, Fionna," Van said reluctantly. "You may go."

As the door closed behind the girl, Van turned slowly to look at Edward's silent figure. In the light

from the window she could see the golden stubble of
beard on his face. His eyes were as blue as sapphires—
and as hard. Blue and gold he was; Saxon, with no
trace of Celt about him.

And she loved him. Alan's kiss this afternoon had
told her that with painful clarity. She had not married
Edward to save Morar. It was no longer possible to
hide behind that convenient excuse.

He looked so tall as he stood there next to the
window watching her. So unyielding. "Did you see
Mac Cailein Mhor?" she asked in a clear, steady voice
that was forced out with all her remaining self-control.

"Yes."

"And what did you go to see him about, Edward?"
Her heart was beating heavily still. She wondered that
he could not see.

"I have been planning for some weeks to import food
from Ireland in order to feed Morar," he answered. "I
went to see the duke about the feasibility of getting
food into Lochaber and Badenoch as well." His eyes
were unfathomable as he watched her face. "The Duke
of Argyll may be a Campbell, but he is also a Highlander and a Scot. He has no wish to see the innocent
suffer for this unhappy rebellion. He has agreed that
the Campbell militia will help get food into the areas
that need it."

The room was filled with an intense silence. Van
stared at her husband, her slender hands opening and
closing on the folds of her yellow silk gown. Finally,
"You have been planning to import food for some
time? You never said anything to me."

"You must know that I have been visiting all the
clan and checking the food supplies," he answered.
He had not moved from his post by the window.

"Aye, but . . ." Her voice trailed off. She had not

wanted to know what he was doing, had tried to avoid him as much as possible, had been so busy hiding from the knowledge forced on her today by Alan's kiss . . . "I suppose I was too concerned about my mother to take much notice," she said faintly.

"So I had thought. That was before I realized you were simply staying as far away from the 'lord conqueror' as you decently could."

It was a moment before she realized he was quoting her own words back at her. She had called him a lord conqueror, she remembered. She looked now at the flinty expression on his face and understood that she had hurt him deeply.

Oh, God. What a stinking, rotten, disgusting mess she was making of this marriage.

She turned her back. She could not bear to look at him, could not bear to see that expression on his face. She closed her eyes. "I wish we were at Staplehurst," she said. "I wish none of this had ever happened."

She heard the sudden sharp intake of his breath. "Do you mean that?" he asked.

At the note in his voice she opened her eyes. "Of course I do. The prince has brought us nothing but sorrow."

"Not that." His voice told her he was coming closer and she turned to face him. He was looking impatient. "Do you mean what you said about wishing to be at Staplehurst?"

She thought of the beautiful golden stone house, the green fields, the horses in their pastures, the peace . . . to be there with Edward, to be able to love him in rightness, with a whole heart. To be able make music again. "Oh, yes," she cried in an aching voice. "Oh, yes, Edward, I do!"

He was looming over her, the golden stubble on his cheeks very evident now he was so close.

"Christ." Then he was holding her against him, holding her so tightly that her ribs ached. She didn't care, but flung her own arms around his neck and blindly lifted her face to his. She kissed him passionately and saw in his narrowed, concentrated eyes what was in his mind. The strength gave way in her knees and she swayed against him. Everything in her gave way. He might do with her as he liked. She didn't care about herself anymore, could not bear to be only herself, alone. So lonely. It was so lonely without him. Edward. She quivered all over as he unhooked the gown Fionna had just fastened, and reached up eagerly to draw him to her when he came to her on the bed.

He slid into her slowly and they lay very still for a long time, holding each other, scarcely breathing, afraid to move because that would trigger passion and they did not want passion just yet, only this quiet, this blissful, quiet union. Finally, however, the male in Edward could take no more, and he stirred and moved, and very shortly had brought them both to a familiar precipice from which they plunged wildly to earth, together.

"I will send the *Sea Queen* to Dublin as soon as she returns from France," Edward said to Van as they sat together in the office the following morning going over lists.

"There will be an influx of refugees into Morar once word gets out what you are doing," Van said.

He was looking at a paper, a very faint frown between his brows. "I don't care about that," he said absently.

Van's eyes were troubled. "What will the government say?"

His frown deepened very faintly. "I don't care about that, either." His eyes looked steadily into hers. She was seated on the opposite side of the desk, directly across from him. "I will give no shelter to Charles Stuart, though, Van. I promised the duke and I mean to keep that promise. Do you understand me?"

"Yes." It was the greatest effort of her life to sustain that blue gaze.

"I don't care about these other wretched souls," he went on. "Shelter as many old friends as you wish. But not the prince." There was a long silence as their eyes held. Then, "Do I have your promise on that, Van?"

Her face was bloodless. The skin under her eyes looked bruised. He knew what he was forcing on her but he felt it was necessary. "Do I have your promise, Van?" he asked again.

Her pale lips moved. "Yes," she said. "I promise."

It was the night of June 21, the shortest night of the year, when Niall and Charles Stuart walked over the moor to the summer shieling in South Uist, where Flora MacDonald was tending her brother's cattle. Neil MacEachain hid them in a barn while he went to talk to Flora. The moon was bright as Niall and Charles watched the schoolmaster cross the yard and enter the small house.

"If we do not get off this island very shortly, MacIan," the prince said somberly, "we are done for."

Niall knew he was right. The hounds were yapping at their heels and escape across the sea was their only hope. In the semidarkness of the barn the two pairs of eyes, one light and one dark, met and held. "I shall never forget you, my friend," said Charles Stuart.

Niall's teeth flashed white in the blackness of his beard. "I will hold your highness to that promise when you are come into your own." After a moment the prince grinned back. "Here is MacEachain," Niall said, his eyes swinging over Charles's shoulder to the man approaching them from across the yard.

"Come with me," said the schoolmaster, and the two figures followed him to the shieling, where they entered through the low door, ducking their heads in similar gestures. They were greeted by a grave-faced girl in her early twenties, who curtsied to Charles.

"Mistress MacDonald's stepfather is Hugh MacDonald of Armadale in Skye, your highness," MacEachain explained. "He is an officer in the militia and could certainly issue Flora a passport to cross to Skye to see her mother." MacEachain looked at the girl. "And, Flora, could you not also get a passport for a servant to accompany you?"

Flora MacDonald's serious young eyes looked troubled. She looked at the prince. "I would like to help you, your highness, but my stepfather is a captain in Sir Alexander MacDonald's regiment. It would go hard with him should Sir Alexander find out that I had assisted in this deception."

"Sir Alexander MacDonald of Sleat is one of the two great lairds of Skye, sir," Niall explained in a brief aside to the prince.

"Aye," said Flora. "And he is for the government."

"Sir Alexander is at Fort Augustus, Flora," Neil MacEachain said persuasively. "And you have good cause to go to Skye to visit your mother. There is no reason for anyone to know of your part in this affair."

Still the girl hesitated. Niall held his breath. If this

chance should fail, they were doomed. He felt it in his bones. The hunt was too close for them to escape it much longer.

The prince smiled at Flora, training on her all of the legendary Stuart charm. Ragged and bearded though he was, the charm was still potent. Thousands of men had gone to their graves during the last one hundred years because of the Stuart charisma. "I beg you, Mistress Flora," he said. "Will you not help your prince?"

Flora was no more proof against that plea than Alasdair MacIan had been. She wavered visibly and then, against her better judgment as well, she said, "Yes, your highness I will help you."

It was only then that Niall discovered that he had been holding his breath.

Flora agreed to leave for Benbecula immediately to secure the passports to cross to Skye. Niall, the prince, and MacEachain made for the hill of Hekla, where they could look across the shining water-patched lowlands of South Uist to the ford that led across to Benbecula. They settled themselves under a large rock and tried to get some sleep.

They waited for the entire day of the twenty-second. There was no word from Flora. By nightfall they were restless, as well as extremely hungry. MacEachain volunteered to go to Benbecula to try to discover what had happened to Flora.

Charles and Niall spent a very long night under their rock. Niall dozed fitfully, dreaming of Jean. He fell into a deeper sleep close to morning and, as happened too often, the nightmares moved in. He woke from the horrors of Culloden to find the prince's hand on his shoulder, shaking him roughly. He opened his eyes fully and saw Neil MacEachain approaching their rock. Niall sat up, fully alert.

"What has happened?" Charles demanded as soon as the schoolmaster was within earshot.

"Flora was detained at the ford by the militia the other night, and they arrested me as well," MacEachain explained breathlessly. "However, all is well now. Mac-Donald of Armadale, Flora's stepfather, arrived in Benbecula and he will issue passports for Skye. We are to meet Mistress MacDonald at Rossinish to make the crossing."

The trip to Rossinish, through closely guarded country, to a shore under constant patrol, was a new chapter to be added to Niall's collection of nightmares. It had begun to rain again, heavy and merciless, and they sheltered under rocks as best they could, dodging the militia, getting thoroughly drenched and bitten by the midges that had come out with the warmer weather. At last they reached the bothy near Rossinish where they were to wait for news from Flora. Wrapped in their plaids, a weary Niall and Charles lay down in front of a smoky peat fire and slept like schoolboys.

In the morning they were visited by two young MacDonald militia men, who told the prince that a boat had been made ready and they were to be the crew.

"God bless the MacDonalds," Charles said with a laugh when the two youngsters had gone out into the yard.

"The MacDonalds are not traitors, whatever the service they may be forced to join," said Niall of the militiamen.

For a brief, glorious moment, it seemed that Benbecula was free of the hunters. Lady Clanranald arrived at the bothy during the course of the afternoon, along with Flora and her brother Angus. They found Niall, the prince, and the two young MacDonald militiamen cooking dinner. There was a great deal of laughter as the whole group sat down to eat, particularly when Lady Clanranald disclosed the news that they had decided to disguise Charles as a woman servant in order to throw off suspicion. His name was to be Betty Burke.

It was Niall, who had gone to the door for a breath of air, who first saw the man running toward the bothy. The runner brought fearful news. General Campbell had just landed on Benbecula with a force of fifteen hundred men.

The merry party immediately broke up and, on the advice of Lady Clanranald, moved hastily to another bothy on the shore of Loch Uskavagh. The news at the loch, however, was no better. Captain Fergusson, leading an advance party of General Campbell's men, was at Lady Clanranald's home at Nunton. Further news was that the hated Captain Scott was also approaching the area with another large company of men. According to the scout, the government forces in the area amounted to about twenty-three hundred men.

Lady Clanranald departed immediately for home to try to save her roof from burning. Left in the bothy, Flora and the men made their plans. Flora's passport was for herself, a maid, and a manservant. Charles was to be the maid and Niall the manservant, and the prince, with numerous curses, donned the women's clothes Lady Clanranald had supplied.

The boat was in the loch, a small shallop of less than eighteen feet, and they waited until the sky darkened to board. They had to row for the first four hours, but then the wind came up and they raised the sail.

At two o'clock the following afternoon they landed on a beach near Kilbride. They were in Skye.

Lady Margaret MacDonald, wife of Sir Alexander MacDonald of Sleat, was entertaining Lieutenant MacLeod of the local militia in her dining room when word was passed to her that the prince had landed on her beach. Sir Alexander was a staunch government supporter and Lady Margaret was a Jacobite. She had no wish to see the prince taken, but neither did she wish to compromise her husband's position. Lady Margaret was in a quandary. In desperation she sent for her factor, MacDonald of Kingsburgh, and the two quickly made their plans.

Niall, who had been the one to bring the news of their landing to Lady Margaret, was dispatched back to the beach to send Flora to the house to talk to Lieutenant MacLeod. The militia had orders to search all ships coming from the Long Island. Flora must show her passports and convince the young man that it was not necessary for him to physically inspect the boat's passengers.

Kingsburgh, the prince, and Niall conferred on the beach and it was decided the fugitives should spend the night at Kingsburgh's house. Niall was dispatched back to Sir Alexander's to fetch Flora and bring her as well. Flora bade farewell to a charmed and well-fed Lieutenant MacLeod and a nervous Lady Margaret, who provided them with horses, and set off with Niall for the house of Kingsburgh, some seven miles distant. About halfway there they caught up with the prince and Kingsburgh, who were on foot.

It was Sunday evening and there were people on the road coming home from church. Niall saw immediately the astonished looks directed at Kingsburgh and his odd, gawky companion. As Niall and Flora came up behind them, Charles waded across a small stream, lifting his skirts immodesty high. The sight would have been funny, Niall thought, had it not been so dangerous. He spoke to Charles in a low, urgent tone. "For God's sake, sir, take care what you are doing or you will certainly discover yourself."

Charles looked around, startled, and then he grinned. At the next stream he deliberately let his skirt hang so long it trailed in the water.

It was nearing eleven o'clock when they finally reached Kingsburgh's house. They fell into bed, exhausted. Niall felt as if he were in heaven; it was the first time in months that he had slept between sheets. But the morning brought no further comfort. Militia units were stationed all over the shores of Skye.

"You are not safe here," Kingsburgh said. "You must get away from Skye."

"And go where, for God's sake?" Charles demanded angrily. He too had enjoyed his night in a comfortable bed and was loath to leave.

It was Niall who answered. "We must get across to the mainland, sir." Niall looked at Kingsburgh. "Is that possible?"

"I can get you to Raasay, I think," Kingsburgh returned, frowning. "The Laird of Raasay's eldest son, young Rona, will help. Raasay was with your highness's army, you will remember, but young Rona was left at home to fabricate an appearance of government loyalty and so save the estate from confiscation. From Raasay you may be able to cross to the mainland."

"But where on the mainland are we to go?" Charles asked impatiently. "There are government troops all over the west."

"Not in Morar," said Niall. "Morar is presently

under the protection of the Earl of Linton, who is married to my sister."

"Linton!" said Charles, clearly surprised. "The Romneys of Linton are Whigs, MacIan, and no friends to the Stuarts."

"And that is why no one will look for you in Morar, sir." Niall's light eyes were glowing. "My sister will help us. There is a cave we both know of that is perfectly hidden. If we can go to ground for long enough, the hunt may go elsewhere. Then, with the seas clear, the French will be able to send us a ship."

Charles looked thoughtful. Then he said slowly, "Very well." He gave Niall a weary smile. "It is a destination, at least. Let us go to Morar."

28

The first shipload of food arrived from Ireland at the beginning of July. Van watched with admiration and pride as her husband efficiently directed the unloading of the yacht, the organization of the foodstuffs for various destinations, and finally the loading of the ponies that were to deliver the food to the glens. She was at his side for the three full days that the entire operation took, serving as interpreter between him and the Gaelic-speaking clansmen who were their workers. Edward had picked up enough Gaelic to make himself understood most of the time, but he still had difficulty understanding what was being said to him.

It was a beautiful, warm summer day when the last of the ponies was finally sent off. Van and Edward stood together on the shore of the loch and Edward said, "Do you know, in all the time I have been here, I have never been down to the sea?"

Van's eyes widened in astonishment. "You have not?"

He shook his head slowly, his eyes still on the glistening, pure waters of Loch Morar.

Van's eyes, the same gray-green color as the loch, suddenly sparkled. "Let's go now," she said. "We can taken the dinghy."

Edward looked down at her and smiled faintly. "I

think we deserve an afternoon to ourselves." He gestured toward the boat. "After you, my lady."

Van glanced down at her clothing and laughed. She was wearing trews and brogues and her hair was done in a single thick braid. She did not look at all like a countess. Edward was dressed almost as casually as she, in breeches and boots and a white open-necked shirt with no coat.

"Thank you, my lord," she replied mockingly, and preceded him down the incline to where the small boat lay moored. Edward pushed off, and they were out on the water, alone. The only sound in the world seemed to be the slap of the oars on the water and the cry of the birds in the mountains. The sun was warm, the sky a deep cobalt blue with a few high white clouds. Van drew a deep breath. She was happy.

"What a marvelous place to grow up in," Edward said.

Van looked at her husband as he rowed them so easily through the water. He had rolled his shirt sleeves up and the sun glinted on the golden hairs of his bare arms. He was looking about him as he spoke.

"Staplehurst is beautiful too," she said.

"Yes. Staplehurst is beautiful. But in a very different way from Morar. Staplehurst is man's beauty." His eyes met her. "Morar is God's," he said.

His skin was tanned golden from the summer sun, his blond head bleached even fairer than usual. How she loved him, Van thought. Just seeing him walk into a room made her want to cry. She smiled into his blue eyes and said, "Wait until you see the beach."

The glittering white beach of Morar was everything she had said it was. Edward stood perfectly quietly, gazing about him, and Van felt as if she had been able to give him a fabulous present. The sand was perfectly smooth, except for the little arrow-like footprints of the birds.

"Niall and I used to chase the waves," she said.

Edward sat down on the sand and began to pull off his boots. "Let's walk along the shore," he said, and she smiled in delight.

They walked hand in hand down the beach, letting the cold, clean water roll up around their bare feet, and Van talked of her childhood.

"Niall and I used to bring our ponies down here," she said, watching her bare feet splash through the oncoming wave. "We would gallop up and down the beach, playing tag. And we would make marvelous castles in the sand, then gallop our ponies over them." She laughed. "We would come home with our hair full of sand and Mother would have to wash it." She swung Edward's hand and turned her face up to the sun. "I get dark as a Gypsy in the summer," she said. "Look." And she raised her arm to hold it alongside his.

Edward's skin was warmly golden. Van's was deep olive, shades darker than his. She stopped walking and looked up at him, her light gray-green eyes more astonishing than usual in her tanned face. He smiled down at her contentedly. She slid an arm around his waist and leaned against him as they began to walk slowly back down the beach.

"You and Niall are very close," she heard his voice say above her head.

"Um." She loved the feel of his big body against her, loved the salty, sweaty male scent of him in her nostrils. "There were only the two of us, you see," she said. His arm was draped across her back and she looked down at the large, beautifully shaped hand on her shoulder. It was ringless, save for the gold signet on his little finger. "Were you lonely, being an only child?" she asked.

"Not really. I had my dogs and my horses and when I was seven I went away to school."

"At seven!" Van stared up at his profile. "How dreadful. You didn't mind?"

"The first year was hard." His serene expression never altered. "I missed my home, of course. But after that I rather enjoyed school. I liked having so many friends."

Not for Edward the loneliness of being an outsider, Van found herself thinking. The future Earl of Linton had probably been the center of admiring attention all his life. "Did you study hard?"

"Not as hard as I should have, I'm afraid." There was a distinct note of amusement in his voice.

"And then you went to Cambridge?"

"Yes. I was at Cambridge while you and Niall were knocking down sand castles with your ponies. Then I went to France and to Italy. I came home when my father died."

"How did he die?" Van asked quietly.

"He was kicked in the chest by a horse. It must have punctured a lung, or something of that nature. He died a few days later."

Van's arm tightened around his waist. "Did you miss him?" she asked softly.

"No." He smiled down at her, thanking her for the comfort that was not needed. "I saw very little of him when I was growing up, sweetheart. He was not a man for children. My mother missed him, though, and I was sorry for her." They had reached the entrance to the loch. He turned to look once more out at the sea. "I would like to be more important to my children than he was to me," he said quietly.

For some absurd reason, Van felt as if she were going to cry. "You will be, m'eudail," she said. "You will be."

The following day a message came to Edward from a Campbell militia regiment stationed near Mallaig, that the prince had crossed to the mainland. Flora MacDonald was a prisoner on Captain Fergusson's sloop *Furness* and MacDonald of Kingsburgh had been arrested and was on his way to Fort Augustus. Edward was advised to look out for the prince in Morar, as it was believed he was accompanied by Niall MacIan.

The message from Niall came to Van early on the morning of July 9. Lachlan MacIan was the bearer. Niall had come to his father's cottage in the middle of the night, he said. Van would find her brother at the cave.

"There is someone with Mac mhic Iain," Lachlan added in a low voice. "I was to tell you he has brought the prince."

Van wondered if she looked as sick as she felt. "Thank you, Lachlan," she managed to say calmly. "I will let you know if I need you."

Edward was writing letters in the office when Van, dressed in trews once more, took a pony and some food and headed for the cave at the head of Loch Morar.

Niall was keeping a lookout and saw her before she saw him. She gave a visible start of surprise when he rose before her out of the heather.

"Niall!" she said. Then, as the full magnitude of his appearance struck home, "Dhé! You look awful!"

Niall looked down at himself. He wore an incredibly ragged kilt and extremely dirty shirt. His hair had grown and he had a beard. But his eyes were laughing at her and his smile was the same and she slid off her pony and ran into his arms.

"I've been so worried about you," she said fiercely.

"We have been leading them a merry dance, never fear," he said into her ear. Then, urgently, "Tell me, Van, did Mother go to Jeannie?"

Van nodded. "Aye. She did, Niall. And they are in Rouen now, not Paris. Mother writes that all is well."

"Thank God." He smiled at her a little crookedly. "We had a chancy time of it, and I would not like to think of Jeannie being alone should I be caught."

Van felt her stomach clench. If Niall should be caught . . . "We have been trying to get to Morar for weeks," she heard him saying. "If we can only go to earth somewhere quietly, the hunt may move elsewhere."

She hoped he could not see that she was shaking. "You want to stay here?" she managed to ask.

"Aye. You wrote to me that there would be no government forces in Morar. Is it so?"

"So far. Of course, everyone knew the prince was in the Isles. Now that you are back on the mainland, the hunt will concentrate here." She stared at her brother out of troubled eyes. "Edward just received a message from the militia near Mallaig that you are to be looked for in Morar. It is known that you are with the prince, Niall."

He was frowning. "Are the government sending troops to Morar or are they relying on Linton?"

Van answered slowly, "I believe they are relying on Edward for the present. He has no love for the prince, Niall. He would turn him in if he knew he was here."

"Well then," Niall said as he gave his sister his most charming smile, "we will just have to see to it that Edward does *not* know." He took her arm. "Come along now, and greet your prince."

Charles looked almost as ragged and dirty as Niall, but he greeted Van with a grin and made a joke about his beard. "I have not had the opportunity to shave since I discarded Betty Burke," he said with a laugh. Charles's two-week beard was redder than his hair and his shirt was actually dirtier than Niall's

"I brought you some food," Van said. "I see I also should have brought some clothes."

"We have four shirts between us," Niall said cheerfully. "The other two are wet from yesterday's rain."

Van brought the food into the cave and watched as the two young men ate hungrily. After they had finished she asked them to tell her about their escape from the Long Island. Niall obeyed, with interjections from the prince, and Van listened in cold horror as she realized for the first time how perilously close they had been to capture. Charles and Niall made it sound like a schoolboy's adventure, but she knew all too well that what they were describing was a matter of life and death.

"Flora MacDonald and MacDonald of Kingsburgh are made prisoners, did you know that?" she asked when the story was concluded.

The prince looked distressed. "No. I did not know that."

"Mother wrote to me that Cumberland has come down hard upon the Highlands." Niall's voice was grim. "Are things quieter now?"

"No." Van's face was strained. "Cumberland is at Fort Augustus and he is as busy about his work of devastation as ever. They have herded all the cattle they can find into the fort and they are selling it to agents from England."

"Dhé!" said Niall. "Without cattle the clans will starve."

"My husband has imported food from Ireland," Van said clearly. "The fist shipload of meat, butter, cheese, and salt came last week. The *Sea Queen* has since gone back to Dublin for another cargo."

"Your husband?" said Charles. "The Earl of Linton?"

"The Earl of Linton." Van stared into her brother's eyes. "Edward went to see the Duke of Argyll and the duke agreed to allow the food to be distributed in Lochaber and Badenoch."

"Mac Cailein Mhor agreed to that?"

"Aye. He is a Campbell, but he is Highland. He does not believe in starving innocent people."

"And what of Cumberland?" asked Niall

Van answered slowly, "I do not believe the Duke of Cumberland was consulted on the matter." Niall gave a sour smile.

The prince spoke. "The Earl of Linton may be a Whig and an enemy, but I applaud his humanitarianism, my lady."

Van gave Charles a long and enigmatic look. Then she said quietly, "Thank you, your highness."

As she made ready to leave some time later, Van asked Niall, "For how long do you plan to stay here?"

"For as long as we can," came the disconcerting reply. "My hope is that they will concentrate the search elsewhere and the French will get a ship in to us."

Van's face was very pale. "Niall, I cannot come out here too frequently. I promised Edward I would not assist the prince, and if he ever finds out what I am doing . . ."

Niall frowned at the look in his sister's eyes. He could not ever recall seeing Van looked like that. "Are you afraid of him, then?" he asked incredulously.

"What I am afraid of, Niall," she replied, "is that, should he find out that I have betrayed his trust, he will never forgive me." The expression on her face was indescribably desolate.

There was a long, heavy pause. Then, "I am sorry, my sister, to put this burden on you," Niall said soberly. "But our duty to our prince comes first."

Van looked at her dearly loved brother and did not tell him that what she was doing was not for the prince's sake but for his.

29

Edward was not at the castle when Van returned. Morag told her that he had received a message that the food they had sent to the Loch Arkaig area had been confiscated by government troops who were in the area to search for the prince. Edward had taken Alan Ruadh and gone to see what could be done to get the supplies back.

Van was relieved she did not have to face him so soon after seeing the prince and Niall, but felt doubly guilty knowing he was out on a mission of mercy.

He did not come home that night. Van put together a package of more food and a collection of her father's shirts and kilts to send out to the cave with Lachlan. On the theory that the fewer who knew about the cave the better, Lachlan was to be their only messenger. He had fought bravely at Culloden and was devoted to Niall. Lachlan was safe.

Van did not see Edward until almost eight o'clock the following evening. She was sitting alone in the great drawing room, a book she was not reading in her hands, when the door opened and he came in.

His boots were dirty and his cheek was scratched. "Dhé, Edward!" Van said, her book dropping unregarded into her lap. "I was beginning to worry about you."

He did not kiss her but came to drop wearily into the big chair that used to be her father's. "Christ," he said, "my feet." He stretched his long legs out in front of him and looked at her. "A horse. A horse. My kingdom for a horse," he quoted humorously.

He looked so long and large, stretched out there in her father's chair. "Morag said you went to Loch Arkaig?" she asked tentatively.

"Yes." He smiled at her, the slow, deliberate lazy smile that she had come to know meant he wanted something. "I'm starving, sweetheart," he said. "Alan and I have had nothing to eat all day but a little oatmeal."

Van jumped to her feet. "I'll order you some meat and bread," she said, and went to pull the bell rope.

Morag appeared almost instantly with a large tray laden with food. She set it on the table before the empty fireplace and Edward said, "I think we could have a little fire too, Morag." Van watched with secret amusement as Morag moved to pile the wood expertly onto the hearth. The clan MacIan, she thought, with centuries of distrust of the Sassenach bred into their bones, had all fallen neatly under Edward's spell.

Van watched him eat while she sipped a cup of tea. Finally, when he had finished, he poured himself another glass of wine and said, "There were about five hundred troops at Loch Arkaig looking for the prince. It was thought that he might have tried to join Lochiel."

Van spoke out of a constricted throat. "Is Lochiel at Loch Arkaig?"

"I don't know. Possibly. At any rate, the country is being closely searched."

"And the food?"

Edward put his wineglass down so hard that a little of the deep red claret splashed onto the polished wood. He stared at the fire and appeared not to notice. "The food that had not yet been distributed was in Ewen Cameron's cottage near to Achnacarry—or the remains of Achnacarry. The soldiers confiscated it, which was why Ewen sent for me."

"And did you get it back?" Van asked.

"Yes."

Van deduced, from the set of his mouth, that his encounter with the military had not been pleasant. "What happened, Edward?"

He shrugged and did not meet her eyes. "The captain was a bloody little sod," he said. "Kept quoting his orders to me." His eyes finally swung around to her face. They were a brilliant blue. "I'll tell you this, Van," he said softly but with contained violence, "I was not proud to be an Englishman this day." Then he pushed back his chair and went to stand by the chimneypiece, one hand on the mantel, looking down into the fire. "At any rate," he continued, "the food has been restored and will continue to be distributed." There was a long pause. Then, "The Camerons have been hit very hard," he said.

"As the MacIans would have been were it not for you." Van stared at her husband's back, her heart filled with turmoil. He had done so much for them. The thought of the cave and its inhabitants scalded her with guilt, yet what else could she do? Edward had said there were five hundred troops in Lochiel's country. "Where else are the soldiers looking?" she asked. "Do you know?"

"There are patrols all over the areas about Loch Quoich and Loch Eil, I believe," he replied. "They have information that the prince came ashore at Mallaig, so that is the area they are searching most carefully." He was still staring into the fire. "Van, if Niall is taken with the prince, there will be little I can do."

And that is precisely why I am hiding him from you,

Van thought a little hysterically. She bit her lip and said with forced calm, "I understand that, Edward," She got up and went over to him by the fire. Putting her arms around his waist, she laid her cheek against his back and murmured, "If you've finished your wine, let's go upstairs."

As she watched him undress in front of the small bedroom fire, she asked, "How did you scratch your cheek?"

"A branch caught me." He grinned at her. "Alan tells me I am becoming as good a mountaineer as a Highlander, though."

He stripped to the waist and Van looked at him, at the breadth of his chest and shoulders. His arms were tanned, and the V at his throat where he had taken to wearing his shirt open. His hair had bleached to the color of ripe wheat. He looked back at her, smiled, and stretched himself like a giant cat. "I will never grow accustomed to sleeping on the hard ground wrapped only in a plaid," he said. "That bed looks very good," He began to cross the floor. "And so do you."

"I doubt that Niall has seen a bed in months," she said before she could stop herself.

He halted as abruptly as if he had walked into glass. Then, "It is by his own choice, Van," he answered slowly. "My offer to get him away to France still holds good."

"But he will never go without the prince, Edward! Don't you see that?"

His eyes were steady on her face. "I see it. Perhaps I even understand it. But there is nothing I can do about it, Van. It is his choice. He will have to live with the consequences."

"Or die with them," she said bitterly.

He regarded her with courteous interest. "Are you by any chance asking me to help the prince to escape?" His voice was polite, curious, as if the question was of little importance to either of them. She did not answer but her eyes dropped, unable to look anymore at that carefully courteous face. "If it were at all possible, you know," he continued pleasantly, "I would kidnap Niall and forcibly send him to France. I am well aware that his shadow stands between us, and that it will continue to do so for as long as he remains in danger. But there are some things a man may not do—even for the woman he loves. I gave my word to the duke not to assist Charles Stuart to escape. I have many faults, Van, but betraying my word is not one of them."

Van wished she had never brought up this subject. The memory of her own promise to him was vivid in her mind. He would never forgive her if he found out what she had done. But he was right. The shadow of Niall stood between them. More than he knew. She felt possessed by a devastating hopelessness. She had been sitting on the edge of the bed and now she stood up and took a step toward him. "Oh, Edward," she said sorrowfully.

He caught her in his arms and she pressed against him, running her hands up and down the smooth broadness of his back. It was as if her hands had released a dark flood of hot passion in him; she felt it, felt it sear into her. Half-fainting, she let herself be lifted up in his arms and carried to the bed.

Niall and Charles remained at the cave for over a week. The area surrounding Morar was crawling with government troops and Van knew she could not even suggest that her two dangerous visitors should try to leave. Morar was for the moment the only safe refuge from the hunters.

Then, on July 16, ships appeared in Loch Morar. Van was working in the vegetable garden when Donal came running to tell her the news. "They are coming up the loch, Lady Van!" he cried. "Six of them. Big ships, my lady; very big."

Van put down her trowel. "Where is Lord Linton?" she asked.

"Up the glen looking at cattle, my lady."

"Get him, Donal," Van ordered. Donal took one look at her face and fled.

Dhé! Ships in Loch Morar! And Niall and the prince only a few miles away. They must be warned to stay in the cave. Van looked around. "Maire," she called to the girl who was working with her, "fetch me Lachlan. Immediately."

Maire ran and Van herself began to walk swiftly back to the castle, her heart thudding so hard it took her breath away. What could this mean? She entered the castle through a side door and went to her room to tidy up. If she had to confront English troops, at least she would do it looking like a lady.

She changed her dress and smoothed her hair and went to wait for Lachlan in Edward's office. "Thank God," she said as the slender, dark clansman came in the door. "Lachlan, go out to the cave and warn Mac mhic Iain to keep inside, that there are enemy ships in the loch. I will get more information to him when I can, but for now he is to remain inside!"

"Aye, my lady."

They would never see Lachlan from the water, Van thought as the clansman moved swiftly away. He was like a shadow, silent and stealthy and insubstantial. He would warn Niall.

Now that she had got the message safely off to Niall, she wanted Edward. Where was he? She went to the window half a dozen times and the last time the sight that met her eyes froze her blood. A great war ship was anchoring off the shore right in front of the castle. Van watched, petrified, as a boat was lowered and men were rowed to the shore.

Dhé! They were coming to the castle. Where in the name of God was Edward?

It was a white-faced Morag who brought her the news. "My lady, General Campbell would like to speak to you."

Van raised her chin. "I will go to the drawing room, Morag. You may show him up in five minutes."

"Aye, my lady," replied Morag, whose eyes were twice their usual size.

Van was sitting in her mother's chair, her back ramrod straight, her head high on its lovely long neck, when General Campbell came into the room. She saw his eyes go around the huge, beautiful drawing room before they came to rest on her. Van had chosen her setting quite deliberately. Let the Campbell see he was not dealing with ignorant peasants. She stared him straight in the eye and asked coolly, "And to what do we owe the honor of this visit, General?"

He crossed the floor toward her, over the Persian rugs, past the Titian portrait of one of her ancestors, and stopped before her chair. Van did not ask him to sit down.

"Lady Linton," he said, "I am quite sure you know our errand. We are in search of the pretender."

Van raised an elegant black eyebrow. "Well, he certainly is not here, General." She gestured gracefully about the room.

"I did not think he was in this castle, Lady Linton,"

Campbell replied a little shortly. "I do think, however, that he may be in Morar."

Van's cool eyes never wavered. "Morar's loyalty is pledged to the government by Lord Linton."

"I have no doubt of Lord Linton's loyalty, Lady Linton," the Campbell said, with the very faintest of stresses on the word "lord." "However, the pretender is thought to be in the company of your brother, and the MacIans will consider that their first loyalty is to Mac mhic Iain. Lord Morar and the pretender may well be hiding somewhere here in Morar without Lord Linton's knowledge."

Van concealed her hands within the folds of her dress so he should not see how they were shaking. "What—?" she was beginning when she heard the door open and Edward's bright head appeared around the fire screen at the door. Van closed her eyes briefly. Thank God.

"General Campbell," she heard her husband say pleasantly. "I see you have brought quite a company to visit us."

"My lord." John Campbell of Mamore took the hand Edward was extending and smiled back at the earl's suntanned, good-humored face.

"Sit down, man," Edward said, and General Campbell, with a quick glance at the silent Van, complied. Morag came in with wine and glasses on a tray and Edward poured a glass for himself and for the general. Van declined. She would have liked the wine but was afraid her hand was shaking too much to hold the glass.

"I was just telling Lady Linton that we think the pretender may be hiding in Morar," General Campbell said to Edward.

"Indeed?" Edward seemed perfectly relaxed and

appeared to be taking no more than a polite interest in his visitor's words. "I am over the estate all the time, General, and I can assure you that I have seen no sign of the pretender."

"I do not doubt you," Campbell returned a little grimly. "But he is thought to be with Niall MacIan, my lord. You have been in the Highlands long enough, I think, to know the loyalty a clan feels to its chief. They would shelter him and never tell you of it."

"That may well be so." Edward seemed completely unperturbed as he sipped his wine. "You have had no luck elsewhere?"

"None. The surrounding area has all been thoroughly searched. There is a cordon of troops around Morar, my lord, and we do not think he has gotten through. Captain Scott is in the lower part of Arisaig. I have six men-of-war in the loch here, all with troops aboard. If the pretender is indeed in Morar, we will find him."

Van felt cold. Icy cold. Her husband was regarding General Campbell with perfect serenity. "If you feel the pretender is in Morar, then of course you must look for him. But"—the merest hint of steel appeared in that pleasant voice—"I do not want to hear of one cottage burned or one man, woman, or child hurt on my property. I hope I make myself clear, General Campbell."

"Perfectly clear, my lord." The Campbell rose to his feet. "I shall be sure your message is given to all the proper authorities."

"One thing more." Edward was on his feet as well. "If my brother-in-law should ever come into your hands, I should be grateful if you would inform me immediately."

Campbell looked once more, swiftly, at Van's silent figure. Then, "Of course, my lord," he said.

Edward walked with the general to the door and Van sat as if frozen, her brain working furiously. Niall and the prince must get away from Morar. The search here would be too concentrated. They must get away.

She forced herself to look calmly at her husband as he came back across the room toward her. "Campbell of Mamore is a decent sort," he said. "If he is in charge, there will be no plundering."

"Van forced a laugh. "I never thought I'd see the day I'd be grateful to a Campbell."

"Van." He was leaning against the chimneypiece and staring at his linked hands, a thoughtful frown on his face. "Van," he said again, "Campbell isn't going to find anything in Morar, is he?" And he raised his eyes and looked at her.

Her face was pale under its tan, but the gray-green eyes that met his were clear and truthful. "Not that I know of, Edward," she answered steadily.

Satisfied, he dropped his hands and nodded. "If they find Niall," he said, "we may be able to free him before they get him to Fort Augustus."

She was now very pale. "Do you think so?" she asked hollowly.

He poured a glass of wine and went to her side. "Drink this, sweetheart. Try not to worry so. If it is at all possible, I'll save Niall's skin for him. I promise you that."

Van sipped the wine and felt her stomach heave. I will not be sick, she said to herself fiercely. I will *not* be sick. She gave the wine back to Edward, looked up into his concerned eyes, and wanted to cry.

That night Van sent two messages, one with Lachlan to the cave and one with Donal to Donald Cameron of

Glen Pean. Niall and Charles read Van's letter by the light of a burning stick; they were afraid to light a fire for cooking lest it be seen.

"Campbell is in Loch Morar and Captain Scott is in Arisaig," Niall read out loud. "There are camps and sentries posted all over the hills from the head of Loch Eil to the top of Loch Hourn." Niall looked at the prince. "Van says our best chance is to go southeast, to Sgurr nan Coireachan, and from there to try to break through north. She has sent a message to Donald Cameron of Glen Pean to meet us at Sgurr nan Coireachan tomorrow night. He will guide us from there."

"Where is Sgurr nan Coireachan?" Charles asked.

"That great hill you can see from here, sir," Niall replied. "It marks the border between the Camerons' country and ours."

Charles nodded and gave Niall a rueful grin. "It was too peaceful here to be true, MacIan. It looks as if we must be on our travels again."

"Aye, sir, that it does," Niall replied with an answering smile. "And we'd best be gone before daybreak."

"Give my thanks to your mistress," the prince said to Lachlan. "Tell her her prince shall never forget her loyalty or her courage."

Lachlan nodded, bowed his head, and melted away in the darkness. Half an hour later, Niall and Charles were on their way as well.

30

Niall and the prince did not make it to Sgurr nan Coireachan. On their way they saw a flock of MacIans moving cattle away from advancing government troops. A clansman told them there were five or six hundred soldiers already at the head of Loch Arkaig. If Niall and Charles continued on their present course, they would run straight into the path of the enemy.

The two fugitives lay in the heather all day, their only food some milk and bread given to Niall by his clansmen. No one had asked Mac mhic Iain who the unknown young man accompanying him was. At sunset they moved off, deciding it was now too dangerous to attempt to find Donald Cameron of Glen Pean. Instead, the two young men moved cautiously north-ward and, shortly before midnight, in a hollow between two hills, they were surprised by a man on foot coming straight at them. The late-night traveler proved to be none other than Cameron of Glen Pean, who had received Van's message and was in search of them.

Donald had spied out the enemy's dispositions, and by paths forbidding even in full daylight, took them to a hill overlooking Loch Arkaig. There was a militia camp not more than a mile from where they lay, but the hill had already been searched, Donald said, and they remained safely hidden there for the whole of the

long hot day. They started north again once it was
dark.

Niall had never been more sensible of the feeling
that God was with them as he was during that perilous
escape from Morar. They hid during the day and moved
only at night. From the head of Loch Eil to the top of
Loch Hourn there were enemy camps every half-mile,
with sentries posted and regular patrols combing the
hills. Sometimes they came so close to the camps that
they could hear the soldiers talking. The going was
treacherous. Charles walked between Niall and Cameron of Glen Pean and more than once the two sure-
footed Highlanders saved him from a dangerous fall.

It was early on the morning of July 21 when they
passed safely between two sentries in Glen Cosaidh,
the outer post of the cordon surrounding Morar. For
the moment, they were free of the net.

By August it was clear to the English command that
their quarry had escaped the trap. The Earl of Albemarle, who had succeeded the Duke of Cumberland as
commander-in-chief of the king's army in Scotland,
gave order for regular patrols to go out from Fort
Augustus to search the west for the Old Pretender's
son. Burning and looting and murder accompanied the
soldiers wherever they marched.

In Morar they were safe, but word reached them of
what was happening in the surrounding country. Van
tried her best to go about her daily rounds calmly, to
speak quietly, to hide from Edward the anguish and
the fury that were growing within her as each atrocity
was reported. She felt at times as if she had a tiger
hidden within her, a tiger whose existence she must
keep out of sight even though it lashed and cried out
for release.

It was mid-August when Lachlan appeared with the information that Lord Edward Sackville was north of Morar, in Knoidart, with a large party of soldiers, laying waste the country and driving off all the cattle they could find.

"A few of the Knoidart clansmen made off with the colonel's baggage horses, Lady Van," Lachlan told her somberly. He had found her supervising the distribution of clothing for the clan. The government had banned the wearing of the kilt and Edward had sent to Ireland for clothing, as the clansmen had no other garments aside from their traditional garb. "In revenge, the soldiers sacked the area," Lachlan went on. "They first raped the women and then forced them to watch the bayoneting of their husbands, sons, brothers, and fathers."

Van's knuckles went white. "God curse them all," she said.

"Aye," replied Lachlan. He looked at her from under frowning brows. "The word is that they are coming to Morar."

"I will speak to Lord Linton," said Van immediately.

Lachlan's face lightened. "Aye," he said with perfect confidence. "Lord Linton will know what do do."

Van waited until they were alone in their bedroom that evening before she related to Edward what Lachlan had told her that afternoon.

He pressed his fingers to his temples as if he had a headache. "Sackville, did you say?" he replied. "He's the Duke of Dorset's son."

"Do you know him?" Van asked.

He shook his head. "I know Dorset. I know Sackville was wounded at Fontenoy." He was sitting in the chair before the empty fireplace, his fingers still pressed to his temples.

"Too bad he wasn't killed," Van said.

"If it wasn't Sackville, Van, it would be someone else." He sounded very weary.

The tiger with Van began to pace up and down. "A duke's son," she said. "There is perhaps some excuse for the soldiers, who are ignorant, brutish recruits from the slums and stews of the country. But a duke's son, Edward! A man of education. There is no excuse for him. None."

"No," he said. "There is not."

"Well? What are you going to do?" She could hear the rising shrillness in her voice, feel the tiger she was trying so hard to keep hidden coming ever closer to the surface.

"I will ride to Knoidart tomorrow," he said. "They won't come to Morar if I can help it."

"When is this going to stop, Edward?" Her voice cracked. She was perilously close to screaming.

He looked at her. "They want Charles Stuart, Van. Albemarle has sworn that for the chance of laying his hand on the pretender he would walk barefoot from pole to pole."

She stared at him, her breath coming short and hard through flared nostrils. "Where did you near that?" She was standing at the footboard of the bed with half the distance of the room between them.

"I received a letter from my mother today. She directed it to Inverary and the duke was kind enough to send it on to Morar." Even in the dimness of the bedroom light his eyes looked blue. "She had further news," he continued. "It seems Cumberland's popularity in England has faltered as word of what is happening here in Scotland has gotten out. When he returned to London in July he was welcomed like a hero, but the tide is beginning to turn."

Van took a step toward him. "How?" she asked tensely.

"Well, it seems that when it was proposed that the duke become an honorary freeman of a city guild, the aldermen replied, 'Let it be of the Butchers' Guild.' "

Van's head went up. "Ah," she said.

"But the aldermen's reply is not going to change government policy, Van. For as long as Charles Stuart is free, there will be soldiers in these glens."

Van took another step toward him. "Would not the best thing for all be for the prince to escape?"

There was a long pause. When he answered at last his voice was very weary. "Should the prince escape, Van, there will always remain the possibility of all this happening again. For as long as there is a Stuart pretender, the Highlands will be involved in plots to restore him."

"No," Van said. Her voice was profoundly bitter. "We have learned our lesson, Edward. There is no way the Highlands will ever rise for a Stuart again."

The expression in his eyes was as weary as his voice. "Would your brother agree to that?" he asked. "Or Lochiel?"

Van looked back at him and did not answer.

"And the MacIans and the Camerons would follow their chiefs," he continued, "and it would all happen again." He pressed his fingers against his temples once again. "No, I am afraid that the best thing for the Highlands is that Charles Stuart should die."

The following morning Van watched Edward ride out on the horse he had had shipped to Morar from Ireland. She smiled a little as she remembered the look on his face when the animal had been unloaded. He was missing his own horses badly.

He was doing so much for them all, had given up so much. And she loved him so. But she wondered if the day would ever come when they could live together without the shadow of this war and this retribution there to darken and distort what they felt for each other.

She was not free to love him. At night she lay against his big, warm, life-giving body and felt despair and guilt welling up within her. How could she love him when she knew betrayal was in her heart? All she could do was live from day to day, waiting, waiting always for some word, some sign, that her brother was safe. Perhaps then she could begin to live again.

Like so many Highlanders who had fought at Culloden, Alan MacDonald had been hiding and running and hoping somewhere in his travels to find a ship to take him to France. His father had escaped, he learned from clansmen in Lochaber. The wounded chief had boarded a French ship in Poolewe that had been searching for the prince. Alan hoped to have similar luck but it was mid-August and he was still in the Highlands.

It was his longing to see Van once more that prompted his decision to return to Morar. Perhaps he could get a ship from Arisaig, he told himself. And so he began to make his way west, from Loch Garry, where he had been in hiding for weeks, toward Knoidart and so to Morar.

Alasdair MacIan's kilt and shirt were filthy and ragged by now, and Alan's red beard was long and shaggy. He had been mistaken for the prince more than once by clansmen who had only seen Charles from a distance. Alan had often thought of how he would put that resemblance to use should the occasion ever arise.

He had made it to Knoidart when he was surprised by a party of Sackville's soldiers who were out rounding up cattle. He turned to run for the hills, where no English soldier could follow a Highlander, but Alan's luck had run out. He felt the musket ball thud into his back. The pain was terrible but he fought the mist that was distorting his vision. Dimly he could see a face leaning over him.

"Villains," he said in the last great effort of his life, "you have slain your prince."

Edward stared at the arrogant, aristocratic face of Lord Edward Sackville and made a heroic attempt to hold on to his temper. The colonel was dressed magnificently, in a fine scarlet broadcloth coat looped with gold, its blue lapels turned back to show the snow-white lace at his throat. Edward's own clothing was beginning to show definite signs of wear.

"Your men's behavior flouts all the conventions of war," he managed to say evenly. "You are dealing with a civilian population, Colonel. Your regiment's behavior has been thoroughly reprehensible and I protest it to you strongly."

Lord Edward's haughty, thin-nosed visage remained unmoved. "This is not an ordinary war, Lord Linton, as you are well aware. There is only one way to deal with this cursed country and that is by fire and sword. Nothing else will cure their damned vicious way of thinking."

Edward's eyes began to get very blue. "I might remind you, Colonel, that this 'cursed country' is part of Great Britain and that these civilians whom you are molesting are British citizens." His voice was restrained but the sting in it brought a spot of color to Sackville's thin cheeks.

"They are damn rebels, is what they are!" the colonel retorted hotly.

"Nor," Edward continued as if he had not heard, "did I ever expect to see an English officer degenerate into the role of executioner."

They were alone inside Sackville's tent. From outside Edward could hear the lowing of the great herd of cattle the English had collected to drive back to Fort Augustus.

"You will retract those words, sir!" Sackville said sharply.

"I will do no such thing." Linton's eyes were like ice, his mouth a thin line in his suntanned face. "And I tell you now, Sackville, do not dare try to cross your troops into Morar or I will have you up before Parliament." The hold Edward had been keeping on his temper was beginning to slip. He hoped very much at that moment that Sackville would challenge him to a duel. He would like nothing more than to put his sword through the bastard's black heart.

Sackville read the look in Edward's eyes very well and took a slight step backward. He did not want to challenge Linton, either politically or personally. The earl had the edge over him on both counts, and he knew it.

"I have no intention of entering Morar," he was beginning, when a soldier appeared at the door of his tent.

"A search party has just come back with a dead body, Colonel," the man said with visible excitement. "They think it is the pretender!"

"What! Where?" Sackville was out the door of his tent in a moment. Edward followed more slowly. One body, the men had said. If it were indeed the prince, where was Niall?

A horse was coming into camp with a body tied across its back. Sackville issued a sharp order and the body was lifted off and laid stretched out upon the ground. Edward walked over and looked down.

The dead face was young and the hair and the beard were distinctly reddish in color. Edward looked at the ragged kilt and filthy shirt. The height was about right. It could be Charles Stuart.

"He said, 'Villains, you have slain your prince,' " one of the soldiers was telling Sackville. Edward knelt down and looked into the dead man's eyes. Then, with gentle fingers, he smoothed them shut.

"What do you think, Linton? Have you ever seen the Old Pretender's son?" It was Sackville speaking. His face wore a strangely greedy look. Capturing the prince would be a major coup for him.

Edward scarcely made an attempt to conceal the distaste he felt. "No, I have not." He looked once more at Sackville and then said slowly, "By all reports, however, this man fits the description."

"Yes. He does. But I would like to be certain." Sackville walked over to stare down at the dead man on the ground. What a plum for him should this truly be the prince! "Is there no one in the area who can identify the pretender?" he asked.

"You have killed every man who could possibly have fought in his army," Edward replied.

Sackville's thin nose looked even sharper. He gave Edward a vicious look and did not reply.

Edward also looked at the figure on the ground, but the expression in his eyes was not greed but pity. After a moment Edward said, "My wife has met the Young Pretender. Perhaps she may be induced to come and identify him."

"Your wife," said Sackville. "Morar's daughter . . .

Yes." He stared at Edward. "Will you send for her, my lord?"

"I will ask her if she feels up to the task," Edward replied, and looked once more on the still face of the red-haired young man before he went to find his horse.

He was back in Morar by early afternoon. Van was in the garden and he sent Morag to find her and ask her to return to the house. He waited for her in the office, an abstracted frown on his face.

She came in, looking alarmed. "What is it, Edward? you are back very soon. Did you see Sackville?"

"Yes, I saw Sackville." He gestured to a chair. "Sit down, Van."

She was very pale as she took the chair he had indicated. "Is he coming to Morar after all?"

"No." His mouth smiled reassuringly, although his eyes remained grave. Van's face did not lose its expression of apprehension. "Sweetheart," he said gently, "Sackville thinks he has got the prince."

"Got the prince!" Her eyes were huge and fearful. "And Niall?"

"There is no sign of Niall." She relaxed visibly and he let out a long, slow breath. "What they have got, Van, is actually a body they think may be the prince."

Her black brows drew together. "A body. A dead body?"

"Yes." And he told her what had happened on the hillside. "Needless to say, Sackville hopes very much that it *is* the prince," he concluded, "but he needs another source of identification."

Van stared at her husband's contained face. "Do *you* think it is the prince, Edward?"

"I don't know. The description fits, certainly, but, you see, I have never met the prince. Nor has anyone in Sackville's command."

"And I have." Her words were slow and drawn out.

"And you have." She could not quite fathom his expression. "If you feel you can do it, Van, Sackville would like you to come and look at the body. If you feel you cannot, I will be glad to tell him so."

She stared intently into his face, trying to understand what he might be thinking. His eyes were unreadable. She drew a sharp breath. "I will come," she said.

"Very well." He looked at her dirt-stained dress. "Why don't you change into trews and I'll have a pony made ready for you?"

"All right." She shot another look at his face before she left to go to her room to change.

They arrived back at the English camp late that afternoon. Colonel Sackville stood at the opening to his tent and watched the tall blond English earl crossing the ground toward him. His eyes went to the slender black-haired girl at Linton's side. "Lady Linton," he said formally. "I am grateful for your assistance in this matter."

The girl's great light eyes flicked once across his face. The colonel felt color sting into his cheeks. There was no doubt at all what the Countess of Linton thought of him. "Where is he?" she asked in perfectly cultured English.

"In the tent over there." He looked at the earl. "If you will come this way?"

Linton nodded. "Are you ready, Van?" he asked his wife.

"Yes." She walked steadily between the two men, her eyes on the tent which might hold the body of the prince. She did not know what it was she hoped to see. If it were indeed Charles Stuart, then this ugly chapter in her country's history might finally be closed. Niall could be got away to France. But to see him in the hands of these Sassenach, their bonnie prince. . . She drew a deep, steadying breath and walked with Edward into the tent.

He was lying on a blanket on the ground and she recognized him instantly. She went white to the lips at the sight of that dead face and her hands clenched into fists at her sides. Dear God. Dear God. Dear God. It was Alan.

From a very long way away she heard Edward's voice. "Do you recognize him, Van?"

"Aye." Her own voice was deep and husky and full of emotion. She went down on her knees and bent to press her lips to the dead man's forehead. It was cold as ice under her mouth. *Ailein, Ailein, Ailein,* her heart cried out in silence. She rose to her feet and looked at Sackville. "It is the prince," she said clearly, and walked out of the tent.

"Well, there's no doubt that she recognized him," Sackville said with satisfaction to his second in command after Van and Edward had left once again for Morar. "She went white as a ghost."

"Looks as if it's the Young Pretender, all right," Lieutenant Morton replied. "What do we do now, Colonel?"

"Cut off his head and send it to London," Lord Edward Sackville replied. "The last of the bloody Stuarts." He smiled thinly. "We shall be heroes, Morton. I'll get a letter off straightaway to Lord Albemarle."

"Yes, sir," replied the lieutenant, and turned to go and order the disposition of Alan's remains.

* * *

The ride back to Morar was silent. Van's mind was filled with memories of Alan. He should have stayed in Morar, she thought hopelessly. I knew he should have stayed.

"Will you be all right?" Edward asked her when they reached the door of Creag an Fhithich.

She looked at him in surprise. "Aren't you coming in?"

"I want to tend to Fitz," he replied, patting his horse's neck. "I have not quite managed to convince your clansmen that horses require more care than ponies."

"I shall be fine," she replied, her attention focused fully on her husband for the first time since she had seen Alan. He was regarding her with polite concern. "Is something wrong, Edward?" she asked hesitantly.

The golden eyebrows rose. "No." There was just the slightest gleam of irony in those blue eyes. "You've had a shock," he said. "Try to get some rest."

"Yes, I will," She watched him lead the horse and pony back down the drive, the faintest of frowns between her brows.

31

Alan's head was sent to London and for several weeks the hunt for the prince cooled. Throughout the end of August and early September a few lonely patrols were sent out from Fort Augustus to struggle through the mountains to search for Charles, but otherwise the west was quiet. Albemarle abandoned Fort Augustus himself and moved his headquarters to Edinburgh, a location far more comfortable than the tent city which he had inhabited at Fort Augustus.

On September 6 the prince, Niall, Lochiel, and his brother Dr. Archibald Cameron were all safely hidden in a cave high on the slopes of Ben Alder. This cave was the headquarters of Cluny Macpherson, head of the clan Macpherson, and from this mountain eyrie Cluny had been ruling for months in perfect safety.

Cluny's cave was far more luxurious than Niall and Van's cave in the hills above Loch Morar. The cave on Ben Alder, concealed by a grove of holly, was constructed on two levels and was roofed with turf. Against a great slab of gray rock behind it, the smoke from its chimney was invisible, and with a fire to warm them, six or seven people could find room to play cards and cook their meals.

The fugitives were physically comfortable yet they were restless. They had been on the run for five months now. What they needed desperately was a ship to France.

The hunt had quieted but there were still navy ships in the waters of Arisaig and Sleat. Neither Edward nor Van thought much of the fact that two ships flying British colors had cruised into Loch nan Uamh. It was in the late afternoon of September 6, while Niall was on Bel Alder eating his dinner, that Van discovered that the ships were not English but French.

The news was brought to her by Macdonald of Boisdale. Fortunately Edward was out, so she met him in the office.

"The two ships lying in Loch nan Uamh are not English but French," Boisdale informed her immediately. "They are in search of the prince, my lady. Can you get word to him?"

"Dhé!" said Van. "The prince is not near Morar, Boisdale. It will take a little time to locate him."

"Aye, so I told the French officer."

"How did they find you?" Van asked. They were speaking in low voices and in Gaelic.

"The ship put a party ashore to contact someone who could get word to the prince. There were directed to me."

"And no one suspects they are not English?"

"They fly the British flag, my lady, and the ships look just like English ships. There is a militia camp near Arisaig, but they have not been curious."

"The militia will not recognize them for impostors, but the navy will. They cannot remain for too long in Loch nan Uamh." Van's body was taut with tension. At last a ship . . . if only she could get word to Niall in time. "Listen to me, Boisdale," she said. "Tell the French officer to lie offshore for a while and then to be back in the loch in two weeks' time. I will have the prince at Loch nan Uamh by then and they can take him off."

"Aye, my lady."

As Boisdale prepared to leave, Van smiled ruefully. "You look so strange without your kilt," she said. "I cannot get accustomed to seeing Highlanders in breeches."

MacDonald of Boisdale raised his chin proudly. "Wait until the prince returns, my lady. Then we will drive the Sassenach out of our glens forever. The chiefs and the tartan will be restored when our bonnie Charlie comes again."

"Aye," said Van, and watched with somber eyes as the MacDonald turned and left the office. Then she set out herself to look for Lachlan.

Lachlan left for Cameron country to get word of the prince on the night of September 6. On September 10 a letter arrived for Edward from London, delivered by a Campbell from Inverary. The letter was not from Edward's mother, however. The seal was official. Van accepted it, fed the Campbell messenger, sent him on his way, and sat down to wait for her husband and to worry.

Edward did not return to the castle until nine that evening. He had taken to spending long hours out in the hills and the glens of Morar, evaluating, as he said, the potential for farming in this rocky Highland soil. Van, however, had a growing suspicion that one of the reasons for his extended hours away from the castle was that he was avoiding her.

She had almost given him up and gone to bed. She was so tired these days, weary with a fatigue she had never felt before. She was also nauseous in the mornings and food had lost all attraction for her. She was beginning to suspect that she might be with child.

She heard his step behind her coming across the drawing-room floor and turned her head to peek around the high back of her chair. The castle drawing room was so big, she thought. How could one man's presence seem to fill it as his did? Sunshine and energy and strength walked into a room with Edward. Van felt some of her own weariness lift. She smiled up into his face and said lightly, "Have you eaten? Shall I order supper for you?"

He shook his head. "Glen Alden shot a stag this afternoon and he feasted me well." MacIan of Glen Alden was one of Morar's most important tacksmen.

Van stared at her husband in wonder. He was sunburned and carelessly dressed and his once-polished boots were worn and scarred. Eating stag with Glen Alden, she thought. The sophisticated and immaculate Earl of Linton. He stretched his long legs in front of him and gave her a faint smile. "What have you done with yourself all day?"

She answered slowly, "A letter came for you, Edward. From London. It looks very official." She took the letter from the mantel and brought it to his chair.

He did not change his relaxed posture while he ripped the seal and read what was inside.

"What is it?" Van asked a little breathlessly. Without answering, he handed the letter to her.

It was precisely what she had thought it would be. Precisely the message she had been dreading and preparing for these last weeks. Lord Newcastle had written to inform Lord Linton that the man slain in Knoidart, the man whom his wife had identified as the Young Pretender, was not Charles Stuart at all. Charles

Stuart must therefore be presumed to be alive and still hiding somewhere in Scotland.

Van lowered the letter and looked at her husband. He was gazing at the top of his boots, seemingly perfectly relaxed. His hands, ringless save for the one signet, were resting lightly on the chair's arms.

"Edward," Van said. "I am sorry."

His head lifted slightly and he looked at her. His face was perfectly contained. Van thought she would have felt better if he had been angry. "I'm glad you didn't try to say you had made a mistake," he said.

"No. Of course I knew it was not the prince." He was so composed, so . . . distant. "It was Alan Mac-Donald," she said. Her voice trembled and then steadied. "I would probably have married him if I had not met you."

That surprised him. His eyes widened just slightly and she dropped to her knees by his side. "He died saying those words, Edward," she said. "What else could I do? I could not betray the last great selfless act of his life. He loved me. I think I might have loved him were it not for you."

She knelt there, her face upturned to his. A memory flashed into her mind of one other time she had knelt thus, the time his mare had died. She thought, from the flicker of expression in his eyes, that he was remembering that time too.

"You should have told me." His voice was very quiet. She searched his face, trying to read his mind.

"How could I tell you? I know how you feel about the prince. You would have been honor-bound to inform the government of the truth. And if you did not tell them, then you would be an accessory as well as I. I could not put you in such a compromising position. Surely you can see that?"

The expression on his face did not challenge. "But I knew all along it was not the prince," he said.

Van felt shock run like lightning through her body. Her lips parted. "What?" she said faintly.

"I knew all along it was not the prince," he repeated. "It was I who closed his eyes. Charles Stuart's eyes are brown."

Van thought of the greenish-hazel of Alan's eyes. She stared at her husband and her shoulders slumped. "You never told me you knew."

"No. I was hoping, you see, that you would tell *me*. That you would trust me." There was a long pause as she stared at him hopelessly. "It was obvious that you knew him," he said at last. "If I had realized that, I would never have brought you to Knoidart. I did not mean to hurt you."

"But why, Edward?" She was completely bewildered by now. "Why, when you knew it was not the prince, did you give me the chance to say that it was?"

"Christ," he said. "I don't know. I knew you would identify him, of course. It was a perfect opportunity to have the hunt called off for a while." He smiled but there was no humor in it. "I'm sick of all this, Van," he said. "I'm sick of being made to feel I belong to a race of executioners. I wanted to run Sackville through that morning. I was hoping that the prince *would* get away in the interim, I suppose. Hoping that this whole bloody 'pacification of the Highlands' would come at last to an end."

Van stared at her husband, her heart in her eyes. "I do trust you," she said. "I trust you more than anyone else in the world. And I love you . . ."

He reached for her, pulled her up onto his lap, his arms cradling her close, his lips in her hair. "I know," he said. They sat quietly for some minutes, Van with her eyes closed, feeling perfectly sheltered and safe. He spoke into her hair. "One day soon this will all be over," he said. "One day soon you will make music again." She pressed closer to him, and his arms around her tightened.

It had begun to rain by the time they went upstairs to bed. It beat against the windows of their bedroom, hard and relentless, sweeping in from the sea to cover the loch and the land. Van tried to ignore it, to seek refuge in her husband's nearness, his pulsing strength, the safety of his great body.

There were French ships in Loch nan Uamh and she had not told Edward. "I trust you," she had said to him, and she did. She trusted in his wisdom, in his kindness, in the breadth of his vision, and in his perception of morality. She did not think that he would betray the ships' presence to the government.

But she could not burden him with that decision. She lay in his arms, listening to his heartbeat, and thought of what he had said earlier. He had known all along that Alan's body was not that of the prince. What would happen to Edward if the government became aware of his deception?

He would be accused of helping the prince to escape. He would be labeled a Jacobite. People would say that his wife had converted him. He could even be arrested himself.

The military leaders in Scotland were not happy with the Earl of Linton; she had seen that in various ways over the last six weeks. They were not happy with his shiploads of food, with his protection of Morar, with his outspoken disapproval of their tactics. They would love a chance to vindicate their own actions, to put Edward in the wrong.

He could not be implicated in the prince's escape.

For his own sake, he must be kept ignorant. He must be able to swear, with a clear conscience, that he had known nothing of Charles Stuart's movements at any time.

Would he ever forgive her?

"Listen to the rain," his voice said softly into the darkness above her head. It beat so hard now against the glass that it drowned out the sound of his heartbeat. Edward's arms were a refuge for her no longer.

32

Lachlan discovered from a clansman of Lochiel's the whereabouts of the Cameron chief, and made for Ben Alder in order to search him out. Van had told Lachlan to first find Lochiel, as he was the person most likely to know the whereabouts of the prince.

For so long now the Highlands had been covered with troops and guarded like a city in a siege, that the easy going he had surprised the MacIan clansman. The government, however, was now convinced that the prince had gone to the east coast to make his escape, and so the guard on the west had been relaxed.

Lachlan was accosted by a MacPherson clansman on the slopes of Ben Alder and, once he had identified himself, conducted to the cave where the MacPherson chief was entertaining royalty.

Lachlan's message put the prince and his entire party into holiday spirits. "What fine, brave women these Highlanders are," Charles said to Niall. "Your sister has the heart of a lion."

Niall thought of that other brave woman, Flora Mac-Donald, now in prison in Edinburgh, and a little of the spark left his eyes. Van was putting herself into danger for them, but he did not see how it could be helped.

They left Ben Alder at one in the morning on the thirteenth of September and began their final journey through the Highlands, going north at first between Ben Alder and Loch Ericht, then west through the Ben Alder Forest and past the south end of Loch Laggan toward Glen Roy. They moved at night and lay hidden and rested by day. They crossed Glen Roy and the river Lochy by moonlight, in a boat that leaked badly the whole way, and came for the last time to Lochiel's ruined house of Achnacarry.

"We are to hide in the cave at Morar and get word to my sister we are there," Niall said as they sat in the moonlight eating the cow Archie Cameron had killed and the bannocks Lachlan had baked. "She will let us know when the French ships reappear."

The whole party of fugitive Jacobites marched through the mountains the following night and by morning they were in Morar. It was the seventeenth of September, eleven days after Van had sent Lachlan to find them.

Edward had missed Lachlan. Van made the excuse that the Highlander had a girl over near Achnacarry and that he was off visiting. To her relief, Edward seemed to accept the explanation. When Lachlan's absence extended to a week's time, however, he mentioned it again. This time Van said that she thought Lachlan had probably got married, a possibility he had thought might happen. Edward looked a little puzzled, but she did not try to embroider the tale further, knowing the less said in a lie the better, and he had once again let the matter drop.

Van had been going out to the cave every morning for the last three days, and on the morning of the seventeenth she found what she had been looking for. Niall and the prince were there, with Lochiel and his brother, Dr. Cameron, Lochgarry, and John Roy Steward. She flung herself into Niall's arms.

"The ships are to return to Loch nan Uamh very shortly," she said as she huddled with the men inside the cave. "MacDonald of Boisdale is to notify me the moment he sees them. I will then get word to you."

"I will go to keep watch also, my lady," Lachlan offered.

Van hesitated and then agreed. "All right, Lachlan. It will be best if you keep out of Lord Linton's way for a while. He thinks you are at Loch Arkaig, getting married."

Lachlan looked distinctly startled and Niall grinned. "Just hope Margaret doesn't hear that, my boy," he said.

"Aye," replied Lachlan so fervently that even Charles laughed.

Lachlan was concealed in the undergrowth on the south shore of Loch nan Uamh, with the sun of mid-September striking low across the still water, when the first sign of sails appeared, moving silently up the loch from the Sound of Arisaig. The flag was British. Lachlan waited breathlessly while the ship anchored. After a short pause a boat was lowered and began to row toward the shore. Lachlan went to meet it.

The French lieutenant who first greeted Lachlan spoke adequate English, although he had to struggle to understand Lachlan's accent.

"Where is the prince?" he repeated impatiently, not comprehending Lachlan's explanation but hearing only the name of the man he was searching for.

"In Morar," Lachlan replied as distinctly as he could. "He is waiting for you in Morar. He will meet you here tomorrow night."

"In Morar." The Frenchman's brow cleared. "To-morrow night. Very well. Tell his highness that we will call in Loch Morar tomorrow night after dark. We will anchor one-half mile up the loch. Do you understand that?" The Frenchman looked intently at Lachlan.

"No." Lachlan made one more attempt. "The prince will come here tomorrow night."

But the Frenchman shook his head. "It is not necessary. We can come to Loch Morar. Tomorrow night."

Lachlan gave it up. "Tomorrow night. One-half mile up the loch. Aye. They will be there."

Satisfied, the Frenchman nodded and returned to his boat. Lachlan did not wait to see him taken aboard before he slipped away to make the journey over the hills to Morar.

The French ship would be anchoring within view of the castle. Lady Van was going to be angry, but there had been little Lachlan could do. Besides, Lord Linton would not stop them. Lachlan was very sure of that. Lord Linton was too good a man to wish ill to Mac mhic Iain.

Van did not get out to the cave until the afternoon of the nineteenth. A grim-faced Niall met her with the news of the new rendezvous.

She was furious. "You could not possibly have been stupid enough to tell them to come to Loch Morar," she said to Lachlan, her eyes blazing like a tiger's. "You know Lord Linton's position! You know how unsafe Morar would be!"

"I could not help it, my lady," Lachlan replied wretchedly. They were speaking in Gaelic. "The French soldier could not understand me when I tried to explain. All he would say was that they would come to Loch Morar. Tonight. One-half mile up the loch."

"In full view of the castle," Van said to Niall.

"Only if you look from the west windows," Niall

replied. "Can't you keep Linton away from them, Van?" Niall's mouth was set in a thin, straight line. "Occupy him with other matters," he said.

Two pairs of light eyes met. "You don't understand, Niall," Van said. "I am not afraid of Edward's stopping you. I am afraid of his being implicated. After all he has done—for me, for you, for Morar—we owe it to him not to compromise his integrity in the eyes of his government. He does not deserve to end in the Tower, Niall!"

"No one need know that we sailed out of Loch Morar," Niall replied.

"These things always get out," Van said grimly. "The *L'Heureux* has already taken aboard a number of Jacobite fugitives. It is not likely that they will all hold their tongues."

"And your own safety is at risk as well," Dr. Cameron said gravely.

"The ship will be in Loch Morar this evening," Charles said impatiently. "What, then, do you suggest we do?" His question was directed to the group in general and for his answer there was silence.

Finally Van spoke. "You must leave from Loch nan Uamh as originally planned. With the watch on the west lifted, Edward can reasonably say he had no knowledge of your activities."

The men exchanged glances. Then Lochiel spoke. "Very well, Van. We have waited for five months, we can surely wait another day or so."

But Van was shaking her head. "No. You must go tonight as planned. I will meet the French ship in Loch Morar and redirect it to Loch nan Uamh. It is a short sail around Arisaig—you will be able to board well before dawn. But you must leave for Loch nan Uamh immediately."

The men were nodding and looking distinctly relieved when Niall said, "It's a good plan, Van, all except for the part of your meeting the ship. There is no need for you to go yourself. Send Lachlan."

Van's eyes narrowed ever so slightly. "No. There can be no confusion this night, Niall. I speak French and Lachlan does not." She smiled at her brother, a brief, flashing smile of gaiety and reassurance. "Do you not worry. I will dress as a clansman and bundle my hair under a bonnet. No one will know the messenger is Lady Linton."

Irresistibly, Niall smiled back. "Our father would be proud of you, my sister," he said.

Van bowed her head, but it was not of her father she was thinking.

The prince's party prepared to leave for the shores of Loch nan Uamh, the very place where he had landed fourteen months before, where Alasdair and Lochiel had first pledged him their support.

Charles held Van's hand in his for a moment before he left the cave. "God will bless you for your true heart and your bravery," he said. He flung up his head and pronounced ringingly, "I promise you, I will be back!"

Niall and all the other dedicated men who had followed him so faithfully cried out strongly, "Aye!" and "God bless your highness!" But Van looked at the bearded face of their bonnie prince and thought fiercely: May you never return to Scotland, Charles Stuart.

"He has the right," she had told Edward once. But as she looked now at the man who was taking his leave, she saw only the devastation his coming had brought to the Highlands. No one had the right to do that to anyone else, she thought. He would go back to Europe, to the life he had led there, but the country that had rallied so loyally to his call was in ashes. Her father was dead. Lochiel and Niall and all these others, who had not counted the cost, were condemned to the land of exile. No, she thought bleakly as she watched the party of men disappear into the mountains, I pray I never see Charles Stuart again.

All the way back to the castle she thought about how she was going to keep Edward away from the loch that night. A dozen plans, all of them fallible, presented themselves and were discarded. She finally decided she would instruct Alan Ruadh to bring news of soldiers burning and looting in the north of Morar. That would get Edward away from the castle for the night and give her time to accomplish her errand.

When she got home she sent for Alan Ruadh, who proved surprisingly reluctant to fall in with her plans.

"Lord Linton may be a Sassenach, Lady Van, but he has been a good chief to us," Alan said stoutly. "I am not liking to lie to him."

"I know, Alan," Van said. "I feel the same way. But it is for his own good, don't you see? I do not want him involved with the prince's escape. You don't want to see Lord Linton arrested, do you?"

"Na," said Alan, but he still looked reluctant.

"Your chief is Mac mhic Iain," Van said sternly. "He is the one who commands your loyalty, and it is he who will be escaping this night, Alan Ruadh."

"Mac mhic Iain is our chief," Alan agreed, "and as his father's son, I honor him as such. But the one who has been a father to the clan these last months is Lord Linton." He looked at her wretchedly. "What am I to say to him, my lady, when he sees there are no soldiers?"

"Tell him you were acting under my orders," Van said. "He will not hold it against you, Alan. Tell him it was my command."

The clansman's brow cleared slightly. "He is a good man, Lord Linton, and I would not wish him to be angry with me. I will do as you say."

"Good," said Van. "Come with the news at seven o'clock. And you must insist that you start out immediately!"

"Aye, my lady," said Alan resignedly, and took his leave.

Van sat for a long time staring at the large terrestrial globe which sat in the corner of the library, where she had interviewed Alan. Edward was going to be so angry with her, but she did not see what else she was to do.

Alan came promptly at seven as arranged. Morag showed him into the drawing room, where Van and Edward were sitting, and he delivered his story in a mixture of Gaelic and English that was very effective.

Edward frowned. "Soldiers in Morar? Soldiers from where? We have heard nothing of soldiers for weeks."

"I do not know, my lord," Alan replied. "But they are saighdearan dearg, and they have burned the cottage of Fergus of the Loy. They are moving toward Glen Achon, and there is a village there, as you know. The people are fearful. They know all too well what the saighdearan dearg did in Knoidart."

Edward's expression became grim as he too remembered Knoidart. "Will you come?" Alan asked, and Edward rose to his feet.

"There won't be anything happening at this hour," he said to Van, "and if I leave now, I'll be there in the morning to put a stop to whatever plans the bastards might have in mind."

There was such an aching cramp in her heart. He was so good, and to be deceiving him this way . . . Very briefly her eyes met Alan Ruadh's and she knew he was thinking the same thing. Van straightened her back. It was for his own good. It had to be done. "Very well, Edward," she said. "I think you are right."

"Were the soldiers from Fort Augustus?" Edward asked Alan.

"I do not know, my lord, where they are from," Alan replied simply. "But they have burned Fergus of the Loy's cottage."

"All right. I understand. Wait here, Alan, and I'll go and change." After Edward had left the room, Alan and Van waited in perfect silence, avoiding looking at each other. The earl was back in fifteen minutes, wearing a much-used riding coat and boots. "Let's go, Alan," he said, and as Alan turned to leave the room Edward bent over Van's chair and kissed her briefly. "I'll sort this out, sweetheart," he said comfortingly. "There must be some kind of mistake."

"Yes," Van said, "I'm sure there is." She smiled at him a little unsteadily and went to the window as soon as he had followed Alan out the door. From the front window of the drawing room she eventually saw them come out the door of the castle and begin to walk down the path toward the loch. They would cross the loch, she knew, and take to the hills on the other side, going north toward Knoidart. After they passed out of her sight, Van went to sit again in her chair and stare sightlessly into space. She felt like a traitor. But it's for his own good! she kept repeating to herself. It's for his own good.

The question was, would Edward see that?

An hour after Edward had left, Van, dressed in trews and with her hair hidden under a bonnet, went down to the loch herself and got into the other boat.

She rowed herself down the loch some quarter of a mile and waited near the shore, leaning on her oars and watching down the loch toward the sea.

She did not have long to wait. At about ten o'clock a ship came into sight, moving silently up the quiet waters of Loch Morar. Van waited until it had anchored and then rowed out to meet it.

She was taken aboard almost immediately and demanded to speak to the captain. Her interview with that individual, conducted in perfect French, was short and to the point. The ship was to sail back to Loch nan Uamh immediately and there it would find the prince and a few of his faithful friends. Loch Morar was not safe. It was the home of the Earl of Linton, an Englishman and loyal Government supporter. Van emphasized this latter point several times. The earl would like to see the prince captured. Morar was not safe. They must go to Loch nan Uamh.

In less than half an hour the French ship had weighed anchor again and sailed down the loch on its way around the Arisaig peninsula to Loch nan Uamh. Once there, it took on its royal cargo and, between two and three in the dark of a September morning, it sailed southwest out of Loch nan Uamh and into the Atlantic.

33

Van did not sleep at all that night. Nor had she eaten much the previous evening, but even so the nauseous feeling that had been haunting her mornings of late reappeared. She was pale-faced and big-eyed when she met Lachlan in the library at seven-thirty in the morning to hear his tale of the prince's escape.

"You have done well, Lachlan," she praised him. "Mac mhic Iain will remember always your loyalty and your service."

The thin, dark face of the MacIan clansman glowed briefly, like a candle. Then, "I will be returning to my father's house, my lady, if that will be all right. He is old and he will have been missing me."

"Go," Van said. "And if you and Margaret are wishing to marry, there will be a new cottage for you near to your father's"

A rare smile flitted across Lachlan's face, he gestured quickly, in gratitude, and was gone.

All the way home the clansman's head was filled with pleasant thoughts. He had done well, been loyal to his chief and his prince, and it looked as if his reward was to be sweet. He was perfectly happy until he arrived at his father's cottage to find the Earl of Linton waiting for him.

Lachlan had thought the Earl of Morar's anger was

to be feared, but one look at Linton's face set his heart to slamming hard against his ribs. Edward was gray with rage. "I want to know where you have been," he said to Lachlan in the hardest, coldest voice the clansman had ever heard.

Lachlan glanced at Alan Ruadh, who stood to the side of the earl, looking like a beaten dog. "Is all safe?" Alan asked in Gaelic.

"Aye."

"Then tell him," said Alan.

"Yes, tell me." Linton's voice was under perfect control which, for some reason, made him even more frightening. Lachlan looked up at the blond-haired Sassenach who seemed to tower above him and then looked down again at his feet.

"Lady Van said to tell him," Alan repeated. Edward moved very slightly and both Highlanders looked at him in fear.

"Where have you been, Lachlan, these last two weeks?" Edward asked again, and this time Lachlan told him.

When Lachlan had finished his story an eerie silence fell upon the three men. Alan and Lachlan exchanged nervous glances and then looked cautiously at the earl's face. They looked hastily away and prayed he would not murder them.

"It was my fault, my lord," Lachlan finally said bravely. "I should not have let them come to Loch Morar. Lady Van had said Loch nan Uamh."

Edward's blue eyes touched Lachlan's face very briefly, then went to Alan's. Both men winced away from his look. "I do not want to see either of you until I ask for you." His voice was perfectly expressionless. "Is that clear?"

"Aye, my lord," they mumbled in unison.

Without another word, Edward turned and walked off down the glen. The two men stayed where they were, grateful not to have been thrown out of Morar, grateful still to be alive.

All the way home, over the mountains that had become so familiar to him these last months, Edward struggled to gain control of his temper. He very rarely lost it, usually managed to remain calm and in command, no matter the provocation. He was afraid of losing his temper, he was afraid of what he might do should he lose control of himself. He remembered vividly the time he had come upon a tenant boy torturing one of his dogs, and drew a long, deep, steadying breath. He had been younger than the boy, and smaller, but if one of the workmen had not dragged him off, he might have killed the tormentor.

He must not lose his temper with his wife. No matter what she had done, he must not lose his temper. "I trust you," she had said to him. She had lied. What else had she lied about? All these months, when she had lain so trustingly in his arms, she had been lying to him.

Nothing and no one mattered to her except her brother and the goddamn bloody prince.

All of her promises to him—they were worth nothing. Their marriage was worth nothing. This war had defeated them. Once, perhaps, they could have built something together, but not now. She felt she could not trust him, and he could no longer trust her.

She had lied to him. She had broken her word. At his side his hands closed slowly into fists and then opened and closed again.

He did not go to the castle when he arrived back

home, but went instead to the stable and saddled up Fitz. He said not a word to anyone as he mounted and rode the horse along the path to the loch and then headed west, toward the sea.

When Edward had not returned to the castle by teatime, Van began to feel really frightened. She had had no word from Alan Ruadh, either, and it was only by chance that she walked down to the stable and found that Fitz was gone.

"Lord Linton returned hours ago, my lady," one of the boys who looked after the ponies told her. "He did not say anything, just saddled the horse and rode away."

"Rode away!" Panic began to set in. "Rode away where, Fergus?"

The boy gestured down the loch and Van's heart quieted a little. He had not left her, then, if he had gone in that direction. He must know what had happened. She had to make him understand . . . Without pausing to think it through clearly, Van ordered a pony brought to the castle. She herself ran back up the path to change into trews as quickly as she could. Within twenty minutes she had set off after her husband.

He was standing near the edge of the sea when he saw her pony coming. His hand tightened convulsively on his horse's bridle and then relaxed as the horse pulled against the sudden pressure. He had needed Fitz this day, needed the familiar, calming presence of an animal to help him get hold of his own raging emotions. He had thought he was all right, was even thinking of returning to the castle, when he looked up and saw her approaching. Rage boiled over in his heart once more.

She slid off the pony and finished the last few yards on foot, stopping some ten feet from him, her light eyes scanning his face. They stood thus for almost a full half-minute, the only sound the slap of the waves and the crying of the birds, the two of them holding the reins of their horses and staring at each other across the pure white sand that separated them.

The air on the beach seemed to grow thick and hard to breathe, as though there were a storm coming. Van wet her lips and said in a low, throbbing voice, "I'm so sorry, Edward. But I could not tell you. I could not implicate you in any way. Surely you see that?"

But he was not listening, or rather, he was listening only to what he expected to hear. "You could not tell me. I see that well enough."

Van had never seen him in such a fury. He was white to the lips. She began to feel very frightened. He was looking at her as if he hated her. "Edward," she tried again, "don't look like that. Listen to me . . ."

In the grim white face before her the blue eyes darkened and blazed. This was not the ice-cold temper she had witnessed in him before. This was something quite different. It took all the courage she possessed not to back away from him.

"No!" he said, and the suppressed violence in his voice was terrifying. "I am through listening to you, Van. Through listening to your lies. You have done nothing but lie ever since we married."

"Edward!" It was a cry of pure pain. She even took a step toward him. "That's not true!"

"Do not come any closer." There was the flash of something frightening in his eyes. "I am not quite . . . responsible at the moment, Van," he said. "Go away."

She hesitated, not sure what she ought to do. Fitz, sensing the tension in the hand that held his bridle, threw his head up and down and pawed the ground. "I don't want to see you," her husband said. "I came here to get away from you. Will you please go back to the castle and leave me alone."

"Very well," she said quietly. Then, "I love you, Edward. That is not a lie." She turned away to mount her pony and so did not see the spasm of anguish that crossed his face at her words. But he said nothing, only stood in silence and watched her ride away. When she was quite out of sight, he turned and buried his face in his horse's mane.

Van was thoroughly exhausted by the time she returned to the castle. It was a tremendous effort to drag her body up the stairs to her bedroom. She took off her clothes with shaking hands and crawled into the bed, where she fell asleep almost instantly.

She awoke at dawn and was aware, immediately, that he was not beside her. She sat up and was struck by a wave of nausea. There was nothing in her stomach to come up, however, so she spat only a little yellow bile into the basin next to the bed. She lay back down again, feeling terrible.

Had he come home at all last night? Surely he was not still down on the beach?

Morag came in an hour later. Van, who was lying perfectly still to control the nausea, watched the girl as she poured fresh water and lit the fire against the cool morning air. Ever since she had married Edward there had been a fire in her bedroom, Van thought. She teased him about being a soft-living Sassenach, but she loved the luxury of a fire. The sight of Morag lighting the logs brought tears to her eyes.

"Morag," she asked in a thin voice, "did Lord Linton return last night?"

"Aye, Lady Van." Morag did not look at her. "He

slept in one of the other rooms. And he left again an hour ago."

"Left!" Van tried to sit up and the nausea attacked again. She lay back and concentrated her will against it. "Where did he go?" she asked after a minute, having won this particular battle.

"He did not say, my lady. Just that he would be gone for several days."

Van closed her eyes. "Thank you, Morag," she said, and did not open them again until she heard the bedroom door close.

By ten o'clock she was able to get up without being sick and she forced herself to take some tea and bread and butter. Then she sent for Alan Ruadh.

He sent back word that he would come only if Lord Linton was not at the castle.

"He was that angry, Lady Van," Alan told her wretchedly when he finally put in an appearance. "When he saw there were no soldiers, I told him the truth of it, just as you said," Alan shivered. "Even Mac mhic Iain did not have such a temper," he said.

"What did you say, Alan?" Van asked. "Try to remember the exact words."

Her father's foster brother frowned in thought. "I said you had told me to get him away for the night, that the prince and Mac mhic Iain would be boarding a French ship in the loch."

Van's face had grown thinner over the past few days. "And what did Lord Linton say?" she asked

"He asked if Lachlan had been involved in this affair and I said that he had." At the expression on Van's face he added hastily, "You said to tell him all, Lady Van."

"Aye," she replied wearily. "What happened next?"

"Next we went to Lachlan's house and waited for him," said Alan

Dear Christ, Van thought. So he knew all about the last two weeks, knew that she had been the one to send a message to alert the prince and Niall of the ship's presence. No wonder he had accused her of lying to him.

"What did Lachlan tell his lordship?" Van asked bleakly, and was drearily unsurprised by the answer.

So he even knew that she was the one to send the boat out of Morar to Loch nan Uamh. She had done it for his sake, but she was beginning to fear that he would never believe that.

He had looked at her as if he hated her.

"I don't want to see you," he had said. "Leave me alone."

She dismissed Alan and settled down to wait for Edward to return.

Three days passed, then four, then five. The *Sea Queen* returned from Dublin with a cargo of food and clothing and she helped see it unloaded and the goods distributed. There was no word from Edward.

It was while Van was staring out the window at the graceful lines of the *Sea Queen* as it rocked gently in the loch that the thought came to her. She should be the one to leave. She should board the *Sea Queen* and go to France to join the rest of her family. Her departure would have the added value of diverting any suspicion of complicity in the prince's escape away from Edward. That way, should governmental scrutiny fall on the Lintons, it would fall on the right one.

The more she thought about it, the more she realized that she ought to go. If Edward should want to find her, he would know where she was. If he should want to divorce her, she would have given him the means.

No one would expect an Earl of Linton to remain married to a Jacobite traitor.

She would go to France.

That night she sat down to write him a letter:

Edward, my love:

I have gone to join Mother and Niall in France. I do not want to leave you, but I think that, under the circumstances, my leaving will be best.

I know that you are angry. You have every right to be angry. But I wish you could understand, just a little, why I acted as I did.

Niall would not desert the prince. And, truly, I think it was best that the prince escaped. His execution would have made a martyr out of him, Edward, and Scotland does not need any more martyrs. I think you were coming to that conclusion yourself.

I did not want you implicated in any way with this venture. As it stands, you can take any oath that is asked of you that you knew nothing of Charles Stuart's activities and that you had nothing to do with his escape.

That is why I sent the ship from Loch Morar to Loch nan Uamh. I did not want you involved at all.

Edward, I am so sorry that it had to be me, but when word was brought to me of the ship's presence, I had to act. Niall is my brother. I cannot say I am sorry I helped him.

There is a line of poetry that has been going through my mind for over a year now, like the chorus from a Greek tragedy. "O God! O God! That it were possible/ To undo things done, to call back yesterday!"

What I would give to be able to call back those happy days we had together at Staplehurst. When I think of you, do you know the picture that comes most often to my mind? You and Marcus in the sun at Staplehurst. Do you remember that day? You were showing off for me, you said.

But the sad truth is that we cannot go back, however much we might desire to do so. You and I can never go back to what we once were. We can only go on.

Whether we go on together or apart is up to you. If you wish to find me, you know where I am. If you wish never to see me again, I will abide by your decision.

Know this, however. I will always, always love you.

Van.

She left the letter on the mantel in her bedroom with instructions to Morag to see that the earl got it. Then, with one portmanteau of clothing, she boarded the *Sea Queen* and gave the captain orders to take her to France.

34

Frances stood at the tall narrow window of the house the MacIans were leasing in Rouen, her grandson in her arms. Between the rooftops she could just see the glint of the river Seine, down which *L'Heureux* had sailed, bringing back to his family her son Niall.

In her arms the baby stirred and Frances looked down with melting tenderness into the dark little MacIan face. How Alasdair would have loved to have seen this child.

With the thought came the pain, the long, cramping pain that was Alasdair's endless absence. She breathed deeply and floated with it, and the baby opened his dark gray eyes and looked at her.

What a godsend this child had been to her, Frances thought. First there had been Jean, fearful and in the last stages of pregnancy, to be seen to. And then the baby himself, Alasdair's grandchild. Without him it would have been unbearable.

Little Alasdair began to squirm and she lifted him up until his soft, fuzzy, baby head was under her lips. She closed her eyes. Oh, the healing power of a baby.

She turned to take him to his nurse to be fed and

so did not see the distant sails of the *Sea Queen*
come gracefully floating up the river.

Van had never felt so physically wretched in all
her life. The nausea brought on by pregnancy had
only been compounded by the rough September
seas of the Channel, and by the time the *Sea Queen*
came to anchor she did not know if she had the
energy to walk down the ramp and onto dry land.

She managed it, however, her head high under
the gaze of Edward's crew. The captain, an elderly
man who had been in service with Edward's father
as well, insisted on escorting the hired carriage that
took her the few blocks from the quay to the house
where her family was lodged.

It was a house that belonged to one of the Rouen
merchants who were making a fortune manufactur-
ing the new cloth known as Rounnerie. The merchant had met Lochiel's brother Fassefern in Paris
and, upon learning of Jean and Frances, had offered them the use of his old house. He was in the
process of building himself one far more magnificent on the outskirts of the city and had been flat-
tered to rent his old one to two countesses. Frances
had been delighted at the opportunity to get Jean
away from Paris, and so they had come to Rouen.

Having relinquished her grandson to the care of
his wet nurse, Frances proceeded to the small salon
and picked up her sewing. She was making an exquisitely stitched gown for the baby and she seated
herself in the light from the window to work on it.
The house was very quiet. Niall and Jean had gone
out together to do some shopping.

She heard the front knocker sound and her head
came up with curiosity. They kept very much to

themselves, the MacIans, and did not see many people in the town. There was the murmur of voices and then steps came down the hall. The salon door opened and Van was there.

"Hello, Mother," she said. And fainted on the merchant's best carpet.

The day after Van left for France, a messenger arrived at Creag an Fhithich with a letter from the Earl of Linton to his wife. The news it contained was brief and to the point. Edward had ridden to Fort Augustus to report that he had heard rumors of the prince's escape. The officer whose tent he had shared at the fort had come down with small-pox and Edward was going to wait a few weeks before he returned home to make certain he was not carrying the germ himself.

When Morag learned from the messenger that the earl would be returning in a few weeks, she decided to wait for him rather than send the *Sea Queen* on another errand to France to deliver his letter.

Van awoke with lead in her limbs, wondering how she would meet another day. The morning nausea was subsiding and she found herself rather missing it. At least her physical misery had given her something else to think about.

She felt as if she were living in limbo, a gray, dreary, cheerless limbo. Three weeks had passed and still she had heard nothing from Edward. In her heart, she had thought he would follow her. She had believed that what was between them was too strong to be lost in this quarrel. It seemed, however, that she was wrong. He was not going to forgive her after all.

He did not know about the baby. Would he take her back if he knew? she wondered. The temptation to write to him was tremendous, but she resisted it. She had told him she would abide by his decision, and she must keep to her word.

The maid came into the room with a can of water and Van faced the necessity of getting out of bed and meeting the day.

"I'm worried about Van," Niall said to his mother that evening after his sister had gone early up to bed. "She is so quiet and listless. And too thin. I was looking at her wrists at dinner." He frowned. "There has been no word at all from Linton?"

Frances shook her head. "None."

Niall's frown deepened. "Dhé!" he said. "Linton knew when he married her what her loyalties were. How can he be so surprised?"

Frances sighed. "I don't know, darling. One never does know what is going on inside another person's marriage. All I do know is that they quarreled and Van left. And I know that she loves him and that is why she is so miserable."

There was a long pause. Frances and Jean continued to sew and Niall frowned into the fire. Then he said gruffly, "I have been thinking I ought to write a letter to Linton myself."

Frances and Jean both stopped stitching and stared at him.

"It is because of me that all of this has come about," Niall continued. "I am thinking perhaps I should write to try to explain."

This was a great concession on Niall's part, as

both his wife and his mother knew. "I think that would be a good idea, darling," Frances said. "If you are . . . conciliating."

Niall looked up from under his brows, a somber and ironic look. "Yes, Mother," he said. "I know."

He was as good as his word, and the following morning sat down at the merchant's old secretary and wrote a letter to his brother-in-law. He was dreading having to write it, but in the end it proved much easier than he had anticipated:

My dear Linton,

I am writing to you because I am concerned about my sister's health. She does not know about this letter, and would be angry if she did know, but I feel it is necessary.

She is missing you badly. She is ill from missing you. I understand your anger over her part in the prince's escape, but I ask you to put it away from you and come to her now.

I do not know if she has told you this, but her one concern all through the entire affair was to protect you from suspicion of complicity. "Edward does not deserve to end up in the Tower, not after all he had done for us." That is what she said to us all that afternoon in the cave when we learned the ship was to call in Loch Morar. It was Van who insisted that the ship be redirected to Loch nan Uamh, and so it was—at some risk both to herself and to the rest of us. But her only thought, as I said before, was to protect you.

As to her helping us at all—she had no choice in the matter, Linton. She is a MacIan, a Highlander, and her father's daughter. She is not one to hide behind the shield of womanhood, my sister. She will act according to her conscience, always. If you wanted a soft and docile wife, you should not have chosen Van.

As for me, I must thank you for your great generosity toward my land and my people. When my father first told me of Van's wish to marry you, I could not understand it. Van and a Sassenach! I could not understand it at all. Now I do.

You are still a Whig and a Sassenach and I a Jacobite and a Celt, but I thank you, Edward Romney.

Come to Van.

Yours most sincerely,
Niall MacIan
Earl of Morar

The letter reached Creag an Fhithich three hours before Edward finally returned home. The one smallpox case had turned into a small epidemic and Edward had feared to leave Fort Augustus until he was certain there was no chance he was incubating the disease.

He was given Van's letter first, then Niall's.

He sailed for France on the evening tide.

It was a breezy, chilly autumn day, but the sun in the small walled garden behind the house was warm. Van was sitting on a bench, ostensibly reading a book, when the door from the house opened and someone else came out into the garden. She heard a step crunch on the graveled walk and looked up.

The sun was in her eyes and the first thing she saw was the halo of his hair. Her heart began to pound so fiercely she thought she might suffocate. She squinted her eyes, trying to see his face. She stood up.

"Edward." Her lips moved, but only a whisper of sound came out. He seemed like a great golden god as he came toward her across the garden. As he reached her the sun went behind a cloud and she was able to see his face. All the air was suddenly squeezed from her lungs. He said her name, and something else she did not hear, and then she was in his arms.

He did not kiss her, just held her against him, and her own arms went about his waist and clung tightly. Her cheek was crushed against his shoulder. She shut her eyes tightly and concentrated solely on the feel of him against her. It was a few moments before she even realized he was speaking.

"I am so sorry, sweetheart," he was saying. "So sorry. I was so stupid. So criminally stupid."

"No." Her head moved slightly in a negative shake. "No, you had a right to be angry, Edward. I understood that."

"Let me look at you." His voice was distinctly unsteady and she moved away from him reluctantly as he put his hands on her shoulders. He frowned and said, "You look ill. Are you all right, sweetheart?"

"Yes." She reached up to touch his face, running her fingers across the planes of his cheekbones, the line of his mouth. "I am perfectly all right," she said. "Now."

"I was caught in Fort Augustus by a smallpox epidemic," he explained. "I did not even know you had gone until yesterday. I returned to Morar to find your letter. And Niall's."

Van's eyes widened in sudden understanding. "Smallpox," she said. "Are you all right, Edward?"

"Yes, but I could not leave until I was certain I was not infected. I did not want to bring it to Morar. I wrote to tell you, but you had gone. Morag did not want to take the responsibility of sending the *Sea Queen* to France with my letter and decided to wait for me to return home."

"Oh, Edward." Van's voice quivered. "And all this time I thought . . ." She broke off and nestled once more into his arms. "You said you didn't want to see me," she said into his shoulder. "You looked at me as if you hated me."

"I lost my temper." He put his cheek against her hair and held her closer still. "I rarely do." He laughed a little shakenly. "I'm afraid of myself when that happens. That's why I went away. I wanted to calm down. I knew I was in no fit state to think clearly. I was in no fit state to see anyone. And by the time I had regained some perspective, I was stuck in Fort Augustus."

"I should have stayed in Morar," Van murmured. "I suppose I was not thinking clearly myself. I thought if I left, it would give you grounds to divorce me."

"Divorce you!" Rough hands on her shoulders forced her to look up at him. "Did you really think I would divorce you?"

"Well," she replied, sustaining that blazing look, "I thought the only honorable thing to do was to offer you the opportunity."

After a minute a slow, reluctant smile spread across his face. "Niall said that you would always act according to your conscience."

"Did you say that Niall had written to you?" Van asked wonderingly.

"Yes. He wrote me a very courageous letter. It made me understand how much you must love him, because it was quite clear how much he loves you." He gave her a half-comical, half-shamefaced look. "I was jealous of Niall, do you know that?"

Van's eyes were clear and beautiful. "You have no

cause to be jealous of anyone," she said. "It is you that I love."

He cupped her face between his hands and bent his head until his mouth was touching hers.

There was no passion in their kiss, only the deep, healing power of love. There would be time enough for passion later, they both knew. For now they wanted something else. They sat down together on the bench, held hands, and looked into each other's eyes and laughed. It was then that Van told him about the baby.

At first he was full of guilt for having left her. Then he was concerned for her health. Finally, when he had been reassured on both those counts, he was absolutely delighted.

"I must write to Mama," he said. "She will be so pleased." He grinned down at her, looking for a moment no older than a schoolboy. Van felt her heart would burst with the love that swelled up in it.

"I will give you a dozen children," she said.

He laughed. "Don't make rash promises, sweetheart. We'll take them one at a time, I think."

The sun was turning his hair into gold and making a brilliant dance in the blue of his eyes. There was laughter still in the corners of his mouth. Van was suddenly dizzy with love and when he kissed her again the wild blood began to race through her veins. They saw no one as they went into the house, dark after the brilliance of the sunshine, and they proceeded without interruption up the stairs and into the privacy of Van's room.

"Was there anyone in the house when you came?" Van asked him, quite some time later.

"Your mother. She directed me to the garden. Then,

with her usual exquisite tact, she disappeared." He was lying back against the pillows, his arms clasped behind his head. His eyes laughed at her. "She must have cleared out the entire house."

Van remembered Frances sending Niall and Jean upstairs in Glasgow to "spend some time alone." She smiled back at him a little sadly. "Mother understands."

He spoke softly. "She is still missing your father?"

Van's answer was simple. "She will always miss my father." She looked at her husband, at the wide, muscled shoulders, the strong column of neck, the thick fair hair lying touseled on the pillow, and for a moment she understood completely her mother's grief. Should she ever lose Edward . . .

"Van," he was saying, "I want to go home to Staplehurst. Will you come with me?"

The question shook her from her reverie. "Of course," she replied, surprised that he would even ask.

"I was not sure that you would want to return to England," he said slowly, watching her out of suddenly guarded eyes. "You have all the reason in the world not to."

"Your life is in England, Edward," she answered after a minute. "I know that England is your home."

"And you?" he queried gently. "Will it ever be home to you, Van?"

She leaned over him so that their faces were very close and her hair streamed down around them, enclosing them in a tent of black silk. "Wherever you are is home to me," she said. His eyes lifted, and then he pulled her down on top of him.

Van's entire family, with the exception of baby Alasdair, was gathered in the salon when she and Edward finally made their way downstairs. Niall shot one look at his sister's radiant face before he rose to shake hands with his brother-in-law. "Glad to see you, Linton," he said sincerely.

"I was caught in Fort Augustus by the smallpox," Edward explained as he took Niall's thin hand in his own larger grasp. "I sent a message to Creag an Fhithich, but for some reason Morag did not forward it here."

Enlightenment dawned in Niall's eyes, so uncannily like his sister's. "So," he said.

"Morag does not excel at acting on her own initiative," Frances said regretfully. Then, when Edward looked her way, she gestured to the small, elfinly pretty girl beside her and said, "May I introduce my son's wife, Jean."

Edward went to bow over Jean's hand. She looked up at him out of big brown eyes and smiled shyly. "I am so happy to meet you at last, Lord Linton."

He gave her one of his most charming smiles, and replied, "Since we are to be family, please won't you call me Edward?"

"I would like that," replied Jean, her shyness completely banished by that potent smile. Van grinned and looked at her mother, who was rising.

"Dinner is ready," Frances said firmly.

For the first time in months, Van felt hungry. "Oh, good," she said innocently, "you waited for us. I'm starved."

Niall snorted and Edward looked amused. "Come along to the dining room, darling," Frances said serenely, ignoring the men. "I've ordered your favorite dinner," and she led the way out of the salon with ineffable dignity.

Van ate hugely, and after dinner, when they all

returned to the parlor, she sat in a chair near the fire, letting the talk swirl around her and feeling full and sleepy and content. It was only when Edward began to talk of Scotland that she came awake.

"It was not just the Jacobite cause that went down at Culloden," he was saying to Niall. "It was a whole way of life. The government set out to break the clans, Niall, and I fear they are going to succeed."

"It is not so!" Niall replied. "The clans will follow their chiefs, no matter what the government says."

"The chiefs who still live are in exile," Edward said steadily. "The tartan and the kilt are outlawed. The glens have been emptied. Those who are left are leaderless." He held Niall's eyes. "It is my hope that in a few years Parliament will pass an Act of Indemnity and you may return home. But it will not be the same. I may have saved Morar for you, but still it will not be the same."

Niall glanced around the room and there was the flash of something wild and hunted in the movement of his head. Edward looked at him sympathetically. He guessed shrewdly that his brother-in-law had been happier during the months he had been hunted through the Highlands than he was in his comfortable exile in France.

"I will work for an Indemnity Act," he promised, "but it will take time. In the meanwhile, you could begin to act as your own agent here in France. Morar's cattle have been untouched. I have been experimenting at home with cattle breeding and I will be happy to send north some stock that I think will improve your breed. Your father always relied on a French agent to sell his goods; you will do better if you see to it yourself."

Niall's face wore a still, arrested expression. "Do you think so?"

"Yes," Edward grinned. "I've been known to do a bit of huckstering myself, so I know what I am talking about, you see."

"Yes," said Niall, "I do see. And it would give me something to do with myself!" This last was said almost violently.

His brother-in-law's blue eyes met his in perfect comprehension. "I know," said Edward softly.

Niall squeezed the small hand of his wife which had slipped into his. "You are going back to England, then?"

"Yes," said Edward, looked at his wife, and smiled very faintly.

"I must get someone to see to Morar, then." Niall's face was grim. "Someone to keep the clan together until I can return."

"I will go to Morar." It was Frances' voice and they all looked at her in surprise.

"I was rather hoping I could persuade you to come to England with us," Edward said after a moment. "I know my mother would love to see you."

Frances smiled at him. "Thank you, Edward, you are very kind. But as Niall said, someone is needed at Morar."

"It doesn't have to be you, Mother," said Niall. "It would be too lonely for you. I'll find someone else."

"But it won't be lonely at all," said Frances, and as she spoke she realized the truth of her words. "I have been lonely here in France," she went on. "Your father has seemed so far away. But in Morar he is close." Her eyes looked dreamy, her face very young. "Besides," she said, "it is what he would want me to do, to look after his people for him."

Niall got to his feet and went to the window, where he looked out at the foreign scene. The rest of them sat in silence until he turned around once more to face them. "I wish I could go with you, Mother," he said. The pain in his voice was raw.

"You were in Paris for three years, darling, at the university," Frances said gently.

"I know." He gave her a crooked smile. "But somehow it was not the same."

No, it was not the same, Van thought, watching him. Nothing would ever be the same for any of them again. In a sense, all the MacIans were doomed to exile, for the world they had known and loved was gone, and nothing would ever recall it again.

But the land remained, and for as long as she lived she knew something in her would miss the mountains and the lochs and the heather. No other place would ever call to her as did the glens of her own country. But what she had said to Edward was true: home to her was no longer a place but a person.

It had been so with her mother, she realized suddenly. The wild Scottish mountains must have been exile to the young English girl who had first arrived as a bride twenty-five years ago. And now it was the mountains she wanted, because they were the land of her love.

Perhaps one day she would come to feel the same about Staplehurst, Van thought, and looked at her husband.

At the window Niall drew a long, steadying breath. When he spoke his voice was light. "Ship me the Titian portrait, Mother. We can live for five years on what the sale will bring in Paris."

"I hope you will not need to wait five years," Edward said, and Niall turned to him with suddenly bright eyes.

"Well, for God's sake, Linton, see about getting yourself reinstated in the government, will you? I don't want to wait five years either!"

"I will do my best," Edward said gravely, and Niall grinned.

"I will have an agent of mine buy the Titian," Edward said to Van when they were once more upstairs in her bedroom. "Don't tell Niall. He can buy it back from me when he gets on his feet again. Or, better yet, we'll give it to Alasdair as a wedding present."

Van was already undressed and in bed, lying propped up against the pillows. "Thank you, m'eudail," she said softly. "What a good idea."

What grace of spirit Edward had, she thought as she lay against her pillows watching him undress in front of the fire. He had known that to offer Niall money would hurt his pride and so he had thought of this graceful way of assisting him.

Edward finished unbuttoning his shirt and threw it on a chair. The firelight cast a golden glow on his bare shoulders and arms. Van smiled and asked the question she had been thinking of for the last few hours. "Do you think Signore Martelli would give me lessons again?"

He seemed to freeze and then his head came up and he looked at her. "Would you want him to?" he asked in an odd voice.

Van's fingers were unconsciously flexing on the brightly patterned quilt that covered her. "Yes," she said.

"Sweetheart." He crossed the floor and sat beside

her on the bed. His eyes were brilliant. "I was beginning to be afraid you would never play again."

She was looking at her fingers on the quilt. "I know. It was as if all the music had been knocked out of me." She looked up at him with wide, grave eyes. "These last months I felt as if I were being torn in two. There was you, and then there was Niall." She reached up and touched his face. "I was so torn," she repeated. "There was no room for music in me."

"I know."

Her fingers moved caressingly along his cheekbone. She thought of Staplehurst, and the harpsichord, and the horses, and realized, wonderingly, that she was looking forward to going. "When can we leave for Staplehurst?" she asked.

"Tomorrow?"

She smiled with satisfaction. "Tomorrow," she repeated.

"Christ, Van." Her eyes widened at the tone of his voice and she stared up at him, her attention fully focused on him now. "Have you any idea of how frightened I have been?" he asked.

"Frightened? You?" She was astonished. "Frightened of what, Edward?"

"Of losing you. Do you think I did not realize how . . . how absent you were at times? Oh, not physically, but . . ."

"I know," she said softly.

"I was afraid the wounds were too deep, the division between us too wide."

She put up her other hand and held his face between her two palms. He was so completely beautiful, she thought. Inside as well as out. "It was never you," she said. "*You* were never part of that."

He put his hands over hers and moved her palms to his lips. He kissed them and then stood up to finish undressing. Van snuggled back into the bed. She had eaten so much at dinner and she was so sleepy . . . The bed sagged as he got in beside her. How lovely it was to have him there, she thought drowsily. She had been so lonely this past month.

She opened heavy eyelids to look at him. He put an arm around her and settled her comfortably into the hollow of his shoulder. "Go to sleep, sweetheart," he murmured, and even in her extreme drowsiness she could feel how his hard body was alight with laughter. She opened her mouth to say something, but before the words came out, she was asleep.

About the Author

Joan Wolf is a native of New York City who presently resides in Milford, Connecticut, with her husband and two young children. She taught high school English in New York for nine years and took up writing when she retired to rear a family. Her previous books, *The Counterfeit Marriage*, *A Kind of Honor*, *A London Season*, *A Difficult Truce*, *The Scottish Lord*, *His Lordship's Mistress*, and *The Rebel and the Rose*, are also available in Signet editions.